Stealing Terry
A Tale of the Fairypocalypse

ADDISON LANE

Stealing Terry
A Tale of the Fairypocalypse

Addison Lane
www.addisonlane.net

Lee Milverton
www.leemilverton.com

Printed in the United States of America

First Printing: August 2012

ISBN 978-0-9839538-3-8

Library of Congress Control Number: 2012912031

DEDICATION

Special thanks to my betas: Mom, Jayce, Adrienne,
Sandra and David. As well as to my supporters and
crackpot marketing team: Kay, Lauren, Lexi,
Marcy, Dad, Sheena and Jamie.

Chapter One.

Ashton Harriet had a murderous gleam in his eye. His cheeks were bright red, nostrils flared. Fergus edged towards a heavy oak armoire on the far side of the room. As an officer of the Air Guard, Harriet was permitted to carry a firearm. In fact, Fergus could see two strapped to his hips. He wasn't so sure that the armoire would shield him from a bullet, but thanks to having a *kelpie's* innate strength, he thought shoving it at Harriet wouldn't be a problem. He wondered if it would provide enough of a distraction that he could jump over the sofa and escape into the corridor.

Only a half hour before, Fergus had been down at the dock markets, picking up fresh fish and vegetables for dinner. Technically, he wasn't supposed to be leaving the Count Palatine's penthouse, as he and his best friend Terry were wanted for burning down New Peiling's slums four months prior. The actual culprits had been the anti-hybrid vigilantes, the Knights of Evalach. Yet, while Terry and Fergus were innocent of the charges, they'd been framed by the Knights, so leaving the penthouse was a gamble.

These days, the relationship between hybrids and humans was especially strained, what with Paige Harriet – Ashton Harriet's mother – running for governor. She was notoriously anti-hybrid, and her son was no different. It had always been an uncomfortable dynamic, ever since New Peiling was founded in the years following the Cataclysm.

Even now, no one could agree about what caused the disasters that had halved the human population. A number of humans took a religious stance, calling it an act of God, while many hybrids believed that humans had been too selfish and careless, and nature had finally reacted.

It was because of the Cataclysm that hybrids even existed. There was no better option for the disembodied fairy souls than to latch onto human children and bond with them. The humans hadn't taken this well.

Fergus had been hiding out at the penthouse for a few weeks along with his companions from the ill-fated adventure to the wilds beyond New Peiling, Pip and Three, and his former band mates, Raja and Terry. The Count owed him. After all, it was Fergus who had convinced his head of staff, Deirdre, to return to the penthouse unharmed after her girlfriend (and fellow maid) Audrey had been exorcised by the Knights. The Count had not been keen on it, but Terry and the other founding members of Bandersnatch had thrown their weight around, forcing his hand.

Still, Fergus felt like he was going to pull his hair out if he had to be stuck inside another minute, so he'd jumped at the chance to run the errand in Deirdre's place. He figured if he kept the hood of his jumper up and made it fast, there was no reason to single him out of the crowd. There were plenty of tall, dark-haired men around, after all. The only thing that might give him away was the white sheen to his eyes, courtesy of his kelpie fairy-soul. But he'd been careful about not looking at anyone too long, or drawing attention, so the shopping had gone down without a hitch.

It was the first time he'd been to the lower level since he and his friends had returned to New Peiling from the wilds, and though he'd seen the devastation of the fire before, it was still staggering to see the remains of the slums. The place he'd grown up in seemed both home and alien to him. He'd been busy mulling over that when he nearly ran into the Air Guard's Captain and Vice-Captain on the penthouse steps. He considered dropping the groceries and running, but Captain William Guillory had stopped him, and from there, things just went from bad to worse.

Fergus didn't know how, but Guillory had gotten wind of their plans to leave the city and tracked them down to the Count's. He hadn't wanted to let the Captain in, but he'd found himself trapped, and it was either stand outside all day, or face the fact that Guillory was going to enter with him. Once inside, Guillory had announced that he was taking a hiatus from the Air Guard in order to be the pilot for their voyage, and Fergus could *feel* the hatred coming off of Harriet in waves.

It was bad luck that the Vice-Captain had cornered him, but as far as bad luck went, it couldn't have been much worse. He couldn't hear anyone in the adjoining room or hallway – the others still downstairs arguing with Guillory.

"This is all your fault," Harriet snarled, advancing on him.

"How is it my fault?" Fergus asked, narrowing his eyes and resting a hand on the cabinet.

Harriet grabbed him by the front of his shirt, jerking him forward. The Vice-Captain was slightly taller than he was. He was a handsome man with long black curls; however, the ugly scar across his temple was a salient reminder that he was not to be underestimated. Fergus grabbed his wrists, trying to push him back without being rough.

"You *know* why!"

"No," Fergus replied," I really don't."

"The Captain resigned because of you. He said he'd met a young man who interested him."

"That's not much of an excuse."

Harriet's eyes narrowed further. "He said he wanted to keep an eye on you. *You*," he spat. "Why you of all people? What's so special about *you*?"

Fergus didn't reply.

"Did that mangy cur put a spell on him?"

Fergus glared. "Screw you. We didn't do anything to him."

"You've tricked him. Why else would he want to help you? What other reason does he have to believe in someone like you?"

"We didn't do anything!" Fergus shouted, shoving Harriet and sending him crashing backwards over the sofa. He moved to jump over the back of the couch and make for the door. No sooner had he hiked up his leg than he found himself looking down the barrel of a revolver. He froze.

"You're not going anywhere. I could kill you right now, and no one would be able to do anything about it."

"The Count will have your stupid hero arrest you."

Harriet laughed. "I think not. Besides, my mother would have me out by dinner."

He drew back the hammer. Fergus swallowed as he heard it click.

"Am I interrupting something?"

Rosslyn Weber stood in the doorway, his limp blonde hair falling into his eyes. Fergus shivered at his expression.

"You know, if by some chance you shoot and don't kill him, I'm going to shut this door and . . . " He paused, sneering. "Well, perhaps you'll be the one disappearing."

"Is that a threat?" Harriet whispered, his voice shaking with something that went beyond insult or anger.

"Get up and go," the blonde replied coolly.

Harriet moved to sit up, mouth forming a white line. Fergus started to relax when he saw the flash and burst of smoke, followed by a deafening explosion as a bullet zoomed over his shoulder and embedded in the armoire behind him. Pieces of wood splintered and shot off into the air, pelting him in the back of the neck. For a second, Fergus thought his heart had stopped. Rosslyn took a great stride into the room. However, the Vice-Captain had already righted himself, dusting off his suit and tucking away the revolver.

"Sorry," he drawled, returning Rosslyn's smirk from before. "Slipped."

Rosslyn said nothing, but his face was a blotchy red as Harriet sauntered past him through the door. Fergus took a gulping breath and sagged down behind the couch, fingers pressing into the embroidered fabric. He hiccupped and then let out a little curse before a second hiccup escaped him. Clutching at his chest, he looked up to see Rosslyn looming on the other side of the sofa.

"Thanks," he managed, standing up. His hands were shaking. He shoved them into his pockets. "Seems like he doesn't like us very much."

"He doesn't like any hybrid. He's Paige Harriet's son."

Fergus said nothing for a moment, leaning back on the balls of his feet. "Guess he is . . . That election's coming up soon, isn't it? Do you think she's gonna win?"

"I'm quite sure of it."

He said nothing, nodding and staring down at his worn-out trainers. "So why does she hate us so much?"

"I believe that her husband – his father – was killed by a hybrid," Rosslyn said with a shrug. "I don't know the details, but they've damned us all thanks to that."

Fergus chewed on his lip, feeling glad he'd be out of the city soon. "I should probably go see what's going on down there, huh?"

"Don't bother. Guillory is going to be your captain whether you like it or not."

"What do you mean?"

"No one is more stubborn than William Guillory. I have no idea why he's set his mind on this, but he has, and I don't know the man who could change it. So I suppose he will be the captain of this mysterious voyage."

"Yeah," Fergus said, trying to edge around Rosslyn to the door before he could fire off any more uncomfortable observations. Going back to his room and his guitar sounded very nice at the moment. He thought maybe his hands would be still if he could just lay them on a pick and strings.

"What about Ursula? And your friend – Raja, right? What about his little girlfriend?"

"Evelyn has been missing for weeks. There's no hope there, you know? Better for him to just get away."

"They've exorcised – or tried to exorcise – a lot of people in the last year," Rosslyn observed.

Fergus stopped. The doorway was just a few steps away. He pursed his mouth. "They have," he agreed as mildly as he could manage.

"I guess it *is* safer to go."

"We aren't running away," he replied, bristling.

Rosslyn was silent a moment too long for Fergus's liking, but before he could press, the blonde turned away and began examining the hole in the armoire.

Fergus didn't feel like rehashing the point. He was doing what he felt Flynn, his murdered best friend, would have wanted him to do. Besides, Ursula was the one who'd said they were better off apart, there wasn't anything *anyone* could do for a hybrid who'd been exorcised, so Evelyn was a lost cause, and Fergus didn't particularly care what role "Ainslee's son" was supposed to be taking in all this. They hadn't seemed so interest in rallying to him a few weeks ago. In fact, he recalled that they'd implied he was too dull-witted for the job. His mother's intrigues were none of his business, and he had his own life to live, which he was going to do by pursuing the puzzle that Flynn had died over.

He let out a low sigh and walked down the dark corridor with its odd assortment of surrealist paintings. He tried very hard not to look at the one of Terry in the raw as he turned right at the corner and continued to the room at the very end.

It was made up in pale spring greens. Given that it was almost autumn, this didn't seem entirely appropriate. He thought maybe the decor was a cover for the fact it was the darkest room on the floor. It looked like it had been a child's room. There were places on the wall where old drawings might have been plastered at one time. They'd been peeled off since, but the rug still had juice stains, and there were crude watercolor scribbles in some of the corners. Fergus sat on the bed, running his hands through his dark brown hair, before throwing himself onto his back.

The Count's penthouse was fancy. There was no getting around that. Even the rooms that had sheets over all the furniture were nicer than any Fergus had ever stayed in, including Ursula's apartment, and there were plenty of rooms to spare, so they'd been allowed to pick the rooms they wanted. Terry had chosen the room next to this one, which was how Fergus ended up in here, though he would have preferred a view of the square and its mermaid fountain.

He hadn't slept in a room all by himself for a long time. Not since before Flynn had been killed. Even with Terry next door, he still couldn't quite relax. Fergus threw his forearm over his eyes. He'd barely slept at all the night before, or the night before that. He kept dreaming about Flynn and Audrey and Evelyn. The three of them would stand at the end of a rotting pier calling his name, and he would just watch as the wood crumbled into the ocean. He would watch as their heads and hands disappeared under the foamy waves. Then he would turn, and Rosslyn would be there saying, "But you're Ainslee's son."

There was a knock at the door. He jumped and sat up, feeling ruffled. "What do you want?"

"Thought you might want some friendly company," Terry said, peeking inside.

He sounded injured, and Fergus felt guilty. He sat up the rest of the way and tried to smile, but felt too tired to make it genuine.

"Heard the gun go off?"

"The great ass returned to the drawing room smelling of gunpowder, and then Rosslyn came in. They're still shouting. I hope Rosslyn curses him."

"Yeah. Me, too." Fergus flopped backwards. "Do people really feel safer knowing that lunatic is watching over the city?"

"Gotta wonder what it'll be like if Guillory really does come with us," Terry remarked, coming over to sit beside Fergus.

Once upon a time, Terry had been the bassist of Fergus's now defunct band, Everyday Resources. He was one of the three pupils Fergus's mother had taught to transform into their fairy forms – Terry's being a *gytrash* specifically – and had established Bandersnatch with Ursula and Rosslyn after Ainslee killed herself. He was a tall man in his early 20s with wild auburn hair, straight features, and pale grey eyes. Terry was a lot of things, and Fergus had only recently realized how few of them he was aware of.

He felt a little stupid for trusting him again, given that Terry had been lying to him consistently for years, but he was comforting to have around, and he was the one person his mother had known first who seemed to prefer Fergus to Ainslee.

"Is Guillory really doing this because of me?"

"Because of you?" Terry asked, looking legitimately surprised.

"That's what his lackey shot at me for."

"I dunno. Who knows what Guillory thinks he'll accomplish?"

Terry lay down across the pillows. The two of them stared at the hangings in silence. Though Fergus and Three had given the room a tidying, it was still pretty dusty and moth eaten. He could see bits of the ceiling through the thinning velvet overhead.

"I wish we could just go now."

"Yeah," Terry agreed, sounding as tired as Fergus felt.

"Hey, Terry," Fergus muttered, looking away. "We aren't running away, right?"

"Running away from what?"

Fergus was silent for a moment before nodding. "Yeah, right? Running away from what?"

Terry sat up. "Are you having second thoughts?"

Fergus paused and then looked up at him. "No, I wanna go. But what about you? Do you *really* want to go to the middle of nowhere with me? What about Bandersnatch and the city and Baba Yaga?"

Terry's mouth scrunched to the side. "Badb Catha."

"Yeah. I mean, what about all that?"

"I suspect the Count has been longing for that role for some time. I'm kind of sick of it."

"Of him wanting it?"

Terry shook his head. "No, of being 'Badb Catha' – the one doing the dirty work."

"You know, I always wondered why people seemed . . . "

"Afraid of me?" Terry frowned, looking away. "If I did stay, I might end up putting all of Bandersnatch in danger. I'm probably next on Evalach's list of 'Evil Fairies to Exorcise.'"

Fergus's heart missed a beat. He swallowed, looking away.

Terry touched his shoulder. "Well, I wouldn't be easy to catch, so don't worry." Sighing, he dropped his hand into his lap. "This city is going to Hell. I'm sick of it."

"What happened to doing the wrong things for the right reasons?" Fergus asked quietly.

Terry shrugged.

They were silent for a few minutes before Fergus finally said, "Go get your bass. We'll play a little while."

•   •   •

Fergus and Terry were recruited to help in the kitchens that night along with Three, who was the only one there on a voluntary basis. Despite their help, only Terry was asked to go to dinner with the Count. Fergus and Three stayed down in the kitchens with Deirdre, Pip, Raja, and the grumpy old cook, sitting on pots or counters or the floor as they could. The cook noisily slurped down her stew, periodically casting glares at no one in particular, like a dog defending its food.

Fergus wasn't sure if it was her presence, or that he had been excluded from dinner upstairs, but the atmosphere was bad. He poked at his stew without interest.

"Cheer up," Deirdre said in her usual no nonsense tone. "At least you'll have some money when you set out."

Fergus jabbed at a carrot. "How come he wanted Terry up there?"

She shrugged.

He noted she hadn't touched her meal either. Though she had returned to the penthouse, and though she was as strict as ever, he noticed that Deirdre's cheeks had grown hollow. He wondered if she was just going through the motions, but then he thought that wasn't all bad. He'd personally found that if he forced himself to continue on normally, repetition usually won out over his misery. Then again, even though his mother and Flynn were dead, their fairies' souls were floating around somewhere. Someday, they'd attach to new humans.

Maybe they'd remember him, if only just a little. Sometimes, he recognized things he'd never seen before, or remembered places he'd never been, which he thought was his soul's memories. So he hoped that maybe someday he might be able to meet them again, even if they were in an entirely different body, and even if they were a very small part of who they were when he knew them. Deirdre didn't have that option.

Then there was Raja, who was essentially in the same boat as Deirdre. He'd been exceptionally quiet since the Knights had taken Evelyn. Fergus and

Terry tried to ply him with songs and drinks and talk about magic and other countries, but he'd been steadily listless. But Fergus had noticed that Deirdre was nicer to Raja than anyone else besides the Count. He'd even seen her bringing him extra food.

"What?" she asked waspishly, and he realized he'd been staring at her. Her hair was short now, sticking out haphazardly, and he had a feeling she'd just grabbed a pair of scissors and started chopping. At his silence, she glared even more. "What is it?"

"Why did you cut your hair?" he asked, putting his bowl aside.

Deirdre frowned, but it made her seem more like herself, and he felt a little relieved.

"I felt like I needed to. It doesn't look very good. I shouldn't have been so careless."

"Who said that?"

She lifted her chin and gave a little snort.

He sighed. "It looks okay."

"One of the painters I modeled for told me not to return until it grew out."

"It wasn't that guy, was it?"

"If you mean the Count, then no, and you should be more respectful. Besides, he prefers male models."

"Yeah, sorry," he muttered, careful not to add the, "whatever," on the tip of his tongue.

"Are you finished? Give me your bowl."

Fergus handed it over and watched her go put it in the sink with her own. The cook was also finished. Dumping hers in with the rest, she picked up her bag and hobbled out without even saying, "good night." Fergus turned to the others. Raja was staring into space again, his bowl yet full. Pip and Three were arguing. Fergus cleared his throat softly, venturing a, "Hello," in their native language. Pip stared at him for a moment before sneering and returning to the dispute. Three gave him an apologetic look, mouthing, "Not bad."

He sighed and stood, pausing next to Raja and putting a hand on his shoulder. Raja blinked up at him sluggishly and then forced a weak smile, swirling the oily surface of the stew with his spoon.

"We'll probably be able to go soon."

"Seems like it," Fergus agreed.

"I don't really want that *human* piloting us."

Fergus blinked, taken aback.

"Sorry," Raja muttered. He turned his electric blue eyes on Fergus for just a moment before looking away and moving to stand. "I think I'll take a walk."

"Do you want company?"

He shook his head and went to pour out his soup.

Fergus sighed again and shoved his hands into his pockets. He left the sounds of Pip's and Three's argument and Raja's and Deirdre's gloomy silence behind as he stepped into the hallway and ran straight into Ursula.

She let out a hiss of irritation, righting herself and brushing her sleeves before looking up. Her face immediately went blank as she stared up at Fergus. She looked less pale than when he'd last seen her, though her features were still pinched, the weight not yet returned to her cheeks. Her shoulder-length black hair was pulled up into a rough bun at the nape of her neck, and most of it had come out. She looked windblown and alluring, and he felt his stomach twist, his throat growing tight, before he turned and started to walk away.

"Fergus," she called softly.

He paused, on the verge of bolting, and jammed his hands into the pockets of his hoodie. "How's Toby?"

"The fish are fine," she said, sounding disappointed. "I put them near the window with some of those moon snails. They light up the aquarium nicely, and it helps keep the snails longer." She hesitated before adding, "You won't be collecting them anytime soon, I imagine?"

"Probably not," he agreed, resisting the urge to turn around.

"Did you know? It's quiet without you."

"I'm sure Dominique would keep you company."

She snorted. "She's taken an interest in one of her girls – Cindy Starlight, or something ridiculous like that."

"Isn't that the one who can swallow swords?"

"I'm surprised you can remember that."

Fergus was beginning to feel like this was getting too familiar, and getting overly comfortable around Ursula was a one-way ticket to pain, so he shrugged and didn't reply.

"You'll be leaving soon, then?" she asked in a softer tone.

"Dunno, but hopefully."

There was a moment of silence, in which he risked a glance at her over his shoulder. She caught his gaze, and he cringed, quickly looking away again.

"Come by before you go?"

"Yeah, maybe I will," he replied and started towards the stairs.

He took the steps two at a time, and if she said anything else, he missed it. He wished he'd said nothing at all, because conceding that much made him want to go and see her. Just entertaining the idea caused that traitorous spark of hope to flare up, like maybe this time she would change her mind. She'd forget she wasn't into monogamy, or decide he was worth the exception. But she wouldn't and thinking about it made him feel sick.

He stepped inside his room and walked over to the bed. For a moment, he just stood there, staring at it blankly, and then he grabbed a pillow and struck the frame. It exploded into a flurry of feathers. Fergus watched them drift and settle around his feet. Despite his outburst, the room was very quiet. He scooped the feathers from the bed and sat down, head in his hands.

There was a hot, prickling sensation just under his skin. He'd been experiencing it every time he got angry recently, and it was becoming harder to convince himself that he shouldn't give into it, but he forced himself to breathe slowly and deeply until the feeling subsided. Then he kicked off his shoes, wriggled out of his jeans, and slid halfway under the covers. He'd be less irritable if he just got a little more sleep, he thought, and tonight would be the night he'd catch up. Then losing his temper wouldn't be an issue.

Yet as he tried to drift off, he kept recalling how his mother had been angry most of the time and about how she had wound up transforming too often and started losing her mind because of it. His fingers tightened in the sheets, and he took steadying breaths. That wasn't going to happen to him. He wasn't going to go crazy. He *wasn't* like her. Still, when he finally fell asleep, he dreamed of cold black water and people screaming.

•   •   •

Fergus felt even grumpier the next morning when he went outside to pick up the bottle of milk, loaf of bread, and paper that were routinely left outside the penthouse between six-thirty and seven. The penthouse was just close enough to the edge of the city that a little sunlight managed to peek through the streets, casting a dim light on the fountain. It would have been nice if he wasn't feeling tired and prickly. He stifled a yawn and tucked the bread and milk under one arm, opening the paper.

Paige Harriet's Growing Popularity: Preliminary Polls Show Over 65% Approval.

Fergus glared at the photo of a smiling woman with dark hair, glasses, and a broad jaw line. She looked like her son. He wondered if that made her handsome. She had a politician's smile, which didn't meet her eyes, but she wasn't bad looking. He found that annoying, so he crumpled up the paper and was about to go inside when he heard a familiar voice.

"Good morning," Guillory called from the bottom of the steps.

Fergus stopped and blinked down at him groggily. "What are you doing here?"

"I thought we'd start preparations."

"Who said you were gonna help us?" Fergus demanded.

Guillory smiled. "Is that still an issue? I thought we'd settled it yesterday."

Fergus glanced around. "Your flunky's not here."

"No, he has business to attend to. He's the acting Captain of the Air Guard now."

"So what do you want, then?"

Guillory proceeded up the steps. He was tall and tawny and formidable. Fergus felt a little uncomfortable standing so close to him. He straightened, feeling he should hold his ground, but edged away despite himself.

"You and your friends will need papers. Proper papers."

"What for?"

"Many cities won't let you disembark without them. Unless you're planning on staying in the airship the entire time, I think it would be a good idea."

"Aren't they still looking for Terry and me?"

Guillory's smile faltered a little. "No, it seems not. It seems they aren't concerned with last spring's arson anymore. However," he continued, perking up again, "even if they were, I'm vouching for you, so it'll be fine."

Fergus didn't feel like picking a fight this early, so he just shrugged and opened the door to let Guillory through before going to dump the paper in the sitting room and heading off to the kitchens with the milk and bread. Guillory trailed after him.

"Why are you following me?" he gritted out, putting down the bottle of milk a little too forcefully. It clattered angrily against the countertop, and he had to check to make sure he hadn't cracked the glass.

"Well, I need you to stir your friends, of course. The sooner we set out, the better. The immigration office can be very crowded."

Fergus counted back from ten. "Fine. Just stay here and don't touch anything, okay?"

Guillory was already inspecting a rack of knives imported from a city with a name Fergus couldn't even pronounce. He sighed in exasperation, but left the former Air Guard Captain to it, taking the servant's passage up to the next floor to wake the others.

Pip and Three were sharing a room. He headed there first, pausing outside the door a moment and listening before knocking. He was pretty sure they weren't sharing it for romantic reasons, but he wasn't entirely certain. It sounded like someone was up and moving around, so he gave a little tap. There was a pause, and then the door opened to reveal a sleepy Three. Her black hair was sticking up weirdly. Part of it had been bleached blonde; the rest was streaked with blue. She stifled a yawn.

"Hi, Fergus," she mumbled. "Pip's still asleep."

"Can you get him up? Guillory's here, and he wants us to go with him to get papers."

She rubbed at one eye, seeming to take a moment to understand him, and then blinked. "Oh, yes. Okay."

"Meet you in the kitchens," Fergus said and proceeded down a winding corridor to Raja's room. He rapped on the door, but Raja didn't answer, so he decided to peek inside. The room was empty. He felt a prickle of anxiety go down his spine. Probably Raja had just gone for a morning walk, but Fergus didn't like anyone being unaccounted for. Lately, that could very well mean all kinds of really bad things. Fergus frowned to himself before heading towards Terry's room, but ran into Terry halfway there.

"What's up?"

"Guillory's here," Fergus replied. "Says he wants to take us to the immigration office to get papers. 'Proper papers.'"

"Sounds like him. Did he say what he was gonna do if someone tried to arrest us?"

"Said he would vouch for us." Fergus paused and then added, "Harriet hasn't come back for us, so I guess his word's good. He also said the arson case was dropped."

Terry scowled. "Figures."

"Maybe we should have testified."

"No point worrying about it now," Terry said, starting past him.

"Have you seen Raja?" Fergus asked.

"Nope. Not since before dinner. You missed Rosslyn dumping a glass of wine on the Count."

"I ran into Ursula."

Terry gave him a wan smile. "I figured. Well, don't worry about her. C'mon. Let's go find Raja."

Chapter Two.

The immigration office was on the top level of the city. New Peiling's middle city, where the penthouse was located, was nice enough. It was cleaner than the lower level and lighter, too. The architecture was newer and thus not in any desperate need of repairs. However, its middle class charm paled in comparison to the top level where every one of the sleek white buildings was exposed to daylight, their rooftops soaring into the clouds. All of the good parks were on this level, along with the best libraries, museums, galleries, and archives.

It was not a place where hybrids were typically welcome. A number of signs and postings littered the streets, declaring laws which by and large would be all too easy to break for someone who wasn't well acquainted with the level, and for a hybrid, committing a misdemeanor once was grounds for permanent expulsion from the top level.

Fergus's mother had been born on an upper-middle level of the city and often played in Erstwyre Park as a child. She'd brought him to the park to play when he was young, as well, and he'd continued to visit even after she'd disappeared, so he was familiar with most of the ridiculous rules. He wondered if they'd passed any new ones in the last five months.

He was first out of the lift, squinting at the sunshine glinting off of the glass fountain in the center of the square. Beyond the fountain was the courthouse and official city library, and just a little ways to the right of those lay Erstwyre Park. The air was thinner on the top plate, but it smelled so much cleaner. Fergus stretched his arms over his head and took a deep breath. He wasn't used to the altitude, and he felt momentarily light-headed. The wind was also stronger here, and he wished he'd worn a hoodie.

Guillory was last out of the lift. He moved to the front of the group and started across the square towards the large government building. Fergus didn't know where the immigration office was exactly, but he knew that a number of official buildings lined the block behind the courthouse, and it was down that street that they progressed. The walk was dotted with trees, which cast dappled shadows over the concrete. He held his arms close to his body, fending off goosebumps.

The top level was always very quiet. There were never as many people out and about as in the lower levels. He wondered if he just never came at the right time of day.

"It's chilly!" Three said. She was wearing several layers, but none of them covered her arms, which she rubbed briskly.

"Usually is," Terry replied.

"This is probably the tallest city we've ever visited. The other islands are wider."

"I heard there are cities where everything is on the same level," Fergus said.

"There are. Lancaster is like that, actually. Well, it's kind of tiered, but not like this. It sprawls down the cliff face, and all the buildings built against that are stacked, but basically nothing's covered up like here."

"What about Clohaven?"

"It's more like this, but also a little broader, so not as tall. Plus, it's in the middle of an island chain, so it's well protected, and all the city offices are down near the harbor."

Fergus nodded. Once upon a time, before he was even born, his father had run away to Clohaven. That was the only thing he knew about that man. His mother had never kept any pictures, and aside from telling him – at 12 – what had actually happened, she never spoke of him. He wondered if he was still there.

"It's only a little further," Guillory said, not looking back. He sounded very chipper. Fergus wondered how he could be excited about an adventure that he still was in the dark on.

The group lapsed into silence, pausing at the edge of the block to watch an old man on an antique bicycle slowly pedal by. The wind drifted through the trees, reshaping the shadows on the walk. On the opposite corner, a young woman with a child stood tossing breadcrumbs to a small army of sparrows.

Across the way was a large cathedral. Its shadow loomed over the street, spiky and intimidating. Like the other buildings, it was white to the tips of every turret. He could see that its windows were stained glass, but it wasn't illuminated at this time of day, and he couldn't make out the images.

There was a gathering on the steps. Fergus slowed as they crossed the street and drew nearer. The crowd wasn't small considering the hour and venue, and it seemed more people were migrating to the church from the streets around them. Even the young woman and child stopped feeding the birds and drifted that way. Fergus stopped. At the top of the steps was a man in a suit. He had greying hair and quivering jowls. His voice was loud and his accent as polished as Ashton Harriet's. He kept moving his arms wildly as he spoke.

"And what of Trevor Fennis? Never seen again, was he? He was lured down into the quagmire and consumed by the beasts! Softhearted fools like Whitehurst are deceived by appearances. Though they may look like us, they are monsters! Never forget this! Look how they turn on each other. They even burned down their own level. Nothing is sacred to them! They seduce our youth and infect them! Their entire quarter is a blight on our fair city!

"Only Paige Harriet is prepared to deal with this sickness! Only Paige Harriet is strong enough to rid our city of the vermin! To the islands with them! We must be rid of them one way or another! Harriet will take them away from us! Away from our children with their sickly, demonic souls!"

Fergus was too shocked to even be angry. He blinked, mouth gaping, and just stood there listening as the man continued to preach about how the hybrids should be rounded up and sent away, listing instances of hybrids who had lost their minds and attacked humans, lobbying for harsher punishments for hybrid criminals, pointing out neighboring cities who had forced the hybrids out, and how they had seen fewer hybrids cropping up since.

It all came back to Paige Harriet and her plan to systematically clean the lower city. For the first time, Fergus realized that this woman really did have an agenda, and she had the resources to follow through on it. He felt sick to his stomach.

Someone yanked on his arm, and he turned to Terry. His mouth was a thin white line, eyes narrowed dangerously. He said nothing, but dragged Fergus away from the assembly. The others were nearly at the top of the next block, but they didn't chase after them. Terry's fingers were so tight on Fergus's elbow, that he was pretty sure he would bruise, but he didn't say anything. He was still too appalled by what he'd just realized. The words kept going round and round his head: *monsters, vermin, scourge, islands* . . .

He wasn't human, and he didn't want to be human, not it if meant being like that guy, because he *wasn't* a brainless, rabid animal.

Plus, the man's facts were all wrong. No one had *eaten* Trevor Fennis, though he had been killed by hybrids, and it was the Knights of Evalach – the vigilante humans who were responsible for the deaths of at least three people Fergus had been close to – who burned down the lower city.

Moreover, New Peiling was as much his home as that man's or any of those assembled. He'd been born in this city. He'd lived here his entire life. Maybe he didn't have a specific home anymore – the apartment he'd grown up in had been consumed by the fire – but this was still where he had grown up, and depending on what happened in their quest, he planned to return here yet. If the humans had such an issue with the hybrids, maybe *they* should go. There were plenty of other cities around, and they, at least, were more likely to have the money to pick up and go somewhere nicer. But then, this wasn't about finding somewhere better. This was about getting rid of the hybrids.

Three had once told him that other cities had handled things in this way: sending the hybrids to adjacent island colonies. Her description hadn't been very nice. It sounded more like internment camps to him.

The shock was finally replaced by anger. His jaw was so tight it hurt, his chest burned, and he found his hands were shaking. His skin began to prickle. He wished it had been Paige Harriet instead of Trevor Fennis at the gala that night. If someone could just get rid of her, idiots like that would have no one to rally to. Someone should round up all the anti-hybrid humans and shove them over the edge of the upper city, or load them all up on a ferry and send them off to nowhere. See how they liked it.

It wasn't like things weren't bad enough in the lower city. Even rich hybrids like the Count weren't free to do whatever they wanted, or be whatever they wanted. All of the Count's influence was behind the scenes. If he'd ever wanted to run for office, it would've been impossible. Fergus had lived in poverty his entire life, struggling to make ends meet, forgotten by the humans in the darkness and decay of the lower city. That was what the humans thought of as 'tolerance.' Now they didn't even want to extend him that?

Screw them, he thought. He hoped an airship crashed into the upper city. He hoped it landed straight on Paige Harriet.

"Don't say it. Don't say anything," Terry said very quietly, voice pinched. "Whatever you're thinking, save it."

Fergus drew up to his full height. "And why shouldn't I?" he snarled. The tingling sensation grew stronger.

"And for Chrissake, do *not* transform here. They'll shoot you in the head."

He didn't like to hear it, but he knew it was true. He stopped. Ducking down a moment, he ran his hands over his face and took deep breaths. He tried to think of anything besides tearing Paige Harriet and that stupid soapbox guy limb from limb. He thought of dark, cold waters and moonlight smeared across the surface.

"Count with me – in threes, okay?" Terry suggested, hand on his back.

Fergus nodded.

"Three, six, nine, twelve, fifteen . . . "

By the time they reached 72, the feeling had subsided, and Terry helped him up. The others were out of sight.

"Damnit, we lost them," Fergus sighed.

"Don't worry. I think it's just around the corner. The buildings all have plaques on them anyway, so I'm sure we can find it."

Terry started forward. Fergus stared after him, wondering if he'd been dealing with this anger all along. He felt like maybe he *had* been too naive back when he'd refused to help Terry take those Fennis-filled crates to the docks. Maybe Terry was the one who'd been right all along, but if so, why was he following Fergus? He realized he was falling behind and took a few jogging steps to catch up.

"Terry?"

"Yeah?"

"Do you hate this city?"

Terry glanced at him, brows rising in surprise, and then his mouth twitched. "Yeah, I kinda do."

"Is that why you're coming with me?"

His expression changed, the wryness sliding off of his face to be replaced with something unreadable. It was a look Fergus recognized. It didn't have any specific meaning, but Fergus knew that if he kept pressing, Terry was going to start lying. He felt a little disappointed.

"Hey, never mind. You're coming. That's what's important, right?"

"There it is. Look, Three's waving," Terry said and began to jog.

Fergus watched him go, filled with fresh misgivings.

•　　•　　•

Beathag's was located several blocks in from the express lift to the upper city. Since the arson carved out a huge chunk of the slums, the back of the shop was now exposed to daylight. It also had a great view of the tent city that had popped up in the cleared out areas and even on top of the rubble in a few places. On the corner across from the magic shop was an old convenience store with a glass front and neon lights. It had the same streamlined look of convenience stores on nearly every level of the city.

Beathag's was completely different, however. Fergus had thought at times that it looked like a living thing, or at least enchanted.

He'd often imagined walking towards the door and being gobbled up. Its ancient brick façade had pieces of dead ivy stuck to it. An aging, hand-painted sign hung over the doorway. There was a window beside it, presently the new home of Fergus's fish tank. The fish were happily floating together with the glowing moon snails. Once, the two lanterns to either side of the door had been perpetually lit. Now, though, there was sunlight enough to illuminate the shop, and they were both dark, which gave Fergus an oddly hollow feeling.

On top of Beathag's was the Labyrinth – a burlesque parlor. The stairs leading to the entrance were in the alcove just left of Beathag's door. There was a wooden placard affixed to the brick above the entryway with a faded painting of two women pressed together. He thought he could see the Labyrinth's proprietress – Lady Dominique – sitting by the window, smoking a long pipe. She seemed to be talking to someone, and he wondered if it was Ursula and almost lost his resolve.

It was still the middle of the day, though, and the open sign was up. Of course, she might have found a new shopkeep. He wasn't sure how he felt about that, though it'd been months since he'd worked there. If she hadn't hired someone, he would certainly be surprised, since she didn't like doing the work herself.

Trying to mentally prepare himself to meet his replacement, he forced himself to walk across the street and enter the shop. The bells over the doorway jingled. It still had a strange, earthy smell that was painfully familiar. He sidled through two packed columns of dried snakes and powdered claws, emerging on the other side of the shop, which was lit by several oil lamps. There was an old grandfather clock behind the counter and a large display of pickled frogs in jars beside the register. Last time he'd been here, it had been shells.

Ursula was not behind the counter. As he suspected, she'd found a replacement. It was a young man with a high, sloping forehead, a broad nose, and dark eyes with long lashes. It took Fergus a moment to remember his name.

"Gavin?" he asked, unable to hide his surprise.

"Hi, Fergus. How've you been?" he asked, smiling.

Fergus was too stunned to see Gavin at the register to feel discomfited. Gavin had once been a friend of Flynn's and a member of Niamh – a scholarly society of hybrids who'd been searching for Tír na nÓg before being hunted down by the Knights of Evalach. Audrey and Evelyn had also been active Niamh members, but like Flynn, they were dead now. For an academic society, membership was high risk.

He wondered if, like Raja, Gavin had dropped out because of Audrey's and Evelyn's exorcisms. Unlike Raja, however, he looked to be in good spirits.

"Fine. Just fine. You're working here now?"

"Since last month. I get a discount. Helps with university."

"Oh yeah, you're still enrolled, huh?"

Gavin nodded. "Two more years."

"How's . . . Jane?"

Gavin's expression fell. He swallowed, but wasn't quite able to make himself smile. Instead, he looked down at his hands on the counter. "Well, she's recovering."

"Recovering?"

"After all that . . . She took it hard."

Fergus could still remember the last time he'd seen Jane: red hair askew, face pale and drawn, eyes bulging with barely contained hysterics. She was a very pretty girl normally, but that night, she'd been frightening.

"Have you seen her since Evelyn?"

Gavin nodded. "I've been trying to check in on her. She's almost entirely alone in that penthouse."

"She doesn't have maids or anything?"

"She fired most of them. Only kept the one she grew up with."

"That sucks."

"She'll pull herself together. It's just hard to accept things have come to this."

"To Paige Harriet?"

"Something like that, yeah. Hey, are you looking for Ursula?"

Fergus nodded.

"She's in the backroom. I guess you already know your way around."

His mouth twitched into a half-smile as he went around the counter to the doorway leading to the back of the shop and Ursula's quarters. He walked past the bedroom that they had shared up until the fire, past the little kitchen and the shower with its overly large tub pressed up against the wall, and down the corridor to the sitting room where she kept her personal materials.

Ursula was sitting in a faded red and gold armchair, poring over a book that was nearly the size of the table it was resting on. She had her legs drawn up under her, her skirt trailing over the front of the chair. Her fingers were linked in her hair, holding it back from her face, and her green eyes were narrowed. He cleared his throat softly, and she blinked, looking up.

For a moment, he didn't think she recognized him, or maybe she didn't believe he was actually there, but then she straightened and stretched out her legs. The toes of her right foot linked around the toe of her left, the only sign of her discomfort as she stared at him without blinking.

"Hi," he said, pushing away from the doorframe, but not entering the room.

"Hello," she repeated.

Silence resumed as she continued staring at him. All the regret he'd seen the night before was gone from her face. He suddenly felt very stupid. He wondered why he'd even come.

"I have a few things for you," she suddenly said.

"What kinds of things? Did I forget something?"

"No, but there were still a few things I wanted to give you. Wait here."

Fergus nodded and stepped aside to let her pass. He'd been in this room many times before. There was a supply closet near the bathroom, but its bench was very small, so she'd often let him use the table in here to crush, grate, or slice ingredients. The room was white, though the paint was cracking all over, revealing a dull, yellow coat beneath.

The walls were lined with glass cases full of books and telescopes and orbs and other magical items that he didn't have the vocabulary for. It was like her bedroom, which also had stacks of books all around, except neater. He thought perhaps the books in her bedroom were the ones she needed less often.

He drifted over to the table, peeking at the book that she'd left open. The page was filled with complicated runes. He couldn't make heads or tails of the explanations, except that they called upon the elements.

Ursula cleared her throat sharply as she returned. She walked up to him and put a few things down on the table on top of the book, looking at him expectantly, so he moved closer to examine her offerings. There was a pouch, a small book, photographs, and a clip of money. It looked like a lot of money.

"I can't accept that."

"You'll need clothing – warm clothing. Autumn is right around the corner, isn't it? What will you do when winter arrives? You'll need to be properly outfitted. Probably some of your companions will, too. You'll also need other supplies. I've prepared a list for you."

"I think Three and Guillory are taking care of that."

"Well, check what they have against my list. You'll be glad you did."

He sighed. "Okay, so what's the rest of this?"

She picked up the book and held it out to him. "This is a beginner's book on magic. I want you to read it. I don't know if you'll be able to make use of it, but you should try. Your mother was a magical virtuoso. Maybe you also have some latent talent."

"Probably not."

"Even so, read it. Study it. Do what you can."

"Okay, fine. What's in the pouch?"

"Medical items and a few other things that if you read this book you'll grasp the uses of. At least if you can't, then Terry will know what to do with them."

Fergus put down the book and picked up the pouch, peeking inside. There were a few bottles and flasks and a roll of bandage. He turned his attention to the photos without touching them.

"I made copies of a few things." She was staring at him expectantly again.

Hesitantly, he reached out to pick them up. There were five in total. The first was the photo of his mother and Ursula from her personal album, which he'd seen before. The next was the one that he'd seen on the page just after with Terry, Rosslyn, and Ursula sitting with Ainslee. Rosslyn and Ursula looked a lot younger. Terry looked only a few years younger. Judging by his mother's face, Fergus thought he probably had been about 13 at the time.

He turned to the next photo. This one was of his mother and a boy with dark, unruly hair standing near the docks with another older woman. Ainslee's hair was halfway down her back, and she had her hand on top of the boy's head, smiling down at him fondly. The other woman also had dark hair, though it was marked with grey.

He looked up at her.

"It's my auntie and Ainslee and you. You were about . . . Maybe three or four then? Do you not recognize yourself?"

"No, I do. I'm just surprised you have this."

"Well, I did take the photograph."

He nodded and looked back at the picture. He had a dozen or so photos of his mother and himself from when he was a baby until he was about seven, but none after. It was strange seeing her with Ursula's aunt. It made their history seem more real. He really had grown up self-absorbed. He hadn't even known that his mother worked at Beathag's, though people tended to do so many little jobs around the lower city that keeping track was difficult. A few years ago, Fergus had been holding down three.

But his mother had made his ignorance possible. She'd worked doubly hard so that he wouldn't have to think about anything but himself. When she'd died, she'd ensured that the people she'd taken care of would do the same for him. All along, Ursula, Terry, and even Rosslyn had been watching over him. He felt foolish having only realized it now.

The next picture was of his mother in profile. He couldn't see what she was looking at, but her face was warm and soft. He thought it might have been the water, but he hoped it was him. She was a little horse-faced, which was especially noticeable from the side, but despite that, she was easy on the eyes. He flipped to the final photo and the warm feeling guttered out.

He had never seen his father before. All he knew was that his name was Owen and that he'd run away to Clohaven before Fergus was born. The picture was more faded than the rest, but he could make out light brown hair and blue eyes. Judging by the photo, most of his features came from his mother, but he was of a similar build and had the same blue eyes as his father. His father had his arm around Ainslee, and they were standing near the fountain in front of the library on the top level.

Somehow, he expected anxiety in his father's body language, but this must have been long before he'd figured out Ainslee was a hybrid. He looked perfectly comfortable, like any other young man in love. Fergus wanted to rip the picture in half. He realized his hands were shaking. His crazy mom and his deadbeat dad.

What a lovely couple, he thought bitterly.

Sensing his mood, Ursula took the picture and slid it to the bottom of the stack, neatly holding them out to him. He wanted to leave the picture of his parents, but Ursula was staring at him again, and he felt it would be ungrateful. Reluctantly, he tucked them all into the book, took the clip of money and bag, and stepped away from the table. Ursula reached out to him, hesitated, and let her hand fall, looking away.

"Seems there's nothing left to say," he said, staring at a crack in the casing to her left.

"Fergus, wait," she said, reaching out and catching his arm.

He stopped, turning to meet her dark green eyes. There were tears caught in her heavy lashes. She looked very small and fragile. He thought it was a bad idea, but he stepped closer anyway.

"What is it?"

"I want you to stay," she said, taking advantage of his proximity to clutch his shirt. She looked up at him imploringly.

"Stay? Stay and what? What is there to stay for, Ursula?" he asked, trying to keep his voice level. His heart was bouncing around in his chest. Hope kept springing out despite reason telling him not to set himself up for failure.

"Stay for me. Stay for us, Fergus. You would stay if I asked, wouldn't you?" she asked. "I want you to stay with me. I miss you."

"I miss you, too," he replied, reaching out to cup her face in his hands. He could feel her arms snaking around his back. "But what about what you said before?"

She shook her head. "I don't know, but maybe if it's you . . . "

He leaned forward to kiss her, and the fantasy snapped back into reality.

She neither spoke, nor looked at him, but steadfastly stared off into space. Fergus let out a sigh. This time, he really did go, only glancing over his shoulder once. He thought he saw her wiping her eyes.

Chapter Three.

Fergus had sometimes wondered where Audrey had fit into the Count's menagerie of beautiful and talented help staff. It wasn't that she was ugly; she definitely had been cute enough. She also was very intelligent. He'd picked up that much just from seeing her at the one and only Niamh meeting he'd attended. Still, one former butler was a famous model, Deirdre was a popular artists' model, and Terry was one of the founding members of Bandersnatch. He'd sometimes thought maybe it was because of Deirdre.

However, he soon found out what had made Audrey special: she wasn't just smart, she was an engineering *genius*.

The Count, Rosslyn, and Guillory went on daily excursions to the island that hosted the Count's factory. As they continued their preparations, it became clear that they would need an airship not just capable of flight, but also of navigating the ocean.

The Count and Audrey had been working on a model before she'd been murdered. It had been fairly far along, but not completed, which meant that the Count was left alone to fine-tune the last parts. While he seemed competent, he wasn't a genius, and though Fergus had hoped to leave a week after they'd gotten their papers together, the delay took longer.

Given that this was the prototype built without Audrey's expertise, Fergus thought it probably was going to be less reliable than his other airships, and the reason he was letting them use it was because it was very likely to malfunction and crash. Terry seemed to agree with this assessment.

Still, as he stood on the tarmac, looking up at the airship, he was impressed by how *cool* it was. It was made of a dark, near-black wood. The sails, styled like fins, were on the sides of the ship, though the Count explained that it was possible to deflate the balloon and use it as a third sail, if absolutely necessary. The white balloon on top was covered in bright, merry banners. On the back were two brass propellers. On the side was the word *Returner* written in gold. Fergus noticed that the Count's crest was imprinted under this.

The *Returner* was a lot smaller than the *Pulsatrix*, which they'd made the unsuccessful voyage to the country in. This only confirmed Fergus's suspicions that while it looked good, it probably wasn't that safe. Still, it was all they had.

He adjusted the pack on his shoulder. It was heavier than he'd expected. With Ursula's help, he'd bought some winter clothes, more jeans, and other basic supplies. Besides this, he also had about ten of Flynn's journals. Strapped over his chest, also on his back, was his guitar. If bounty hunting didn't pay off, he could still busk. Terry had also brought his bass, though there was no way Raja could bring a drum kit. Fergus wondered if he could borrow some barrels from the ship's stores, or pots from the kitchen.

But maybe Raja didn't feel like making music. Recently, he seemed to participate more to placate Fergus and Terry than because he wanted to. Fergus watched him climbing up the ladder with a little furrow in his brow.

Terry, Guillory, and the Count were still in the middle of a last minute discussion. Three and Pip were already following Raja inside, aided by the bare bones crew that Guillory had strung together. Fergus started to follow, but was stayed by a hand on his shoulder. He turned to look up at Rosslyn, who had his other hand outstretched. Four vials – one purple, one green, and two in varying shades of red – rested on his palm.

"Take them," he said.

Fergus frowned in consternation, but took the vials. "What are they for?"

"One is for injuries, one is for poison, one is to poison, and the last will start a fire if it touches oxygen. A large fire."

"That seems kind of dangerous for a rocky airship."

"I've sealed it carefully. As long as you keep it packed in your clothing, there shouldn't be any problems."

"Dunno if I wanna set anything on fire," Fergus replied, skeptically.

"Fire has many uses, Fergus."

"Okay, I guess." He slid the bag from his shoulder and tucked the vials in between his jeans and jumpers.

Rosslyn didn't reply. He loomed over Fergus with a torn look.

"Is there something else?"

"Yes, I," Rosslyn started and then hesitated. He cleared his throat and then reached into his jacket to pull out an envelope and a book.

"I can't," Fergus said, but Rosslyn quickly shook his head and pressed them into his hands. He looked down at the book: *Basic Alchemy and Potions Making*. "Rosslyn, you know I . . . I mean, it's me. I don't think I'm gonna understand it."

"It was my father's. I read it when I was about eight, and I understood it well enough. Just apply yourself, and you'll pick it up."

"Your dad's? But what if there's another crash? What if it gets lost?"

Rosslyn's expression became instantly more familiar. His mouth twitched into a crooked, unpleasant line. "I'm trying to break myself of this sentimentality habit. I suppose if that's what happens, it will be an excellent test of my progress."

Fergus sighed and then stuck these items into the bag as well. He stood back up.

"And I have a bit of a favor to ask," Rosslyn said rather abruptly.

"What is it?"

"There are certain ingredients in that part of the world . . . "

"Want me to pick 'em up for you?"

"If you happened to come across them, I would reward you for them on your return."

"Do you have a list?"

Rosslyn gave him a self-effacing smile and held out a slip of paper. "Thank you," he said briefly and, looking a little flustered, hurriedly shuffled over to the Count.

Fergus once again shouldered his backpack and started up the ladder. There were several levels to the ship. From the deck, he went down a set of stairs leading to the control room with its brass instruments and large forward-facing window. Passing this, he arrived at a second narrower staircase leading down to the cabins. At the bottom of this stairwell and to the back of the airship were the kitchens and other amenities, along with the engine room.

A crewman with bright red hair stood at the landing, herding him off to the left towards a line of doors. He pushed open the second one down. Inside was a room with two sets of bunk beds built into the walls. Raja was already sitting on one of them.

"Just the three of you in here, sir," the crewman informed him.

"You can just call me Fergus."

The man gave him a funny look and shrugged. "Let me know if you have any troubles. The name's Orson."

Fergus nodded and stepped into the room to put his pack on the bottom bunk across from Raja. Raja looked up and gave him something that might have been construed as a smile had he been shutting his eyes.

"Think it's just you, me, and Terry in this one. The Captain has his own quarters at the end of the hall, and those other two are in the room next door. Seems even smaller than this one."

"And the crew?"

"In the rooms between those two and the Captain. I get the feeling we're going to end up recruited. This is a pretty small airship, but the crew is *really* small."

Fergus snorted a little. "Well, it'll help pass the time, I guess."

"It's a little claustrophobic. It's kind of like . . . " Raja abruptly stopped, looking away.

"Like what?" Fergus asked, cocking his head.

"Nothing," Raja said, lapsing into silence.

Fergus sighed. Through the wall, he could hear something heavy drop, and then excited shouting in a foreign language. He started to go see what Three and Pip had gotten up to when Terry came in.

"You've saved me a top bunk," he said cheerfully, looking between Raja and Fergus.

Raja didn't respond, and Terry came over to toss his equally meager pack of earthly possessions onto the bunk over Fergus's.

"We'll be taking off soon," he said, as though there hadn't been even a second of awkwardness following his greeting. "It might be rough with an airship of this size, so you probably should hold tight. Looks like these bunks are made for that, though." Terry put a hand on his hip, studying the beds. "Or for *that*," he muttered.

"That better not be *that*," Fergus replied with a distraught expression.

"I'm sure they only did it in Guillory's quarters," Terry said and kicked off his shoes, clambering into his bunk. A moment later, he leaned down over Fergus's. "Did you ever read those classic adventure stories? You know, the ones from before the

Cataclysm? With boy detectives and camps and that sort of thing. They often had bunks."

"You're in a really good mood," Fergus muttered, still wondering if his bed had been defiled by the Count.

"We're off to a new start. It's an adventure. Besides, I always sort of wanted to be a sky pirate," Terry replied with a dreamy expression, and Fergus couldn't tell if he was joking or not. He caught Fergus's look and gave him a rueful smile. "I had a normal life once upon a time. Those Baldini comics were my favorites."

"My mom gave me a few copies once when I was about 12 or 13."

"Where do you think she got them?" Terry asked, smirking.

Though the remark was light, it reminded Fergus that much of the Terry that he had known until a few months ago had been a lie. He shifted uncomfortably. The ship gave a little shudder, coming alive.

"Hey, do you want to watch it take off?" Terry asked.

He looked so enthusiastic that Fergus forgot to feel doubtful. He nodded. Terry hopped out of the bunk, sliding back into his shoes.

"What about you, Raja?"

Raja did not reply. Fergus started to walk towards him, but Terry caught him by the wrist and shook his head.

He'll come around, he mouthed.

They left Raja to hurry up the stairs, pausing outside the control room. They could hear shouts coming from speakers within the room – some from Guillory, others from outside. All sorts of lights were coming on, and things were buzzing and whirring. Guillory barked out instructions, which made about as much sense as Three and Pip's arguments, as crewmen rushed by.

"Ah, Terry, Fergus," he said, catching sight of them over his shoulder. "Just in time. We could use a few more hands. Terry, will you go help above? And Fergus, what I need you to do is monitor that machine right there. Yes, that one. Very good. Now, what I need you to tell me is if the dial goes below that first notch to the right, or if it goes beyond the first to the left. If we let them go too far either way, well, the city will be enjoying quite the fireworks display."

Fergus doggedly studied the dial on the panel in front of him. It was golden with a white background and two black notches to either side of the top mark where the dial presently pointed.

"If it goes too far either way, I may also need you to help me by grabbing that grey lever to your right and giving it a pull. That will shut down the power to the propellers, so at least those won't catch fire."

"Is this ship actually safe?" Fergus asked, his face puckering in alarm.

"My *Wyrd* is much safer, but we can't be flying public vessels on a private errand. Now, keep a steady watch. Once we're in the air, we should be fine."

Fergus turned back to the dial, willing it to remain upright and let nothing catch on fire. The ship began to vibrate even more violently than before. Out of the corner of his eye, he could see that they were slowly rising. He hadn't seen their ascent on the *Pulsatrix*. The storm had made it unbearable for him, so he'd spent the take off hiding under a pillow. However, without the bad weather to mar things, it was actually incredible watching the airship rising into the clouds.

He almost forgot to watch the dial, which tilted first a little to the right and then a little to the left, but luckily never passed the first notch on either side. The airship jolted, throwing him against the doorframe, and the clouds began to cut past them with surprising speed.

"All right back there?" Guillory asked without turning.

"Yeah," Fergus said, rubbing his shoulder. "Just fine."

"I think we're steady now. You can go and have a look up top if you like. Be sure to hold onto the railing."

He made his way up to the deck. It took a bit of pushing to get the door open, and the moment he let go, it ripped out of his hands, striking the side of the ship with a loud *bang*. Fergus stumbled out onto the deck, making a grab for the railing. Birds flashed past, white streaks against the sky, though he noticed that the ship seemed to be slowing as it evened out.

By the time he got to the forecastle, he didn't feel so worried about being outside, and the flocks of birds were easier to watch. In fact, he took a moment to observe them gliding through the clouds. Mainly, it was gulls wheeling along, though they passed a couple of sea hawks, too, cutting through the sky and disappearing in the blink of an eye.

"Wow," Fergus murmured, both hands gripping the railing, as he watched a hawk dive below the ship.

"Makes you wish you could fly, huh?" Terry said, joining him.

He nodded. "This is a lot better than last time."

"Well, the weather's not bad."

"Is it going to get bad?"

Terry glanced at him and shrugged. "At least this one can sail in the water, so that might help."

Fergus felt a little stab of anxiety.

"Hey, we survived one crash, right? What's another?"

"Ha ha," he replied, but he did feel a little better.

"Come on, I want to show you something," Terry said.

Releasing the railing, he made his way over to a mast leading up to the crow's nest. Terry began scaling it with a rope ladder. He clutched the pole with his legs as he climbed. It didn't look particularly safe or easy. Fergus was fairly sure that if he lost his grip, he would be blown away entirely. However, Terry made it to the top okay.

"C'mon, Fergus!" he shouted down.

Fergus stared at the rope whipping around in front of him and then looked back up at Terry.

"Just grip with your thighs. You'll be okay," Terry called.

His stomach flip-flopping, he took the rope, mimicking Terry, though climbing at half the speed. He kept imagining tumbling free into the wind and falling hundreds of meters into the ocean. He definitely couldn't survive that. He squeezed his eyes shut and forced his hand to slide up the rough twine and grip. Slowly but surely, he made his way to the top where Terry grabbed his arm and hauled him into the crow's nest.

"The view's even better up here."

He could see the sea below, broken up by thin clouds. The sunlight glinted off the ocean's surface.

There was no land to be seen. The wind ripping through his clothing and hair was cold, and despite having the mast at his back, he found himself gripping the side of the crow's nest with white-knuckled hands.

"You really do like flying," he managed after a moment.

Terry smiled. "I do, but it's pretty much impossible to get into the piloting school in New Peiling. I mean, if you're like us. You have to at least finish high school, and then you have to have good marks to get into the program. Probably the Count could have arranged something, but I didn't want to owe him any favors, you know?"

Fergus nodded. His eyes were watering.

"Seems like they're going to need our help, though, so it's a good opportunity to learn," Terry added. "Are you okay?"

Fergus nodded again. "Yeah, just trying to get used to it. Seems like you've been on a few airships before."

"The Count'd sometimes let me go on errands for him to Lancaster and Clohaven."

"Guess that's why you knew where to go on the *Pulsatrix*."

Terry nodded.

They lapsed into silence. The wind muffled most sound anyway, so Fergus didn't mind. Terry leaned against the railing with his eyes closed. Fergus, meanwhile, was trying to coax himself into letting go of the railing, or at least to loosen his death grip. After a little while, he decided to mask his insecurity by crouching down and hooking his legs through the slats. Sitting down, he felt a little safer. He leaned his forehead against the railing and rubbed at his eyes with the heels of his palms.

"Hey, Terry," he finally said.

"What's up?"

"There's something I've kinda wanted to ask you for a while," Fergus started and then stopped, feeling jittery all of a sudden.

Terry looked down at him expectantly.

The words crammed into the back of his throat, unable to break past the barrier of his nerves. He cleared his throat, averting his gaze. It was hard to ask Terry for the truth. He was afraid of being lied to again. He was afraid of making Terry angry. He was afraid of something he couldn't name. Still, he wanted to know.

"How much of all that was the truth?"

Terry's expression tightened, turning into something inscrutable. "What do you mean?"

"I mean, all the stuff you told me about you: about how you wound up in the lower city and about Flynn. Was there anything that was true about that? Why did you lie about my mom and Rosslyn and Flynn?"

Terry looked away. This time, he couldn't escape. Of course, he could just refuse to answer until Fergus went away. Fergus's brow furrowed. Somehow, he had to make sure that didn't happen. He reached out and tugged on the leg of Terry's jeans.

"Was anything true, Terry?"

Terry sighed, running a hand over his face. "Of course. It's easier to hide a lie within truths."

"So what was true?"

Terry stared into the distance, sighing again. "I did follow a classmate down to the slums. His parents kicked him out. I knew my parents were gonna do the same, so we ran away together. I was about 12."

"That young?"

"How old were you when you knew?"

Fergus thought back, but he couldn't recall an exact moment of realization. He just had always known. He shook his head. "I don't remember."

"Probably, since your mom was a hybrid, you just assumed you were, too. Most people up there realize around puberty. I knew from when I was about 11. Started showing signs at about nine or ten, though. I managed to hide it for a pretty long time. They were working it out, though. It's pretty rare that they don't."

"How?"

"You start to change. Rosslyn says we're more like humans than fairies, you know? But we're not entirely like humans, either. It's hard to explain. For someone like you, maybe you could fit in."

"What's that supposed to mean?"

"Nothing. It's not a criticism, Fergus. Maybe it's just that you're more . . . empathic. You've probably figured out by now that fairies aren't that interested in other people's welfare. They do whatever is most amusing at any given moment, or what will benefit them most. To me, thinking like that's always been natural. It's why I was able to make it down here from 12 on. The guy I went down with wasn't."

"What happened to him?" Fergus asked, forgetting to be irritable.

"Killed himself. We were lonely and starving. We had no place to go. We stayed in abandoned buildings and stole food when we could. We did odd jobs for rough guys, and sometimes they gave us a few dollars, but a lot of the time, they gave us . . . It was hard. I knew my parents weren't gonna let me come back. I'd outed myself, you know? But my friend – even though they told him to never come back – he couldn't accept that this would be his life. How many 12-year-olds could? He wanted to believe that being their son was more important than being a hybrid. That they'd just been in shock when they told him to go."

"Did he try to go back to them?"

Terry nodded. "They hadn't changed their minds. He was in rags, didn't even have shoes, hadn't showered in weeks . . . Hadn't eaten properly, for that matter. Who knows if they could even recognize him? He came back down. Stopped talking. It's a pretty sure sign."

Fergus slowly nodded.

"He jumped from the building we were sleeping in."

"Did you . . .?"

Terry looked away and didn't reply. Fergus let it drop.

"What about your family?"

"Moved to Lancaster the last I heard."

Fergus rubbed at his eyes. A flock of seagulls drifted by. He considered how to shift the topic back onto the lies Terry had told before they wound up straying into an area that ultimately led to silence.

He took a deep breath before asking, "And my mom?"

"I met her when I was about 15 or 16. I was just doing odd jobs – a lot of them were bringing messages and packages around for people. So I wound up at Beathag's a lot. I got to know Ursula. I was thinking that maybe I could . . . well, maybe if I got on her good side, she'd provide me with a little stability. Her aunt had died, so I thought she might be vulnerable. Your mom kept getting in the way, though. Maybe she just wanted to draw me away from Ursula, but she offered to teach us. Ursula brought Rosslyn. She'd been studying under him at the Count's – something her late aunt had set up. Your mom started teaching us what she knew, but I'm not really like them."

Fergus looked up. "Not like them?"

"Not like Rosslyn or Ursula. Ursula probably already told you what she thought of Ainslee. Rosslyn was similar. He idolized her. He loves anyone who's clever. She was clever and . . . well, you know your mom better than I did."

"Are you going to say compassionate?" Fergus asked, sounding bitter.

"You don't think so?"

He bit his lip. "It's not that I don't. She wasn't a bad person. She was a good mother. When I was a kid at least. She started to change, though. She changed a lot." He shook his head. "I don't really wanna think about that. So you knew her all along. Why did you lie?"

"For Ursula," Terry replied. "She panicked when she realized what had happened to Flynn. The Knights found him, so they could just as easily have found you. You were protected by your ignorance, by the fact you were no one. If you decided to learn more about Bandersnatch, or if you wanted to join Niamh, you'd be upping the chances of discovery. I told her that it was your right to make that choice, but she wrote to Rosslyn, and then it was two against one."

"That's why you told me so much about them? You weren't entirely warning me away, were you?"

Terry nodded. "I wasn't entirely sure I should, honestly. Ainslee would have wanted us to protect you, of course, but you weren't a little kid anymore. I didn't want all our efforts to go to waste, but I felt like it wasn't fair to you, either. Our lives have been kinda similar, don't you think? I learned things. I learned magic, I learned who's who, I learned politics, I learned to defend myself, I learned and learned, and that's why I'm here now instead of prowling around the docks stealing fish. Knowing is what's let me make decisions to get here. For me, keeping you in the dark was the same as controlling you. I know Ursula doesn't have an issue with that, but I couldn't agree."

"Huh," Fergus muttered. "Rosslyn was right about that, I guess."

"About what?"

He shook his head. "Never mind. Why did you lie about Flynn, then?"

"I thought you might listen to me if you could relate to me, so I said I knew him, and I told you a revised story of how I wound up in the slums." Terry said this with a kind of candidness that made Fergus's stomach turn. He pressed his forehead to the planks.

"Why didn't you tell me what happened to him?"

"I'd just found out myself, and even I didn't know all of it. I was worried you would go after the Knights, or that maybe you'd attack the Count. If you did, Deirdre would have hurt you at the least. The Count was starting to take interest in you, but he wasn't invested yet. A lot of his good manners are because of Ursula, and through Ursula, Rosslyn, too.

"That would have been the only thing that kept her from killing you in that situation, but she still might have hurt you pretty badly. Plus, accidents do happen. Around that guy, they happen a lot." Terry let out a long sigh. "I wasn't lying about the band. I hadn't had fun like that since I was 10. Being with you guys made me feel a little like I could live out some of the teenage years I'd lost."

"I can see that," Fergus replied. "So, are you telling the truth now? The absolute truth?"

"That's up to you to decide."

His mouth twitched downward. "I don't want to play games."

"I can't make you trust me," Terry replied, looking down at him evenly before snorting softly and looking away. "It's probably best if you don't entirely."

"Is that why you're here? For Bandersnatch? Or something like that? It's not for my mom, is it? I told you, you can shove that."

Terry laughed, and Fergus felt ruffled. "No, it isn't for Ainslee. Everyone here has their own reasons, even if they haven't figured them out yet."

"I don't get it."

"Why are you here, Fergus?"

"Because of Flynn. I wanna finish what he started."

"And that's the only reason?"

He paused, thinking. There were a lot of reasons. Finding that there was a world outside of the dark bowels of New Peiling had made him want to see more. Maybe there was a place out there that could become his new home. Maybe there was someone out there who might suit him better than Ursula. At least getting away from her and the city might make him stop wanting her so badly.

The known was so depressing, it was hard to feel anxious about the unknown, and so searching for something else seemed natural. And maybe he wanted to prove that he was as clever as his mother, or that he deserved to be the one to solve Flynn's puzzle. There were a lot of reasons.

"What about you, though? Why are you here?"

"A lot of reasons," Terry replied flatly.

"Are you gonna keep lying to me?" Fergus asked softly.

Terry shrugged. "I want to see where you'll go – how far you'll go – if you're just allowed to go. I think there's something I can learn from that, too. So I'll protect you until you get there – however I can."

Fergus stared at the deck below. He felt a little empty, and he couldn't help but wonder how much of this new story was the truth. Finally, he said, "I can't stop you from lying, but I dunno if I can trust you if I can't be sure you aren't."

"I know." Terry turned to him and simply added, "I'm sorry."

"Are you gonna tell me someday?"

"I'm here because I want to be. Isn't that enough?"

Fergus slowly nodded. "Guess it'll have to be."

For a moment, he thought Terry's eyes looked very sad.

"I'm gonna go down and check on Raja."

"I'll join you in a little while," Terry replied.

"Yeah, don't fall, okay?" Fergus said, standing up and locating the rope to slowly climb back down.

Chapter Four.

Terry, Raja, and Three took quickly to helping out on deck. Fergus, however, found that the only thing he was particularly adept at was tying knots. Pip had no talent whatsoever for manning an airship and had been relegated to the kitchen. More often than not, Fergus found himself shuffled down right along with him. But it wasn't until Raja or Three came down to the kitchen that their concoctions even smelled edible.

Fergus wasn't sure which he preferred. He found moving around outside difficult, but staying inside became cloying, especially since Pip refused to talk to him outside of curt, monosyllabic answers. It made time spent together pass very slowly.

Fergus sat on a crate, peeling potatoes. Pip was bent over a book of recipes, following each line with his finger. He seemed intent on getting it just right, which Fergus thought would be a nice change of pace. Pip seemed to have a knack for burning even the simplest things. He was muttering to himself. Fergus wondered if he should offer to help read. Maybe that was part of the problem. However, he also knew that Pip could easily make this quiet preparation into a punishment, so he held his tongue and tried to focus on the grimy, pockmarked vegetable.

This would be nicer with Three. She'd fill the silence with chatter about her village and her parents and places she'd been. Not Pip, though. Fergus would like to have asked the boy why he was so very surly, except he had the feeling there was a legitimate reason for it, and maybe prying wouldn't do him any favors.

He let out a little hiss of pain as the knife skidded off of the potato's surface and nicked his thumb. Pip didn't turn around, though he did lift his head a little, like he'd thought about it. Fergus let out a long sigh and put his thumb in his mouth, sucking on the cut. It made him think of meat, which was something they were missing. Because there wasn't an easy way to store it, there was a very sad lack of fresh meat. Dried meat – while more appetizing than potatoes – didn't quite do it for Fergus. He wondered how long it would be before they reached a city where they could eat properly and stretch their legs.

"Hey, Pip," he started.

Pip's shoulders tensed. He was silent for a moment before uttering a soft grunt.

"How long is it before the next city?"

"Don't know."

Fergus frowned. "You don't know? You've come through this stretch before, right? So where are we landing next?"

Pip was quiet for a moment too long before replying, "Sovnik."

"Never heard of it."

"It's a small city in the mountains. It's very cold there."

"Is it nice?"

"No. It's cold and remote."

Fergus took a deep breath, closing his eyes and counting back from 10. He forced himself to not scowl as he opened them again. "What's after Sovnik?"

"After that, we will stop in Ping City."

"And then?"

Pip glared over his shoulder. "After that, we will stop in Utsujima. That will be close to where we are going."

"Is that where you're from?"

Pip hunched even closer to the counter.

"Guess you're not looking forward to that."

"I am not from Utsujima, but I am from a place near it."

"So what city are you from?" Fergus asked.

"I don't want to talk about it," Pip said and started reading again.

Fergus decided to leave it at that, finishing the peeling and moving on to chopping the carrots, because the only other vegetable they had on hand was onion, and he was hoping that if he put that off, Pip would do it and spare him the stinging eyes. Probably Pip was putting it off, too, because he kept reading silently.

"What's next?" Fergus asked, chopping his second carrot very slowly.

Pip gave him a look, but took the hint and moved over to the pot on the flame, checking the broth and putting a scoop of rice in. However, having done this, he did not pick up the second knife and start the onions, but rather returned to his book.

"You can stick the vegetables in when you're finished," he mumbled.

Fergus began cutting even more slowly.

Their battle of wills was derailed as the kitchen door opened, and Three walked in. She looked between the two of them with a smile, as though she'd caught them happily engaged in conversation instead of silently warring over who would chop the onions.

"Are you done?" Pip asked, looking up from the book.

"Yup," she replied and walked over to sit on a crate near Fergus. "How's the stew?"

"Still chopping." Fergus replied, trying to smile, but his mouth just twitched and refused to lift in the corners.

Three blinked at him and then looked up at Pip. "Are you helping, Pip?"

Pip froze. He looked away from Three. "I have a headache."

Three's expression softened. "You should have said so! Go lie down. I'll take care of the rest."

Fergus tried not to look irritated as Pip slunk off.

"He's still getting used to you," she said, picking up a knife, a chopping board, and an onion. "I think he likes you. He usually likes the people I like."

"I think that's why he doesn't like me," Fergus replied.

Three shrugged and offered him a wan smile. "It's been just the two of us for so long. It's harder for him than it is for me."

"Why?" Fergus asked, lowering the carrot and knife.

Three glanced at him and then at the door. She shifted uncomfortably, knees drawing closer together, and bit her lower lip.

"You must understand . . . " she started and then trailed off.

"It's hard to understand something no one's ever said anything about," he replied, running his thumb over the leathery bands of the vegetable without looking.

She sighed, lowering her face. Her dark hair fell over it, obscuring her features.

"Hey, if it's *that* awful, you don't have to tell me."

"I want you to understand him, though," she replied, still looking down. "He won't ever tell you. He doesn't care if he's misunderstood, but I do. I care about him, you know?"

He nodded, though she couldn't see it.

"Remember how I told you about how different cities treat hybrids? In New Peiling, you all live in the slums. My village was nothing but hybrids, and their powers were revered. Pip grew up near a city." She stopped and poked at the onion with her knife, slitting its skin without removing it. "Hybrids are powerful, and some humans want that. They want that magic at their disposal. There's . . . a black market in that area. It's near where we're going."

Fergus was starting to feel uneasy. "Hey," he started, but she didn't stop.

"Men raided his village and took a number of children. Probably they intended to sell most as servants, or even adopted children."

"And Pip?"

She looked up and took a deep breath. "Maybe that's what was intended, but the master of the household . . . " She turned away.

"Jeez," Fergus said softly.

Slowly, Three nodded. "It's like that."

"So, how did he get out of there?"

"He did what he had to. He's . . . Well, going back will be difficult for him. It's been a long time, but there may still be people looking for him."

"So he's scared of people."

"Yes," Three replied. "Especially men."

"Guess I can't blame him," Fergus said, shaking his head.

"Please don't mention it to him, okay?" Three suddenly said, standing up and dropping the onion.

"You don't have to worry about that," he replied, a little surprised by the sudden movement. "But he trusts you, and you're human. Isn't that kinda weird?"

"He didn't trust me at first. It took a long time. We've been through a lot together," she said, sitting back down and not meeting his eye. She picked up the onion and rubbed it on her trousers.

"Is this about the man you're looking for?" Fergus asked, starting to chop the carrots again. "I remember you said you were after some guy, right?"

"*That* man is long gone, but our target is connected to him. He was the head of staff at that place. He caught up with us before. We were lucky to escape, but I know he's somewhere out there, looking for us still." She peeled back the skin of the onion. Her nails caught in the flesh. "But we'll be ready next time."

He felt the hairs on the back of his arms rising and hurriedly cleared his throat. "So, uh, Sovnik, huh? Have you been there before?"

The blank, dark look on her face didn't fade. She stared at the onion without answering.

"It'll be the first foreign country I've been to."

"Really?" she asked, coming out of it. Her eyes still looked far away, though, and Fergus wondered what she was recalling. He wasn't sure he really wanted to know.

He nodded. "Yeah. First time I ever left New Peiling was when we met you."

"There isn't much to Sovnik. It's high in the mountains. There's probably already snow there, even. The city isn't very big. Still, it does have some interesting things."

"Like what?"

"They're very fond of dancing," Three said, chuckling. She looked more like herself, and Fergus relaxed. "And they have great beer. Oh, and there's this amazing lake a mile or so from the city where people ice skate."

"Skate?"

"You know, sliding around on ice."

Fergus snorted. "Why would people do that?"

"Because it's fun. I hope the lake will be frozen when we arrive. I bet you'd like it if you tried it," she replied, slicing the onion and squinting back tears.

Fergus went to put his vegetables in the broth and picked up some of the onions to help her. "Did you ever ice skate in your village?"

"The lake only froze once when I was a kid, but we did skate that year." She laughed. "Well, we tried to, anyway."

"Maybe you skate, and I'll watch." He paused before adding, "With some of that amazing beer."

"Well, if you won't skate with me, you at least have to try dancing with me."

"I don't know how to dance," he replied, shaking his head.

"But you're a singer!"

"Not the same thing."

"Hey, Fergus," she said softly, her hair falling into her face again. "Sing for me?"

"Okay," he said, thinking for a moment before deciding on a song about the sun rising over the docks of New Peiling.

She smiled softly and quietly put the onion into the stew.

•   •   •

After dinner, he returned to his bunk, flopping on the hard mattress and sliding the magic book Ursula had lent him out from its spot against the wall. He was on chapter three, though he felt like chapters one and two had hardly sunken in at all. He opened the book, and the stack of photos fell onto his chest. He sat up, gathering them, while trying to keep the one of his parents on the bottom. The door opened with a bang, and Fergus jumped. The pictures flew out of his hand, landing on the floor next to his bed. He looked up to see Raja standing there, looking contrite.

"Sorry, it got away from me," he said, stepping inside and carefully shutting it.

"No problem."

"Were you sleeping?"

"No, just thinking about reading," Fergus replied, putting the book down and leaning over the side of the bunk to gather the photos.

Raja walked over, squatting down. "Let me help."

"Thanks."

It was harder for Fergus to reach the floor, so he only recovered one before Raja started to hand the rest to him. Fergus held out a hand, but Raja suddenly stopped, cocking his head.

"I know this man," he said, extracting the photo from the pile. "I've seen him before."

"Probably when you looked at me," Fergus replied, scrunching his mouth to the side. "I mean, he is my dad."

"No, I've seen him in person. He's important."

Fergus snorted softly.

"Owen Crawford!" he suddenly exclaimed. "Wait, he's your father?"

Fergus stared at Raja and then slowly nodded.

"You're sure?" Raja asked, looking down at him skeptically as he handed back the photographs.

"I look like my mom," he said, shrugging and tucking the photographs back into the book. He looked up. Raja was studying him. "What?"

"Maybe I can see it."

"So how do you know my dad?"

"He's always making really big donations to the universities. Plus, he's a pretty important politician in Clohaven," Raja said, going over to sit on his bed. "And he's rumored to be 'the benefactor.'"

"The hell is that?"

"Well, you probably can guess the lower universities tend to favor hybrids, but materials are often still so expensive that a lot of students wouldn't be able to go without scholarships." Raja kicked off his shoes, sliding back against the wall with his legs drawn up against his chest. "But there's one anonymous donor who gives a lot every year. Whoever it is, that donation alone takes care of 10% of the student body." He paused seeing Fergus's blank expression and smiled. "That's a lot of money."

"And you think that's Owen Crawford – my dad?"

"Most people do. He's conservative, but he's not without sympathy for us."

Fergus shook his head. "It must be someone different. I don't think it could be my dad. He ran out on us. Totally disappeared."

"Maybe so," Raja replied slowly. "There are probably plenty of Owens around and a lot of Crawfords in Clohaven."

"And I don't even know his last name. It might not be Crawford," Fergus added.

Raja nodded, but the look on his face said he thought otherwise.

"I mean, seriously, how could it be? He *abandoned* us, Raja. How could someone like that be super generous and pay for hybrids to go to school? Doesn't seem likely."

"Maybe he's hoping you'll be one of them," Raja replied, resting his chin on his knees. "There's always more than one side to a story. I don't know much about his personal life. Still."

Fergus sighed, flopping backwards. "Well, good for him. Lot of good that's done me, though, so he can shove his charity."

"You know, my dad died."

He looked up, but said nothing – partially shocked that Raja had said anything about his family and also worried that saying anything might cause him to clam up again.

"On an airship like this," Raja added quietly. "We immigrated to New Peiling when I was about 10, but he didn't make it."

Fergus stared at the bunk above before putting his hands over his face, fingers threaded. "Sorry," he muttered.

"You're not really, but I guess I can't blame you."

Fergus's mouth twitched, but didn't find its way to a smile. He let out a slow sigh.

Raja had already fallen back into silence. Fergus wasn't sure what he was doing, but he didn't really care. He felt like being alone, but he didn't want to say it to Raja of all people, so he rolled onto his side and stared at the book between the arch of his stomach and the wall. He picked it up, giving it a wistful look. Somehow, though he wanted to study, all his motivation had been sapped. He tucked it back between the bed and the wall and rolled onto his stomach, still staring at the lacquered wood.

Raja's mattress gave a faint creak, and he could hear the sound of curtains being drawn. The gentle vibration of the ship, the soft call of the crew as they came and went outside the door, and the golden light in the cabin were lulling to his unfocused mind, and he drifted off before he knew it.

•   •   •

He was walking down a narrow path through a misty forest. By the greyness of the light, it was either dawn or dusk, but because of the trees blocking the skyline, he wasn't sure which. The tall grass on either side of the path caught on his jeans, leaving seeds in the seams. He saw a couple of deer grazing near a thicket to his left and paused to watch them until they caught sight of him and bounded off into the trees.

As he continued, the trees began to grow taller and the brush tumbled out onto the path so that soon he had to pick his way through the bushes to continue. The weeds and wildflowers grew up to his knees, and when he reached to push them away, nettles bit into his fingertips. He cursed and stuck his hand in his mouth, trying to suck the tiny darts out.

He could hear a bird warbling in the distance and the chirp of crickets. The light beyond the mist was yellow-orange, and he thought that it must be nearer to night than morning, because fireflies had come out, leaving long trails of green light between the leaves and shadows of the bushes. He was growing tired, or at least his mind reasoned that he should be tired, and he began to lag, each step slower than the one before.

The path started uphill, turning rockier. The leaves on either side went from green to orange and yellow, falling off in piles on the forest floor. They were slick with dew, and he kept slipping on them.

It felt like hours had passed when he finally reached the top of the hill. Before him lay a mossy glade. The light had grown dimmer, filtered out by tall pine trees, which allowed only thin, slanting rays to illuminate the rich green of the lichen covered earth. He carefully started towards the beams of light, his feet making sucking sounds in the wet earth. The glade was oddly silent and still, like there was nothing but him and the trees, and the trees were holding their breaths.

Beyond the glade, the dirt path resumed, wider than before, though the trees on either side were sparer. A few red-orange bushes lined the path, but the forest looked very brown to him, like it was not mist but dust that obscured the way. He suddenly felt very lonely and afraid. He wanted to turn back, but he didn't dare look behind him. He just knew there was something terrible there, so he tried to walk faster.

Stumbling, he broke from the path into the forest where the fog turned green and the trunks of the trees black. The heather was orange and red and lit up by large clusters of fireflies, and he knew he had gone the wrong way, but he still couldn't look back, because something would be there – something that he never wanted to see.

He plunged ahead, forcing his legs into an off-kilter jog. There, at the edge of the forest, was another meadow. All the leaves – each a brilliant red hue – were on the ground. In the middle of this red sea stood a lone, gnarled figure in a cloak. He heard a laugh that sounded like frogs croaking. It made his hair stand on end. The hood fell back, revealing a head of white hair that seemed to glow against the fog and the redness of the leaves.

The old witch woman turned and smiled at him with pointed teeth. She lifted a bumpy finger and pointed behind him. He shook his head, refusing to look. She began to advance on him. He stood his ground, continuing to shake his head with increasing force. She swung her staff at him, striking him in the rib cage. He heard something crack and cried out, falling backward. Strong arms caught him.

His mind told him to close his eyes or look away, but his gaze kept creeping upward. He stared into his own blotchy face and milky eyes, and he screamed.

The leaves melted away, turned to liquid – hot and wet and thick, pooling around his ankles. Fergus tried to free himself. He could hear people screaming – could taste their blood coating his tongue. The old woman was laughing in the background with a chorus of a hundred golden-eyed frogs. His throat burned; he couldn't breathe.

"Fergus! Hey, Fergus!"

He blinked.

A figure leaned over him, lit from behind by a single lantern. Still caught up in the nightmare, he let out a muffled scream and lashed out. Terry grunted in pain and staggered into the light. Fergus sat up, gasping for breath, and stared at him for a long moment before his mind supplied connections. Raja parted his curtain, blinking against the light and looking annoyed. Terry prodded at his cheek as he got to his feet.

"Last time I try that," Terry muttered.

"What's going on?" Raja yawned.

Fergus stared at the two of them, his mind finalizing the situation. He was in their cabin, it must have been the middle of the night, and all of that had been a bad dream. He ran a hand over his face. Terry and Raja were both watching him bemusedly, and he could feel his face going red.

"Sorry," he mumbled. "Bad dream."

"Yeah, well, you probably woke half the crew there," Terry replied, glaring.

"Sorry," Fergus repeated, lying back down and putting his hands over his face. He could still see his own bloodless face drawing closer.

"Are you okay?" Terry asked.

He nodded and heard the curtains on Raja's bed swing closed again on their metal rings. This was punctuated by a little yawn. The light went out, and there was silence for a moment before he felt his mattress depress. He lowered his hands to look up at Terry's silhouette.

"You can hit me in the morning, if you want," he mumbled.

"I'll live. But you know, this isn't the first time."

"I've never hit you before," Fergus replied a little more loudly than he'd intended. He heard Raja make an irritated sound and lowered his voice. "I haven't."

"No, I mean, with the shouting."

Fergus was glad for the darkness hiding their faces. Still, he turned away. "It's just nightmares."

He heard Terry sigh. For a moment, they said nothing: he stared at the wall, and Terry (he presumed) at Raja's drapes.

"We'll probably dock by tomorrow evening. I think we're staying the night in Sovnik."

Fergus nodded without replying.

"You know, if something is on your mind . . . "

"It's just nightmares," Fergus repeated.

"Okay."

He stood and used Fergus's bed to leverage himself into his bunk. The springs creaked softly, and Fergus could see the faint impression of his body between the slats overhead. He said nothing more, but Fergus thought that perhaps he also spent the rest of the night awake.

Chapter Five.

Sovnik was a river of red roofs running along the side of a mountain. Pip's description seemed totally off to Fergus, who found the little white houses and autumn foliage charming. Unlike New Peiling, it was a single-layered city, and the late afternoon sun shone on all of the rooftops, catching the curl of smoke rising out of hundreds of chimneys.

"Gothic architecture," Guillory said over his shoulder as Fergus came into the control room. "One of the few places where most of it's original," he added, turning back to the window. "Don't let on that you're a hybrid."

Fergus bristled. "Why's that?"

"They're a bit superstitious in these parts. Very religious."

"What, so like, you're saying they're some kinda pitchfork-wielding mob waiting to happen?"

Guillory chuckled. "Oh, it's more modern than that, but I imagine it's like wandering around the upper city back in New Peiling. It's best to keep a low profile."

Fergus crossed his arms, leaning on the doorframe, and studied Guillory's shoulders and tousled brown hair. "What do you know about that?"

"I'm no expert on quality of life for hybrids, but I'm not ignorant either, Fergus."

"Yeah, guess not."

Guillory gave him a passing glance. It was one that Fergus was learning meant he should hurry along, because if he didn't, he was going to get a lecture about the right way to do things, which ultimately would end with the unspoken disappointment that he hadn't testified against the Knights for the arson.

"Gonna go help up top," he muttered, quickly extricating himself.

He didn't go up top, however. He lingered in the stairwell leading to the deck. Admittedly, he was still afraid of being swept away by the wind, and he imagined it would be far more likely during takeoff and landing. Of all the unpleasant ways to die, he thought being blown from the deck of an airship and falling into the trees was near the top of the list.

So he sat on the steps and hummed quietly to himself, leaning against the wall and trying to judge by the vibrations and the popping of his ears for when it'd be safe to go up. He could hear shouting above and footsteps hurrying over the wooden boards. The airship began to vibrate more violently, and then it began shaking so hard he was almost knocked off his step. He grabbed onto the railing, clinging as the airship skidded and slowed to a halt.

Up top, the air smelled crisp, but the undertones of loam and crops ready for harvest and fallen leaves and wood smoke slipped through. It filled him with a peculiar emotion. Autumn in New Peiling was never this charming. Rather, it was cold, wet, and increasingly darker as the days grew so short that daylight only lasted a handful of hours. Sovnik was bright and welcoming. Pip's description was definitely wrong.

He took a deep breath, closing his eyes, and welcomed the prickle of goosebumps running up his arms and down the back of his neck.

"Nice, huh?" Terry said, coming over. His cheek was dark purple and swollen where Fergus had clipped him the night before. Spiderwebs of red, broken blood vessels poked out from the bruise.

Fergus cringed. "Does it hurt?"

Terry snorted. "Of course, it hurts. Since when does being punched in the face not hurt?"

"I'm really sorry."

Terry shook his head and gave him a good-natured smile. "Just don't do it again, or I really will punch you back."

"So what's the plan?" he asked, watching the crew hurry below to prepare the ladder.

"Well, basically, we can do what we want, as long as we're all back here by noon tomorrow."

"What about hotels and stuff?"

"It's every man for himself. Part of the crew will probably stay here. Well, everyone who wants to save some cash."

"What will you do?"

"The Count gave me this letter," he said, showing an envelope to Fergus. "So if we want, we can stay with a friend of his. Dunno if I will, though. I've

73

never met her before, and you can never tell with the Count's contacts."

Fergus nodded.

"Still, I think we'd get a free dinner."

"Free food is good," Fergus said with a nod.

"So let's have a look around, and then we'll try to find this place," Terry suggested.

It was colder than he'd expected, and Fergus wished he'd worn more than a jumper. He pulled his hood up and tucked his hands into his sleeves. The autumn sky was a rich blue. The afternoon sun blazed against the rust-colored tiles, making Fergus squint. They made their way through the rows of quaint little buildings up a cobbled lane to a square before an old church. The other buildings had newer looking tiles, but the church's roof was made of dirt or heather. It looked strange and inefficient. Fergus wondered if it leaked often.

Terry walked past him towards the fountain at the center of the square, scaring a small battalion of pigeons into flight. Fergus wandered after him, still trying to make sense of the church's roof.

"Looks like there's some stands over there. Why don't we check them out?"

Fergus followed his gaze to a brief row of stalls framed by white sheets. He shrugged and started that way. As they grew nearer, he could smell something warm and sweet. His stomach growled. Terry walked up to the first stand, which looked to be selling pastries. The next stand over was selling sausages; the one after that blown glass; then candles and an assortment of trinkets; and the final stall was heaped high with fabrics of every imaginable color and pattern. He wished he had someone that would like that kind of souvenir.

He turned back to Terry who was pressing a hot, greasy roll into his hand.

"What's this?" he asked.

"Meat bun, she says," Terry replied, biting into an identical lump of fried dough.

Fergus took a bite and let out a sound of pure joy.

Terry snorted and choked. He pounded himself in the chest, trying to right himself between chuckles.

"We haven't had anything this good in forever," Fergus sighed, swallowing.

"It hasn't been that long. What are you gonna do on this next leg? It's the longest of all."

"Dunno," Fergus said and took a bite that nearly finished off the bun. He fished around in his back pocket for his wallet. "Ow muj?" he asked behind his other hand.

"Two for fifty cents," Terry said, wiping his mouth on the sleeve of his jacket.

Fergus looked between the delicious buns and the roasting meat in the next stall. His stomach growled again. He popped the rest of the meat bun into his mouth and dug around in his wallet. He still had a good bit of cash. He wondered how many buns and hunks of barbecued meat he could buy with it.

"Save your cash."

"But I want to eat more," he replied, giving the meat a worried glance. He scooted a little closer.

"There's bound to be more stalls around," Terry replied. "Besides, what will you do if you spend all your money on food right now, eat it, and then get sick? We still have a free dinner coming, you know."

Fergus was fairly sure he could eat ten meat buns and still be ready for dinner, but he didn't want to spend all his money here if there were more stands to try, so he nodded and allowed himself to be talked into a single skewer of roasted beef. He and Terry took their snacks and started for the other side of the square.

"It's a lot fresher than the meat in New Peiling," he observed, licking each finger in turn to make sure not an ounce of grease got away.

"Well, the farms are closer here," Terry replied. He was scrutinizing the numbers on the doors as they passed by, and Fergus realized he must be looking for the Count's friend's residence.

"What number is it?" Fergus asked, wiping at the side of his mouth with the back of his wrist.

"Two-fourteen. Seems like it might be at the top of the hill. I'm thinking it's probably that white building up there," he said.

Like the church, it also had a strange, old-looking roof and white walls, but there was no steeple, no glass windows, no cross. Actually, as Fergus looked up at it, it looked daunting. He frowned, brows knitting.

"It is pretty big . . . "

"What's wrong?"

Fergus's mouth twitched. "Nothing. Just got a funny feeling."

Terry shook his head. "Probably from eating too fast."

"Well, we haven't had fresh meat in ages," he replied, letting the conversation settle back into an easier place. But as they ascended the hill, Fergus's apprehension only grew.

It definitely looked like the kind of place the Count would like. As they drew closer, Fergus could see that it was more like a castle than a church. It was far fancier than the rows of homes trailing down the hill from it. The best description Fergus could come up with was "pointy" and maybe "jagged." It had several spires, and the front was covered in rough moldings depicting knights hunting a unicorn.

It was rather gruesome, Fergus thought as he followed the line of men on horses to the unicorn resting quietly under a tree and then down the side of the building to the men descending on the creature with hounds and spears. It didn't make him feel any better about the place, but Terry was already ringing the doorbell. He crammed his hands into the pockets of his jeans and tried not to look at the art of the dying unicorn.

"Maybe they're out," Fergus muttered as seconds stretched into minutes, and five minutes became ten.

"It's a big house. It might take them a few."

Fergus ground the toe of his trainer against the stones. He was a little afraid that if he said anything more, Terry would suggest he return to the ship, and he didn't want to be excluded. Still, he wished Terry would propose they return, but he kept waiting until a short boy opened the door. He had pale grey eyes, black hair, sallow skin, and an unwelcoming expression. He stared up at them without speaking. Terry began to dig around inside the breast of his jacket until he procured the envelope. The boy reached for it.

"I think not. I'll give it to the lady of the house, if you please," Terry replied, holding it out of reach.

The boy scowled, but stepped back to usher them through. They followed him down a long corridor under vaulted ceilings. The building was made of white stone, which made it seem cold and unlived in to Fergus, like it was a gallery or museum. It was surprisingly light, however, with dozens of tall, glazed windows to the right, casting long beams of light onto the paintings to the left. The afternoon light was intense, and it obscured some of the images.

However, he thought that at least one of the paintings looked very much like the Count's work. Since Terry had once told him that the Count never sold his paintings, but tended to horde them in his penthouse, he thought that perhaps this woman must be a very good friend.

The corridor ended in a set of stairs leading to tall glass doors. The boy opened one door and stepped aside, gesturing for them to pass. Fergus nodded to him as he went through. The boy stared back moodily, and he couldn't help but think of Pip. Inside, a tall woman sat in a chair by the window. This room was also white, though there was a fireplace across from the door, crackling merrily and casting a red-golden hue on the walls. The furniture wasn't white. It was made of black lacquered wood with colorful cushions that looked oddly worn in the pristine environment. As they entered the room, the boy gave a loud cough, and the woman looked up.

She had long brown hair, presently piled on top of her head in a messy bun, intense hazel eyes and heavy lashes. He thought he had never seen a woman quite this beautiful before, and so he just stood and stared at her. Terry walked up to her, offering the letter. She took it and picked up a penknife from the table beside her, slitting it open, though her bearing was of one who already knew what she'd find inside. Still, she went through the motions of reading it from start to finish before she slid it back into the envelope and set it on the table.

"Please have a seat," she said, beckoning to the sofa. "My name, as you already know, is Darya Abel."

Terry held out a hand. "Terry Bridges, and this is my friend Fergus Irvine."

Fergus offered a little nod as she shook Terry's hand. Her attention flickered to him only briefly, though there was something speculative about the look – something that made him shiver. He quickly looked away, turning his attention to the large windows looking down onto the town. With the sun setting over the ruddy rooftops, it looked like it was on fire.

Terry tugged at his sleeve, pulling him towards the sofa. He reluctantly followed. The white space made it difficult for his eyes to settle on something besides their hostess. He stared at his hands instead.

"And how is Evan these days?"

For a moment, Terry didn't reply, but then something clicked in his eyes, and he smiled. "Rosslyn Weber is back in town, so I suppose he's happier than usual."

"Really? Mr. Weber? That's a bit surprising . . . "

"I imagine no one was quite so surprised as Rosslyn."

Fergus blinked at Terry and then realized that they were talking about the Count. He managed to bite back an incredulous, "Evan?" It was a very regular name compared to "The Count Palatine."

"They are a lovely couple, though. I remember a few years back . . . They did seem very happy."

"I imagine they still are . . . in their way."

"And whatever happened to that other man who was working for him?"

"He's due to present the Count's new airship model in Clohaven next month."

Fergus found the gossip difficult to feign interest in. His eyes kept searching for something to fix on as he nodded in time with Terry. He figured it was rude, but he wasn't very interested in the Count's love life, nor his airships. He wished the couch was facing the window. Then he might at least watch the sun setting over the city, which would be a rare treat. However, all he could see of it was the golden light slipping further down Darya's face and throat until it was obscured entirely.

The boy returned, silently lighting candles throughout the room. Fergus noticed that not a single lantern was in use, nor did Darya seem to be using any kind of electricity. He wondered if she was trying to create a warm atmosphere. However, the candles did little more than make the room look like the inside of a church, and Fergus felt increasingly antsy.

"Will you be staying the night? We have plenty of rooms, and we haven't had any guests for a while," Darya said, and Fergus realized he'd missed a rather large chunk of the conversation. He didn't feel particularly sorry.

Terry glanced at him. "I certainly wouldn't be adverse to your hospitality. Fergus?"

He glanced at Terry to keep from looking at Darya, because she was giving him another look that made him want to jump out the window and run straight back to the airship. He swallowed and started to smile, but she interrupted him.

"At least stay for dinner, won't you?"

Fergus looked between Darya and Terry and then forced the corners of his mouth up the rest of the way. "It sounds great."

She smiled and clapped her hands. "Matthias, make sure there are place settings enough for two guests."

The boy stared at her sullenly and then nodded, disappearing up the steps on the other side of the glass doors.

"Well, I imagine you two will want to tidy up! I know I simply must. Matthias will be back shortly to show you where you might refresh yourselves."

The skirts of her dress made a swishing noise as she stood. Terry stood, too, which Fergus took as a cue. Not a moment later, Matthias was back and glowering. He seemed to realize what was desired of him without being told, because he nodded to Fergus and Terry and walked away, going back up the hallway to an alcove that Fergus had missed before. A winding set of stairs led up from it.

They followed Matthias to the second floor and down another dark hallway to what he could only assume was the guest room. Matthias opened the door and stared at them expectantly. Terry went in without hesitation, though Fergus glanced at the boy as he passed.

He got the impression that he wasn't going to leave and wondered if Darya had sent him here to listen in on them. He decided not to say anything important. It seemed Terry was of a similar mind, because he began talking about how nice the city was, and Fergus half-suspected he'd gotten stuck in meaningless small chat mode. He didn't chime in, and so Terry eventually stopped talking and rolled up his sleeves to wash his arms and face. Fergus sat on the bed as he waited his turn.

He noticed a large painting over the bed. For a moment, he thought maybe this, too, was the Count's work, but there was something slightly different about the brushwork. It was less precise and more emotive. The painting was mostly in black. A low setting sun illuminated the figures from behind. He stood to get a better look. It appeared to be a number of men on horses, but as he drew nearer, he realized that the figures were far stranger and more lurid.

The Wild Hunt, he thought.

He noticed the paunchy face of a frightened man in the foreground: a drunkard caught out after dusk – their prey. It reminded him a little of the Count's rendering, because it had that same terrible quality of the alluring and the grotesque. Fergus frowned and stepped away from it.

"All yours," Terry said, coming out of the bathroom.

"Thanks," he said.

He splashed cold water on his face and then stared at himself in the mirror – at his milky white eyes and the rivulets seeping down his cheeks. He would leave as soon as dinner was finished. This place was giving him the creeps, and though he couldn't think of how to explain it to Terry, he knew that he didn't want to stay the night.

Matthias brought them down to a grandiose dining room. A long marble table stood at the center of it, and at the center of the table was a cascading river of candles – some new and some melted down to their bases. Fergus got the impression that Darya entertained more than she let on. He also got the feeling that she'd known they were coming, because the meal that was brought out did not look like it'd been thrown together last minute. The point was punctuated by the fact that a young girl who looked markedly like Matthias sat in the corner with a harp before her.

Fergus gave Terry an uncertain look, but it went unseen as Terry followed Matthias to his designated chair. They were on either side of the head of the table, he noticed as he hovered behind his chair, waiting for Darya to arrive.

She entered in a dress that made the previous one look like a maid's frock. He caught Terry giving her an approving look and felt annoyed. His irritation only increased as Terry moved to pull back the chair for her. Fergus waited for Terry to sit before taking his own seat. This entire thing felt stuffy and ostentatious, and he wished he'd stayed with the others on the airship.

However, he sucked down a sigh and tried to look politely interested as Terry and Darya resumed their discussion of politics and trade. He noted that Terry's take on the political side was less opinionated than what he was familiar with. He stared into the candlelight, trying not to look bewildered as Terry deflected questions and played stupid. He was doing a very good job of seeming like he hardly knew a thing at all.

Darya turned on Fergus. "And what about you? What do you think about the state of New Peiling?"

Fergus dropped the Brussels sprout he'd been playing with and looked at Terry, but he received no guidance, so he set his fork down and tried to come up with an answer.

"Well, I'm . . . not really a fan of Paige Harriet."

"The city will probably go to her, though, don't you think?" Darya asked, fixing him with an unblinking stare.

"Yeah, seems like people are scared enough of us, so they'll probably vote for her."

"You know, the vote is in only a couple of months. Will you be back in New Peiling for it?"

"Probably not. We're heading further east."

"What exactly are you planning to do in the East?"

Fergus cast another furtive glance at Terry. He had his impassive face on, and that was cue enough. Fergus tried his best to avert the question. He wished he'd paid more attention to the earlier conversation.

"Well, you know the Count. He wants to show off his airship, and Rosslyn asked me to look for some things for him on the way."

"I suppose there *are* a number of rare ingredients that simply don't come to this side of the world," Darya said. "But if you are heading east, you should visit my brother."

"Your brother?" Terry asked.

"Yes," she smiled, turning to him. "You see, our father was a merchant. He met my mother on his travels, and she talked him into moving here in the final years of his life. He'd picked up an illness that he simply couldn't shake, and she thought the rest would mend him. He left the company to my brother and me. I run things in the west, and my brother is in charge of the office in Ping City. I'm sure he'd love to have you."

Fergus picked up his fork again and pushed the vegetables around on his plate, staring at his Brussels sprouts and trying to channel his thoughts to Terry, which were mainly along the lines of, *No, no, no, please no.*

"I'm sure by the time we get there, we'll be glad for a friendly face," Terry said.

Fergus inwardly cursed.

"It's decided then. I'll write him tonight. I'll send a letter with you, too, just in case you arrive first."

Fergus forced himself to smile and eat one of the Brussels sprouts, turning his attention to the girl in the corner. Unlike her brother, she looked very happy in her work. In the candlelight, she was very pretty, though also very young. But there was something about watching her fingers drumming the chords – about the light striking the strings – that reminded him of the painting in the guest room. He suddenly felt uncomfortable.

He swallowed awkwardly, washing down the greens with the wine. That's when he noticed the hearth over Terry's shoulder. It was unlit, but there was another painting over it, and this one was definitely the Count's hand.

It was a portrait of Darya and a man who looked much like her standing in a garden filled with white roses. Like Darya, the man had sharp hazel eyes that seemed, even in dried oil paint, to know too much about Fergus. He had the same unfamiliar, yet unmistakably beautiful features, though there was something about him that seemed even more dangerous than Darya.

"Do you like it?" she suddenly asked. "Darling Evan painted it for us before Declan went away to Ping City." She sighed, and for a moment, her face looked like a regular woman's. "I do miss him."

"You have a lot of art," Fergus replied.

She smiled. "I have no talent for it, but I do appreciate it. Don't you?"

"Some of it," he carefully answered. "The one upstairs was interesting."

Her eyes lit up. "Oh, did you think so?" She put down her knife and fork and leaned forward on the table.

"Uh, yeah, it was great," he replied, forcing another smile. "It reminded me of one the Count did."

She nodded. "I've seen that one." She paused, glancing at Terry with a rather predatory look.

He smirked a little. Fergus wanted to kick him under the table.

"Evan, Declan, and I were friends in school. We were all sent to the same boarding school in Lancaster, you see."

Fergus nodded. He couldn't imagine the Count as a child. He thought he must have looked like a small demon with blonde curls.

"You might say we shared an interest in the topic."

"The topic?" Fergus asked, looking to Terry, who shrugged.

"The Wild Hunt, of course. You must have some interest in it, too," she added, turning her attention back to Terry. "It's quite romantic in its way. A little squalid, but isn't that part of the allure?"

Terry smiled. "Of course."

"Do you like hunting?" Fergus asked, thinking of the unpleasant moldings of the dying unicorn.

"Actually, I rather do. Evan used to come and visit us here for a week or two in the summers. We'd all go out riding in the hills. I've always been very fond of hawks, and we'd often catch a few things to bring home for dinner. But that was hardly the exciting part."

"Which was?" Terry asked.

"Well, I feel a little silly saying it now, but we would often play as though we were fairies in the Wild Hunt. Oh, it was a bit dangerous – the way we raced around, scaring farmers and cows and anything else that we could spook." She laughed and picked up her fork and knife again. "Perhaps we hoped we could spirit ourselves away."

"You must still have some interest in it," Terry ventured.

She looked up and fixed him with a scrutinizing look. The moment stretched too long not to be awkward, and Fergus was grateful when Matthias came to take the plate of vegetables away and replace it with a plate of pork chops. He waited as the boy continued replacing the dishes until all three had been exchanged. Darya gave him a little nod and then looked slowly between Terry and Fergus. She was wearing a sly expression, which made him feel a lot less hungry despite the warm, fresh meat sitting in front of him.

"If you are interested in the Hunt, you should certainly meet my brother. I hear they play a game of it over there."

Fergus fingered his knife. "What do they hunt?"

"I imagine they mostly just run around scaring drunk humans. It's quite harmless." She smiled at him, incisors flashing.

He nodded slowly.

"And that's it?" Terry asked. He looked all too interested, sitting forward and watching Darya with curious eyes.

"I'd be glad to tell you more after dinner," Darya said, picking up her knife and fork.

Fergus followed suit and allowed most of the conversation that followed to be lost to the sound of the harp. He found his attention kept returning to the shifts and gyrations of the strings in the candlelight. She was playing folk songs; at least, that's what he guessed they were. They had a kind of universal familiarity about them, though he could swear he'd never heard a single one before.

He was grateful when the final round of food appeared. He was still a little hungry, though his appetite didn't seem to be sticking with him tonight. Then Matthias placed a meat pie in front of him, and suddenly his appetite was back with interest.

"What's this?" Terry asked, picking up a fresh fork.

"I'm afraid I can't tell you," Darya laughed. "You see, it's a local delicacy, but if I told you what was in it, you probably wouldn't try it."

"That's a little suspicious," Terry replied, tone good-natured.

"You should try it on the merits of its taste rather than its ingredients," she replied with a smile and picked up her fork, delicately slicing into it.

Fergus cut out a chunk of the strange pie and put it in his mouth. It was *really* good. It was just the right mix of sweet and salty, and the meat practically melted on his tongue. He swallowed and tasted something refreshing and minty in the back of his throat. He unabashedly took another bite. However, before he could take a third, he suddenly felt queasy.

He stared down at the meat pie for a moment. It looked moist and delicious, and he thought he'd vomit if he took another bite. Actually, he thought he might be sick anyway.

"Are you all right?"

He looked up. Terry was watching him with a frown.

"Yeah, just maybe ate too much. It was all so good," he replied, swallowing reflexively.

"Oh dear, do you need to rest?" Darya asked. She looked amused, and Fergus thought he might hate her a little.

He shook his head. "I might just head back, actually. Sorry to cut the evening short."

Darya moved to stand, and so he pushed his chair back, too. "I'll have Matthias see you to the door. I do hope you feel better."

He nodded and glanced hopefully at Terry. He didn't miss the fact Terry didn't offer to come with him. Turning back to Darya and her long neck decorated with shimmering gold bands and her well-fitted dress, he decided it was fair enough. Terry probably hadn't had a chance like this in some time. Still, he felt a little annoyed that his concern was so short-lived.

He cut a path through a sea of niceties wherein Terry finally did offer to go with him, but without much feeling behind it, and he assured them that he'd be just fine. He tried not to be angry when Terry looked satisfied, and he tried not to feel uneasy when Darya gave him a look that seemed to strip him bare. He quickly extricated himself, following Matthias down the hallway to the door, not bothering with a good night, and started down the street.

He was halfway down the hill when he finally couldn't hold it in any longer and stopped to throw up behind a row of mums.

•   •   •

Fergus wasn't feeling better by morning, and Terry wasn't back yet. Despite being nauseated, he let Three drag him to the lake. It was still too warm for ice, so Three found a couple of long sticks, which Fergus initially thought would be makeshift fishing rods. However, Three pulled out a knife, sharpened the ends, and then rolled up the cuffs of her trousers and waded into the water. He stared after her for a moment, but cold water had always made him feel a little better, so he kicked off his shoes and rolled up his jeans, following her in.

The water was freezing.

He gasped in shock and backpedaled, tripping and falling on the bank. He could feel mud seeping into his jeans.

"Are you okay?" Three asked, straightening up to look at him.

"Yeah," he muttered, standing up and trying to wipe the mud from his pants. All he achieved was dirtying his hands, but he washed them off in the water and eased himself back in. "God, that's cold."

She laughed, pulling her hair over her shoulder, and returned to surveying the shallows. "We used to do this a lot. Pip hates it, though. He hates being cold."

"And you don't?" Fergus muttered, staring into the muddy shallows, trying to find a fish to spear. He couldn't see much of anything, though.

"Don't move around. You'll stir up the mud."

"Maybe they're hibernating."

"Just stand very still and watch. They'll come. It's not that cold yet," she replied, not looking at him.

"So, basically you're used to this cuz Pip hates doing it?" Fergus asked. Thick, frigid mud welled up through his toes. His feet stung. However, he did feel less queasy.

"No, he always helps – well, not today – but he usually helps. It's just that I don't mind. I lived closer to the north on a farm, so I was outside most of the time. It was a lot colder than this."

"Guess that makes sense."

Three didn't reply. Her hand moved faster than he could follow. The stick was thrust with such accuracy that it barely even splashed as it broke the surface. A moment later, she pulled the spear free with a fish wriggling at the end.

"There's one!" she cheerfully said, yanking the fish free and throwing it onto the bank. "Well, if we can catch a couple more, you, Pip, and I will have some breakfast."

Fergus glanced at the fish gasping in the grass and felt sick again.

She frowned at him. "You're a little green. Maybe enough for Pip and me?"

He smiled weakly.

"Hey, *are* you sick? Fergus! Why didn't you say anything?" she exclaimed, lowering her spear and started towards him. She took one step and slipped. Fergus didn't even have time to blink before she disappeared backwards into the water. She reemerged a moment later, spluttering, her hair stuck to her face.

"Jeez, are you okay?" he asked, starting towards her.

That's when he noticed that her shirt had slipped. He could see the end of a long, crooked scar peeking out from the hem. Moreover, the wet fabric was sticking to her chest, and he thought he could see something square and dark against her skin. She pulled the hair out of her face with both hands and laughed.

"Yeah, but it is pretty cold, now that—" She stopped, following his eyes and quickly pulled her hair over her chest. She gave him a strained smile. "Well, maybe one fish is enough. Don't want to catch a cold, right?" She pushed herself to her feet with the spear.

"Three . . . "

"Do you think we might have time to stop by an inn? A hot bath might do us both some good."

"Three," he repeated.

She sloshed past him, climbing onto the bank, and picked up the fish. "Yes?"

He stared at her back for a moment. Water was pooling around her bare feet in the grass. He had definitely seen a nasty scar, and he thought it was leading to a metal plate in her chest. He bit his lip.

"Yes?" she asked again, turning to him with a brittle smile.

She didn't look like the girl who could make fire in the air, climb the rigging faster than any of the male crew members, or snare a fish on a stick. It scared him.

He gave himself a little shake. "Are you okay?"

"Of course. Just my pride."

He nodded uncertainly. "We've waited this long to take off. I'm sure we can wait a little longer. Let's go into town and see about a bath."

•   •   •

Guillory was not happy about the delay in the schedule and made little effort to hide it, but Terry still wasn't back when Fergus and Three returned from the town. A hot bath hadn't done much for his stomach, and he wasn't feeling particularly obedient when Guillory ordered him to help scrub the deck, but he bit his tongue and joined the others anyway. He felt lightheaded from not eating, but the thought of filling his stomach made him want to empty it again.

Making sure that Three had her back to him, he gave up on scrubbing to lean against the railing, squeezing his eyes shut.

"Slacking off?" Terry asked jauntily.

He opened his eyes, turning to the redhead, and frowned. Terry smelled of rosemary soap, but underneath that was Darya's perfume, sweat, and blood. He swallowed thickly, feeling his stomach twist.

"What's wrong?" Terry asked, leaning on the railing.

He could already feel the muscles in his throat and stomach contracting. He leaned over and threw up between his hands. It was nothing more than bile, but his body seemed unwilling to move on from that.

"Oh man, Fergus." Terry's hand was heavy on his back, rubbing up and down.

"Please . . . stop . . . " he managed. With Terry up close, the smell of blood was overwhelming.

He could easily imagine the hurt on Terry's face, but he was already stuck in another bout of dry heaving.

"I *knew* you were sick!" Three rushed over, coming between him and Terry. He could see Terry slipping off out of the corner of his eye. "Fergus, just come on. We need to get you in bed."

"I'm fine," he gritted out.

Three wouldn't hear of it. Ten minutes later, he was in bed, pretending to be asleep just to get her to give him some space. It took an additional five for her to decide to go back up top – just in time for Terry to return. He'd changed clothing and washed up. Fergus didn't know what he'd done with his dirty clothing, but he couldn't smell blood anymore. He slowly rolled over.

"You look pretty rough," Terry said quietly. "How long's this been going on?"

"Since last night."

Terry didn't say anything, but he looked a little white as he climbed into his bunk. Fergus leaned over the side of the bed, fumbling around for the glass of water Three had left for him. He sipped at it, leaning up just enough not to choke.

"You aren't gonna help with the take off?" he muttered into the glass, lowering it to his stomach. His head was hurting now, and he could still feel acid in the back of his throat.

"Thought I'd have a little nap."

"Not much sleep last night?"

There was a pregnant pause before Terry snorted. "No."

Fergus was quiet for a moment. "And the blood?"

"Thought we'd do a little hunting."

Fergus's thumb slid down the front of the glass. He said nothing.

"We let it go," Terry mumbled.

The airship began to shudder, and Fergus rolled over onto his side, swallowing back the burn. His stomach was cramping, the muscles aching. He could taste bile rising at the back of his throat again and swallowed harder.

"Are you gonna be sick again?" Terry asked, peeking over the edge of the bunk.

He shook his head, putting down the glass, and pressed his hands to his eyes. "Nothing left," he muttered.

"Sorry," Terry said quietly.

"Maybe you can just punch me or something – knock me out."

"I can do a little better than that," Terry said, and Fergus heard him shift, searching around in his bag. He reappeared with a little vial, holding it down. "Drink this."

"What is it?"

"Just a sleeping draught. Go on."

Fergus sat up and took the vial, uncapping it and throwing the sour potion back.

"How long does it–" he started to ask, but was unconscious before he could finish.

Chapter Six.

The first leg between New Peiling and Sovnik was nothing compared to the journey between Sovnik and Ping City. As promised, they'd already been traveling for twice as long. The worst part of it was that they'd been living on potatoes and onions for the last week, and though there was plenty of dried meat, the idea of putting another hard, smoky chunk in his mouth made Fergus feel ill. He felt cheated. He hadn't had a *good* dinner since he'd been sick, which made it feel like that much more of a loss. Vegetables had never been his favorite, and his jeans were starting to feel loose.

Besides this, Terry was being weird about the evening they'd spent at Darya's. He was wearing that indifferent expression that told Fergus he knew something, but he wasn't going to share. Also, he seemed to be making sure Fergus was never out of his sight for too long and put an especial effort into roping him into helping on deck, mainly with cleaning, as that was the only thing Fergus was good at.

However, Fergus was perpetually nervous about being blown overboard, so Terry had also been making time to visit the kitchens. This did not ease Fergus's skepticism, but he wanted to know whatever it was that Terry wasn't saying, even if it meant scrubbing until his fingers hurt and constantly fearing for his life.

"You know, there are runes on this airship, Fergus. You think you're gonna be blown away, but you're not," Terry said for what may have been the 200th time, but Fergus still hunched as he scrubbed, keeping close to the railing.

"I wish we could just sail on the water," he muttered.

"That'd take even longer."

"I know that, but I'm good at swimming. I'm bad at falling."

Terry laughed, reaching out to ruffle his hair, and fell straight into the railing with a grunt. Fergus gasped as he was tossed right behind him. The brush slipped from his fingers, sailing over the railing and disappearing into the clouds below. The ship shuddered, a dark trail of smoke extending from the rear. Fergus gripped the railing tightly. He could see trees and mountains below and not a drop of water. He let out a little groan.

Guillory's voice rang out over the loudspeaker. "Everyone, stay calm. Crewmen, to your stations. We'll be making an unscheduled stop at Jarpur. I repeat: everyone, stay calm. Men, to your stations. Everyone else, hold on tight. This is going to be bumpy."

"Maybe we should go below," Terry suggested, peeling himself away from the railing and stumbling towards the door.

Fergus nodded and followed after. "We're gonna crash, aren't we?"

"No idea," Terry said, pressing his hands to either side of the stairwell to steady himself as he hurried down one flight of stairs and then the next to the bunks.

Pip was coming up the hall at a run, a carrot in hand. "We're going to die," he squeaked, brandishing the vegetable at them. "Where is Three?"

She poked her head out of the next door down. "I was just cleaning up. What's going on? What broke?"

"No idea. Just get ready to land," Terry said, pushing open their door and herding Fergus in.

Pip flashed past as the door closed, and Fergus heard the other door slam shut and muffled shouts next door. The door swung open again, and Raja stumbled inside.

"What broke?" Raja said, tripping on his way to the bed.

"No idea," Terry repeated. "You okay?"

"Fine," he said, rubbing his chin and clambering into his bunk.

Fergus pressed himself to the wall and closed his eyes. Terry joined him, clutching onto the footboard. None of them spoke, but waited breathlessly as Guillory called out orders, and the ship shook and bounced. It became momentarily more violent, and Fergus grabbed Terry, dragging on his shirt.

"Fergus, you're choking me," Terry hissed, trying to loosen his fingers, but Fergus wouldn't let go. "Calm down!"

The ship rolled from side to side, nearly sending Raja rolling out of his bed. Fergus fell onto his side, losing his grip on Terry's shirt, and nearly tumbled out of the bunk, but Terry grabbed him and hauled him back up. The ship began to slow, smoothed out, and then came to a surprisingly gentle stop.

"See? Good work, men!" Guillory's voice crackled brightly.

Fergus's hands were shaking as he slid out of the bunk onto the floor. "These things are death traps," he muttered, putting his hands between his knees to hide their trembling.

"Let's go see what's going on," Terry said, hopping over him and dragging at his shoulder until he got up. The three of them made their way to the control room where Guillory was shouting orders.

He paused when he saw them. "Might be a day or two, boys. Looks like the engine malfunctioned. We may need to make some replacements."

"Do we have the money?" Fergus asked, stepping out of the way for a crewman who hurried past.

Guillory's no nonsense expression faltered. "Well . . . "

"How much would it cost?" Three asked from behind Raja. She stood on her tiptoes, peeking over them. Raja moved out of the way, letting her into the room.

"That's a good question, and I'm not sure."

"What if it's too expensive?" Fergus asked. "Are we gonna be stranded here?"

Three gently slapped him on the arm. "We can make some money, you know."

He stared at her blankly.

"Come on, we'll go check out the local job boards," she said. "We'll just round up a few drunks, and we'll fill our purses quickly enough."

"Count me out," Raja said. "I'm no good at that kind of thing."

Three stopped, turning around, and put her hands on her hips. She pursed her mouth and then looked at Terry.

"Don't worry. Raja and I will do a little busking and see what we can drum up. Right?"

Raja looked relieved as he smiled at Terry. Fergus thought it had been a while since his face had looked that open. He felt a twinge of guilt.

"Well, come on, Fergus. We'll get Pip and check it out," Three said.

She grabbed him by the arm and pulled him from the control room. Pip was already standing by the stairs. He and Three exchanged a little nod, and then the three of them headed up to the deck to disembark.

Jarpur was like nothing Fergus had ever imagined. As they made their way through the city gates, they found a thriving marketplace crammed between the scalloped, weather-stained buildings. Hundreds of people milled around the market place. There was so little space that the stands were running into each other and spilling out into the path.

The sheer range of color made his eyes hurt. From the black lacquered pots to the women in rich blue and gold robes, his eyes couldn't find a place to settle. He edged his way around piles of what was either spice or dye. They were bright red, yellow, green, and earthy purple, which didn't seem natural enough to be spice, except they smelled amazing.

His mouth watered, but he was quickly distracted as a man shoved a bunch of bananas in his face. The merchant spoke rapid-fire, going on and on, even though Fergus was sure it was obvious he didn't understand a word. He definitely didn't want any bananas, though, so he shook his head mutely and backed away, putting a large middle-aged women between himself and the banana man.

There were fresh mangos, strings of peppers the color of dried blood, live chickens squawking and adding feathers to the chaos, dainty handmade slippers that would have looked great on Ursula, wooden charms that smelled of incense, fine silks, bags of goldfish, fireworks, and all sorts of prayer candles. He looked at the fireworks longingly.

A young man with eyes as blue as Raja's stepped out in front of him, holding a statue of an androgynous god with many arms. His fingers played in the air before it like a magician's, and though Fergus couldn't understand him at all, he gathered that it was supposed to be good luck. He decided to try his earlier tactic of smiling, shaking his head, and escaping, but the young man put his hand on Fergus's shoulder and pressed the idol closer to his face, slipping into a conversational tone.

"That's okay," he said, holding up his hands. He bumped into the people behind him, who complained, but didn't budge.

"Fergus, come on." Pip was suddenly there, grabbing him roughly by the elbow and dragging him free of the merchant.

"Thanks," Fergus sighed.

Pip shrugged and hurried on.

"You guys okay?" Three called, glancing over her shoulder. "Looks like there's a square or something up ahead."

"What if we can't read the signs?" Fergus called out, ignoring the frown of an old man who'd wedged his way between them.

Three missed the question. She hurried on ahead, Pip not far behind her. Fergus struggled against the crowd, starting to lose sight of them, but as he reached the end of the street, the mass of people began to thin out. The street twisted upwards. Ahead, he could see brightly painted buildings sticking out of the trees, seemingly right on top of each other. Strange music drifted down from the corner where an old man sat cross-legged, playing a string instrument.

Fergus hurried past him with a little backwards glance, catching up with Three and Pip at last.

"Have you been here before?"

Three shook her head. "There's a bigger city east of here, which we've been to, but not here. I was hoping there might be some kind of town hall or something . . . " she trailed off, looking around, and then turned back to him, holding up her palms.

"Wait, I think that may be a police stand," Pip said, pointing up ahead.

Fergus and Three looked up to see a white building at the top of the hill. There was a wooden bench in front of it where two men in tan uniforms were smoking.

"Only one way to tell," he said with a shrug. "Let's take a closer look."

They followed the ebbing crowd up the hill past a line of barbers sitting on cushions. Fergus rubbed his chin, which was feeling a little rough; it was dangerous to try for a close shave on a rocking airship. A few of the more timid shopkeepers had set up stands here, mainly women and their daughters, who watched them uncertainly. There were bunches of wilted looking greens, but some also had steaming pots of fresh food.

He drew closer to one such stand, breathing in the sweet, buttery curry. Lumps of chicken bobbed amidst the red-orange sauce, glittering with beads of oil. His stomach growled, and he felt a little sick from hunger.

"Keep moving," Three said, lightly slapping him on the arm as she walked past.

The old lady attending the stand giggled, and he gave her a sheepish grin, rubbing the back of his head, before hurrying after Three. They stopped across from the white building with its scalloped doorway, looking between each other uncertainly. None of them could read the sign next to the door, and the two men were speaking in an unknown language. Pip elbowed him in the back, pushing him forward. He glared back at the boy, but shuffled across the street to the officers.

They didn't look up until he was right in front of them. They stared at him expectantly, but there was a tension in their mouths. He gave them an uneasy smile and then held up his fingers as if to smoke. The man on the right snorted. His mouth crooked up, and he searched around in his pocket, pulling out a carton of cigarettes and tapping one out for Fergus, who bobbed his head thankfully as the other man pulled out a box of matches to light it.

Fergus brought it to his mouth and inhaled deeply. It tasted different from the cigarettes he was used to. There was something almost woodsy about it. He turned his head to the side, exhaling smoke through his nose.

"Foreigner?" the man asked.

He turned back to the man and nodded. "You can understand me?"

The man stared at him for a moment before nodding. "I speak many languages. Where are you from?"

"New Peiling."

He turned to the man who'd given Fergus the cigarette, exchanging a rapid explanation. Fergus only understood the "New Peiling" part. The man nodded, looking up at him thoughtfully.

"So what are you doing in Jarpur?" the man asked.

"Our airship broke down, so we've got to wait around to fix it. We were wondering if there were any jobs available."

"Jobs, is it?" The man took a long drag, squinting up at Fergus. "There are many jobs, but I think maybe you have an idea to come here."

"Is this a police stand?" Fergus asked, looking up at the building.

The walls looked to be made of mud or clay, though they were painted white. Unlike the building next to it, the paint had no chips in it at all.

"Yes, it is," the officer replied, leaning back. "So what job do you want?"

Fergus felt his face heating up. He felt a little stupid asking for bounties like he was some tough guy. He was saved from having to say it by Pip's abrupt appearance to his left.

"Bounties."

He smiled awkwardly. "Yeah, like he says."

The man rubbed his impressive moustache. "Of course, we take care of most of the crime, you know."

Fergus's smile faltered.

"But this is a big city. So we have some bounties, yes."

"Can we see your list?" Pip asked. Fergus wished he'd be a little less no nonsense.

The man nodded, but didn't get up, and Fergus thought perhaps he wasn't going to until they all finished smoking. He tried to will Pip not to look impatient, schooling his own exasperation. The man turned to his partner and began to, Fergus assumed, narrate the conversation. The second officer nodded, glancing at them now and then.

"He wants to know what you can handle. We have several lists. This is a large city."

Pip glanced at Fergus. "Non-violent criminals."

Fergus felt a little ruffled, but didn't protest. He didn't really feel like chasing after murderers anyway.

"But with a good reward," Pip added.

The man stuffed out the rest of his cigarette. Fergus took the last drag of his own.

"Okay, come with me."

The inside of the station was not nearly so immaculate as the outside, and it smelled of old smoke. There were several doors, but the man stopped by the front desk where a fresh-faced boy about Pip's age sat looking overly alert and hopeful. The officer spoke to him, and he nodded enthusiastically, unlocking one of the desk drawers and pulling out a file. He handed it to the officer who spread it on the table. There were dozens of papers with photographs and what must have been write-ups. The man and Pip began to go over them.

Fergus glanced towards the door. Three was standing outside, peeking in. He gave her a curious look, and she receded from sight. He turned back to Pip who was asking for a sheet of paper, sketching a couple of faces and jotting down notes.

"I wish you luck," the officer said as he and Pip finished talking and ushered them to the door.

Outside, Pip showed his notes to Three and Fergus. "Two cases. One is a man called Basu. He's broken into a restaurant several times. It seems like they have a feud. He stole the lock box a few days ago and disappeared. It's likely he's already left the city. Then there are two men named Ray and Amit. They have also been accused of a string of robberies."

"So where do we start looking?" Three asked, exchanging papers with Fergus.

He looked down at Ray, who looked like a pretty nice guy. Unlike Basu, he had no tattoos, nor did he seem particularly athletic. He looked average and friendly. His cousin looked younger, but equally non-threatening.

"This guy is a criminal?" Fergus asked, looking up.

Pip gave him a withering look and turned back to Three. He didn't look so confident, however, as he opened his mouth to speak, said nothing, and then looked away from her.

Three nodded. "I see," she said softly before looking to Fergus. "They're in the red-light district."

"Well, that's not surprising. What's the prob—" He abruptly stopped, recalling what Three had told him, and cleared his throat. "Well, that's no big deal. I can go and have a look around. Probably you should stay with Pip, Three. I mean, he's underage, and you're a girl, so it's no place for you two."

Pip spluttered.

Three frowned. "I don't think you should go alone."

"Well, you'll just be outside, right? So if they ran, you could nab them."

"You can't speak the language," Pip said.

"Neither can you."

"Maybe Raja could, though," Three said, tugging at her hair.

"But he doesn't wanna help us," Fergus reminded her. "We can do this. I mean, what would you do if Raja wasn't here?"

"We try to avoid jobs in cities where we can't speak the language – it makes it a lot harder. But we'd probably pay off a kid to gather information for us, and then we'd see if it was good. If it was, we'd wait for the right moment and make the capture, and if it wasn't . . ." She cleared her throat. "Well, we'd probably have to find the kid and ask him again for the right information."

Pip snorted.

"So why don't we do that?"

"Because," Pip said, poking him in the chest, "we don't have any money."

"We've got enough for a kid," Fergus said, pulling out his wallet and peeking at its contents. Not enough for engine parts, he was sure, but enough that if someone had offered the sum to him when he was orphaned, jobless, and alone, he'd have taken it. More than enough. "How much do you have?"

"Nothing," Pip said, backing away.

Three's mouth twisted, but she sighed and pulled out her own change purse. It sagged, looking thin and deflated.

"Never mind. I've got it," he said. "Okay, let's find a kid."

•   •   •

Jarpur's red-light district was different from New Peiling's in that there was an easily distinguishable separation from the rest of the city. Whereas the brothels and gambling venues and seedy clubs tended to run together with regular shops and residences in lower New Peiling, the red-light district in Jarpur started with a black gate and ran a single long strip down to the other end, which ended in a matching gate.

Their scruffy informant had told them that a popular courtesan was hiding Ray and Amit in one of the nicer brothels. The kid had added point-blank that it would be difficult for a foreigner to get in, but Fergus felt he had to at least try. If he could find it, of course. All he knew was that it had a faux gold exterior.

The top of the street was nice. The brothels looked like fancy hotels or even small palaces. Several of them were gold, though, and he couldn't read any of the writing, so he wasn't sure which one he was looking for. Now and then, a girl drew back a curtain and peeked down at him, but disappeared as he looked up, leaving only the ghost of her silhouette.

However, by the time he'd walked halfway down the street, the scenery drastically changed. The buildings became shabbier. Women lingered in the doorways – small, sad spots of faded color against the gaping shadows. A hollow-eyed woman who could have been his mother's age called out to him, and he shrank back.

"What are you doing?" Pip muttered.

"I can't find it," he replied through gritted teeth, turning away from the desiccated brothels. He saw movement out of the corner of his eye. Three dropped down into a nearby alleyway behind Pip.

"It was the last golden one. The one on the right."

"The last one was on the left."

He heard Pip smack his forehead.

"Oh, you mean on my right *now*."

He started back towards the top of the street until he found the building. It didn't look like a brothel. It looked like a mansion. There was a tall arched doorway leading to two smaller ones. Above them was another set of matching arched enclaves with screens. He could see figures moving behind them, illuminated by candlelight. The third story had what looked like a walkway – also behind a screen – and two towers with a multitude of small, pointed windows.

Though most of the façade was golden, there were turquoise strips here and there, and the entire thing was patterned in an elaborate floral design. He gulped and wondered if he could afford to even go in. They'd gone back long enough to try to pool together their resources and change, but even his nice clothing seemed unsuitable for a place like this. Still, here he was, and he wouldn't know if he'd be turned away or not unless he tried, so he took a deep breath, steeled himself, and walked up to the door where a burly man with a large beard was standing. He gave a polite nod to the man who asked him something he couldn't understand. He stared for a moment, wondering what he should do.

Of course, if he was in New Peiling, he could ensure entry with a nice payoff, so he pulled out his wallet and took out some cash. He didn't hand it over, but watched to see if the man looked interested. He did, though he also looked suspicious. His arms remained crossed over his chest. Fergus's mouth twitched, and he glanced over his shoulder. He couldn't see Pip or Three, and he wasn't sure what to do.

He wasn't sure if it was rude to just hand the guy a bribe, but he wasn't reaching for it, so Fergus tried to politely hold it out. The man stared at him for a moment and then laughed. Fergus couldn't tell what he said, but he didn't seem to be saying, "leave," so he took a few more bills out of his wallet and then offered those. The man stared at him for a long moment, looking less amused. His eyes flicked from shoes to hair, and Fergus was glad he had changed out of jeans.

Nodding, the bouncer reached out to take the money. He pushed the door open and gestured for Fergus to enter. The inside was even more intimidating than the outside. Rich purple and blue carpets with gold threading covered the floor. The walls were unadorned, but they, too, had golden patterns. The room was airy, though the air was thick with something sweet and dizzying. He felt his fingers tingle just a little as he breathed it in. All along the outer wall, couples lounged on cushions around tables piled high with fruits and meats and drinks.

His stomach rumbled, and he chewed his lower lip. A woman in a green brocaded outfit with a golden veil met him halfway. She looked mildly surprised by his appearance, but she smiled nonetheless and motioned for him to follow her.

She sat him at a lone table with a bottle of wine. He sat on one of the red silk pillows and looked around, at a loss. He could hear others talking, though he couldn't understand, and the screens hid them from view. At least he was near a window, so he could look outside while he waited. His eyes were growing heavy, and he wished that the evening was windier, because the incense was suffocating.

He leaned back and took a breath, wondering how he was going to pull this off when he couldn't speak the language and couldn't stay for more than 30 minutes. His worrying was interrupted by the gentle *clink* of metal.

A girl in red stopped before his table. Both her wrists were hidden under an impressive collection of bangles, which matched the beads at her throat and the heavy tassels on her ears. She smiled and sat down across from him. Taking the wine and uncorking it, she poured two glasses. Her hands were small and painted with brown flowers. She pressed one glass to him and leaned back, smiling again. Her mouth was very red. Lifting one hand, she pulled back the veil of her headdress a little.

"Hi," he said, rubbing the back of his neck.

"Hello," she replied.

He started. "You understand me?"

She gave a little nod.

"Really?"

She lifted her hand, stifling a laugh. "I studied abroad . . . once."

"Then how come you're . . .?" He stopped, motioning vaguely.

"That is a long story," she replied. "Let's not speak of it."

He nodded stupidly and picked up the glass of wine, raising it in a brief toast before taking a long drink. "What's your name?"

"Indu."

"Fergus. Nice to meet you."

"What are you doing in Jarpur, Fergus?"

"Just passing through. We're on our way to Ping City."

"Oh, are you an airship captain?"

"Something like that."

"It must be lonely on those ships," she said softly, offering him a coy smile.

He felt his face burn and cleared his throat. "A little, yeah."

"You look tense."

"I've just never visited anywhere like this before."

"I can tell."

He ducked his head, scratching it.

"Did I offend you?"

"No. I guess it is kinda obvious."

"It's not bad." She leaned over, taking out a silver incense burner and lighting a stick.

He frowned a little.

She glanced up. "Do you dislike it?"

"No, just not used to it. What is it?"

"Just incense."

He watched the silver-purple plume of smoke gently snake into the air. His head was swimming. He took a deep breath, though it didn't help.

"I can put it out," she offered.

"No, it's fine," he lied, forcing a smile. "Actually, a friend recommended this place. He goes by Ray. Do you know him?"

Indu raised an eyebrow.

"He said he might actually come here tonight," Fergus said. He felt like he was babbling, but he couldn't seem to stop. "Him and his cousin."

Her brow remained arched. "He and his cousin are sitting two screens away. Did you not see them?"

His cleared his throat. "Oh. Must've missed them."

"Should I bring them over?"

"Bring them over?" he repeated dumbly, fumbling for a save. "But then I'd have to share you."

She laughed. "In a way."

"No way I'm letting that happen." He tried to give her a cocky smile. "I can talk to them later."

"You are very charming," she said, adjusting her headdress again. "Are you sure this is your first time?"

He grinned sheepishly. "So . . . "

"So," she repeated, giggling. "I'm sorry. You look a little like a puppy."

"Are you teasing me?"

"Maybe," she replied, mouth twitching. "You are making it very easy."

"Seems like you're the charming one," he said, shaking his hair out of his face.

"Shall I charm you more? Perhaps a dance? A song? Do you like poetry?"

"Uh . . . I like songs."

"Do you like to sing?"

"I dabble," he replied with a shrug, glancing away.

"I think it's more than that. Will you sing for me tonight? I have never had someone sing for me."

He fumbled with his tie, loosening it. "Y-yeah."

"I would like a love song."

"L-love song," he repeated. The tips of his ears were burning now.

"Yes, a love song. A sweet one. It doesn't have to be long." She picked up the wine bottle, refilling his glass. "Will you?"

"Okay, yeah, a love song it is," he said, picking up the glass and taking another drink. He knew plenty of romantic songs. He'd written quite a few for the long line of exes he'd had since 15. It seemed a little unfair to sing her a song about another woman, though. "Don't stare at me. Let me think for a few minutes."

He leaned back into the cushions, tapping his fingers against his knee as he looked through the slats at the moon. Her bracelets clinked together as she shifted, waiting. The incense stick burned down first by one inch, then two. Then it was halfway down the stick, the ashen line at the top perilously hanging on. A tiny breeze sifted in through the screen, knocking it free. He wondered if she was using it to time their meeting. He wondered how much one incense stick of her time was worth.

"Okay, are you ready?" he said. "It's gonna be short, though."

"That's fine," she replied, sitting up a little. She looked expectant, but there was something hopeful in her large, dark eyes. Something that made him feel a pinch of regret that was too deep for him to entertain for more than a second.

He cleared his throat and began. "There's a piece of the moon in Indu's eyes. She could swallow me up in their blackness. Just show me that moon in her sweet, dark eyes. That'd burn way all the sadness. Let me pretend that this moment could last forever. Let it last forever and a day. Cuz when I'm looking at my pretty Indu, I just gotta stay. You don't know how the moon trembles in her eyes. Don't know how she smiles. So let me go with this moment and float away in her gaze."

He stopped.

Her face was lowered. A little sniff escaped her.

"You okay?"

"Yes," she quickly said, looking up, her eyes red-rimmed and bright. "Yes, fine. It was very nice, Fergus. Thank you."

"Uh, it's nothing."

She laughed, blinking, and looked away. "The moon is very apt."

"What do you mean?"

She shook her head, taking a deep breath. "I will do you a favor."

"Jeez, you don't have to. It's a freebie."

She shook it more vehemently. "No, I want to. I will help you. You are no airship captain."

"Huh? Wait, how did you . . .?"

"May I see your hands?"

He held them out.

She reached out, holding them palm up.

"The calluses are wrong. They're larger on your fingers than your palms. Besides, what crewman could think of a song like that so quickly and sing it so nicely?"

"Oh." He bit his lip.

She lowered her voice, leaning over the table. "Neither Amit or Ray speak your language, nor can you speak ours. You must have come for the bounty.

What is a musician doing hunting criminals, though?"

"Well, I did come here on an airship, but it's in need of some repairs, so . . . "

"I see. I can only help so much, but I will do what I can. Please wait here a moment." Her skirt rustled as she stood.

He looked up at her. "Be careful," he said, for lack of anything better.

It seemed to be enough, because her mouth twitched as she nodded. She disappeared, taking their empty wine bottle with her. He couldn't see where she went, but he could hear her voice nearby. He sat back, drinking the rest of his wine, and wondered what she was up to. He was starting to feel sleepy and muddled again. The incense had nearly burned to its end, and he realized the tips of his fingers had gone from tingling to numb. This did not worry him as much as it usually would. Instead, he stared at them a little dazedly and then rubbed them together.

Indu reappeared with a sly smile. "It is done."

He blinked and then suddenly sat up, which made his vision prickle. "What did you do?" he whispered.

"Drugged their wine. They will leave here soon. I believe they may be up to their usual business tonight."

He nodded slowly.

"Come with me. You should act like you are drunk."

This wasn't too hard, because his knees were especially wobbly as he got to his feet. She moved closer, offering an arm, which he gratefully took. His legs felt numb, too, and making them move properly took all of his concentration.

She led him to the front where the woman in green stood. They began to speak. Indu sounded like she was complaining. Fergus blinked owlishly, looking between the two of them. The woman in green frowned at him, eyes narrowing. Indu moved away from him, moving her hands rapidly and sounding increasingly annoyed.

The woman nodded and turned her frown back to Fergus. She held out a hand expectantly, and Fergus stared at it for a moment before realizing she wanted him to give her something. He pulled out his wallet, taking out the rest of its contents, and put it in her palm. Her fingers snapped around the bills, and she turned away, barking out a final order to Indu.

"Come back, if you ever return to Jarpur," she said, her fingers playing with her veil.

"Are you sure that'd be okay?"

"She won't remember you, but I will."

"Thank you, Indu."

She gave him a brief smile and walked away. He went back down the corridor, tucking his empty wallet into the back pocket of his trousers with some difficulty. Outside, the guard gave him an amused look and said something unintelligible but obviously disparaging, but since Fergus couldn't understand him, he just smiled and nodded, continuing on his way. A few buildings down, Three and Pip slipped out from an alley, falling into step beside him.

"So?"

"They're coming. Said they were up to their usual business tonight."

Three frowned at him, putting a hand on his shoulder. He stopped, swaying.

"Are you drunk?"

"Not at all. I only had a couple of glasses of wine."

"Are you sure?"

"Uh, yeah. Come on. We should wait at the top of the road." He started walking again. He was pretty sure it wasn't a straight line, but he tried to use speed to hide that fact.

Three said nothing as they reached the end of the district. Pip was giving him an incredulous look.

"What?"

"You *are* drunk."

"How the hell could I be drunk on two drinks?" His tongue felt swollen, the words slurring together, which annoyed him, since it seemed to prove their point. "Look, I can touch my nose. So I'm not drunk."

Pip didn't look convinced. "There is something wrong with you."

"Just stay back this time. Okay, Fergus? Let us handle the rest."

"I can help!"

"Be quiet, you idiot. Someone's coming!"

They fell silent, straining their ears. Sure enough, voices issued from down the road. Three men passed through the gate, not even glancing their way.

"Not them," Three muttered.

They let out a collective sigh.

"Anyway, Indu drugged their wine, so we can probably just follow 'em a little while, and the drink'll do the rest," Fergus said.

"Are you sure she didn't drug you?"

"Hey, she's a nice girl."

"She's a . . . "

"Shh! Someone else is coming!" Three hissed.

They stopped arguing and listened. This time, it was only two voices. Amit and Ray passed through the gate. The three shrank back against the wall as Ray glanced their way, pausing for a moment. Fergus held his breath as Ray studied the shadows and then shrugged, jogging a little to catch up with Amit.

"Let's go," Three whispered, slipping out of the shadows and padding after them as silently as a cat. Pip followed. Fergus, however, found himself weaving like a drunken bull. Pip turned back, saw him stumbling, and stopped to drag him back towards the side of the road.

"Ow," Fergus grumbled.

Pip didn't release him, but dug his fingers in more sharply. Three was already several yards ahead, and Amit and Ray were moving slower and slower. It seemed they weren't doing a very good job of putting one foot ahead of the other, either. Fergus wanted to say, "told you so," but Pip was forcing him to move a lot faster than he presently had the coordination to manage. He kept stumbling, and it was all he could do to stay on his feet.

Ray leaned against the side of a building, wiping his forehead with the back of one wrist, and Fergus stared, wondering when they had stopped. Three made her move. The buttons of her jacket flashed in the light, and Ray let out a little cry, crumpling. She turned just in time for Amit to strike her in the back of the head. She stumbled and fell to her knees.

Pip released Fergus with a shout, rushing over with one of his slips of paper. It zoomed through the air, began to glow, and then caught fire. It missed Amit, whizzing past his ear. Amit turned and pulled something out of his belt, throwing it at Pip, who deftly dodged.

Fergus tried to make his feet hurry, but instead they became tangled, and he fell on his face. When he looked up, Amit was squaring off against Three and Pip. Ray was getting up, too. Fergus let out a shout, as Ray launched himself at Pip, catching him off-guard. The two went tumbling, fists and legs flailing. Three shouted his name, but her eyes remained on Amit. He tossed a second knife. Fergus saw its blade glimmer in the moonlight.

Three sidestepped it, lunging at Amit and kicking. He managed to stumble out of the way, but she clipped him with her side. She was knocked off-course and he to the ground. That seemed as good an opening as anything, so Fergus stumbled to his feet, sprinting forward. He half fell on Amit as he was getting up. Amit gracefully turned, sending him sprawling on his face.

Their shouts were drawing attention. Lights came on in windows, and people were starting to gather. Pip had managed to subdue Ray. Fergus wasn't sure if he had knocked him out, or if it had been the drugged wine. Whatever the case, he definitely wasn't going anywhere, and Pip was rejoining the fight. Then Pip started shouting and grabbing at Three. He saw the fear in her eyes, and suddenly the two disappeared into the crowd.

Fergus stared after them, but before he could call out, Amit's fist connected with his cheek. The people in their bright clothing swirled together for a moment before he hit the ground. Amit's foot connected with his stomach, and he grunted in pain, curling around it. A second kick followed it, and Fergus reached out, grabbing his leg. Amit tried knocking him free, but Fergus clung as though his life depended on it. He wasn't sure that it didn't.

Amit called to Ray, but Ray was still lying in a heap. He let out an angry exclamation and finally kicked free of Fergus's grip. Fergus didn't know what he was shouting, but the look in his eye said it all. He reached into his belt for one last knife. Fergus tried to scramble out of the way, but his arms and legs felt numb. He held an arm over his face, closing his eyes.

Amit let out a shout, and he opened his eyes to see a police officer tackling him to the ground, knocking the knife out of his hand. Another officer ran up behind him, going to check on Ray. Fergus slowly sat up. The first officer struck Amit in the back of the head, and he stopped struggling long enough for the cop to bind his hands behind his back. It was the man from earlier in the afternoon. He looked down at Fergus.

"Not bad," he said. "Though not very subtle."

"Sorry," Fergus mumbled, rubbing his head.

"Can you stand?" the officer asked, hauling Amit to his feet.

"Yeah, I'm fine."

"Come by tomorrow. We will have the papers for you to collect in the morning."

A third officer pushed through the crowd, going to help the second get Ray on his feet. Fergus watched the five of them depart. The crowd began to disperse, leaving Fergus sitting in the middle of the street.

He tenderly poked his stomach and winced before rolling to his feet. His lip had been split open during one of the falls and blood dripped down his chin. He rubbed it away and began to limp back towards the city gate and the airship. By the time he got there, he could feel his hands and feet again, though they stung as though they'd been asleep. His lip had also scabbed over, but his head was pounding in exchange.

He slowly made his way up the rope to the deck. One of the crewmen called out to him, and he waved a little before limping towards the door. Pip and Three lingered at the bottom of the stairs. Pip was squatting, his arms around his legs. Three paced, hugging her stomach. She stopped when she saw him.

"Fergus!"

"What the hell, guys?" he growled, limping down the steps.

"I am so sorry. I really am sorry," Three said, her eyes welling with tears.

"What did you split for?" he demanded.

Three swallowed, biting her lip and glanced at Pip. He uncurled from the floor, shrugging, and left without another word.

"Yeah, well, I didn't need your help anyway," Fergus called after him.

"He's sorry, too," Three said quietly.

"Kinda hard to believe that."

"He's ashamed! We both are."

Fergus said nothing. He couldn't think of a reason they shouldn't be.

"It's just that Pip saw him. Or he thinks he did."

"Him?"

"That man. The one we're looking for – the one looking for us. He thought he saw him in the crowd and panicked. We both did."

"Well, was it him?"

"I don't know. I panicked. I'm sorry."

"Okay. Fine. Stop apologizing. So you didn't see him?"

She shook her head.

"I thought you wanted to find him, though. Why'd you run away?"

"I don't know," she said weakly, hair falling over her face. "I don't know. I panicked. I remembered what happened last time, and there were so many people around . . . "

"What happened last time?"

She looked up slowly. Her eyes were red, mouth trembling.

"Fine, don't answer."

"Wait! Just wait." She reached up, slowly undoing the buttons along the shoulder of her top and peeling back the cloth to reveal the top of the scar he'd seen that morning at the lake. "He did this. I would have died, but Pip's magic saved me."

Fergus stared at the jagged scar leading down to the edge of a metal plate, which he could only assume extended over her heart.

"Oh," he said at last.

She began buttoning her shirt up, though her fingers shook. "Magic and a little science . . . that's all that's holding me together, like this airship, like New Peiling. We don't know when it will give."

"You mean . . . ?"

"I was afraid to fight him unprepared. I was afraid to do it with civilians around. With you around."

"I guess . . . yeah, that makes sense."

"There's no other reason that we would have left you. Please believe me."

He shook his head. "No, it's fine. It turned out all right, didn't it?"

"Did you take him down?"

"Well, the cops did, but I definitely softened him up for them." He gave her a lop-sided grin. "We can claim the bounty in the morning."

She smiled and put a hand on his shoulder. "You should get washed up. Sleep in. We'll go and fetch the bounty."

"You sure? What if that guy's around?"

"We'll be careful. Anyway, you've earned your rest." She dropped her hand, moving past him. "Good night, Fergus."

Chapter Seven.

Fergus sat on a hard wooden chair in the center of a large bazaar. Across from him, amidst a pile of apples, sat an old man on a cushion playing a sitar. As Fergus looked around, he realized that none of the stands were selling anything but apples, which had spilled into the aisles, forming shiny red mounds. He craned his head back and could see that the roof of the bazaar was plastered in posters of gods with blue skin and multiple arms and elephant trunks.

The gods moved from poster to poster, pausing to chat with their neighbors and making a lot of noise. He tried to get up, but the blanket that had been tucked around his shoulders was too heavy.

"Don't struggle," Terry said, approaching him with a brush full of shaving cream. He was stripped down to his shorts.

"Why are you naked?"

"I'm not," Terry replied, lifting his chin and painting cream over his cheek. "It's very hot."

"Don't you have a lighter blanket?"

Terry ignored him, coating his face. The cream seeped into his mouth, tasteless and thick. He spluttered and tried to spit it out. Terry flipped open a switchblade and leaned over him. He could hear the metal scrapping against his skin. He swallowed convulsively, drawing sharp bursts of air through his nose.

"Terry," he said through gritted teeth.

Terry paused; the blade hovered close to Fergus's eye. His mouth was just visible below it, set in a firm line.

"Can't breathe."

"It wasn't so bad, was it?" Terry asked. The blade disappeared from his hand. He reached forward, pulling Fergus's head up, fingers threading through his hair.

"You're getting shaving cream in it," Fergus complained.

"You have bad energy."

"What?" he asked sharply.

He was now looking down at Terry, and his hands were around Terry's throat. He could feel his pulse jumping against his thumbs. Terry's stared up at him impassively. Droplets of blood were forming on his cheek.

"You're bleeding."

"It's not mine."

"Whose is it, then?" Fergus asked.

"Theirs, isn't it?" Terry replied.

Fergus released him and slowly stood back. The apples were melting, forming red sludge that pooled in the aisles, mixing with the dirt, and turning into a muddy, sanguine river that seeped towards his feet. He stumbled backward, but there was something there. He could feel its cold breath on his neck. The river of blood began to rise and pick up speed, flooding around his ankles.

Something bumped into him, and he saw a blue eye bobbing on top of the muck for a moment before being carried away by the current. Hands, still twitching and grasping, drifted behind it. He jerked away, trying to avoid their grasp, but whatever was behind him kept him from moving. Wrinkled fingers grabbed his ankle.

"No!" he shouted, kicking violently.

Terry blinked at him slowly, safe above the deluge on his wooden chair.

"Terry, help me."

But he realized that Terry was not looking at him, but whatever was behind him. He started to turn.

"Don't look," Terry said.

Screaming filled the bazaar. Hundreds of voices shrieked in unison. Fergus didn't want to look back, but once started, it seemed he was magnetically compelled to keep turning. His breath came in sharp gasps. He turned and turned. Something wet and black was at the edge of his vision. He opened his mouth to scream, but nothing came out.

He awoke with a jolt. His heart drummed painfully in his chest, and he couldn't catch his breath. The planks of the top bunk swam in his vision and then settled. He took a deep breath and slowly sat up. From beyond the curtain, he could hear Terry and Raja moving around, talking quietly as they dressed.

He flopped back onto his pillow, closing his eyes, and tried to control his breathing. Bits and pieces of the dream swam behind his eyelids, though for the life of him, he couldn't recall what he'd seen that made him feel so jumpy.

"You awake, Fergus?" Terry called.

He cracked an eye open. He could see Terry's silhouette on the other side of the fabric. "Yeah," he mumbled.

"Well, get up, then. We'll be docking in Ping City today. Looks like we might have some rough weather on our hands, so we'll need everyone to help out."

Fergus sat up and pulled back the curtain. He winced at the thin light coming through the cabin window, running a hand over his face.

Raja pulled a long white shirt over his head, something he'd picked up in Jarpur, and turned to Fergus. "Looking rough."

"Thanks," Fergus grumbled and slid out of bed. "I didn't . . . " he paused, and Terry and Raja both turned to him inquisitively. "Um, never mind."

"Have something to eat," Terry said, tossing him an apple.

He caught it with both hands and stared down at the gleaming red skin. It made him feel unaccountably nervous, so he put it down on his bed with a brief, "thanks," and set off for the shower to splash his face.

The cold water didn't refresh him. He stood, staring at his white eyes in the mirror, watching his pulse twitch in his throat, and felt strange and unfamiliar to himself. He thought maybe washing up might help clear his head, so pulling off his shorts, he sat on the low stool and filled the tub with fresh water to pour over his head. He repeated the process a few times before putting the bucket down and locating a block of soap. The door opened behind him.

"Privacy," he grumbled.

Terry snorted and went over to the sink to get his toothbrush. Fergus didn't turn around, but he didn't tell Terry to brush outside, either.

"'ow's za bruise?" Terry asked around the brush.

"Almost gone," Fergus replied, looking down at the spot where Amit had kicked him. The skin was still yellow, but it hardly even hurt.

"'at's good," Terry said and then paused to spit into the basin. Fergus heard him splash some water on the brush and then put it back in his mouth.

"You're taking your time today," he noted, washing away the soap.

Terry spat again. "Just wanna look nice for the ladies."

Fergus rolled his eyes and then realized Terry couldn't see him doing it. "I thought we were gonna visit that Declan guy."

"Well, he might be as good looking as Darya."

Fergus glanced over his shoulder, frowning.

Terry laughed.

"Whatever," he muttered. "But why are you really here?"

"You looked a little out of it. Just wanted to make sure you didn't slip and crack your skull open."

"Newsflash: I wake up every day without cracking my head open."

Terry was silent for a moment. Fergus could hear him washing his toothbrush.

"Did I wake you?"

"Not this time," Terry said and began to gargle.

"Then what are you so worried about?"

Terry spat again. Fergus could practically feel him leaning on the sink. He sighed impatiently and refilled the bucket a final time.

"You probably don't wanna hear this."

"Well, I do now."

"Just . . . your mom. She complained of nightmares a lot before . . . "

"I've only turned twice. She was doing it a lot more than that, right?" Fergus replied more hotly than he'd intended.

Terry was silent for a moment before quietly replying, "Yeah, that's true."

"Bad dreams are still just dreams," Fergus said as he dumped the last bucket over his head. "We're gonna have to lock up a lot of people if nightmares are the main symptom of insanity. Gimmie a towel."

Terry tossed one, landing it on his head.

"Thanks," he grumbled, scrubbing his hair.

"Hey, if you don't wanna see Darya's brother, I'd understand. I can go alone."

"Why wouldn't I?" Fergus asked, standing up and wrapping the towel around his waist before turning to Terry.

Terry looked away. "I dunno. You didn't seem to enjoy visiting Darya."

"If you don't want me to, then I won't."

"No, it's not like that," Terry quickly said, glancing at him, though not meeting his eyes. "Never mind. It's nothing. Come up when you're ready."

"Yeah, I know," he replied, watching Terry leave with a twinge. He sighed. "Nothing is ever *just* nothing, though," he muttered to himself as the door shut.

•   •   •

The labyrinthine streets of Ping City would have given New Peiling a run for its money. The buildings were crowded together and so tall that even if they weren't in plates like in New Peiling, they still didn't let in any of the late afternoon light. Not that there was much to enjoy in the first place. It had been drizzling since they landed and windy enough that Fergus had pulled on a second jacket over his hoodie.

They'd disembarked at a landing strip by the harbor. Pip and Three led the way through houseboats and skiffs towards the city proper where Fergus could smell a mixture of fish, boiled meat, dust, and sweat. They stepped off the maze of boardwalk and started down an alley, narrowly avoiding a bicyclist by flattening against the wall. Fergus found he was standing next to an enclave that looked like a tiny shrine. Incense sticks were burning in front of a rotund statue in bright paint. Pip lifted one hand in a brief gesture of deference as they passed by. They managed to squeeze through the first alley to be greeted by another just like it. Overhead hung spiderwebs of laundry, blotting out the sky. The smell of boiling meat curled out of a window where a fat old cat with a bobbed tail sat glaring down at them.

"Kinda tight, huh?" he said, glancing back at Three.

She smiled and nodded.

"Do you speak the language?"

"Yup!" she replied, edging past him to the top of the line to walk beside Pip.

"Is it your native language?"

"No," Pip replied sharply without turning. "We have learned several languages."

"Sheesh, sorry," Fergus grumbled. "Can we hurry up? That cat's giving me the evil eye."

They turned down another street, which was a little wider and framed by open-front shops and stands of flowers, fruits, and meats. He gazed longingly at the dangling rows of ducks and trays of flopping fish.

"There are so many," he said, stopping to admire a table with at least thirteen trays of different seafood. "What the heck is that?" he asked, reaching out to pick up a shelled thing. An old lady smacked him on the hand from behind the table, and he sucked in a pained breath, rubbing his knuckles.

"It's just a snail. Don't touch anything you don't intend to buy," Pip said exasperatedly.

"He's just getting a feel of the city," Guillory said in a kindly tone. Fergus jumped. He'd nearly forgotten that the Captain had come with them. Guillory turned to the woman and began to speak to her.

"Wait, you can speak it, too?" Fergus asked as the old woman finally laughed, lifting a hand to her face in mock shyness, and Guillory turned back to them.

"Hmm? Oh yes. Well, I have traveled far and wide. You didn't think I was coming here completely blindly, did you?"

"I dunno," Fergus muttered.

"Well, I have a few errands to run, so I'll meet up with you later. Remember, we'll be leaving in a day's time, so be on the ship, or we might leave you." Guillory lifted a hand in salute as he strolled off down a side street.

Terry made a derisive sound. "I'll bet anything he's on the prowl."

"Hey," Fergus said, "you were the one who was trying to freshen up for the ladies."

Terry's scowl faded. "I guess I was."

"Hey guys, if you don't mind, we're going to head off, too. There might be some bounties for us to collect on," Three said.

"You want me to come?" Fergus asked.

Three shook her head. "No, that's fine. You handled the last one, and you've got a friend to meet, right? Leave it to us. Besides, we owe you one for last time," she said, patting his shoulder.

"So, just the three of us," Fergus said, looking between Terry and Raja.

"We should stick together," Raja suggested. "Since none of us can speak the language."

"We did okay in Jarpur," Fergus replied.

"There are a lot of people who can speak our language in Jarpur."

"So do you two want to look around before we head to Abel's house?" Terry asked.

Fergus looked around. "I wanna eat."

"Well, that's no surprise. Anything else, though? There's one of those old cinemas here, I think. Or we could go see something live."

"Live?"

"I hear there's some kinda opera house."

Fergus lifted an eyebrow incredulously.

"That sounds interesting," Raja piped up.

"Count me out. I'm fine on my own," Fergus replied. "I wanna look around here some more."

"You just want to eat," Raja sighed.

"So?"

"Probably better here," Terry muttered.

"What?"

"Go on, Fergus. But let me write down the address for you."

He waited patiently as Terry copied down a note obviously written by Darya. He didn't think the characters looked quite as authentic in Terry's hand, but maybe the people here would recognize enough to point him in the right direction. He tucked it into his front pocket.

"Are you sure you don't wanna come?" Terry asked.

"It might be educational," Raja added.

Fergus made a face. Terry rested an arm on Raja's shoulder, still giving him a hopeful look, but Fergus felt annoyed by their familiarity. He cleared his throat, looking away. "I'll educate my stomach first. Go on. Get lost," he added, giving Terry a little shove that effectively made him stop leaning on Raja. It felt a little better than he thought it ought to have. "Okay, bye," he quickly said, heading towards the smell of boiling meat.

He felt a little lonely as he sat down and made a random gesture at the menu, which earned him a heaping bowl of noodles and sliced pork, but he did his best to drown out the feeling by gulping down the soup as fast as he could before having another bowl. He was feeling pretty full, but there were still too many interesting smells around to give up yet, and he hadn't had anything for breakfast.

The dim afternoon light was nearly gone, and the streets were glowing with a mix of neon lights and lanterns. He wandered to a stand with broiled fish on sticks. They were a little too salty, but he still finished one off before heading over to another stand where a pretty girl about Pip's age was selling little balls covered in sesame seeds.

She looked up at him from under heavy lashes, smiling shyly. Her dark hair fell into her face, and he was reminded of Ursula, even if he doubted she'd ever looked so innocent in her life. Still, he found himself staring at the girl a moment too long, his stomach twisting up, before she asked him – he assumed – if he wanted some dumplings.

He bought two, though he only ate one. It was doughy, and the center was filled with a sweet paste. The mixture didn't sit well with him, so as soon as he was out of sight of the stand, he handed off the second to a little boy who happened to be running by.

He wasn't sure how much time had passed, but his stomach was starting to hurt, and it was definitely dark above the strings of lanterns, so he began looking for Declan Abel's residence. Most people he showed the address to recognized it, and though he did accidentally circle one block twice, he soon found himself before a modern looking building that rose several stories over the surrounding buildings.

He peered at Terry's writing and then at the sign outside the building, and he thought they looked similar, so he went inside. The floor was marble, though the walls and most of the light fixtures were made of a shiny black material. There was a single glass desk at the back of the lobby, which he slowly approached. He wished he'd worn something nicer than jeans.

The man behind the counter stared at him for a moment before asking in a thick accent, "You are here to see Mr. Abel?"

He nodded dumbly.

The man picked up a receiver, punching in a number. A quick conversation followed before he hung up and extended a hand to his right. "Please take the lift to the 48th floor."

Fergus nodded slowly and backed away from the counter, heading towards a glass elevator marked "Floors 30-50." He glanced over his shoulder at the attendant who was looking at him expectantly and pressed the button. Stepping inside, he stood against the back wall, watching the lobby growing smaller through the clear floor, and let out a sigh. The quick ascent made his ears pop, and he yawned, trying to relieve the pressure. It wasn't long before the number "48" lit up over the doors, and he stepped out into a foyer.

A stone path led from the elevator to the doorway, framed on either side by pools full of goldfish, which were illuminated from below by oscillating lights. A doorman stood on the other side of the path, watching Fergus blankly. He kept his hands behind him and his back very straight. Fergus gingerly made his way over the stepping-stones to the other side.

"Hello," he said to the doorman, hoping the man could understand him. "Um, I'm here to see Mr. Abel." *Please let Terry be here already*, he willed.

The doorman nodded curtly and reached out with one white-gloved hand to push the door open. "Wait inside."

Fergus straightened his shoulders and crossed the threshold into a second foyer. There was a flower arrangement to his left and a coat rack to his right. It looked a little like the Count's penthouse. It smelled a little like it, too. He recognized the lingering trace of Fairy Dust. Fergus moved closer to the flowers, sniffing them for want of anything better to do.

"You must be Terry."

A tall man with olive-colored skin, dark brown hair, and flashing hazel eyes stood at the end of the foyer. He was dressed in an elaborate silk jacket. It looked a little like what some of the merchants had been wearing, but much, much more expensive. Fergus opened his mouth, turning bright red, and said nothing. Darya had been breathtakingly beautiful, but there was something about her brother that made her pale in comparison, and that, he felt, was an uncomfortable thought.

"Terry Bridges?" Declan Abel repeated.

He shook his head. "Fergus Irvine. I'm a friend of Terry's," he paused before adding, "and the Count's."

Declan chuckled. "Evan is taking on airs, isn't he? Don't worry. Darya wrote to me about you, Fergus. I'm glad you could make it. Please come in."

Fergus nodded uncertainly and shuffled to the end of the foyer. The whole place was immaculate. He looked around, embarrassed to even stand on the shiny wooden floor with his broken-down sneakers and jeans. He wondered if he smelled like the marketplace. If he did, Declan was too polite to remark on it. He led Fergus into a sitting room looking out over the city through a wall of windows.

Fergus's jaw dropped, and he forgot to feel embarrassed as he migrated to them. He'd seen New Peiling at night from the deck of an airship once. It was nothing like this. From above, Ping City was a sea of light, each street a channel flowing into the next.

"Wow."

"Nice, isn't it?" Declan said, pressing a tumbler of whisky into his hand.

"Thanks," Fergus said, clinking their glasses together as they both took a drink and returned to looking down at the city. "It's amazing."

"You're from New Peiling, right? I suppose you don't see the city lit up very often. It's so very cluttered there."

He nodded, sipping the whisky. It was spicier than any he'd drunk before, and it burned when it went down, but he kept chipping away at it distractedly.

"This isn't what the old man left to me. I had to build this," Declan said, swirling the amber liquid in his glass. "Nothing quite like what you take with your own hands, though, is there?"

Fergus felt the hairs on the back of his neck rising. He cleared his throat, carefully replying, "No, I wouldn't guess so."

"Let's have a seat, Fergus," Declan said, putting a hand on his shoulder and leading him away from the window. Despite his hesitancy, Declan pushed him onto one of the white leather sofas before seating himself in an old armchair. "Do you partake of the pixies? Mind if I do?"

Fergus shook his head, and Declan pulled out a roll of papers and a little canister. He tapped a little golden dust into the paper and rolled it up, licking the edge and sticking it in his mouth before feeling around for a match. Fergus pulled out his lighter.

"Thanks," he said, as Fergus lit the cylinder. The unpleasantly sweet smell of Fairy Dust began to seep into the room, but Fergus tried to look polite about it. It wasn't a lot at least. "You're not a talkative one, are you?" Declan asked, sliding the tube from his lips with long fingers. He let out an exhalation of glittering smoke. "Strong and silent type, is it? From what I've heard about your mother, it makes sense."

Fergus stiffened, knuckles whitening around his glass. "I dunno if she was really like that," he carefully replied.

"No, I guess not, but all the more reason you are," Declan said, taking a drink of whisky before slipping the cigarette back between his lips.

"How do you know about her?" Fergus asked, forcing his fingers to relax.

"Well, she's a local celebrity. It's a pity she disappeared. We would have loved to have her on for the Hunt."

"For the Hunt?"

"Surely Darya told you about it?" he said, eyeing Fergus.

"A little, yeah."

"Are you interested in hunting?" Declan asked, blowing a smoke ring through his nose.

A bell rang out, saving Fergus from having to answer.

"More guests," Declan cheerfully declared, putting his drink and cigarette aside and getting to his feet. "Just stay here and relax," he added, padding off to the foyer. A few moments later, he returned with Terry and Raja.

"Please, make yourselves at home. The more the merrier. We'll have enough for a grand dinner, if not for good sport," Declan said, going to fill a couple more glasses.

Terry sat down beside Fergus. "Sorry, it took a little longer than I thought it would. Had a run in with one of the actresses."

Fergus raised an eyebrow.

"I'll tell you later."

Declan returned, handing off fresh glasses of whisky to Raja and Terry and sitting back down in his chair. "Will either of you partake?" he asked, picking up the cylinder from the ashtray.

Terry shrugged. "You only live once."

"That's my man," Declan said, a little purr to his voice.

Fergus twitched and took a big drink of his whisky. He choked, turning to the window to hide it. Beside him, Terry took a long drag before leaning his head back and letting out a breath of shimmering fog. Fergus ran his thumb over the rim of his glass and tried to quietly clear his throat of the remaining whisky.

"So all of you – you were in a band together?" Declan said, looking between them. "And what are you doing way out here?"

"We're looking for an island," Raja said before they could stop him.

Declan's brows rose. "An island? Which one?"

"A pirate . . . " Raja stopped. Fergus thought Terry must have elbowed him.

"Oh, White Rock? What do you need there? Is one of you missing a kidney? Or maybe Evan has you smuggling for him?"

"Missing a kidney?" Fergus asked.

"A kidney, a heart, a liver . . . Well, the black market thrives in all forms there. You should be careful. They're always on the look out for a healthy body."

"Really?"

Declan gave him a curious look and then smiled. "Yes, actually. You can buy pretty much anything at White Rock. Luckily for you, I happen to be one of the few people able to arrange for you to dock."

Fergus sat up a little. "You are?"

"Well, I have made a name for myself in this city. I share a certain fondness for dabbling in matters of government."

"So you'll write us a permit or something?"

"If you insist on going."

The bell rang again. Declan stood to greet the new guests: a man and a woman. The man had short, neatly cut hair and was dressed in a suit. He introduced himself as "Lau." The woman with him was a blonde and about ten years older than Declan, with sharp features and pale green eyes, who introduced herself as "Faustine." Fergus guessed that they were married, but they didn't sit next to each other.

"Well, this is everyone, I think," Declan said, lighting up Fairy Dust for both Lau and Faustine. Now the smell was pervasive, and Fergus was beginning to feel ill. Oblivious to his discomfort, Declan continued, "I was thinking tonight's dinner would be light. There is plenty of sport to be had, and it's difficult on a full stomach."

Faustine's mouth twitched, and she shared a knowing glance with Lau. Terry also looked intrigued. At least Raja looked as apprehensive as Fergus felt.

"Are you leaving it a surprise?" Terry asked.

"I just may," Declan replied. "I believe Raja and Fergus have never been on a Hunt before. Is that right?" He turned to Fergus.

Fergus shrugged. "Not really." He could feel Raja trying to catch his eye, but Faustine and Lau were also staring at him, and he felt compelled to act like he had some idea of what was expected of them.

"Then it will be a merry surprise for you, I think. I imagine Ainslee Irvine's son will be quite the Huntsman."

Lau's and Faustine's looks became more intent.

Fergus smiled weakly and looked away.

"What is the 'Hunt'?" Raja finally asked.

"Why, it's the Wild Hunt," Faustine said in a thick accent of her own. "You know of this, do you not, boy?"

Raja turned red. "I've heard of the Wild Hunt, yes. Spiriting humans away to the Otherworld and playing tricks on them and all that, right?"

Faustine chuckled and took a drag without replying.

"Very much like that," Declan supplied. "It's a harmless game."

"I'm in," Raja said, sitting back again.

Fergus stared at him in disbelief.

"That settles it," Declan said happily, releasing another glittering cloud into the air.

Fergus wondered if it would be rude to ask to open a window.

"So then, boys, catch us up. I'm sure Faustine is as eager as I am to hear what's happening in the west."

•　　•　　•

It seemed that like New Peiling, Ping City also stayed busy late into the night. As their group slipped out into the street, there were still a number of people out. It made Fergus anxious. He'd hoped that maybe no one would be around, and then Declan and the others would have to give up this stupid game. He didn't really want to know what they intended to do to the humans they chose to "trick." He could still remember how strongly Terry had smelled of blood after his late night jaunt with Darya.

"Relax, will you?" Terry muttered.

Fergus didn't reply. His stomach was twisted up in knots and his nerves were jangling too violently for him to come up with a quick retort. He mulishly followed the others, who were growing louder and more excited by the moment. Even Raja had relaxed and was joining in with Declan as he burst into song.

"You know, I can smell it when you're freaked out," Terry said, slowing up to put an arm around Fergus's shoulders and shepherd him along.

"I'm not freaked out."

"It really is just a game. No one is gonna get hurt, so you don't have to worry so much. We're not all gonna transform into evil fairies and start eating people. Just give 'em a little spook and go home, you know? Like frightening pigeons."

Fergus nodded, trying to keep his breathing slow and even.

"Come now, Terry. We may have found a good one," Declan cried up ahead.

Terry released him, hurrying to catch up. The others gathered together at the end of the block, whispering and laughing amongst themselves. They were too caught up in their mutterings to notice he'd fallen behind, so Fergus stopped and just stood watching them. It seemed like there was a very long and deep gap between their cheer and him.

Declan and Terry soon straightened and disappeared around the corner. Faustine and Lau were not far behind. Raja spared him only a brief wave as he, too, slipped out of sight. Fergus didn't follow, though. He wondered if he shouldn't just try to find his way home.

He had never been close to many full humans. Most avoided the slums, but for those who didn't, he found the mixture of fear, distaste, and conceit they exhibited made it hard to want to get to know them. But they weren't all like that. Three definitely wasn't, nor was Guillory. Indu hadn't been. She'd even helped him.

Fergus wondered if they were only justifying the humans' paranoia by doing this. He thought of the thing that had been following him through his dreams: the black, unseen presence. There was already something scary in his head. He didn't want to be scary outside, too. He pushed the thought away, replacing it with the notion that he just didn't want to prove the humans right: *Hybrids make trouble; hybrids want to hurt us; hybrids are innately vicious.* He didn't think he was any of those things. He'd avoided being that way his entire life.

He'd seen scary and vicious with his own eyes. He could easily recall his mother in a fit of temper smashing a table to splinters against the wall. She'd then turned to him, but stopped before striking him. She almost always recalled herself well enough to stop before she reached him. Still, recalling the empty fury in her eyes gave him chills even now.

He was snapped out of his reverie by the sound of screaming. Without another thought, he rushed forward, catching the corner and swinging around to see two young guys backed against a wall. One sported a bloody lip. The other was plastered against the wall, a dark spot growing in the front of his trousers. Faustine was laughing and pointing, though the man hardly seemed aware of it. He stared at Lau fixedly, breath coming out in trembling gasps.

Fergus pushed Raja out of the way, putting himself between the group and the humans. Lau's face was shadowed, but he could definitely see his skin ripple, shifting from something swollen and blue to human.

"What are you doing?" he demanded, searching for a face to pin the blame to.

Faustine's mirth disappeared. Raja looked uncertain, but Declan and Terry looked defiant. He turned to Terry.

"I said, *what the hell are you doing?*"

"Calm down, Fergus," Declan purred, stepping in front of Terry and reaching for him. Fergus jerked back. He heard one of the men behind him let out a little gurgle of fear. "Fergus," Declan implored, holding out his palms. "We aren't going to hurt them. We just wanted to make them to run a little."

"They haven't the heart to entertain," Faustine said with a sneer.

Fergus ignored her. "You aren't gonna hurt them? One of 'em's bleeding!"

Declan smiled. His hazel eyes narrowed in the darkness, and Fergus had the impression that they were glowing. "Does that bother you?"

He bristled, brows lowering, and mouth forming a thin line. Just then, one of the men let out a half-groaned shout and began running, which snapped the other out of his stupor. Both sprinted down a nearby alley.

"And here we go," Declan crowed, shoving him out of the way and barreling after them, followed Lau and Faustine.

Terry stopped in front of him. "They're just humans, Fergus. Think of all the things that have happened to you. What's a bloody lip?"

"Terry!"

However, Terry had no ear for him and took off after the others.

"Raja?" he implored, reaching out, but Raja evaded his grip, averting his eyes.

"Sorry, Fergus. But Terry's right. They *are* just humans. Besides, they're just going to chase them around a little. It's like playing tag."

"They don't . . .!"

But Raja didn't let him finish. He scurried off, too, leaving Fergus alone in the alley. He stared after their shadowed figures until they disappeared around another corner, feeling shocked. Someone jerked on his elbow roughly. He turned to see a man in uniform glaring up at him.

"You, noise?" the officer demanded, giving him a shove.

"What?"

"Noise! You!"

"Uh, no, it wasn't me . . . "

"You leave now!" the officer shouted into his face, grabbing the front of his jacket to hoist himself up. His breath made Fergus gag.

"Okay, okay!" he managed, trying not to breathe or vomit.

The man released him with another shove and pointed at the alley. With nowhere else to go, Fergus began to run in the direction the others had taken. He couldn't hear them, and the scents of the city were too strong to smell them. His only guide was the uneasy looks of the people he passed. He wondered how often Declan and his friends played this game. Probably not too often. Even with all the money Declan apparently had, Fergus couldn't imagine how he could get away with regularly terrorizing pedestrians.

Maybe he was overreacting. Presuming he was on the right track, none of these people were fleeing or looking for a cop. Maybe Declan really was only giving strangers a scare every now and then. They'd just chase the guys around until they escaped up a building, or into a bar, and that'd be it.

He wanted to believe it. He wanted to believe that this was what Terry meant, and that Terry also believed that this was all it would be. He didn't, though, because if all they wanted to do was spook some humans, they could have left off with whatever nasty trick Lau had been pulling. If it was just about harmless mischief and bumps in the night, they could have moved on to the next victims. He sped up.

Fergus could see the group up ahead in what must have been one of the very few dead ends in the city. One of the men dangled from a fire escape, legs kicking frantically. He managed to catch the side of the building with one foot and launched onto the landing, knocking a potted plant free from between the metal rails and forcing the Huntsmen underneath to jump back. The man continued up the ladder to the third floor. He paused then, shouting down. There was a little desperation in his voice.

A middle-aged woman poked her head out of the window below and began shouting about the smashed plant. The man on the ladder paused, looking down at her and then to the group in the alley, and began to scurry upward without further hesitation. The woman continued to yell up at him for a few more minutes before an old man across the way stuck his head out and started yelling at *her*. They seemed unaware of the gathering under their windows, standing still and silent as statues. They were too intent on yelling at each other, which continued until a second figure appeared in the woman's window, dragging her away, and she gave one last furious gesture before the window slammed shut. The old man receded back into his home, leaving the alley silent.

Fergus was close enough now that he could make out Raja's wavy hair, Terry's grey eyes, and Declan's wild smile. Terry and Declan were the only two that noticed him, though neither gave him more than a glance. Faustine crouched down between them, leaning over the remaining man, who was sitting with his back to the wall, legs splayed out, and sweat gleaming on his face. Blood dripped down his chin, and his eyes rolled with fear.

It was the look of a creature that knew it was cornered and was simply waiting to see from which side it would be pounced upon.

The smell of blood and fear made Fergus's brain tingle, and he took an involuntary step forward. For a moment, the man looked more like prey than a person, but it was a short moment. A half-forgotten dream passed before his eyes of floating limbs and wailing, and he shook his head sharply, taking two steps back. He clamped a hand over his nose and tried to breathe through his mouth.

Faustine leaned forward, kissing the man. His look of apprehension faded a little as he looked up at her. She put her hands out, taking his cheeks in them. She began to murmur to him, and the man's leg twitched. As Fergus watched, her fingernails elongated and sharpened. Little droplets of blood formed around the tips, trickling down the man's cheeks, but he didn't look away. His features were softening. His eyes were still wide and mouth open, but there was awe in them as he stared up at his captor. She leaned down, and he couldn't see what she was doing, but when she leaned back again, the blood on his cheek was smeared as though she had licked it.

She gracefully rose, holding out her hands. The man reached out to take them, though it seemed his legs wouldn't hold him. He fell to his knees, but Lau appeared at his other side and hoisted him to his feet. He didn't even seem to notice. He only had eyes for Faustine.

Fergus watched in bewilderment. Faustine put the man's hands on her sides and began to sway, coaxing him into a dance. Her arms wrapped around his shoulders, and Fergus could see the sharp edge of her thumb drawing blood down the man's neck. She leaned forward, running her mouth over the wound, and the man shivered and stumbled.

Declan chuckled and stepped forward, pulling the man out of her arms and swinging him around. "A merry lot are we," he sang, as the man tried to keep up with each spin. "A merry lot we are. Come with us, come with us, it's never very far. We'll see the moon and stars and light and drink a brew or three!"

He released the man, sending him spinning into Lau, but the man was regaining his senses, and though obviously dizzy, trying to pull away. Lau locked his hands over the man's forearms, leaning forward, and then his face shifted again. His nose grew bulbous, his brows bushy, thick fangs protruded from his lower jaw. His skin became blue and waxen. Little bumps began to grow out of his gnarled, misshapen forehead.

Fergus gasped. Raja stepped back, pressing against the wall. However, Terry and Declan stepped forward, closing in on the man, until he was surrounded, and Fergus could hardly see him between them. Their captive let out a pitiful whimper.

"I think you've scared him enough," Fergus said quietly, stepping forward.

He ran his thumb over the taut skin between the knuckle and joint of his right hand, trying to calm himself, but his skin was prickling and burning. Something thick and hungry and demanding pressed at the back of his mind, trying to force its way through. Terry stepped back. The others continued to form a barricade around their victim.

Faustine rolled her eyes. "Why did you bring this wet blanket, Declan?"

Declan stepped away from the man, who fell out of Lau's grip, landing on his side. He lay on the ground, shuddering violently and hiccupping. Fergus couldn't see his face, but he could smell him, and for a moment, the world tilted.

"No, he's right. This one's worn out," Declan said with an airy shrug.

"Are we leaving him as is?" Lau asked.

"What else were you gonna do to him?" Fergus demanded.

"Fergus," Declan purred, stepping away from the others and reaching out to take his shoulder.

"Fergus, Fergus, Fergus, we aren't going to do *anything*. We just wanted to dance with him a little. What's the harm in that? He gave us a little chase, but now we're all tired, so we're just going to let him go. No need to get worked up."

Fergus bit the inside of his cheek to keep from shoving Declan. He felt another wave of the hot, rippling sensation under his skin.

"Did you think we would eat him, little boy?" Faustine chuckled, adopting Declan's carelessness. "We do not eat trash," she added, giving him a pat on the cheek as she passed by. He could smell the blood on her fingertips, now on his cheek. He held his breath.

Declan laughed. "You look very worried, Fergus. Trust me, we mean no harm."

Fergus glanced at the man. He was still on his side, but he'd pulled his knees up to his chest and was burrowing his face into them, hands held protectively over his head.

"Scaring someone that much isn't harmless," he quietly replied, looking away. "What *were* you planning to do to him?"

Declan let out a little sigh, releasing him. "Come now, Fergus. We're civilized people. We've no intention to injure this man, and you can see that he's not hurt. Not really. Just a little spooked. So let's leave him and go have a drink to relax."

Fergus narrowed his eyes. "After you," he replied tightly, giving a little jerk of his chin.

Declan gave him a splendid smile and began to stroll after Lau and Faustine. Fergus turned back to the man. He wanted to go and check on him, but he wasn't sure he could. His brain was filling with rage and hunger, and the man smelled so strongly of blood and sweat and fear. He felt a little sick deep down. Despite the fact he pitied the man, his body language kept making Fergus think, "prey." He roughly wiped at the blood on his cheek and began undoing his jacket.

"What are you doing?" Raja asked.

"It's too hot," Fergus muttered, yanking free of the last buttons.

"Hey, are you okay?"

"Don't touch me," Fergus snapped, jerking away from Raja. "I'm fine. He's who you should be worried about."

Raja lowered his eyes guiltily and went over to the man.

"Fergus, calm down," Terry said, pushing away from the wall.

"Screw you."

"Fergus," Terry said a little sharply. "Stop freaking out about this. He's not even hurt, okay?"

"Just cuz he doesn't have any broken bones doesn't mean he's not."

"Damnit, Fergus, he's just a stupid human. Think of all the things they've done to you."

He looked up at Terry, and for a moment, the fury was replaced by a cold feeling. "What they've done to me, or what they've done to *you*?"

Terry's eyes narrowed, lips drawing back. He took a step forward, and Fergus readied himself for the blow, but it didn't come. Instead, Terry grabbed the collar of his shirt, drawing closer.

"Yeah, that's right. What they've done to me. You wanna be buddy-buddy with strangers, fine, but don't expect everyone else to, and don't expect *them* to extend you the same courtesy. Grow up."

Fergus latched onto Terry's arm, not looking away. "You're just proving them right."

Terry sneered. "Since when were you so spineless? Or maybe you're scared of something else."

For a moment, Fergus said nothing. His stomach constricted painfully. His fingers tightened around Terry's arm. "What does that mean?" he managed.

"I think you're the only one thinking about eating humans."

His knuckles stung as they met Terry's cheek. Terry released him, crashing into the wall and crumpling.

"Terry!" Raja shouted.

Fergus didn't turn. He stepped forward, looking down at Terry. Terry cringed, feeling his cheek, and then looked up at him defiantly. Fergus wasn't sure what he wanted to say. Furious words jangled around in his head without forming coherent sentences. He wanted to hurt Terry. He wanted to hurt him a lot more than what his fist could do. He felt so angry, his head hurt.

"So you think I'm gonna lose it like all those other psychos, huh? You wanna be pretty boy Declan's best friend? Good luck to him. Maybe I am crazy, thinking *we* were friends."

He paused, feeling like he'd said too much. He took a step back, horror and guilt threatening to overwhelm him. Terry said nothing, but watched him with an inscrutable expression, and Fergus found he couldn't look him in the face. He had to leave.

"Fergus!" Raja cried.

He shook his head and began to run.

Chapter Eight.

Running blindly through an unfamiliar city was probably not the best idea he'd ever had. Soon, Fergus was out of breath and hopelessly lost. The smells were strange, the buildings unfamiliar, and no one could speak his language. He had no idea how he was ever going to get back to the docks. He wondered what time it was, for the glow of the lanterns distorted the night sky. It felt late, and he was exhausted.

He stood at yet another corner that looked the same as the one before and gave up, sinking against the wall and putting his hands over his face. Maybe he could just sleep here, he thought. He didn't have a lot of money, so if someone robbed him, they weren't taking much. He was too tired to deal with trying to find the airship, and he couldn't begin to tell which buildings might be hotels.

Resting his forehead on his knees, he let his arms fall to his sides, feeling exhausted and miserable.

"Fergus?"

He didn't want to lift his head. It felt very heavy. A firm hand touched his shoulder, giving it a little shake.

"Fergus?"

He forced himself to look up at Guillory. He stared at him for a moment before blowing his hair out of his face. "What?"

"What the devil are you doing here?"

"Going to bed."

Guillory let out a little chuckle, though he sounded uncertain. "Have you been drinking?"

He shook his head, wanting to rest his forehead on his knees again.

"You look awful. Where are the others?"

"Three and Pip went off to drum up some money, and I don't care where Terry and Raja are."

Guillory said nothing for a moment. "Well, if you aren't drunk, maybe you should be. Come on, I'll buy you one, and then we can go back."

Fergus considered. This didn't seem like a terrible plan. He nodded and let Guillory help him to his feet.

They didn't walk far before Guillory pushed open a barred door and waved Fergus up a set of stairs to the second floor. Inside was a regular looking pub. In the center was the bar, and all around it were wooden tables and a few machines that let out clinking noises now and then. Fergus wasn't sure if they were games or gambling machines. There was an actual video screen in one corner playing a sporting match, though the picture was marred by static.

Guillory drew him to a table near the screen and left him to watch the game. For a moment, Fergus forgot about being angry with Terry and disgusted at Declan, or being ashamed of his fairy-soul's instincts.

"Don't see many of them in New Peiling," Guillory remarked as he returned, sliding a beer in front of Fergus.

"Thanks," he said, lifting his mug in a vague salute, before taking a drink. His eyes remained locked on the freckled image overhead.

"What're they saying?"

"No idea," Guillory replied. "It's too fast for me." He smiled as Fergus glanced at him.

"How'd you learn?"

"I've been around the world a time or two. You really must be thirsty."

Fergus paused, realizing he'd nearly finished his drink. "Oh, yeah. Guess it's from running."

"Here, you can have the rest of mine. I've had a few already. I'll order a fresh round."

Fergus gratefully accepted the second glass, pushing the finished one to the side and watching as the foam dripped down to settle in a soggy pile at the bottom of the glass. The beer didn't quench his thirst, and he thought his lips were getting chapped, but it was better than nothing. It felt wet against the back of his throat, he mused as he sipped on his second mug, feeling the bubbles burst against his upper lip. Guillory returned with two more mugs and set them down.

"So, do you want to tell me what happened? Why are you wandering around alone?"

"I dunno," Fergus muttered, staring cross-eyed into his drink.

"You don't know?"

"I don't know if I wanna talk about it."

"With me, is it?" Guillory replied with a chuckle.

Fergus's mouth twitched downward. He lowered the beer to the table. "Do you ever just feel like . . . you don't know where you're standing?"

"How do you mean?"

"Like you don't know who's really with you, and who's just a spectator."

"Oh, well, I suppose everyone feels that way now and then. Until they meet the right friends, that is. Are you wondering about Bridges?"

Fergus gave a noncommittal shrug.

"What are they up to tonight? Looking at you, either you were outright excluded, or you didn't approve. You looked up at the second. Should I take that as, 'didn't approve'?"

"Whatever," Fergus grumbled, hunching over his drink.

"You're probably right to wonder why Bridges is here. You know, he isn't without a reputation. He's been in and out of jail a number of times – before he was even 20. He's clever. He knows how to slip out of trouble, and as a minor, he used that to his advantage."

"And recently?"

"I suppose he learned how to evade capture, but I doubt he's stopped the business that got him into trouble in the first place."

"I don't think he's a bad person."

"But you do think he does bad things."

Fergus didn't reply.

"Probably he's looking to you to show him something – something like what would happen if he was more like you – but he's been that way for so long, he's afraid to jump in with both feet."

"Like me?"

"Have you ever purposefully broken a law?"

"What, you mean like snitching food or fights?"

"How did you feel about that?"

"Well, if the guy deserved it, not too bad."

Guillory let out a snort. "I knew a man who used to say that – who still does."

"If it's Harriet, I might hit you."

Guillory's mouth crooked a little. "In a way, he's like your friend."

"How's that?"

"They've both let circumstance dictate what they feel they can and can't do rather than trying to think of what they might accomplish on their own."

"You're so damned optimistic. Maybe they only *can* do what their circumstances allow."

"I don't think so. Look at you."

"I swear to God, if you're about to say anything about Ainslee's son or whatever, I really will hit you."

"I don't know anything about that, Fergus," Guillory replied. "I know very little about your mother. I may know a little about your father. But let me see if my theory is correct: tell me about your mother. Tell me about being 'Ainslee's son.'"

"Are you a freaking psychotherapist or something?"

"Not at all. I just don't want to spout out 'unfounded optimism' at you."

Fergus stared down at his beer, twisting the base between his thumbs, and watched the amber liquid splash against the sides of the glass. He sighed, blowing his bangs out of his face, and looked up.

"The more I hear about her from other people, the more I hate her. I didn't grow up hating her, though. She was a really good mom. She spent as much time with me as she could. She taught me how to swim. She took me to the parks on the top layer. She tried to show me as much as she could about what was good in New Peiling. I'm not sure what happened," he muttered, eyes trailing to a box of napkins.

"She just started changing. She was mad all the time, or she was sad. She just wasn't right. She started yelling about stuff, and then she started yelling at me. She broke things in the apartment, said she was gonna hit me, and then she'd cry. One day, I came back, she was gone, and that was that. She never came back."

"What happened to her? Do you know?"

Fergus swallowed. His throat felt thick. He picked up the glass and finished the beer, pushing it over to the empty mug, and took up the third. "Dead. Killed herself. I was pretty mad when I found out. There was a lot of stuff I wanted to say to her about what she did, but I guess there's no point in holding onto that."

"So what did you find out about her?"

Fergus shrugged and began to sip the third beer.

"Was it like with Bridges? Maybe things you don't agree with?"

"I don't wanna talk about it."

"Okay, what about your father? Owen Crawford?"

"How'd you know?"

"You resemble him. Same eyes, same build. Same hair – a little. I knew him when he was younger. He resembled you a lot more then."

"I dunno anything about him. Mom hated him. Never kept any pictures of him, cursed him for leaving us, wouldn't even tell me his last name," Fergus said, shaking his head. "I've heard he's some

159

kinda secret philanthropist, but whatever he's like, that's how I know him."

"Well, he's no saint."

Fergus looked up.

Guillory snorted softly. His eyes didn't match the uneven smile. "I've always found him to be a weasel. He says one thing and does another without much compunction. It's a little too easy for him. Well, he is a politician."

"What do you mean?"

"I've never been into politics. Too many people saying whatever they think their listeners want to hear and no sense of justice. Rather, if there is going to be justice, it's only because there's gain to be had. I'm a man who believes in justice for the sake of justice and truth for the sake of truth. Politics have never sat well with me."

"Is that why you've never run for office?"

Guillory nodded. "Can you really imagine me as governor anyway? I don't think I could survive the intrigue."

"But someone like you would be a better leader than someone like . . . "

"Like Paige Harriet? Or Callum Whitehurst? Maybe. Still, being Captain of the Air Guard is different from being Governor of New Peiling. You can't sway the public without saying what they want to hear, and I don't think I could do that, even for the greater good. Truth is too important to me."

"You're all right. For a human."

"Thanks, Fergus," Guillory said without an ounce of sarcasm.

Fergus felt his face turn red and quickly looked away.

"I think you and I are cut from a similar cloth," Guillory continued. "Do you agree? You know right from wrong. I knew that just looking at you."

"I don't always do the right thing."

"What are you? Eighteen?"

"Twenty."

"You get to make some mistakes at 20. The thing is, you know when it's a mistake, don't you? And you don't want to make mistakes. You don't want to hurt others."

Fergus shifted his gaze from the napkins to his glass. Terry's words echoed in his head: *I think you're the only one thinking about eating humans.* He felt a little nauseated.

"Would you say you usually try to look for a way that doesn't harm anyone or thing around you when faced with an obstacle?"

"Yeah, I guess so."

"Would you say that people should be fair because it's the right thing to do, not because it benefits them to do so?"

"Yeah."

"Would you say there's no substitute for the truth?"

"Some lies protect people."

"So we'll say two out of three. But your mother – like your friend – she did things you didn't think were right. You've had people doing things you don't believe in all around you your entire life, right? Father, mother, friends. Still, you believe in what you think is right and try to adhere to it. Why can you do this, but your friend Bridges can't or won't?"

Fergus looked up, studying Guillory's weathered face. "He can. He just is stupid."

Guillory chuckled. "He lets the bad parts of his past limit him. Do you get what I'm saying now? There really *isn't* a reason he can't become more like you. There isn't a reason he has to do anything that hurts others, that's unfair, or that's untrue. He's his biggest obstacle. Well, we all are, but this is his particular method of obstructing himself."

"Okay, I guess I get you. It's not so mindlessly optimistic."

"Probably Bridges does look up to you, but he's so afraid of himself and what he's built his world out of that he doesn't think he can be like you. And your other friend . . . "

"Raja."

"Raja has the look of a man who's lost a part of himself."

Fergus nodded.

"He's looking for someone to show him answers, too. Bridges can turn on the charm. He's good at seeming like he knows just what to do. He's good at hiding his insecurities. He's dishonest to the core: so much so that he can even pull the wool over his own eyes. Your friend Raja sees that, and he's drawn to it, because he doesn't have what he needs in himself to answer his own questions. They're a lot alike that way."

"Is that why they're all buddy-buddy now?"

Guillory glanced up at the ceiling a moment. "Very likely. Bridges may sense that. It may be reassuring to him. You're probably lost, too, but you have your principles. You don't know where you want to end up, but you do know how you want to get there. Maybe you seem unsure, and maybe that scares the both of them. However, in the end, you're three steps ahead."

"That's nice of you to say," Fergus said.

"Oh, I'm not just saying it. I took this chance because of you and *only* you."

"Why?"

"Because I think when you get where you need to go, you're going to fill in all those pieces that will answer your questions and their questions and a hundred other people's questions, and people need the answers you'll provide."

"You're starting to sound like a motivational speaker again."

"Sorry. Well, it might sound ridiculous to you now, but you're a rare sort. Not because of your family or your background or even your abilities, but because of your conscience."

"Yeah, yeah, okay, fine. Enough about that."

"You don't talk about yourself much, do you?"

Fergus lifted an eyebrow.

"Fergus, I'll admit I'm disappointed that you didn't testify against the Knights of Evalach. I've decided to trust you on it, though. You had your reasons, whatever they may be. What I said about believing in you still holds. If you need a friend, I would like for you to rely on me."

"Oh god," Fergus groaned. "You sound like some corny high school teacher."

"I'm serious. I'm here to listen to anything, and if you don't want me to give you 'unfounded optimism,' I swear I'll do nothing but listen."

"Okay, I get it. Can we go now? I'm gonna fall asleep."

Guillory tilted back the rest of his mug, his Adam's apple jumping with each swallow. Fergus looked away, feeling something uncomfortable and wicked coiling in his stomach.

"All right," Guillory said, putting the mug on the table with a clatter. "Let's go."

Fergus stood and found the world was a lot less stable than it had been when he sat down.

"Are you all right?"

He nodded. "Just a little tipsy. Go on."

He followed Guillory out of the pub and down the steps, taking them slowly and holding both walls to keep from falling down. His legs felt tingly and disconnected. His head felt a little like it was filled with bubbles and might just float away. It wasn't a bad feeling at all. It was a rather pleasant state of tipsy, even if it was a state that made it hard to walk without weaving.

Guillory slowed down, righting Fergus where he could, but even he couldn't stop him from bumping straight into a crowd of equally drunk young men. One ran into Fergus and went straight down.

"Sorry," Fergus slurred. He started to reach out to give the man a hand up when one of the guy's friends gave him a shove, shouting at him.

"Now, now, let's not do that," Guillory said, reaching for the guy and slipping into the same language.

Before he could finish translating, though, the man shoved him out of the way and grabbed the front of Fergus's jacket, giving him a shake. His head bobbed back and forth disjointedly. He shoved at the guy to make him stop, and the man fell back against the others, knocking half of them down like bowling pins.

"Uh oh," Fergus said, staring down at the angry, shouting mass of people.

He didn't see the first guy get up, though he didn't miss the fist that caught him straight from cheekbone to brow. He cursed, falling on his rear end. Blood began to well in his vision, stinging his eye.

"What the hell?" he growled, trying to blink the blood away.

Guillory was back in the thick of things, grabbing the man by the arm to keep him from coming at Fergus again. Unfortunately, he wasn't the only one getting involved. More shouting came from down the street, and the young men began to flee in all directions. Uniformed men grabbed a couple, but most scampered up fire escapes and down alleys and out of sight.

An officer descended on Fergus, giving him a sharp kick and forcing him onto his stomach. His arms were jerked back, and he felt something metal and unforgiving snap around his wrists.

"Are we . . .?" he started to ask, but the cop kicked him again, and the question was cut off.

"Bloody . . . Yes, it seems we are," Guillory replied from somewhere behind him.

He heard Guillory try to reason with the officers in their language, but they just yelled at him, too. Fergus was forced to his feet.

"It looks like they're taking us to jail along with that lot," Guillory said, nodding to the two thugs.

The officer gave him a shove, and Guillory stumbled, looking irritated as he righted himself. The man began to bark out orders, and Fergus found himself being herded down the street. Blood seeped from his brow over his tightly clenched eye, down his cheek, and pooled at his chin. He could feel his eye swelling, which at least made it easier to keep shut, though it did nothing to stem his mortification.

He imagined he probably did look like a dangerous criminal as they were trotted along. Drunken passersby stopped to ogle the bloody foreigner being driven along by the cops. Fergus wanted to melt into the ground, but it seemed his luck wasn't good enough for any sudden end to his humiliation.

They were taken to the police station, placed in a cell next to the men who had attacked them, and the cuffs were removed. Fergus rubbed his wrists, glaring balefully at the officer who shouted at him nonsensically.

"I don't understand you," he ground out, tenderly blotting at his eye with the hem of his hoodie.

Guillory started arguing again. Whatever it was he said, it seemed to reach the officer. They gestured for him to leave the cell.

"I'll be back. Just hold tight," Guillory said, leaving with the officers.

Fergus was left alone in the cell with the two drunks on the other side. One of them spat at him, and he considered having a go at them, but he didn't want more trouble, so instead he went to sit in the corner of his cell, trying to lean his injured eye against the cold bars. His pleasant buzz was gone, and he just felt queasy and alone again. He tried not to think about it. He counted backwards, hoping to fall asleep, but his eye ached too much to let him drift off.

He wondered what Raja and Terry were up to. Probably they'd had nice, luxurious baths and sweets and were full up on wine and Fairy Dust and tucked away in soft, cushy beds. He hated them a little. He wondered what Three and Pip were up to. Perhaps they were out hunting down criminals. He wondered if they were having any success. He hoped they were, since Three had said she'd share part of the cut with him to make up for last time. He returned to fuming over Raja and Terry.

Before the moroseness of his thoughts could move on to Ursula, Guillory returned. Fergus stood, coming over to the door and ignoring the jeers of the men in the other cell.

"They say they'll let us out if someone comes and pays the fine. The boys will all be dead asleep. Do you know where Three and Pip are?"

He shook his head. "They might end up here, though. They're out looking for bounties."

"I'd rather not spend the rest of the night here. Plus, your eye is a mess."

"Hurts like hell, too."

"I know you hate to do it, but what about Bridges? Where is he?"

Fergus's mouth jerked into a frown. He wanted to say he would rather rot in this cell than ask for anything from Terry. No, he'd rather *die* here than be the one who backed down.

"I'll deal with him. Just please tell me where he is. We really don't want to spend time here. If they keep us for trial, we'll be in a lot more trouble." Guillory's brows pinched a little, and he glanced uneasily at the cop hovering nearby.

Fergus bit his lip. "They're staying with Declan Abel. It's this big swanky building . . . "

"Abel?" the cop asked. He asked something in the other language.

Guillory answered, his reply far slower and less accurate sounding.

It seemed the cop understood him, though, because he began barking out orders.

"They just upped the bail," Guillory said with a dark chuckle, rubbing his brow. "Abel is a merchant, right? I hope Bridges can talk him into paying."

Fergus considered slamming his face against the bars.

The cop opened the door and pushed Guillory inside. He snapped something at Fergus, poking him in the chest between the bars. Fergus had a brief fantasy of grabbing his hand and breaking his wrist, but he bit his lip, took a deep breath, and returned to his corner. Guillory sat down next to him, leaning his head back against the wall.

"I'm going to beat my head into these bars until I die," Fergus grumbled.

"Come now, it's not that bad. We'll have a good laugh about this someday. These are the stories you'll want to tell your grandchildren."

"You wanna tell your grandkids about how you were stuck in a foreign jail cuz some drunken jerks beat you up? That's messed up."

Guillory just laughed.

•　　•　　•

The cold iron bars provided just enough solace that Fergus was starting to finally drift off when he heard Declan's laugh coming from up front. He sounded very cheerful as he fluidly conversed with the policemen. Guillory got to his feet, straightening his jacket. Fergus curled up tighter in his corner. He wanted to just stay with his nice cool bar, which was far greater solace than the idea of accepting Declan's or Terry's help.

Guillory reached for him, perhaps thinking he was drunk, and pulled him to his feet. He scowled ferociously at the floor. Declan, Raja, and Terry came into view, led by an officer who unlocked the cell. Guillory stepped out. Fergus remained, obstinately glowering.

The officer made a snide remark.

Declan chuckled and replied. Fergus could feel his heart hammering in his chest. He wanted to step out just so he could punch the smile straight off Declan's smarmy face.

"Come on, Fergus," Guillory said, standing in the doorway to keep the officer from shutting it.

Fergus didn't move. He wondered how childish it would be to sit back down and turn his back to them.

"Can we have a minute?" Terry asked.

Declan asked the cop, who gave a little grunt and stepped back.

"Well, he won't go further than that, but he can't understand you anyway. We'll just be outside."

Fergus was left alone with the Terry, the two sleeping drunks, and the surly officer. He didn't move any closer to the door, though he chanced a look at Terry's face. It looked about as bad as his felt. It cheered him a little.

"Some might call that karma, you know."

"What?" Fergus spat.

"Your face. This is the second time you've gone full out on mine, you know."

"If that's all you've got to say, get lost."

"You're just going to stay in there? Cut off your nose to spite your face? Really, Fergus?"

He felt hot all over. His heart was thumping even more violently. For a moment, he couldn't reply; the anger sealed the words in his throat.

"Come on. Seriously. If you stay in here, you're going to end up in their legal system. You're gonna be screwed."

"But maybe a monster *should* be behind bars," he spat. It was petulant, and he knew he sounded stupid and childish, but he hated Terry so much he felt like he might burst into flames just looking at him.

"I'm sorry."

Fergus was on the other side of the cell in two strides. He grabbed the bars hard enough that he felt them vibrate. One of the men in the other cells stirred, and the cop took a step forward, giving a warning command that was lost on Fergus.

"No you're not. You've wanted to say it for a while, haven't you? Sitting up there thinking about whether I'm gonna go off the deep end and eat the crew. Well, you've got perfectly well-adjusted friends now, don't you? So go worry about them."

"I'm sorry."

"Shut *up*."

Terry said nothing, looking down at his feet.

"You and Ursula and Rosslyn can all go jump off a damn pier for all I care. You all act like I'm so freaking indebted to your kindness, and you're all . . . " Fergus paused, unable to think coherently enough to finish the thought.

"We're all what?"

"You'd *all* screw me to save yourselves in the end. Mom and Ursula already showed their true colors, so it's about time you did, too. I'm not a science project, and I don't want fake friends. You can shove your pity."

"Do you really think that?"

Fergus glared at him and turned, going to settle back in his corner. He didn't care about dire warnings of foreign penal systems. He just wanted Terry to go away. He didn't, though. He came into the cell, though not without a hesitant look at the officer, who moved closer, now looming by the door. He frowned, but came over to crouch down a few feet away from Fergus.

"Do you really think that?" he repeated.

"Tell me why I shouldn't." Fergus felt ashamed at how much he hoped Terry would say something to convince him otherwise. He pressed his eye to the bars, looking away.

"Because even though you've been a royal ass to me tonight, even though you nearly broke my jaw, I don't want you to end up disappearing in some prison in a place where you can't even speak the language."

"An ass to you? After you went and terrorized those guys and then acted like I was some stupid little kid for thinking it was wrong? After you accused me of wanting to *eat* that guy?"

Terry didn't reply.

"I'm *not* gonna eat anyone! I'll jump off the airship first."

"That's what scares me," Terry said quietly.

"What?"

"I *said*, that's what scares me."

Fergus lifted his head to stare at him. Terry was hunched over, his reddish hair falling into his face.

"You're the first person I've liked enough to wanna call my friend since Sean."

"Sean?"

"The guy I went down to the slums with – the one who jumped from the window."

Fergus looked away.

"He just couldn't take it, but I'll bet your mom did it thinking she was doing the right thing. 'I'd rather die than hurt my child.' So she up and drowns herself. What am I supposed to think about someone like you with all your stupid ideals, someone that I like who really would do that if push came to shove? I'd rather you *were* more like Declan. That's right. I'd rather you were the kinda person who would eat rather than be eaten. But I don't like him the way I like you." He paused. "You say you can't trust me, but how am I supposed to trust you, Fergus?"

"I don't know."

"What good is nobility if all it gets you is dead?"

"I don't know."

"I know you wouldn't eat anyone, okay? I was stupid for saying it. It was out of line. And I don't wanna stay here in Ping City with Declan. I came this far to find Tír na nÓg with you. With *you*, Fergus. Okay? So stop acting like an idiot and come on before this officer locks us both in here and demands the ship for ransom."

Fergus nodded slowly. He looked up at Terry as he leaned down, offering a hand. "I wanna trust you, Terry."

"I want to trust you, too, Fergus," Terry said, hand still outstretched.

"There are better ways to have fun than hurting people."

Terry's mouth crooked. "Good, wholesome fun?"

Fergus shook his head. "It's more than that. It's about being able to look at yourself every day and be okay with who you see."

Terry's fingers twitched. Fergus wondered if he would retract his hand.

"It's about making a life worth living."

"This is the last time I ever let you get drunk with Guillory," Terry muttered.

Fergus stared up at him, unblinking. "He's not always wrong. The world's full of messed up, angry people, but everyone who decides not to be one of them makes it suck a little less for everyone else. It's gotta pay off somewhere along the line."

"Is this because of my karma remark?"

"Maybe," Fergus replied, reaching out at last to take his hand. "Cuz at least you can see properly."

"You have some luck with the locals."

"Tell me about it," he grumbled, stumbling to his feet.

They walked out into the street where the others were waiting, talking amicably, though Fergus thought that Guillory and Declan both seemed a little tense. Raja kept rubbing his hands over his face and stifling yawns.

"You two are quite the set, aren't you?" Declan suddenly said, biting back a laugh as he turned to Fergus and Terry.

Raja snorted. "You should've aimed higher, Fergus."

"Don't give him ideas!" Terry chided. "Two one-eyed men don't make a full set."

"Well, let's all hurry back. The hour is much too late, and the chickens will be starting up soon. I can never get to sleep once they get going."

"That's okay," Terry said. "Thanks a lot, Declan. We really owe you one, but I think we're just gonna go back to the ship. We're casting off today anyway."

Declan's expression faltered for a moment. "Oh. Well," he said, clearing his throat. "You'll have to pay me a visit when you return. I do want to apologize for tonight, Fergus."

Fergus gave him a wan smile.

"Stay safe, Terry," he added, letting his fingers linger just a moment too long on Terry's shoulder before he jauntily headed down an alley.

"I'm dead on my feet. Let's get going," Guillory said, turning the other direction. Raja began to plod after him. Fergus started to follow, but he felt a tug on the back of his jacket and turned to Terry.

"What is it?"

"You really are the only person I've thought of as a friend in years."

Fergus stared at Terry, feeling his face heat up. He quickly looked away. "Isn't that a sad thing to say?"

"That's why, if there's anything that's bothering you, trust me enough to tell me, okay? Don't bottle it up until it's all too much. I wanna prove to you that I mean it when I say we're friends. I wanna see that you believe it, too."

Fergus opened his mouth and then shut it again. "Okay."

"Don't dilly dally, you two!" Guillory shouted at them. "If I have to pilot in a few hours, you have to man the deck, so you better get to bed!"

Chapter Nine.

The route to White Rock was as brief as promised. Moreover, to Fergus's great relief, Guillory decided the next evening that it would be easier to dock from the sea, and so they moved from air to water. With sea spray coating his face and the fresh ocean air whipping through his hair, Fergus felt much more at ease helping out on deck. It was nice to be close to the water. The morning fog had blown away to the west, and the noontime sunlight was glinting off the metal hulls and balloons of the airships docked at the pirate port.

One of the crewmen lent him a set of binoculars, but he couldn't make out any natural landmarks amongst the ships. There were buildings, though, and since there were buildings, there had to be something solid to attach them to.

"I already told you there isn't," Pip snapped.

"Yeah, but what about the buildings?"

"They obviously aren't directly on the water. They're just sitting on something that does float. Anyway, they aren't made of brick."

"How do you know?" Fergus asked. "You've never been there, right?"

"We've passed by!"

"Calm down, you two," Three said, putting a hand on each of their shoulders. "We'll find out soon enough, won't we? For now, we should talk about you, Fergus."

"Me?"

"Yes, you and how you should handle yourself."

"What the hell does that mean?"

Three dropped her hand, blowing her bangs out of her face. "Well, you were beaten up in the last two cities we visited, and you were pretty sick in Sovnik."

"Hey, Jarpur wasn't . . . "

"I know, and we really are sorry," she quickly replied. "It's just that this is a lot more dangerous than Sovnik or Jarpur or even Ping City. You could say this is the heart of the international black market. They'll sell anything here – the shoes from your feet, your eyes, your blood, *you*. It's not a safe place for hybrids. For anyone. You should assume that anyone you cross is going to be armed. If it isn't a weapon, it'll be magic. So fist fights are going to be a big no-no, okay?"

"Fine, whatever. I don't go looking for fights, you know."

"They keep finding you, though, and you've got to avoid that."

Fergus sighed. "Okay, so organ trade, thievery, murder. What else?"

"That's basically it, but don't take this lightly."

"You should be careful about your eyes," Pip added.

"What?"

"They look discolored. Maybe you could pass for blind, but I don't think you're that good of an actor."

Fergus scowled.

"Pip does have a point," Three said, biting her lower lip. "They've looked white a lot more lately. You should probably keep your hood up and avoid shadowy places."

Fergus let out a longer sigh. "Okay, fine. Jeez." He glanced at Three's face, saw her brow puckering, and tried to soften his expression. "I know you're just worried. I promise that I'm not gonna pick any fights, and I'll hide my face. All we gotta do is gather information about this map and Tír na nÓg. As soon as we've got that, we'll leave."

"That may take a few days, Fergus," Three said softly and then hurriedly amended, "but I trust you. Anyway, no one should go anywhere alone. That's just asking for trouble, so make sure that your friends don't go wandering off, either."

"Pretty sure Terry can handle himself."

"Maybe. Maybe not. This isn't the place to test that."

Fergus's cheek twitched, but he didn't reply. He made a mental note to let Terry and Raja know as he leaned on the railing, looking through the binoculars again. He didn't need them anymore. The city was growing close enough that he could make out the ships and floating structures without the binoculars' aid. Still, it gave him an excuse to avoid Three's worried look. She seemed to get the message, because she let Pip tug her away.

Fergus lowered the binoculars and leaned forward on his palms, closing his eyes against the wind. He could hear the cry of gulls and the roar of an airship passing above and smell the rich, oily scent of brine.

"Pretty impressive, huh?" Terry said, coming up to lean on the railing beside him.

He opened his eyes and nodded. Ahead, he could see a number of ships in at least a dozen designs. Some looked like sea dragons with fins for sails; others were sleek and metallic; and then some – like the *Returner* – were made of wood and cloth, calling back to an earlier period of shipmaking. Their balloons were a cheerful mix of colors. It gave the port a festive appearance, and despite Three's warning, Fergus felt a little less worried.

"I've never seen so many," he said after a moment.

"I've only seen it once before – at Clohaven."

Fergus nodded. "You like airships. Is that why you started working for the Count?"

Terry turned, leaning on the railing. He crossed his arms over his chest, pale eyes casting skyward. "No, actually."

"No?"

"We met at a time when I needed to keep my head down, but I still needed money. Ursula suggested it. They've been friendly for a long time. She likes traveling in higher circles, as you know."

"And what about Rosslyn? You already knew him, didn't you?"

"I did. Our relationship was tense back then. He was already having issues with Olivier. He probably felt threatened by the thought of another male servant for the Count to lust after."

"Sounds like he should have been."

Terry stiffened. "Rosslyn had already left."

Fergus blinked. "Um, that's not what I meant."

They both looked the opposite direction.

"Oh," Terry said at length.

"Yeah," Fergus replied, clearing his throat. "Was that for money, too?"

"Hey now. Let's not talk about money on the side. From what I hear, you never said 'no' to Ursula."

"I did, too! Whenever I had a girlfriend, I always said 'no,'" Fergus replied, feeling a little stung.

"Well, I never had a girlfriend, and Rosslyn and the Count were through."

"Can we not talk about this?" Fergus asked.

Terry shrugged. "I did learn a lot about airships at the penthouse. I'd always been interested, but it wasn't until I started working there that I actually got to spend any time around them. I had no head for the mechanics, so I couldn't learn much from his angle, but I thought he might let me pilot if I stuck around."

"But you didn't."

"Nope. I have my pride."

Guillory's voice crackled over the intercom. "All right, men! All hands at ready. We'll be docking in about 20 minutes. It may tricky, so bear with me!"

"Better get back to work," Fergus said, pushing away from the railing. "Oh yeah, and Three says not to go anywhere alone here."

Terry raised an eyebrow.

"Just passing on the message," Fergus said before hurrying over to help the crew.

•　　•　　•

Pip was right: the buildings weren't made of brick and mortar, but rather wood and thatch. If ever there was a storm, he was pretty sure it would all be torn to bits, though maybe that didn't matter. No one actually lived here. The structures served immediate, temporary purposes: places to join together for drinking, gambling, and other entertainments. Yet some of the tenements were two storeys tall, made of straw and bamboo. They floated on large rafts and skiffs.

All of the buildings were moored to the boardwalk, which was also floating. Fergus got the impression that the shape of the port must have been decided by the airships docked around it. It explained what Three meant about the location always changing.

As they continued along, he saw that the water around the central structures was glowing a soft green just below the surface.

"What's that?"

"Probably what keeps this from drifting apart," Pip replied. Fergus noticed that he was glued to Three's side. He hadn't seen light between them since they'd disembarked.

"Yeah, but what is it?" he asked

"That's what we're here to find out, isn't it?" Terry replied, putting a hand on his shoulder.

"Do we have any leads?" Three asked. She was standing a bit straighter than usual, shoulders held back, and Fergus thought Pip wasn't the only one clinging.

"All I know is what Pip said," Fergus replied, pulling out his worn copy of Flynn's notes. "That the shape of the map resembles this spot."

"It does," Pip replied, lifting his chin.

"Care to explain how?"

"Because I believe that is the tip of Utsujima, and this is the only thing beyond it, so it has to be here."

"Do you think the gate is that green spot?" Fergus asked, stopping to inspect the water. "Lady Gemini did say, 'green.'"

Raja and Guillory nearly ran into him, and he waved his arms wildly to keep from falling in. Terry pulled on the back of his jacket.

"Careful!" Fergus grumbled, glaring at them.

"If you went in, that'd be one way to find out," Raja said.

"Very funny," he replied. "So did that jerk tell you anything?"

"Do you mean Declan?" Terry asked. "He said that if we couldn't find anything the regular way, we ought to try the seers."

"There are seers here?"

"Probably they're just women who have outgrown other lines of work."

Fergus rubbed one eye, making a face. "Okay, so what are the regular ways?"

"Bar talk, mainly, though maybe some of the ladies around may have heard something." Terry looked directly at Guillory.

"No one should split up," Three said firmly, directing the single unit of herself and Pip back over to them. "This isn't like anything you're used to."

"Okay, so Raja and Guillory, you go ask around the brothels, Fergus and I will take the taverns, and Pip and Three will check out the seers?"

Pip snorted. "I think *we* should check out the bars. You're likely to end up drunk and robbed." His eyes narrowed. "Or sold."

"There's bound to be a lot of bars, though," Fergus interjected.

"Which are unlikely to be doing much business at this hour," Guillory put in. "Why *don't* we start with the seers? At least we'll be able to check them off early while everything else is still quiet."

Fergus didn't feel keen on having his fortune told. The last time it hadn't been so dire, but the time before, he'd returned home to find his best friend murdered, and he had a sneaking suspicion that Flynn's phobia of Lady Gemini had generated from more than the eerie prediction of a break up. Whether these fortunetellers were as good as Lady Gemini or not, if they wanted to warn him of imminent doom, Fergus thought he'd rather find out on his own.

However, Guillory was making sense. Why not check that off while they were waiting for the bars and brothels to come alive?

"Okay, fine. So let's find the seers. Where are they?"

"Declan thought they should be near the greenest part of the water," Raja said.

Fergus nodded and turned, moving towards the brightest area of water. The seedier pedestrians began to dwindle as they continued towards the center of the port, which was a relief. The festive air of the airships diminished considerably when presented with the haggard faces of their crews. Some just looked weathered and tough; others were missing eyes, ears, limbs, or even noses (which made Fergus nearly knock Terry into the water); and then there were those who were giving them distinctly calculating looks. He thought that a couple of men might have been following them. He kept trying to look over his shoulder without being obvious about it, which meant that he couldn't tell if it was the same guys or not. It gave him the creeps.

He stopped at a crossroad before a number of veiled houseboats. Cheap incense seeped out from behind silk covered windows and doorways. It was an oddly quiet space. Even the sounds of gulls and the roar of engines seemed muted here, as though everything was being absorbed by the green light below. It hurt Fergus's eyes to look into it, and he noticed Pip and Terry were also squinting. He looked past them to see if the men he'd spotted before were still following them, but he couldn't see anyone nearby, so he decided he must have been imagining it.

"All right, we should split up here, I think," Guillory said. "Three-and-three seems safest. I'll go with Three and Pip."

"Fine by me," Terry said.

Raja and Fergus nodded.

"So which one do we wanna try?" Fergus asked as Guillory began to lead Three and Pip in the other direction.

"Probably the one with the most expensive looking façade," Raja suggested. "It might mean that seer is more successful than the others."

"Or a better liar," Fergus muttered.

"Makes sense to me," Terry said over him.

They proceeded down the walk, pausing now and then to study the fronts of the shops. Most looked about the same: covered in barnacles and stained with algae. However, they did find a couple of taller buildings, which Raja thought meant the seers inside were more affluent. They took some time to study these before deciding on one that wasn't emitting the sickeningly sweet incense. Its veranda was decorated with rows of silver coins that glinted in the breeze.

"If they're not fake," Raja pointed out, "she might have powers worth considering."

Fergus studied the sun-bleached bamboo supports, the delicate straw walls, and the thatch roof. It looked better kept than the buildings around it at least. "How can you tell if they're fake or not?" he asked, eyeing the coins.

"Probably by bending one, but we better not. She's watching us."

Fergus looked up. A woman was sitting behind the upstairs blinds. He couldn't make out her features, but she was definitely looking down on them without moving.

"That's creepy."

The woman disappeared. A moment, later, she pushed aside the purple draperies over the door. Her hair was mostly silver, but Fergus thought it might have been blonde once. She had grey eyes and a wide, toad-like mouth. She stared at them without blinking before lifting a knotted finger and beckoning.

"Are we really . . . " Fergus started to ask. Terry gave him a little shove. "*Fine.*"

"Only one of us needs to talk to her. I don't mind," Raja said as they carefully made their way over the crate path leading to her door.

"I will speak to all of you," the woman said.

"That's not really necessary," Raja said, scratching the back of his head.

"I will speak to all of you," she repeated. She fixed her unblinking gaze on Raja. "You are fine to start. Come in." She held back the draperies, ushering the three of them inside.

The bottom floor looked like a waiting area, though there was no one attending it. There were a few wicker chairs and a table with an ashtray jutting off to the right. Directly ahead was a set of stairs, which the woman began to limp up. Fergus wondered how she'd gotten down so quickly with a bad leg.

She paused, not looking back. "The first may come."

Raja turned to Terry and Fergus. He didn't look quite so confident anymore. "Well, guess I better get it over with. I'll see what I can find out."

"I'm sure it'll be fine," Terry said, putting a hand on his shoulder.

Raja nodded and followed the woman up the stairs. Terry and Fergus retired to the wicker chairs.

"Wish I had a light," Terry sighed, staring wistfully at the ashtray.

Fergus nodded. "What if the gateway really is that green light? Do you think I should check it out?"

"Absolutely not."

"Why not?"

"Because we don't know what it is, and I don't know about you, but just looking at it hurts my eyes. It may not be safe just to swim into it blindly."

"Guess you have a point."

They lapsed into silence, listening to the muffled sounds of the outer port and the waves lapping gently against the houseboat. It rocked a little, just enough to make Fergus sleepy. He stifled a yawn. The wicker chair was hard and prickly, so he couldn't lean back, which kept him from dozing off.

Terry seemed less concerned and crossed his arms on the table, leaning his head on them.

"Let me know when Raja's done," he mumbled.

Fergus didn't reply, but stared with blank fixation at the light illuminating the base of the straw walls. It very likely was the gateway to Tír na nÓg. No one had ever said it would be above ground. In fact, he recalled Jane suggesting that it might be sought out underwater. He rubbed his stinging eyes. Maybe the light *was* dangerous. He felt repelled by this brightness and fascinated at the same time.

It was a little like the smells of the enchanted forest outside of Peygham where Fergus had transformed into a kelpie for the first time. He could still recall the sour honey scent. It had been soothing and unpleasant all at once. More than that, there had been an unnamable alluring quality to it.

He pulled at his lower lip, trying to decide if the similarities in gut feeling were really connected. If they were, they might have to take a swim to find this place. Though if they did find Tír na nÓg below the waves, would they be able to return? Then again, what was the purpose of seeking it out if they weren't going to go in? For the first time, Fergus began to wonder. What was he hoping to achieve? Just seeing it to see it? That seemed a little pointless. Plus, he had nothing left back in New Peiling.

Yet entering the Otherworld would mean giving up all traces of his humanity. It frightened him.

"She says she wants to talk to Terry next."

Fergus looked up to see Raja coming down the stairs. He nudged Terry's leg under the table. Terry lifted his head blearily, rubbing his hands over his face.

"What?"

"You next," Raja repeated.

"Oh, fine," Terry said, yawning as he stood. He stretched his arms over his head. "Guess you didn't learn anything?"

Raja gave him a peculiar look and then slowly shook his head.

"Freak me out, why don't you?" Terry grumbled and walked past him towards the stairs.

"What did you find out?" Fergus asked as Raja plopped into Terry's seat.

Raja blinked slowly, brow puckering in consternation. His lips twitched, but he didn't answer.

"What? Was it really bad?"

He scratched his cheek, staring off into the glow. "I'm not sure. She looked at me and said I was on the wrong path. I asked her what she meant by that. It was really vague."

"They always are," Fergus sighed.

"And then she asked me a question."

"What was it?"

Raja pinned him with that same odd stare he'd just given Terry. Fergus felt goosebumps prickling on his arms.

"What?"

"I . . . " Raja started and then shook his head. "I'd rather not say."

Fergus tried not to groan.

"You'll probably find out soon enough."

Fergus leaned back as much as he dared and let out a long sigh. "Why are we wasting time on fortunetellers?"

Raja didn't reply.

They both stared off into space. Whatever she had asked him, Raja seemed to be intent on turning it over in his mind without sharing, and though it annoyed Fergus, he figured it was Raja's right to tell or not. Instead, he stared at the reflection of the green on the ceiling and tried not to think about how they could be sitting on top of what they were searching for. Luckily, Terry came out sooner than Raja did. He didn't look stunned so much as annoyed.

"You're next," he said, thumbing at the stairs.

"What? Why? Didn't she say anything?"

Terry's mouth thinned. "Couldn't get a useful word out of her, but maybe you can sweet talk her into being sensible."

The woman leaned over the banister. "There is one more left. Come, child."

Fergus cringed. He considered suggesting they just leave now, except that if Terry was telling him to go ahead and try her, he must have thought she knew something, and so Fergus steeled himself.

"Come," the woman said again and then disappeared behind a wall of glittering beads.

Fergus put one hand on the banister and glanced back at Terry and Raja, but they were both staring off into the space. He forced himself to climb the stairs and enter the parlor beyond the beads. It was not particularly mystical. Rather, it looked much like the waiting room with more wicker chairs and a little table in between.

It was not shadowy. There were no candles burning. There was nothing especially mysterious about it at all. It was a fairly average sitting room with a shelf of cute figurines and pretty shells and faded photos, potted plants, and a couple of fat old cats lazing in the rays of sunlight peeking through the blinds.

"It's not what you expected," the woman chuckled, "is it?"

"Not really," Fergus admitted, taking a seat across from her.

"I do not require a show to do my work."

"What was that with the door, then?"

"I knew you were coming."

"Oh yeah? Where's your crystal ball?"

She smiled and tapped her temple with one finger.

"You know, a lot of seers say that."

"You would like some other proof?"

He nodded.

"You seek the Otherworld."

"Didn't the others tell you that?"

She smiled faintly. "You seek it because of a man named Flynn, or you think you do."

Fergus shifted uncomfortably. "How do you know about Flynn?"

"I know many things. How did you find this place?"

"I thought you knew everything," Fergus said, but obliged her by pulling out the map.

She spread it out on the table. "Yes, this is the spot, but the gate here has already closed."

"Wait, what? What do you mean?"

"There is a gate here. It's right below us. It closed decades ago, though."

"So you mean there's no gateway? No hope . . .?"

"Do you want hope?"

"Of course, I do!"

The woman smiled. "There are many gates. This one is closed, but there is another open, even now."

"Well, where is it?"

"You will find it when you stop looking for it, but do you really want to?"

Fergus looked away. "Yeah, of course."

"You are uneasy."

He glanced back at her. "About what?"

She didn't reply.

"So what if I am?"

"What will you do when you find it?" she asked.

"I dunno."

One of the cats awoke. It sat up and stretched, yawning toothlessly, and then lumbered over to the woman. Fergus could hear it purring under the table. It reminded him of Ursula, and while he hadn't thought about her for a while, it suddenly struck him as depressing to think he wouldn't see her again. It wasn't just her, though. It was Pip and Three, because surely Three wouldn't be able to go to the Otherworld. He couldn't imagine a full human living happily amongst fairies. It would be sad not having her around, patting him on the shoulder and grinning.

If he went, he'd have to live as a kelpie all the time, because he *didn't* think it would be very nice to live as a human in the fairy world, and if he was a kelpie, he'd be thinking about the hunger all the time. Maybe his mind would be consumed by it. He'd be like an animal.

"You can only be one or the other," the woman said, interrupting his thoughts. "That decision cannot be avoided."

"One or the other what?"

"If you try to hide from it, it will consume you. If you embrace it, it will consume you."

"What are you saying? That I'm gonna go crazy?"

"You should go now," the woman said. The cat hopped up on the table, and she began to scratch it without looking at him.

"I'm not gonna go crazy," Fergus said, standing up and slapping a hand on the table. It trembled under the force, but the woman neither flinched, nor glanced at him. He could understand why Terry was annoyed now. He stormed out of the room and down the stairs.

Chapter Ten.

"That was useless," he snarled as he stomped down the stairs. "Let's just pay up and get . . . "

A strange man stood across from him, trying to wrestle a half-conscious Raja through the door. Terry was nowhere to be seen.

"What the hell!" Fergus shouted, lunging.

The man released Raja, who toppled into Fergus, and took off. Caught off-guard by Raja's sudden weight, Fergus lost his balance, sending them both sprawling to the floor. Fergus sat up first, taking Raja by the shoulders.

"What happened? Where's Terry?"

"Terry," Raja mumbled, eyes rolling back.

Fergus patted his cheek. "Raja! Raja, hey! Come on, stick with me here!"

"Fergus!" Three leapt through the doorway, followed by Pip and Guillory. "We saw some guys! I think they had Terry! Oh, Raja, is he . . .?"

"I think they drugged him. Where did they take Terry?"

"I'll show you. Three, Pip, you stay with Raja until he can walk and then return to the airship immediately. Fergus, come with me," Guillory said, already heading back through the door.

"Don't worry, Fergus. We'll take care of Raja. Just be careful, okay?"

He nodded and rushed after Guillory onto the floating walk. It wasn't easy to run along the planks. They were stable enough that they didn't sink with each footfall, but they weren't secured, and they shifted with his weight and force. He could see the kidnappers less than 40 meters ahead. They were dragging Terry, who was stumbling, but not trying to fight them off. They must have drugged him, too, but there wasn't time to dwell on that.

It was all he could do to keep up with Guillory, who didn't seem to notice that the walk kept shifting underfoot. He pounded on ahead, closing the distance between the kidnappers, but putting more and more between himself and Fergus. As Fergus sprinted to catch up, he stepped too close to the edge of the boardwalk and lost his balance. He flailed wildly and went careening into the ocean.

The water felt thick and warm around him. It tingled against his skin. Everything was lit by the green light. It was so bright, he couldn't see the surface. He wasn't sure which way was up or down, but as he let out a breath, the bubbles went in a singular direction, so he swam for it. He broke the surface, gasping and grabbing for the planks. Guillory was there, catching him by the arms and helping to drag him up onto the walk. He coughed, wiping at his eyes.

"Are you all right?" Guillory asked, pulling him to his feet.

Fergus nodded, trying to rub the water from his face. His eyes stung, and his skin felt numb. "Where'd they go?"

"That way. Let's go."

Off they went again. Fergus's shoes squished with every step. He ran a little slower this time to make sure he didn't fall in again. Now that he was on dry land and soaked, the air felt very cold. He tried not to think of that as he followed Guillory out of the seers' quarter through a line of thatch buildings that smelled strongly of beer. Small crowds of people stood outside the makeshift taverns, snickering and pointing as they ran past.

Guillory skidded to a stop before a group of young men, grabbing one by the lapels of his vest. "Did a man with a tattoo on his cheek and a redhead pass this way?"

"Oi, let go!" the boy shouted, trying to push Guillory away, but the Captain didn't relent.

"I *said*, did you see . . .?"

"Yeah, we did! Get off me!"

Guillory released him. "Which way?"

The boy pointed to a fork in the path.

"If you're lying, we will come back," Guillory said.

"I'm not lying! They were headed towards the northern docks!"

Fergus started to run.

"Are you crazy? That's where—" the boy shouted.

But Fergus didn't wait to hear why they shouldn't go. Guillory was already passing him, taking the corner at a dangerous angle and sprinting up the walk. Fergus cursed and threw caution aside to catch up with him.

As they left the taverns behind, Guillory finally slowed. The structures around them were decaying. Some were just floating skeletons of former buildings; others were sunken, soggy piles of rotting straw. It looked like there had been a fire or a storm or maybe both. None of the remains looked inhabitable, and yet Fergus saw eyes watching them from between blackened boards and moldering shades.

There were airships docked in both the sky and sea ahead, looming over the ruined shacks. Beyond them, Fergus could see dark clouds gathering. The wind whistled through the buildings, breaking off pieces of straw and thatch and sending them pelting through the air. He swallowed roughly. If there was anything Fergus hated, it was a storm, and he didn't want to see what happened to places like this when a squall hit. They had to find Terry fast.

"Now what?"

"I'm not sure. They might have taken him into one of these shacks, or they might have brought him to the airships."

"So what do we do?" Fergus demanded, peeling his eyes away from the approaching thunderheads.

"Stay right here," Guillory said.

He reached under his jacket and pulled out a revolver. The next thing Fergus knew, he was jumping from the walk into one of the shacks, landing in a crouch, and then lunging upward and out of sight. Fergus heard a startled cry, and then Guillory dragged a man out of the shadows into view. He was heavily tattooed and had a large silver hoop in his nose. His eyes were wide, staring down at the barrel of the gun pressed to his throat.

"Don't shoot!"

"Did you see two men dragging another this way?"

"I didn't see nothing!"

Guillory drew back the hammer. "Did you see two men dragging another this way?"

"I didn't! I swear!"

Guillory let go of the man with a shove, sending him into the water. He was back on the pirate as he surfaced, grabbing him by the collar of his shirt and pressing the revolver to his forehead.

"Where did they go?" he asked very quietly.

Water dripped down the back of the man's bald head. He didn't try to float, but let Guillory hold him above the water. The two were locked in a silent battle of wills, which didn't exactly suit Fergus. The planks under him were beginning to rock as the waves picked up. He swayed and stepped closer to the center. He could hear the echo of thunder growing closer. Seconds ticked away into minutes, and Fergus wanted to say something, but the tension was so thick that he felt he shouldn't even move.

"You don't have to die today," Guillory said in a conversational tone.

"They kill me if I tell."

"And I'll kill you if you don't."

Fergus wondered if Guillory actually would. He doubted it, but the look on Guillory's face made him feel uncertain. He bit his lip.

"Look at it this way: if you tell me, I'll let you go, and you'll have a chance to run. If you don't, it's over here and now."

"They go to the black ship."

"The black ship?"

"The one with 'black' on it. They set sail and make the operation. Then they toss him over."

Guillory released his captive and straightened before nimbly jumping back onto the walk beside Fergus.

"We have to be quick," he said.

Lightning struck close by, illuminating the bold line of Guillory's profile, and Fergus recalled that he'd first met the Captain during a rainstorm. He pushed the déjà vu aside as the first raindrop struck him in the forehead and began to run as fast as he dared towards the line of airships. Pelting rain soon followed the first drops, making the boards slick under their feet and blinding them.

"The weather's on our side!" Guillory called from just behind him.

"How do you figure that?" Fergus shouted back without looking back.

"They can't take to the air in a storm like this!"

"But they can still go by sea, right?"

Guillory didn't reply. Fergus took that as a "yes."

They skidded onto a perpendicular pathway. Before them lay a line of ships, which all looked black in the rain. Fergus put a hand to his forehead, shielding his eyes to get a decent look.

"It's that one," Guillory shouted, pointing to an airship three ships down.

"How do you know?"

"It has 'black' written on it!"

Fergus couldn't make out anything, but Guillory had already started moving again.

"Wait, what's our plan? Are we facing them head on?"

"We'll go by water," Guillory said.

"What?"

However, before he could get an answer, Guillory had already sat down at the edge of the walk and slipped into the ocean, holding the gun over his head as he began to swim towards the airship.

"Jeez," Fergus muttered, but quickly followed.

The black airship loomed above them. He could see lights in its windows, and it looked like people were running around on the deck.

"Probably trying to cast off," Guillory shouted.

Fergus could barely hear him over the drone of rain and waves. He squinted, searching around for anything they could use to climb aboard. Then he spotted the anchor's chain slowly creeping out of the water.

"The anchor!" he shouted.

He couldn't tell if Guillory was behind him or not, but their window of opportunity was closing, and if they didn't make it to the chain before it was out of reach, Terry would be as good as dead. The light from the windows glinted off the wet metal as link-by-link it rose from the ocean. It seemed to Fergus that his heartbeats matched the anchor's steady climb. He gasped, tasting salt, but kept on.

It was right there. He could see the shadow of the anchor several feet below the surface, and then his fingers brushed the cold, rusty iron. He latched onto it and turned to look for Guillory. He wasn't too far behind, but he was struggling.

"Hurry!" Fergus shouted.

This didn't make Guillory swim any faster. Fergus's arms went taut as the chain continued to rise. He hooked a foot into one of the lower links.

For a brief moment, as he looked down at Guillory's tawny head lit up by lightning and growing further away, he wondered what would happen if he had to do this alone. He wondered if he even could take on a cutthroat crew of organ traders by himself. They'd handled Terry and Raja pretty easily. Probably, he'd wind up in the same place as Terry.

Still, he couldn't give up. He had to try, even if his chances were not promising. Holding his breath, he willed Guillory on. He could see the top of the anchor break over the waves. Guillory was still a couple of yards off. The tips of the hooks and then their curves lifted out of the water. Guillory lunged and just barely managed to get his arms around one end. He quickly kicked, wrapping his legs around the other. Fergus let out a long sigh of relief.

It didn't last long, though. The ship was moving, slowly grinding away from the dock. He looked up, blinking against the rain. They couldn't afford to wait until the anchor was drawn entirely. He linked his free foot into another ring and began to climb the chain, pausing for just a moment to look down. Guillory had pulled himself up onto the anchor and was now following Fergus up the chain. Fergus passed the layer of windows, the crews' shouts becoming louder, and then he was at the top, vaulting over the railing onto the deck.

The rain *was* good cover. The crewman manning the anchor was caught off-guard. He blinked at Fergus, wiping water from his face. He opened his mouth to shout, but Fergus struck him in the cheek, knocking him down. It wasn't enough to cut off his cry entirely, though. There was a little flash, and a bullet whizzed past him, splintering the railing.

Fergus jumped, nearly slipping on the wet boards, as the other crewman turned to the commotion.

"Help me up!" Guillory shouted from behind as another bullet struck the deck by his foot.

Fergus turned to see him trying to clamber over the rail. He grabbed the Captain, yanking with all his might, and sent them both sprawling onto the deck. A bullet grazed his leg close enough that he felt his jeans rip and his skin sting. He rolled to his feet. About seven men had gathered – three with pistols. They were shouting, but Fergus couldn't understand them. Guillory shouted something back and then fired. Fergus barely ducked a hailstorm of bullets.

"Just run! Run and hope they don't hit you!"

"What?"

"Don't worry about it! Think of the rain as a shield! Go!"

Guillory raced past him, and rather than stand around waiting to be shot, Fergus took off after him. Maybe the rain was working in their favor. It did make it hard to see, and apparently it made it difficult to reload, too. Two men were fumbling with their weapons as another took aim and fired. Guillory faltered, cursing, but didn't stop. The other men had quickly armed themselves with boards and pipes, and the Captain barely managed to block a pipe to the head with his gun.

Fergus wasn't as lucky. His shoes slipped on the wet boards, and instead of drawing up before the board hit him, he slid straight into it. It connected with his stomach, and he let out a grunt of pain, doubling over. A second blow sent him sprawling to the deck.

They descended on him, and he just had time to roll onto his back and start kicking before a pipe connected with his forearm. He let out a cry of pain, but it was echoed by his assailants, as he kicked the man in the stomach and sent him skidding into one of Guillory's attackers, knocking them both down. The rain pelted him in the face, and with two men still trying to hit him with board and pipe, Fergus didn't dare check on the Captain.

He managed to roll out of the way, avoiding another blow from the pipe, and grabbed the board as it struck the deck next to his head. With a violent jerk, he ripped it from the pirate's hands, immediately swinging it as hard as he could. The board caught the man in the knee, and he let out a grunt, reaching for it, but Fergus swung again. This time, the cry of pain was much sharper.

He moved just in time to block the pipe with his board. The pipe-man lifted it above his head with both hands, and Fergus got to his feet faster than he ever had in his life. He managed to block a second swing. The other man had recovered, though, and as Fergus tried to fend off the pipe, he found the other guy back on his feet and wrestling for the board.

"Aim for the head!" Guillory shouted behind him.

"That's gonna kill . . .!" Fergus was cut off as he was hit in the arm by the pipe.

"Half-strength!"

A man went sailing past him, toppling overboard. It distracted his unarmed attacker. The one with the pipe yelled out a warning, but it was too late. Fergus hit him straight in the chest. The man gasped, clutching at his sternum, and stumbled backward. His legs hit the railing, and he joined the previous crewman in the ocean below.

Overhead, lightning flashed in shorter and shorter intervals. Fergus could see it skirting the surface of the water only a few miles away.

"Fergus, watch out!"

The pipe connected with his shoulder. The board went flying out of his hands, spiraling end-over-end over the railing and down into the water. He cursed, grabbed his shoulder, and darted out of the way as the pipe came crashing down, striking the railing with a resounding *dong*. The next blow caught him in the cheek, and he fell against the railing, his head spinning.

The man loomed over him, holding the pipe over his head with both hands, but over the roar of the rain, Fergus heard a *bang*. The pipe clattered to the deck behind the man as a dark spot began to grow on his arm. Not a second later, Guillory came flying through the air. He kicked the crewman, sending him stumbling over Fergus and into the water.

"They're just dazed. They'll come to in a minute. Hurry!" he said and ran over to swing the cabin door open.

Fergus hauled himself to his feet. He tenderly poked at his cheek and winced. His fingers came away with blood, dripping down his fingers with the rain. He could hear one of the men groaning and turned to follow Guillory down into the cabin. The Captain had already disarmed a crewman at the bottom of the steps and was pocketing the extra firearm. Fergus watched as he struck the man on the crown of his head with his own gun – leaving him slumped in the corner.

"Jeez, you're good."

"When it isn't two-ton shape-shifting monsters, I'm all right," Guillory replied with a wink.

Shouting came from the room beyond, and a moment later, the door swung open. A tall man with a tattoo covering half his face stood in the doorway, holding a knife. Guillory raised his gun. Fergus had a feeling he was out of ammo, but it gave the tattooed man pause.

"We'd like our companion back," Guillory said, drawing back the hammer.

The man gave them a gold-toothed grin and didn't reply.

"Have it your way."

Fergus heard the gun click, but no explosion.

"Thought I might have been out," Guillory said and then threw the gun at the man, who easily dodged.

"And you thought that was gonna work?!" Fergus shouted as two more men appeared behind the kidnapper.

Guillory said nothing, but lunged for the first man's knife hand. The other two slipped around the struggling duo, coming straight for Fergus. He tried to prepare himself, but one tackled him around the stomach, and they went flying straight into a stack of crates. Fergus heard the wood crack, and acrid powder filled the air. He coughed, trying to keep it out of his eyes, and began thrashing wildly, but couldn't get his attacker to let go.

The other jumped in, landing a fist to his jaw and leaving Fergus momentarily dazed. He stopped struggling long enough to earn another to the nose. Letting out a grunt, he shoved with all of his might, pushing the two away, and scrambled out of the debris. He could taste blood dripping down from his nose into his mouth and gingerly wiped at it. For a moment, he thought about having a serious go at the two, but Guillory had managed to wrestle the main kidnapper into the room beyond, so Fergus hopped over them and ran through the door.

One *might* have described it as an operating room, but Fergus certainly wouldn't have. There was a low hanging light, swinging back and forth over a table with white sheets draped over it. Terry lay on top of the sheets, stripped down to his trousers, positioned on his side. Next to him was a silver tray with various utensils on it. Most looked like knives, and none looked particularly clean. There was old blood caked around the handles. As Fergus looked down at the crate of ice before the table, he saw dark stains on the wood.

He dragged his eyes back up to the table. Terry's eyes were shut. His face was very white, and his mouth had a grey tinge to it. There was a single bloody line drawn just below his rib cage, but not quite all the way around his side. Blood seeped from the wound. Fergus could see something pinkish-white peeking out from the cut, and for a moment, he was torn between a terrible, ravenous hunger and the thick burn of bile at the back of his throat.

"Terry?" he said very quietly, putting a hand on his shoulder, but Terry remained still and silent.

He took one shuddering breath followed by another, but it seemed his lungs just wouldn't fill. Static crowded the corners of his eyes. They wouldn't have killed Terry before the surgery – it wouldn't make sense – but he looked sallow and lifeless, and Fergus heard a buzzing in his ears. His whole head felt like it was on fire. He let out a groan and stumbled backward, knocking the crate of ice over and slipping on the chunks. He was suffocating. He released his head to clutch at his chest. Everything was hot and tingling, and Terry was dead.

He was distantly aware that Guillory was shouting at him, but he couldn't stop staring at Terry. He saw one of the crewmen start to grab for him out of the corner of his eye, but the man suddenly shrank back. His vision went white. He felt his knees hit the floor, felt a piece of ice catch him in the kneecap. The buzzing was deafening. His skin burned. He thought someone had set him on fire.

He disjointedly tried to rub at his arms, but they weren't doing what they were supposed to. Nothing was. His body jerked and twisted. He screamed, but it came out strange and feral. Then he blacked out.

He came to in seconds. The room was still. He had to crane his head to the side to look at Guillory and the tattooed man. One of the other men shot at him. It missed and struck the light, sending the entire room into darkness, but Fergus did not find this particularly troublesome. Rather, it was easier to see this way. He lunged for the men. They dropped their weapons, barely avoiding being crushed against the wall, and took off yelling.

But the remaining kidnapper did not leave. Guillory stepped away from him. It seemed the Captain was having a hard time parsing the darkness, but he was careful to keep from putting his back to Fergus or the organ thief. Fergus could see the man's eyes quite well. They glowed a faint yellow – another hybrid. Fergus stamped a hoof, nostrils flaring, and breathed in the heady scent of blood. It was invigorating and thrilling and electrifying, and he was *hungry*.

He slowly backed up, turning to face the kidnapper, as the man stepped forward to face him. Guillory appeared to be edging along the wall, but Fergus didn't particularly care what he was up to. There was a meal standing right there in front of him. He lunged. The man artfully dodged, and Fergus slammed into the other wall. The space was too tight, he realized – the shape distinctly not in his favor.

Fergus snarled, shaking his head. He could see Guillory sneaking towards Terry. Rearing up as much as he dared, he lashed out. His teeth closed on thin air, the force rattling his bones. The sound of his jaws snapping shut seemed particularly loud. It made him feel powerful. He could easily rip the man in half if he wanted to. It annoyed him that the human didn't acknowledge this. Instead, he was grinning and moving closer, fingers twitching in a "come" gesture, so Fergus lunged.

He felt a searing pain in his back. The tattooed man yanked his knife free, and Fergus let out a furious roar, but he was trapped in the corner. The kidnapper grabbed his mane with surprising strength, dragging Fergus towards him, and he could see his own blood on the knife, gleaming in the dim light from the room next door.

He tried to rear, to kick, to escape, but he couldn't reach the man, who grabbed another hunk of mane with his knife hand. The man kept his body pressed against Fergus's, preventing him from reaching around. Closer and closer, he came. Fergus could smell his blood on the blade. It wasn't possible that this little human could overtake him. He was not going to have his throat slit in the backroom of some dingy old airship.

His neck stung where the man pulled at it, but he tried to keep his head up and away from the knife. Then it occurred to him: he still had *one* advantage. With a violent heave, Fergus threw himself onto his side, pinning the kidnapper beneath him. The knife scraped the back of his neck but he was sure he had the man trapped. He could smell the tattooed man's sweat as he finally realized that he should be very, very afraid.

Fergus rolled over, and his captive screamed. The knife dropped to the floor, and Fergus scrambled to his feet. The man lay still, but he was still breathing. It annoyed Fergus. He drew back his lips, making a low, angry sound. He slowly approached the fallen kidnapper, putting one hoof down on his knife. The man remained still, unconscious but alive. Fergus would crush him. He would crush him with certainty. He wouldn't even eat the dirty human. He just wanted to punish him.

His muscles tensed as he prepared to rear, but before he could get off of the floor, Guillory was suddenly there, throwing his arms around his neck.

"Stop! Fergus, stop!"

He paused. His name sounded strange to him.

"It's done! Let's just get Terry back while we can."

He let out an angry squeal, throwing his head.

"Please, Fergus. Think of Terry. He can make it if we just get back to the *Returner*."

Fergus turned his head, eyeing the pale, motionless form on the table. Terry. It was Terry, and Guillory said he was still alive. He wanted Terry to live. He turned back to the kidnapper. He also wanted the man to die.

"Fergus, if we don't go now, it'll be too late!"

That did it. Fergus turned from the man, and Guillory carefully released him, stepping back.

"Go up top. I'll bring him."

Fergus glanced at Terry one last time and then trotted from the room. It was hard to maneuver in the narrow space and getting up the stairs was no easy task. He only just fit through the doorway. The deck was quiet. He cocked an ear. The rain obscured his vision and his sense of smell, but he could hear breathing nearby.

A boom split the silence, and the boards in front of him cracked as the bullet struck. He whirled around, searching out his attacker. A second bullet whizzed by, inches from his eye. He reared and simultaneously tried to back away, nearly falling over entirely in the process.

"Jump!" Guillory shouted, his head just visible from the doorway.

Another shot struck the deck between his front hooves. Fergus turned and jumped over the banister, free falling into the roiling, dark water. He slipped through the waves down into the cold, pressing ocean. Silt and weeds rushed by with the current. It threatened to pull him deeper, and he struggled upwards.

He saw Guillory and Terry break the surface above him in a flurry of bubbles. Guillory seemed momentarily shocked by the fall, and Terry began to slip from his grasp, but Fergus surged forward and gently caught him by the shoulder, surfacing. Guillory spluttered, emerging from the water, and swam over, reaching out to take Terry.

"You aren't going to drown us if we get on your back, are you?" Guillory asked, clutching his mane as he tried to keep himself and Terry above the waves.

Fergus wasn't sure about that. The little voice in the back of his head thought that was a rather good idea, in fact. A fresh human would taste very good, and the storm made him antsy. He wanted to be deep under the water and safe. However, he eyed Terry, who looked even more pathetic now that he was soaked, and gave Guillory a little nudge. The Captain didn't hesitate, but clambered onto his back along with Terry.

Fergus set out for the port. The waves pushed at him, threatening to send him further out to sea, but he fought on. Guillory was yanking at his mane, aggravating the bruises left by the tattooed man, and he wished he could tell him stop. But he realized he was cutting through the water fast despite the waves' interference.

The port grew larger until he was in the space where the kidnapper's ship had been, and then Guillory was clambering up, using his back as a step, and dragging Terry behind him. Fergus wondered if he should change back. His mind felt close enough to human to do it, but then Guillory might be stuck with two people would couldn't walk on their own. He launched himself out of the water, but the planking sagged dangerously under his weight. He tried to take a step forward, and it tilted, sending him sliding back into the surf.

"You're going to have to turn back!" Guillory shouted, getting Terry's arm over his shoulder. "Can you do it?"

Fergus closed his eyes. The water was cold and soothing despite the violence of the storm. Being a kelpie was more comfortable than being human. He was stronger, more alive. Smells were richer. Sounds were sharper. He hesitated. He didn't really want to change back. He wanted to stay a kelpie.

"Fergus, come on! I need you!"

He thought of his human body. It was small and weak and very mortal. He could practically feel it dying, and it was a terrible feeling. It would be better to stay this way, where everything was simpler and less painful. He let the waves pull him away from the walk.

"Fergus!"

Terry's head lolled against Guillory's shoulder. The cut in his side was bleeding again, spreading a mask of pink down his hip. His hand hung limp and white at his side. Fergus thought of Flynn: his face mottled and bruised, his carefree smile slipped into an impersonal line, his body – so full of life the day before – so painfully, gut-wrenchingly still. He could remember touching his face, feeling a whisper of the warmth that had been there only hours before. He'd tried to curl his hands around Flynn's fingers, but they had been too stiff.

He stared at Terry's pale, dripping hand. It came back to him in a rush. The pain was familiar; it was as though it had been days rather than months since he'd last gone from kelpie to man. He screamed, saltwater filling his mouth. His arms, legs, hands, feet, torso, and head – everything was changing in ways that didn't make sense. It didn't last as long as he recalled. He clutched weakly at the side of the walk, tasting bile in the back of his throat, but he swallowed it back with a grimace and began to shakily pull himself onto the slippery planks.

Guillory didn't help him this time, and though Fergus could tell he was impatient, he waited until Fergus had finally dragged his shivering, twitching body onto the boardwalk.

"Can you stand?"

He pushed himself onto his elbows. Everything ached, like a runaway bull had just rammed him straight on. His nose and cheek throbbed, and the cut in his leg burned from the ocean water. Nothing was broken, though, and while he felt dizzy and sick, he had no choice: they had to go now. He managed to get to his feet, swaying and stumbling with the wind. His stomach felt pinched just below his chest, and he thought he might vomit then, but he swallowed again, forcing everything to stay in place.

"Go ahead," he said hoarsely. "Go ahead. I'll catch up."

"And risk you being grabbed, too? Give me your arm."

Fergus couldn't think clearly enough to protest, so he held out his hand. Guillory grabbed it and began to pull him along. It was faster than he wanted to go, and he kept slipping and nearly pulling them both off the boardwalk as he went to his knees. Black motes formed at the corners of his eyes.

"Where is it?" he mumbled, but Guillory didn't hear him.

The Captain moved forward without hesitation, leaving the shacks and the bars behind. Fergus put a hand to his mouth. He could feel the contents of his stomach halfway up his throat. Guillory released him, and he dropped to his knees, vomiting into the ocean. He risked looking up to see Pip and Three sliding down the ladder and rushing over to help with Terry. He wiped the back of his mouth with his wrist and stood.

"You next!" Guillory shouted over the storm, taking him by the shoulder and leading him over to the ladder.

"I can do it," Fergus muttered, though the climb up the sodden rope felt like the longest, most difficult exercise in his life. By the time he got to the top, Three and Raja had to pull him onto the ship. He lay on the deck, shuddering.

"Get moving, men! We've got to cast off!" Guillory shouted, stepping over him and rushing towards the control room.

The crew moved swiftly, and the ship ground to life. Fergus found he couldn't move a muscle. The rain drummed against his head and shoulders. He pulled himself into a sitting position against the railing and watched the lightning crisscrossing the thunderheads in the distance.

"This is it, men! Prepare yourselves! There's an enemy ship out there, and you can bet your mother's heart they'll open fire the minute they see us! Springer, what's your report?"

Fergus dragged himself to his feet. He knew they needed help, but his legs felt rubbery, and his knees kept shaking. He managed to open the door and half-fall, half-climb down the first set of stairs. Using the wall to brace himself, he turned the corner to the control room where he clutched the doorframe.

"Do you really think they're looking for us?"

"Probably. We're being pretty obvious right now, running away like this. Nothing we can do about that, though."

"Will we be okay?"

Guillory raised an eyebrow. "Who do you think you're talking to? Go down with Pip and see what you can do for Terry."

"But I should . . . "

"Go," Guillory said, turning away from him and shouting a whole new string of orders into the intercom.

Fergus minced his way to the second flight of stairs and, leaning over the banister, managed to make it down the second set with only one slip at the bottom. He picked himself up and stumbled towards his room. The ship was moving faster than he'd ever felt it go before. It was hard to stay on his feet, but he made it to the doorway. He dropped into the room, and the airship jerked, causing the door to slam behind him. Pip jumped and cursed.

"Don't scare me!"

"How is he?" Fergus asked, crawling over.

They'd laid Terry onto a makeshift bed on the floor. A stack of towels was next to the pillow.

"Not great," Pip replied. "He's probably in shock. Dry him off. I'll do what I can."

Fergus picked up a towel and did his best to ignore the taste of sick in his mouth and the spinning of the room. He gently did as Pip told him, trying to warm Terry up as he dried him.

"Dry here first!" Pip barked, grabbing the towel from Fergus's hands and blotting the wound in Terry's side. "And get him out of those pants!" He picked up a paintbrush and began to quickly draw characters around the wound, muttering to himself all the while.

Fergus glared, unfastening and pulling the jeans off. He picked up a fresh towel to try to dry Terry's legs.

"Get another blanket when you're done."

He stumbled to his feet, going to pull the quilt off of his bed.

"Don't get in my way!"

"Like I would," he growled, doubling up the blanket and putting it over Terry's lower half.

Pip's muttering sped up as he made strange gestures in the air with his fingers. The ink began to glow a soft green. Fergus didn't dare ask what he was doing, but the wound began to knit together, forming a long, brown scab. Pip didn't stop until the entire length of the incision had scabbed over.

He dropped backward, leaning against the bunk. His hair was sticking to his forehead, which was covered with a fine sheen of sweat. He ran his hands over his face, leaving trails of ink across his cheeks.

"That's the best I can do. What about you?"

Fergus considered for a moment. He was still bleeding and bruised, but as he always found, being in water helped him heal a lot faster.

"I'll live," he said with a shrug.

Just then, the ship rolled precariously, and Fergus barely managed to keep from hitting his head on the bedpost.

"What was that?" Pip asked, eyes wide.

"They've probably found us."

"What?" Pip was on his feet in an instant. There was an explosion overhead, and the jolting of the airship sent him straight into Fergus's bed. He sat up, rubbing the back of his head. "I have to get up there."

"What are you gonna do?"

"Something. Shut up! You watch him! He's been drugged. Make sure he doesn't throw up." Pip climbed out of the bunk, swung open the door, and was out of sight. The door shut with another loud slam.

Fergus was left alone with Terry and the sounds of battle overhead.

Chapter Eleven.

The airship rocked and jerked, sending Fergus sliding across the room several times and causing him to bang his elbow no less than twice. He wondered if the kidnappers were going to sink their airship. He and Terry were probably goners if they did, stuck down in the cabin. He sat with his back against the bed, gripping the edge with one hand. Terry remained silent and unconscious, tucked into the bottom bunk. Fergus hadn't been able to lift him any higher than his own, so he figured that would have to be good enough. If the airship went down, it wouldn't really matter anyway.

It was a long time before the ship stopped rocking, and the shouting and blasts from above went quiet. Slowly, he got up and strained his ears. There was nothing. He went over to their tiny window and peeked outside. All he could see was cloudy sky and choppy sea. He dropped the curtain and let out a long sigh, leaning against the wall. Then, taking a deep breath, he peeled himself away from the wall and went over to check on Terry. As before, he didn't move. Fergus leaned over, patting his cheek, but not even a single eyelash flickered.

He sat down on the edge of the bed and sighed. A few things had come loose. Amongst them were the four potions that Rosslyn had given him. He picked them up. The little tubes gleamed in his hands, their contents roiling back and forth: red, purple, and green. What had Rosslyn said? One was for fire, one for injuries, one to poison, and one for poison. The poisonous one was the purple one. The brighter red was the fire. He stared between the darker red and the green vials, trying to remember which was which.

Maybe if he gave Terry the antidote, he'd wake up. He considered the two vials for a moment longer and then decided he could probably stand both. Fergus uncorked the green vial, putting an arm behind Terry's head to lift him up, and tilted the potion into his mouth. Terry made a soft gurgling sound, but the muscles in his throat flexed. He swallowed.

"There's one," Fergus said, tucking it into his pocket to toss later.

He carefully opened the other vial to make sure it didn't burst into flame, and then repeated the process. Then he put the remaining vials back into his backpack and tucked his things between the mattress and the wall once more. Pulling the covers back up over Terry's chest, he returned to his position on the floor, resting his brow against his knees.

He wrapped his arms around his legs and let out a long sigh. Then he let out a bitter laugh. Even he was surprised by how harsh his voice sounded.

"Our lives suck," he said. "They really suck. They suck so much. Just *why*? Why is it like this?"

He looked up at the shadows over Raja's bunk. Terry continued to breath quietly, evenly. He felt his throat constrict and swallowed roughly.

"Damnit," he said, weakly hitting the floor with his fist. It stung, and it sparked a greater wave of anger. "*Damnit!*" he repeated, hitting the floor harder this time. He grimaced, rubbing his hand. "Everywhere we go, it ends up like this," he muttered to his smarting fist. "And we didn't ask for this . . . " he trailed off, feeling helplessness welling up in his chest. "We didn't ask for this." His skin prickled dangerously. He closed his eyes, taking a deep breath to ease the rush of fury.

"I know."

Fergus jumped, hitting his elbow on the bed frame for the third time. He cursed, rubbing at it, and quickly turned to sit on his knees. "Terry?"

Terry smiled at him wanly. In the dim light coming in through the curtain, he looked very sallow and bruised. He swallowed weakly before asking, "What happened?"

"A lot. Are you thirsty?"

"Yeah, a little."

"Wait here."

Fergus hurried to the kitchen to get a cup of water. The others were still above. He couldn't hear Guillory. He wondered if he was congratulating his crew in person. Certainly, they deserved it. Fergus wasn't entirely sure he wasn't dreaming and that they were about to sink to the bottom of the ocean.

He came back into the room, handing Terry the cup and helped him sit up enough to drink. Terry let out a long sigh as he swallowed and fell back against the pillows. Purple spiderwebs of veins ran over his eyelids. They looked very distinct against his pale skin. For a moment, he thought Terry might fall back asleep and was prepared to return to his guard spot, but at length he opened his eyes and turned to Fergus.

"So what happened?"

"What do you remember?"

"Some guys suddenly came into the shop and grabbed me. After that, nothing." Fergus could see his hands moving under the blanket. "Did they . . . take anything? Where's Raja?"

"Raja's fine, and no, you're still in one piece."

"And? Wait. Lie down. The looming is freaking me out." Terry slowly scooted closer to the wall. Fergus shrugged and kicked off his shoes, lying down on top of the covers. He crossed his arms over his chest and stared at the slats above. It felt like a nightmare now, more dream than real, and he didn't want to rehash it.

"Come on. How did I go from being nabbed to being back here?"

"Guillory and I chased after them. He managed to find the ship they were on, so we climbed aboard. It was kinda messy. We found where you were . . . " He stopped.

"And, and, and. What happened next, Fergus?"

Fergus sighed, putting his hands over his eyes. "I thought you were dead. You looked like Flynn."

Terry said nothing.

"It freaked me out," Fergus said at last. "But we managed to escape from them."

"Did you . . . transform?"

It was Fergus's turn to remain silent.

Terry let out a little sound that was too sardonic to be a chuckle.

"What?"

"Nothing, I just . . . " He snorted softly.

"You just what?" Fergus asked, turning to him.

"I dunno. I guess I feel touched. I kinda didn't think . . . I mean, you freaking out like that because of me is . . . " He laughed again, turning away as Fergus peered at him.

"You mean going after you? Like I was gonna stand back and let them kill you."

"No, not that. That you were that upset. I dunno if anyone has ever really worried about me before. It's kind of nice."

"Shut up."

"Life's not so bad."

Fergus rolled onto his side, scowling. "Some guy tried to cut out your kidneys!"

Terry shook his head. "I don't mean that. I just mean, it's not so bad when there's someone who's actually . . . you know."

"You mean, a friend?" Fergus asked, settling back down.

Terry nodded, closing his eyes. "Hey, Fergus."

"What?"

"Stick around, okay?"

Fergus snorted. "I'm not going anywhere."

"No, I . . . Don't make me embarrass myself by explaining, okay?"

"Yeah, um, okay," Fergus replied, looking at Terry out of the corner of his eye, but he appeared to already be asleep.

•   •   •

"Bad news," Guillory said, walking into the kitchen with more aplomb than Fergus thought bad news should merit.

He and Pip stopped bickering and looked up from the vat of boiled oats they'd been preparing for breakfast.

Guillory sighed, stepping out of the doorway, and walked over to the stove. He paused for a moment, cocking his head as he considered the oatmeal. Fergus thought he was trying not to look disgusted. Admittedly, it did have little black flecks all over where the bottom had burned and Fergus had scraped, which was what had prompted the argument with Pip. Guillory took a deep breath and looked up.

"We spent half the night assessing the damage. The engine is in bad shape. We're lucky it didn't blow entirely. It means we have no power source over land or in water. Luckily, our benefactor provided us with sails, so we're making do with that." Guillory stopped, though it looked like he had more he wanted to say about the Count and his airship. He cleared his throat.

"We're relying on the wind to blow us back to land. I had been aiming for Utsujima, but our direction's changed, so we'll probably end up in the farmlands. I suspect Bridges could stand a real physician looking at him sooner than later. How is he?"

"A little better," Fergus answered. He did seem to have regained a bit of color, and Pip was pleased to say that he'd avoided infection. Fergus thought it might have been due to Rosslyn's potions rather than Pip's magic, but hadn't mentioned it. "He could use some rest, though, and real food."

Guillory nodded. "Since White Rock was closer than expected, it shouldn't take too long, but I'll admit, I can't speak this language."

"I can," Pip replied, poking at the sodden, half-burned oats.

Guillory glanced down at them and shuddered a little.

"More importantly —" he began, sliding around them to grab an apple from the counter. He rubbed it against his vest and took a bite before continuing. " — did you find anything out from that fortuneteller? I spoke with Raja this morning, but he was mum on the subject and said what she'd told him wasn't useful to anyone else."

"She wasn't that useful," Fergus agreed. "She just said that there was a door, and . . . " He trailed off. This was the first time he'd mentioned where they were really headed to Guillory, but he had played a crucial role in rescuing Terry. Fergus cleared his throat. "There was a gateway under White Rock, but it was already closed. She said there were others, and I'd find one when I stopped looking."

"One of those 'the last place you looked' scenarios?"

"I think it was something different, though . . . Well, I guess it could be that, too. It was pretty vague."

"So what is this gateway?" Guillory asked, leaning on the counter.

Fergus glanced at Pip, but he was busy trying to pick bits of burned oatmeal out of the pot with a fork. He took a deep breath, biting his lip. Terry wouldn't want him to tell, but Pip wasn't saying he shouldn't, and he did owe Guillory a big one, or maybe a big two. He slowly nodded, affirming it for himself.

"The gate to Tír na nÓg. It's kind of a long story."

"First mate's on steering. I have time," Guillory replied.

Pip looked up at Fergus curiously.

He hopped up, sitting on the edge of the counter, and fixed his gaze on a sack of rice on the floor, purchased in Ping City. "My best friend was a really smart guy," he slowly started. "He was part of this study group – the same one that Raja was in. They were looking for clues about Tír na nÓg."

"Why?" Guillory asked.

"To go there. To get away from the humans. Life pretty much sucks for us, so you know . . . "

Guillory said nothing, but looked down at his apple.

"He found out about the gateway under White Rock. I guess he was keeping it to himself, though I dunno why. The Knights of Evalach got hold of him. They killed him and . . . " He paused, thinking of Deirdre's and Audrey's role in Flynn's death. "Someone set it up to make it look like a suicide, so the cops wouldn't ask questions. They're eager to believe it's suicide when a hybrid shows up dead. Guess it is most of the time.

"But I found a note in his room. Pip said that it was a map of White Rock, so I thought if we went there, we might find the gate."

"And you found a gate," Guillory supplied.

"But not an open one."

"So what will you do if you find an open one?"

Fergus stared hard at the hemp sack. It was fraying in one corner. There was a green circle with a logo printed on the front and characters he couldn't read around it. He didn't want to answer; he didn't want to admit he didn't know. He shrugged.

"What about you, Pip?"

"I don't know," Pip replied, scraping little pieces of black from the fork and wiping them on the counter. "I don't want to leave Three."

Fergus saw Guillory nod out of the corner of his eye.

"She wants to go home someday, and if you go into a place like that, who knows if you'd ever get back, or how much time would have passed if you did? But I want to see it, in case someday I change my mind."

"What if it closes before then?" Fergus asked, now picking at his cuticles.

"I guess that's fate."

Fergus snorted, and Pip glared at him.

"It'd be a big decision to go," Guillory said, eyeing the apple in his hand. "But I can't imagine you're all headed there just to take a look."

Fergus didn't reply.

"I guess it really exists after all. How strange." The Captain took a bite out of his apple and pushed away from the counter. "Well, for now, let's just focus on repairing the ship and Bridges. And maybe you should start over with the oatmeal."

•   •   •

Fergus went back to his room with two fresh bowls of oatmeal, this time unburned. Raja had pulled the curtains back, and a little sunlight was slanting into the cabin, forming a circle on the floor. Terry was still asleep, turned to the wall, and Fergus felt a little annoyed that Raja hadn't pulled the bed curtains shut for him. He stared down at Terry and then sighed. Probably that second bowl was going to go to waste. He put them both on the floor and reached over to grab his bag from the wall.

Terry shifted just a little, mumbling, but didn't wake. Fergus sat down on the floor with the bag between his legs and began rifling through it. He found the remaining potions from Rosslyn and placed them on the floor. Then he took out the pouch Ursula had given him and removed the items from it. There were two unmarked bottles: one blue and one orange. He had no idea what the contents of either did, but it must have been something medical. Ursula had said that Terry would know what to do with them and resolved to show them to him when he woke.

There were three flasks, as well, all with red liquid inside. These had tiny labels on them. He could barely read her script, but all three said, "topical." He put these items, along with the bandage and Rosslyn's potions, back into the little sack. Then he considered the sack. He probably should start carrying it around, he thought. Only, the bandage made it a little bulky, and he was worried that if he accidentally broke the fire vial, he would be engulfed.

He put the bag aside and dug around under his clothing until he felt the books: Flynn's journals, Ursula's basic magic book, and Rosslyn's guide to potions. The photos were still in the magic book. He carefully tucked them back between the pages as he set all of these down. By now, he'd read through Flynn's journals several times. They didn't illuminate this voyage, but they did make him chuckle and feel a little sad. He remembered a lot of the stories Flynn had jotted down, but he felt a bittersweet tug as he thought of how much better it would have been to reminisce with Flynn in person.

He wasn't in the mood to entertain that little ache, so he put the journals aside and picked up *Basic Alchemy and Potions Making*. Rosslyn had told him that if he just applied himself, he'd pick it up, but it was extremely complicated. The first few chapters were just memorizing different types of ingredients, and he found he simply didn't have the head for it. He thought it might be good as a makeshift cookbook in an emergency, but he thought Rosslyn had overestimated his potential.

Flipping to the first page for what must have been the twentieth time, he once again tried to focus on memorizing the list and definitions, but all too soon, the words began to run together, and his head started to hurt. He sighed and thought about going up to get some fresh air, but it felt disloyal to leave Terry.

He picked up Ursula's book. He'd gotten past the long, dry introduction and most of the first chapter, though he'd had little luck with implementing any of the spells. Still, he had plenty of time to try again, he thought, so he opened it to a chapter on fire spells and picked up his bowl of oatmeal, scanning the steps as he ate the watery mush.

First, he needed a candle. Then he needed something to write with, so that he could copy the runes in a circle around the candle. Last, there was the incantation.

He swallowed the final bite of oatmeal and turned to check on Terry, who was still asleep. The other bowl was surely cold by now, so he picked it up and went to dump both into the water in the kitchen before grabbing a candle and holder from the stores and returning to the room.

Putting the candle on the floor, he went over to Raja's bunk, casting a brief, guilty look over his shoulder, before opening up his bag and looking for something to write with. He found a pencil and returned to the candle. He began to carefully copy the runes onto the floor around it, the tip of his tongue peeking from the corner of his mouth. When that was done, he picked up the spell book, leaned over the candle and rune circle, and began to read the spell in a hushed tone.

"It's a bad idea to practice fire on an airship," Terry mumbled.

Fergus jumped, knocking the candle over. He whirled around, cheeks burning. "Jeez, don't scare me like that!"

Terry yawned and rolled over, rubbing at one eye.

"How are you feeling?" Fergus asked.

"Heavy."

"Probably whatever they gave you."

Terry nodded and let his hand flop onto the bed near his face. "Would've made it easy to drown me."

"It didn't happen, so don't think about it."

He nodded again, but didn't reply.

"You don't have to worry so much. We're all looking out for each other, so it's not like you're alone."

"I know. Or well, I guess I know. It's a little weird still." He rolled onto his back.

Fergus put the candle and book away.

"I haven't been done over like that for a really long time."

He looked up, blinking. "This has happened before?"

"Not this exactly, but something like it. Back before I knew your mom, I was involved with the wrong guys. I told you some of this before, right? One time it got pretty bad. We thought we were gonna die. We couldn't even move. We just laid in that alley bleeding. I'll admit, it was scary."

"Nobody wants to feel helpless," Fergus replied quietly.

"Yeah. Only other time I hurt this much was the first time I transformed."

"It doesn't hurt anymore?"

"It does, but I've learned to cope with it."

"Guess it's easy for you guys now."

"For Ursula and me, yeah."

"And Rosslyn?"

Terry laughed hoarsely. "He hates it."

"Because it hurts?" Fergus asked, putting the pouch in his bag and climbing up onto the bed.

"Nah, because he's embarrassed."

"Why? What is he?"

Terry looked up at him, silent for a moment. "You can't tell anyone if I tell you. At least don't tell him."

"Okay."

"A *boobrie*."

"A boobrie?"

Terry nodded, mouth twitching. "Yeah, one of those big water birds that steals sheep and stuff. First time we saw him, we couldn't stop laughing. Well, Ursula and I couldn't. Ainslee didn't laugh. Rosslyn got really embarrassed about it. Probably more effective in a fight than a gytrash or a *cait sìth*, but . . . well, boobries are pretty weird looking."

Fergus nodded.

"Did he give you that book?"

"No, Ursula."

"Figures. He's rotten at spells."

"Really?"

"He's a genius at potions, but yeah. Well, though I say he sucks at them, he can still do them. They're just not his strong point. He's better with water. Probably you'd find the same."

"Why?" Fergus asked. His back was starting to feel a little sore.

"Because you're a kelpie. Water should be your element. You should practice those spells instead of stuff like fire."

"What about you?"

"I'm not as good as Ursula, but I'm not bad. It came naturally enough."

"Are you boasting?"

"A little."

"Flynn used to practice spells at home. He used a lot of water spells, too."

Terry nodded. "Well, he was a *tarbh uisge*, right? Another water fairy, like you and Rosslyn."

"He could do other stuff, though. He was really smart."

"I was always a little jealous of him," Terry said, looking away.

"Why? You're good at magic, too."

"No, not because of that."

Fergus tried to meet his eyes, but Terry remained firmly turned away.

"Mostly cuz of you," Terry said after a moment. "Do you remember when I first met you?"

"Yeah, it was at an audition. I wanted to be in a band since like junior high. When Mom disappeared . . . I guess it was just something to make me wanna get out of bed."

"Ursula told me you wanted to start a band, so I learned to play bass. The guitar was the most expensive thing I'd bought in years, but I couldn't think of another way to get close to you."

Fergus snorted. "Yeah, you weren't all that good. I thought you could've been, though, and you turned out pretty good, I think."

Terry's mouth scrunched to the side. "Thanks."

"You are a good bassist."

"I learned to like it. Anyway, I'd kinda hoped that we would become friends and roommates, so I could keep an eye on you, but Flynn was already in the picture. You guys were attached at the hip. I dunno. I'd never had any friends like that. I'd had friends, sure, but you know. I felt jealous. I didn't try to get close to you because of that. Well, I know I'm no replacement for Flynn."

"I don't need a replacement for him. Flynn was Flynn, and you are you."

Terry didn't say anything, but Fergus could see him smile a little.

"I kinda felt jealous about you and Raja," Fergus admitted.

"Really? But you've been spending so much time with Three and Pip."

Fergus shrugged and finally shimmied his way to the back of the bunk, resting against the wall. "I like Three. Pip's okay, too, when he's not mad."

"She's cute, though he's kind of a pain in the . . . "

"It's not like that. It's more that she's easy to get along with. She cares about other people. Besides, I think Pip would knife me in my sleep if I tried anything," Fergus said with a little snort.

"Probably," Terry agreed.

"It's really not like that. Anyway, who knows if they're gonna stay with us? They've got their own thing going on."

"What do you mean?"

"There's this guy they're looking for. Well, they saw him in Jarpur. That's why they ran off and left me. Even though they're looking for him, I think they're really scared of him," Fergus said, lowering his voice and eyeing the door.

Terry finally looked back up at him. "They're running away from someone they're looking for?"

Fergus frowned. "It's complicated. This guy . . . They've got a history with him. He hurt Three pretty badly. She's got this huge scar on her shoulder, and well . . . I dunno that much about what happened to Pip."

Terry sat up a little. "You can tell just by looking at him."

"How's that?"

"Well, he's pretty much terrified of being in a room alone with anyone except you, Guillory, or her. He seems pretty unstable, like he's gonna go off at any moment."

"Yeah, I guess he does. Well, he has his reasons."

Terry nodded. "So they want revenge. Guess that means Pip doesn't wanna go to Tír na nÓg."

"No, I think he plans to return with Three to her hometown . . . after they deal with that guy."

"You're right. Even if you wanted her, I don't think she'd ever choose anyone over him. Tough luck."

"If we find that gate, are you gonna go?" Fergus asked, turning to the window. He thought he could see the dim outline of mountains in the distance.

"Maybe. Are you?"

"I . . . I dunno. Maybe. I felt kinda worried when I thought we'd already found it. I hadn't really thought about what I would do, and then there was a gate right under us."

"There was?"

"Yeah, though it was closed, according to the fortune lady. She said I'd find the gate when I stopped looking."

"She said I'd lose something valuable."

"You almost did," Fergus replied. "Do you know what she said to Raja?"

Terry shook his head. "I kinda feel like . . . it wouldn't be bad to leave this world. There's a lot about it that really is bad, and no matter how much we fight it, it seems like the best we can do is make it tolerable. I didn't choose to be a hybrid, but I wound up one anyway. That decided everything."

"The fairies might not be much better," Fergus replied softly.

Black peaks were rising up out of the fog outside, growing larger.

"If we can get in, we might be able to get out. Even if it's a hundred years, maybe things might've gotten better."

"Who's gonna make them better, though?" Fergus muttered.

"Dunno. Guillory, Rosslyn, Ursula, the Count, Three, Jane . . . It doesn't have to be us."

"Guillory, huh?"

Terry gave a halfhearted smile. "Well, he did risk his neck to get me out of there. Guess he's not all talk."

"I can see why he's called 'The Hero of New Peiling.'" Fergus said and slid out of the bed to look out the window.

Dark, craggy mountains, tinged with a hint of green, spilled down to the sea. The landscape looked hard and austere, but there was something elegant about it, too. Like someone had conjured it out of ink and charcoal.

"Looks like we're here."

Chapter Twelve.

They docked at a tiny fishing village unlike anything Fergus had ever seen before. The roofs of the houses were constructed of rounded tiles that ended with floral designs, which had turned green from the ocean air. The walls of the buildings were partially white plaster and partially dark lacquered wood. Bamboo curtains hid the windows. Few of the houses were taller than a storey. Yet to Fergus, they seemed very fancy. He stood at the end of the dock, marveling over the quaint rows of brown and white buildings.

There were a number of cats around. A calico curled around his legs, meowing loudly. He ignored it, turning as Terry laboriously made his way down from the ship. Fergus barely got to the rope in time to catch him as he stumbled onto the pier, doubling over.

"Are you all right?"

Terry gave a brief, pained nod.

Three led the way as they set off to find a doctor. Pip had been recruited by Guillory to ask about repairs. It was a little weird to see them separated, but Pip seemed less anxious than he would have thought, and he didn't think it was because of Guillory. Pip really did look like the fishermen who'd gathered around to see the damaged airship; Three did, too.

She was several strides ahead, bobbing her head in a polite but brief bow as she spoke with the locals. The men motioned inland, and Three waved Fergus and the others to come along as she set out with a quick step. It was too fast for Terry, so every few meters, she had to stop and wait for them. She didn't seem impatient, though. Fergus thought maybe she was a little anxious, but she seemed to be in good spirits as she led them to a little brown building.

"Bring him in here," she instructed, sliding back a door.

Fergus and Raja did as they were told, and with Three's help, they soon had Terry resting in a crisp, white bed at the back of the clinic. She spoke to the nurse for some time. Raja and Fergus stood uneasily by the doorway, not sure what they should be doing with themselves and casting each other hopeful glances, as though the other might suddenly come upon an answer.

Terry meanwhile – in a comfortable, stationary bed for the first time in weeks – had already passed out. Fergus went over to pull the sheet over his chest.

"The doctor is out, but he should be back by tomorrow. The nurse will look at him soon. For now, she says Terry can rest here, so don't worry about a thing," Three said quietly as she rejoined them. "She says you can stay with him if you want, though I suspect he'll be out for some time."

She glanced at Terry. A beam of light struck his cheek, making it look very white. His chest rose and fell rhythmically. She reached out and took both Raja and Fergus by the forearms, drawing them out of the room. Once outside, she let go of them, sliding the door shut behind them, and then adjusted her hair over her shoulders.

"If you like, I'm going to visit an interesting place that's nearby. Do you want to come with me?"

"What kind of place?" Fergus asked.

"A shrine. It's on a lake just past that mountain. It shouldn't take long to get there."

"But what if he wakes up?" Fergus glanced uncertainly at the closed door.

"Probably he'll be busy with the nurse. We can go another time."

"No, it's okay. Let's go now while he's asleep. I'll just take a look and come back." He turned to Raja, who nodded.

Three smiled and led them out and away from the sounds of the ocean towards the forested hills on the other side of the village. There was a thin, stony path leading up the mountain between the trees. Dried out husks of grass framed it on either side. When the wind blew, they whistled and scraped eerily, and the wind did blow, coming off the ocean before dark clouds.

Fergus paused, turning to look at the little houses below between the trees. He couldn't see the water anymore, though he could see the storm blowing in and shuddered.

"Okay back there, Fergus?" Three called from above.

He nodded and continued after Raja, trying to focus on his back rather than the feeling of foul weather. Great roots sprung out of the ground, and the path became narrower. He began to pant, feeling warm despite the crispness of early winter, and had to pause to catch his breath, wiping the sweat from his forehead.

"I thought you said this was a short walk," he called, but Three was climbing steadily upwards, making her way around the stones and roots with the ease of a mountain goat.

He sucked in a great breath and began climbing again. The trail trickled into a gap hardly wide enough to put one foot in front of the other and then into a number of large boulders, but on the other side of those was a flat, well-trodden dirt path easily two people's width. Fergus groaned with relief as he slid from one of the boulders onto the path.

Raja was also leaning against one, holding a stitch in his side. Fergus leaned back, fists on his hips, stretching, before following after Three once more. He paused to put a hand on Raja's shoulder as he passed by. Up ahead, he could smell water on stone. As they wound around the side of the mountain, he could hear it rushing. Two waterfalls spilled out of the mountain, cascading under a wooden bridge.

"Whoa," Fergus said, hurrying to have a closer look. "That's amazing."

Three stopped at the juncture between the two falls and turned, smiling. "We call them the 'Goddess's Hands.'"

"Why?"

"Water is necessary for life. Here, it falls side by side. They say it's like the Goddess is opening her hands to us, letting life spill out of them. Does that make sense?"

Fergus made his way over the slippery planks to her before answering. "Yeah, I guess it does."

"Well, though I say she's a goddess, maybe that's not exactly what she is."

"And that *doesn't* make sense. So what is she then?"

"More like . . . a teacher?" Three replied, tugging her hair and staring up at the dark rocks from which the water emitted.

"Oh. I see, I guess," Fergus replied, rubbing the back of his head.

"She isn't a goddess. She's enlightened," Raja said, coming up behind them.

"Yes, that's it," Three agreed enthusiastically.

"So what's the difference?"

Raja gave him a crooked smile. "How about I explain it some other time?"

Fergus felt irritated, but shrugged. "Fine by me. A storm's coming anyway."

"How do you know?" Three asked.

He shrugged again. "I just do."

They crossed the second bridge and continued along the trail. Up ahead, he could smell something burning. He sped up only to find that the next bend led straight to a steep set of stairs, which were framed by bright orange-red gates leading down the mountainside to the lake below. Fergus let out an exasperated groan.

"There, there," Three said, lightly patting him on the back as she started down the steps.

He let out another whine, but it was ignored, so he began to descend the slippery stone path towards the lake. Three did not touch the gates, and he thought by her body language that maybe they weren't supposed to, but he found that he had to use them as a brace. The stairs were clear of moss and leaves, but it had obviously rained recently, and they were slick and a little bit muddy. They were also very tall and not very wide.

By the time he reached the bottom, both his sides were cramping. He leaned over, hands on his knees, and gasped as they waited for Raja to catch up.

"It's not far now," Three promised, pulling her hair out of her face.

"You said that before!" Fergus grumbled, trying to slow his breathing.

"Okay, Raja? Let's hurry before the storm hits. Even I can feel it now!" she chirped.

She led them down the last part of the path through the trees, which opened up to the lake. Sure enough, at the center of the water was a shrine, connected on either side by wooden bridges set on rock columns. It was painted the same orange-red as the gates leading down from the mountain. There was a dense fog over the water, but Fergus could see bunches of flowers blossoming below the mist.

"Lotus blossoms," Three supplied and began to cross the bridge.

Fergus followed her. The bridge rose and fell in humps, which were wet – the angles just steep enough to make it dangerous. The railing on either side was too low for him to use to balance, so he had to simply half-slide, half-walk down each descending segment. The roof of the shrine flipped up in all the corners, similar to the fisherman's homes, though far more ornate. There were lions and dragons guarding the tiles, and the buildings were not only one storey, but had multiple floors with roofs on top of other roofs.

Moreover, the guardian statues seemed to be gold-plated. The details of each building were so intricate that Fergus had to stop to actually get a good look at what they were approaching. The shrine was made up of several buildings joined together. A few were open to the elements. Fergus couldn't see what was in these little rooms, but clouds of sandalwood wafted from them, along with the sound of men chanting. He thought he could also hear some queer wind instrument being played and a hollow, wooden *thunking* sound.

He gave himself a pinch, half-expecting that it would all fade away, and he'd find himself napping in one of the little chairs in the doctor's office. However, there stood the shrine complex, and before it was Three, waving impatiently for him and Raja to come along.

"Don't step on the threshold," Three said and passed under another gate to a little well.

At least that's what Fergus thought it was, though it turned out to be more like a water fountain with lions engraved into the stone and dippers sitting just on top of the water. Three picked one up and began to wash her mouth and hands with it before passing it on to Fergus. He blinked at her and then down at the water collected in the basin before hesitantly scooping a fresh dipperful.

"You can just wash your hands, if you like," she said.

He nodded, but he was feeling thirsty after their hike, so he mimicked her as best he could before passing it on to Raja. She pretended not to notice his stolen drink.

"Now what?" Fergus asked, lowering his voice.

Three gestured to the open door of the main complex and stepped inside. Incense was thick in the air. It felt very still and cold. To his right stood several stone statues. They had fierce, violent faces, and he shifted away, feeling like they were staring right at him. He bit his lip, glancing at Three, though she had already approached a small altar, tossing a coin and clapping her hands as she began to pray. Raja went over just the same and began a similar ritual before clasping his hands in prayer.

Fergus just watched. He had never prayed before. He had never seen how it could help. It made him feel weird and out of place to watch Raja and Three doing it, their faces intent as they wished for whatever it was they hoped that magic and spirits might give them.

They were taking their time about it, and Fergus was beginning to feel very antsy. The chanting droned on in the background, and the incense was giving him a headache. Plus, he really was starting to feel like the statues were giving him the Eye. He wandered away from the prayer hall and out onto the wooden veranda surrounding the complex. His footfalls sounded much too loud, and he wished the fog would swallow up the noise.

Rain started to fall, forming coffee-black circles on the already sodden wood. He ignored the unpleasant feeling in his bones and shuffled along, peeking into buildings. He could see a small group of men sitting in white and red robes in tidy rows and columns, chanting as one man, wearing some kind of golden jacket over his robes, moved back and forth in front of them, waving a wand with pieces of white paper attached.

He scratched the back of his head, wondering what they were doing, but there was no answer in simply observing, so he continued around the outside of the shrine. As he approached the other side, he came upon a young man in a purple jacket.

"Oh, sorry," he quickly said, backing up.

The young man was leaning on the railing, looking out over the foggy water. He looked up as Fergus spoke, watching him with dark, quiet eyes and something of a devilish smile. He looked a little younger, though not by much. His dark hair had gone wavy from the drizzle, and droplets hung on the strands like a web. He pushed away from the railing, straightened his robes, and bowed to Fergus without speaking. Fergus scratched the side of his neck and bowed back.

"Guess you don't understand me," he mumbled.

The young man shrugged a little, which seemed answer enough to Fergus.

"Sorry to bother you," he said and began to turn.

But before he could escape, the young man tugged the back of his jacket, and Fergus turned to see him smiling, his face growing warm and soft as his lips crooked. He patted the railing expectantly. Fergus edged closer. This seemed to be exactly what the young priest expected, because he relaxed. He reached out, putting a hand on Fergus's shoulder, and then, rather unexpectedly, removed the hand and made a slashing motion over his chest.

Fergus's eyes narrowed. "What? Are you threatening me?"

The priest cocked his head and then gave it a shake. Once again, he made the slashing motion and then reached out to pat Fergus's chest.

"I don't get it," Fergus said. "What? Are you trying to say I've been hurt?" The priest's hand felt warm, even through the layers of clothing. The heat felt soothing. "I'm fine, you know." He paused, trying to think of how to convey that, before touching his chest and holding his thumbs up.

The young man chuckled and took his hand away. The spot felt oddly cold without it. He rubbed his chin, looking up at Fergus thoughtfully. There was a brightness in his eyes that Fergus had rarely seen, except maybe with Rosslyn or Ursula. He lifted a hand to Fergus's bruised cheek, and Fergus flinched. This did not deter the young priest who kept his fingers just a hair's breadth away.

He began to speak, and the warmth from before flooded into Fergus's skin. The sting of the bruise ebbed. He closed his eyes, letting out a little sigh. It was nice to have a little relief. His nose ached less, too.

The priest dropped his hand, leaning on the railing, and Fergus touched his face gingerly. It felt like the bruise was almost gone. It still stung, but it didn't hurt nearly as badly as before. The young man wiped the back of his hand across his forehead.

"Thanks," Fergus said softly.

He glanced at Fergus, giving him a smile that spoke of mischief and a lightness that seemed at odds with the austere, weighted atmosphere of the shrine. He nodded and then pointed below at the clusters of flowers floating on the water. Fergus looked, though he didn't see anything except the flowers, which did seem out of season.

"Sorry, I don't get it," he said after a moment.

The priest scratched his head and pursed his mouth, obviously trying to think of how to convey his thoughts without words. He leaned over the railing and began to move his hands like a puppeteer, dragging up, up, up. Fergus stared in bewilderment. Then he noticed that the surface of the water was rippling. Not just rippling, but it began to rise, like a pebble striking it in reverse.

The priest released the water and put his hand on Fergus's shoulder again, speaking. He had a soothing voice, but Fergus couldn't make heads or tails of the words. He thought he might have said "you" once or twice.

"He senses water in you."

Fergus jumped and spun around to see Three. She slowly walked up to them and gave the priest a deep bow. He smiled and returned it with a shallower one. A brief exchange followed before she turned to Fergus again.

"He says there is water and pain inside you. Maybe you are in pain because of the water?"

"I'm feeling kinda good, actually," Fergus replied, looking between Three and the priest.

Three relayed this to the priest, who shook his head. She turned back to Fergus. "He says it's deep in your mind, or your soul. Well, one word, same idea."

"And why does he care?" Fergus asked, wiping the drizzle from his face.

Three turned back to the young man. Fergus bit back a sigh.

"Well," she said after a couple of minutes, "he says that you are holding onto something that only hurts you. Um, it's a little complicated. Basically, it's like something that you fight and so you don't let go of it? But something you shouldn't give in to either, because that's holding onto it, too. So more like maybe you should accept it as it is and let it be. Maybe that's what he means by the water."

"That makes no sense at all."

"Well, take the water trick he was trying to show you. With magic, he can move it whatever way he wants, but its nature is just to be in this lake, you know? When the magic is done, it returns to being that way."

"Oh my God, Three, you're killing me here."

"I'm really bad at explaining this kind of thing! Just listen. There's something inside you that will be there no matter if you try to force it away or drink it in. Whatever you do, that will still be there, weighing on you. So the only answer is just to let it be there and accept that's how it is."

Fergus raised an eyebrow.

"At least, I think that's what he means."

"Okay, well, maybe we should . . . "

"Wait, wait, there's someone else I want you to meet."

Three turned from him to give the priest another bow. Fergus glanced at her and then did the same. The priest smiled at them both, patting Fergus's arm.

"He says not to worry so much," Three said, chuckling.

Fergus followed her as she began to walk away, glancing once over his shoulder, but the young man had disappeared, as though swallowed up by the fog.

"You know, I lived really close by," she suddenly said.

"Really? How come you aren't visiting your family, then?"

She shook her head, her back to him as she steadily walked around the edge of the complex to the other side. "I can't. If I went, I might not be able to leave, and I can't endanger them like that. If I stayed, Pip would stay – I would want him to – but if we were both there, that man would come, and he would kill anyone who got in his way. Until we get rid of him, it's just impossible."

"That's kinda sad."

"I'll leave a message for them here with the Head Priest. He's an old friend. Actually, he taught me magic. It's not so easy for us humans, you see. For the villagers who'd been visited by the spirits, it was second nature, but for me, it was so hard. My parents came and asked the Head Priest for help, because he was a human like me who could do magic . . . They knew how much I wanted to fit in. He agreed to teach me, and here I am. Talking to him helps me settle things. Maybe you'll find the same."

"Do you think I have something that needs settling?"

She didn't reply, but tucked her hands into the fuzzy pockets of her coat and stepped into one of the buildings. Fergus let out an annoyed sigh and followed.

Inside was dark, but more than dark, it was *red*. It was a little like being in a poorly lit club, except that the red illumination made it feel organic. A lot of his nightmares had this feel about them, and Fergus backed away, suddenly feeling very uneasy. His heels bumped into the raised doorframe, and he stopped, swallowing roughly. Three continued down the hallway, passing between weak rays of light from open doors and into the shadows between.

At the other end of the hallway was a black door, which she stopped just in front of and turned to him.

She stood in a line of red tinged daylight, which made her face look strange and ruddy.

"Come on, Fergus. It'll be okay."

He begrudgingly began to shuffle down the hallway after her, shoulders hunched, staring down at the floor in front of him. Even though he knew it was irrational, he felt afraid to look into the open rooms. It was far too easy to imagine something terrible inside, even though this was a holy place. But the red called to that dark and ancient feeling in the back of his mind. He wondered if part of him didn't *want* to see something horrible. He took a sharp breath, shaking his head.

"What's wrong?" Three asked, clasping her hands behind her and leaning down. "You look uneasy."

"It's just . . . the red. It's weird."

She straightened, scratching her cheek. "You think so? I always thought it felt safer here than anywhere else – warm and protected."

"Maybe," Fergus replied, not meeting her eye.

"Are you afraid of red?"

"I don't know," he replied, surprising himself. "Maybe I am."

"Red is like . . . lying under a warm blanket with a light overhead, or a festival with lanterns and fireworks. Think of it that way – as a good thing."

He nodded.

"Are you ready?" she asked without waiting for a response. She turned and kicked off her slippers, setting them onto a stand to the side of the door. "You, too," she said, waiting for Fergus to pull off his boots and put them next to her shoes. Then she slid the door open and bowed. A thick wave of incense poured out. It smelled less like sandalwood and more like cedar. It was not red within that room, but bright, and he couldn't easily see inside.

"Please excuse our intrusion," Three said, still bowing.

"Come in, child. There is no intrusion in this place," replied a deep, gravely voice.

Three straightened and stepped inside. Fergus followed after her, sliding the door shut behind them.

The room had straw floors, which felt very clean under his socks, like walking on the beach. The entire room – walls and ceiling – was covered in white paper, framed by cream-colored wood, which he could only assume must be lacquered or waxed, because though he could hear the rain droning against it, the paper looked dry. Oddly enough, despite being in a paper house, it was very warm – almost hot. The grey light from outside illuminated the space from all corners, though that wasn't what made it bright.

At the other end of the room was an altar from which the light emitted. There was a rope with strips of triangular paper draped over it and ink paintings on either side. An assortment of small items rested before the altar, but between the light and the incense smoke, Fergus couldn't make them out.

A man stood before it, dressed in white and red robes, but with an embroidered blue jacket over them and a tall black hat on his head. To his right was a young girl also in red and white, though her pants were a higher cut than the man's. She looked up at Three and smiled. The man, too, seemed happy to see her, his expression brightening as he took a few steps forward.

Fergus crept up to her shoulder. The man stood only a few feet away from her. He was brimming with energy, and Fergus thought he might want to hug her, but he didn't, nor did she make any move to close the gap. She bowed again.

"Master Kamo, it's been a long time."

The man chuckled. "So it has, Chizu."

Fergus blinked, scratching his head.

"Your eyes are blue now?"

"Lenses. I can't see a thing without them. Master, this is my friend, Fergus Irvine. We've been traveling together for a few months."

Master Kamo gave Fergus a little bow, which Fergus returned.

"Uh, nice to meet you. You speak the same language?"

The Head Priest chuckled. "I speak many languages. This place may seem very remote, but pilgrims come here from all over the world. It's a necessity."

"Another thing I learned from Master," Three added with a grin, then turned to the priest. "I was wondering if I could speak to you privately, but first . . . Well, I was hoping you and Fergus could get to know each other."

Kamo tilted his head, studying Three. "I'm sure you have your reasons, but it doesn't do any good unless Fergus wants to speak with me."

They both turned to him, and Fergus felt his face heating up. "Um, I don't really mind, I guess?" he said, feeling a little annoyed at Three for putting him on the spot.

"Chizu, would you go and fetch Takafumi in the meantime? He's talking to stranger things each day. He's going to catch cold if he stays out in the rain."

"Is that what he was doing?" Three asked. "Well, he was talking to Fergus, but he looked like he'd seen something in the water."

"Another spirit has taken up residence in this lake. He seems very fond of it, but he's always been a little strange, don't you think?"

Three laughed. "He is your son, you know."

Kamo smiled.

"Is he the priest from before?" Fergus asked.

Three nodded. "He's actually a very powerful medium, though he's only about Pip's age. He can speak with the spirits."

"Spirits? Like the fairies' souls?"

"Those and others. He's a little mysterious that way. I'll go and tell him to come in."

"Master," said the other girl, though her words were slower and choppier, "may I go with Sister Chizu?"

Kamo crossed his arms and nodded.

The girl grinned and hurried over to Three, linking arms with her. The two fell back into their native language as they walked away, leaving Fergus alone with the Head Priest. He bit his lower lip, unsure of what he should do.

"I can see you've been visited by the spirits."

Fergus looked up. "Huh? How?"

"Your eyes. You don't seem blind, so it must be a spirit."

He slowly nodded. "That's right. A kelpie. Do you know what that is?"

Kamo shook his head.

"Um, it's kind of like a horse that lives in lakes and rivers and stuff."

"A water spirit," Kamo repeated. "Yes, that makes sense."

"Your son was saying there was water in me or something," Fergus said, feeling that he should say something and wondering if he was saying too much, or even saying something stupid by admitting that.

"He's good at seeing those things. Did he say anything else?"

"Um, that I was injured, I think."

"Come, Fergus, let's sit down."

Kamo walked over to the wall and pulled back one segment. The roof sheltered the veranda outside. Water dripped down from the awning, creating a screen over the rest of the world. Kamo stepped out onto the deck and sat down. Fergus followed him.

"Should I shut the door?"

"No, it's a little stuffy in there. It needs some airing out. Are you cold?"

Fergus shook his head and sat down, drawing his knees up to his chest.

Kamo pulled out a long, thin pipe and a match. "Do you smoke?"

"Sometimes. Not as much lately."

"It's bad for you, so that's probably best," Kamo said, exhaling a thin stream of smoke.

"So . . . you're not afraid of the, um, 'spirits'?"

Kamo chuckled. "Not your kind."

"There are other kinds?"

Kamo tilted his pipe, dumping out a little ash, and took another long drag. Just beyond them, between the buildings, was a small open-air garden. It had a pond with large orange and white fish in it. The grass and bushes around it looked a little unkempt, and there were old leaves floating on the surface of the pond. It made Fergus think of Toby and his other fish, though he supposed that by now, if the fish were still alive, they were Ursula's, not his. He felt a pinch of homesickness.

"There are spirits in practically everything," Kamo replied at last. "Trees, rocks, rivers . . . all of them have something you could call a spirit. Those are harmless. Then there are other, greater spirits. Some people call them gods, but that's not exactly it either. There are spirits like the creature that has moved into our lake. There are spirits like the one that has visited you.

"Most of them simply must be appeased in some way or another, and they do no harm, but there are those that are dangerous. Perhaps you're thinking you might be one of them?"

Fergus gave a noncommittal grunt.

"Why is that?"

"Because . . . because it's hungry," Fergus mumbled, pulling his knees closer.

"Oh?" Kamo said, breathing out a smoke ring. He tapped it with his pipe, breaking the circle. "Perhaps if I had met that spirit outside of you, I would be concerned, but it's a part of you now. Your face is not that of a dangerous man, so I see no reason to fear your soul."

"It'd be nice if everyone thought that way."

"My ancestors have boasted of special powers for many, many centuries. Even before the Cataclysm, they had powers other people couldn't imagine. Though there was a long time when no one would believe in such a thing, there was also a time when we were venerated. Power that is used for harmony should never be feared."

Fergus nodded, chewing on the inside of his cheek.

"Well, now we live quietly, tending this shrine." He tapped out more ash. "But in the past, our abilities easily rivaled even the most dangerous spirits. We were often called upon to deal with them. Therefore, it's hard to imagine fearing such a thing. But other people are always fearful, because they are powerless in the face of something or someone like you, or so they think. They forget how to live quietly and instead live defensively. Pretty sad, don't you agree?"

"Yeah."

"So, why are you afraid, Fergus?"

"Because I don't feel like I can control that part of me, I guess. It's always there. I feel like . . . like there's two of me, and the other me is just waiting for when I can't stop it, and then I don't know what I'll do." He paused, pursing his mouth, and rested his chin on his knees. "I'm afraid of becoming a monster. I'm afraid of going crazy."

"It's not impossible," Kamo agreed.

Fergus blinked, lifting his head.

"Plenty of people use power in the wrong way and for the wrong reasons. It's not hard to wind up on that path when you really think about it. I think the difference is perhaps that you *do* think about it."

"I was told that I couldn't . . . embrace this or shove it away. That either way I would fail in the end."

"I see." Kamo blew smoke through his nose and then reached into his robes to refill and relight his pipe. He puffed on it for a little while.

"A fortuneteller said it."

"Sounds a little like she was guessing, but her advice wasn't bad."

"Advice? What do you mean?"

Kamo let out a long exhalation, watching the smoke twist and rise up towards the roof, disappearing into the air. "If you embraced that hunger – hunger, wasn't it? – then you would become a monster. Constantly rejecting it won't drive it away, though. It will only drive you mad."

"So what am I supposed to do?" Fergus asked, frustration leaking into his voice.

"Accept it as something that will always be there."

"How does that help?"

"You can accept it without giving into it, and accepting it means that you won't make yourself crazy fighting something that really will always be with you. It may not be pleasant, but enduring it will give you relief eventually."

"I guess I don't understand," Fergus said, chin dropping back to his knees.

"That pond over there," Kamo said, gesturing with his pipe. "Look at how the rain strikes the surface, though it is already full of water. Imagine that the pond water didn't want the rain. What could it do to stop the rain from coming? Nothing, because it's only natural that the rain is there from time to time. Think of it as the water accepting that rain sometimes makes it overly full, but it's necessary to its existence. Without rain, it would dry up.

"Without your spirit, you would die. The pond is still the pond, though, even after the rain. Your spirit may trouble you at times, but instead of fearing it, you should just accept that and wait for it to pass, because when the moment is over, you're still you."

Fergus watched the fish rising to the surface, their mouths gaping hopefully, beyond the screen of rain. "It's not that easy. If I don't fight it while it's bothering me, I might end up giving into it."

"Discipline."

"What?"

"Discipline yourself. Teach yourself to go to a place that is calm and untroubled when you feel something bad growing within you."

Fergus scratched the back of his head. "I don't know how to do that."

"Meditate. If you practice a little each day, it may help. I have taught Three to do it. You may ask her to guide you."

"Okay, I guess."

"Let me give you this," Kamo said, holding the pipe between his teeth and reaching into his sleeve. He pulled out a black beaded bracelet and held it out to Fergus with both hands.

Fergus blinked at him.

"Please accept it," Kamo said with a nod.

He took the bracelet, holding it in the palm of one hand. It felt warm. "What is it? Is it magical or something?"

"Not really. Think of it as a reminder. When a soul is troubled, the problem can't just be wished away with magic. It takes time and effort. So think of this as a reminder. When you feel frightened of yourself, when you feel yourself losing control, you can look at this and think about this moment. Sometimes, we forget things when we don't have a physical reminder. Let it become that for you."

Fergus slid it onto his left wrist. "Okay. Um, is it really okay?"

Kamo nodded, taking the pipe out of his mouth. "Of course. Come now. I should speak with Chizu.

It will snow tonight, and if you stay much longer, you might get caught out in it."

"It's going to snow?" Fergus replied, blinking. "It's not that cold, though."

"Not yet, but it will be soon. I think this may be our first snowfall."

Fergus stood after Kamo, stepping back into the room. He could hear voices beyond it, happily chattering. Kamo shut the exterior door and walked over to open the interior one. The little priestess, Three, and his son were standing outside in the red hallway.

"Are you done?" Three asked, quickly composing herself.

"I think so. Shall we have tea?" Kamo suggested, ushering the three inside.

Takafumi gave Fergus a knowing smile. Fergus wondered what he knew. He looked away.

"Will you come, Fergus?" Three asked.

He shook his head. "I heard it might snow, and I wanna be there when Terry wakes up."

"Okay. Raja already went back, so be careful on your way."

•　　•　　•

The snow arrived before Three returned from the shrine, leaving Pip very edgy. Most of the crew were offered places at nearby inns and homes, which they gladly took. Pip, however, decided to stay on the ship and wait, just in case Three came back. Fergus stayed at the infirmary with Terry. There wasn't a bed for him; the other bed was taken up by an old man who kept complaining of aches. Fergus thought he might have been faking it just to get the nurse to pay extra attention to him.

He sat in a hard, overly straight chair in the corner, trying to lean back enough that he could fall asleep without falling over. He felt exhausted. His head was heavy, his eyes burned, and yet sleep refused to come. He stifled another yawn and rolled one of the beads between his fingers, thinking about what Kamo had said.

In a way, he felt glad that the Head Priest hadn't offered him a magical cure-all. Perhaps it would have been harder to believe in that. He wasn't sure he believed that he could be both accepting and disciplined enough to tame his fairy-soul either, but it seemed more likely since it seemed hard.

He watched the light catching on the beads and tried to think of the fish bobbing at the top of the pond and the smell of Kamo's smoke and the warmth from the prayer hall at his back. It had been very relaxing. He wasn't sorry Three had talked him into going. He was very sorry that he didn't have a bed, though. He thought of just curling up on the floor.

Outside, snow was drifting past the window in large, puffy flakes. He hadn't seen snow very often. It was pretty cold in New Peiling, but the winters tended to be rainy rather than snowy. When it did snow, it usually was just a thin coating that melted by the end of the day. He wondered if this snow would stick. It was gathering on the glass, forming a thick layer.

"'s cold," Terry muttered, pulling the covers up to his chin without opening his eyes.

Fergus sat up. The front legs of the chair clanked loudly against the floor. "Oops," he muttered. "Let me see if I can get you another blanket."

He returned a moment later with a thicker blanket, though the nurse insisted on following him. She checked Terry for fever and then went to retrieve a vial of medication along with a basin of water. She pointed to the basin and then to Fergus, before dipping the rag in and wringing it out, placing it on Terry's forehead. Fergus nodded and pulled his chair closer to take over as the nurse went to check on the old man.

He hummed quietly as he adjusted the wet cloth and then leaned back, waiting for it to warm up, so that he could put it back in the water and start over again. The front door banged open, and he heard Three call out an apology and stomp the snow from her shoes. A moment later, she appeared, flushed and bright-eyed.

"How is . . .?" she started and then lowered her voice. "How is he?"

"Feverish," Fergus said with a little sigh. "Did you get caught in the snow?"

"Sort of. I grew up around here, though, so I know that trail pretty well."

Fergus nodded and checked the rag, as Three pulled a chair over to sit beside him.

"I heard you wanted to learn how to meditate," she said, looking rather excited.

"Dunno if I can, but I might as well try."

"I'll help you. It's hard at first, but if you keep at it, it'll come."

"So your real name is Chizu."

She blinked, cocking her head. "Oh, yes. It is."

"Why do you go by 'Three'?"

"It's easier for foreigners, and . . . "

"And?"

"And well . . . it was kind of given to me. I thought it was a joke at first, because I didn't really think . . . I don't think I'm that kind of person."

"Say it already."

"Because I can kill a man three different ways."

Fergus stared at her for a prolonged moment before replying, "Oh."

"Yeah," she said, looking down at her lap and tucking her hair behind her ear.

"What are the three ways?"

"Magic, hand-to-hand, or . . . Well, I used to have a weapon, but when we crashed near New Peiling, I lost it."

"How come you didn't get another?"

She shook her head. "The man who made it died not long after I received it, so I couldn't get another just like it."

"So I guess you should be 'Two' now. Should I call you Chizu?"

"Someday, but not today. I don't want to give *him* any clues."

"He's probably pretty far away now. You could visit your family."

"I can't. I already said that, right? It's too tempting." She let out a long sigh.

Fergus replaced the cloth on Terry's brow.

"I'm sorry. It's just sad for me. I have a place I wish I could go, but I just can't. I really, really want to go. I want to take Pip and live there. I know he'd be happy."

"He'd be happy wherever you are."

"It would be peaceful and gentle. It would help him. Living like this is hard on him. It reminds him of what he had to do to escape. Even though he must have hated the man who enslaved him, he isn't the kind of person who likes violence. It's painful for him." She tucked her chin into her throat. Her face was half-hidden behind the fur lining of her hood. She looked very young.

"It's a sad world, I guess," Fergus replied softly.

"I don't want to die far away from my home."

Fergus looked up.

"If my body gives out, I want to be home. I know that doesn't really make sense. For someone like me – someone who hasn't been visited by the spirits – it wouldn't matter that much, but still . . . "

"Please don't say that."

"I'm sorry," she replied, hair falling over her face.

"It's not so great to be 'visited' or whatever anyway."

"I know. I know for you it isn't, but it is in my village. People rarely leave. They're born and die in the same place, and they have children in that place. The spirits of those who have died in our village return to those who have been born. Maintaining that cycle is important to us. It's a way to keep our loved ones close. Even though that wouldn't happen for me, I still want to be there."

"You're not just gonna die, okay?" he replied a little sharply, splashing water onto his knee. "Stop saying it."

She glanced up at him timidly and then nodded.

"So what is this guy's name? You guys tiptoe around it like saying it will summon him or something."

Three laughed weakly. "Maybe we're afraid it will."

"Well, it won't, so what is it?"

She took a deep breath, clearing her throat. "Jun Hyo."

"You said it's magic and a little science holding you together, right? New Peiling's been stable for decades, and that airship has gotten us pretty far all things considered. So don't worry so much. You'll take out this Jun guy, and then you and Pip can go back to your home and live happily ever after. For now, though, I think he's waiting for you on the airship. Seemed pretty anxious."

"Oh," she said. "Oh no, I bet he is." She quickly stood up and put her chair back. She paused by the doorway. "Thank you, Fergus."

He gave her a little nod as he wet the rag once more.

•   •   •

"Fergus? Are you awake?"

Fergus groaned and squinted against the light cutting across the room. His neck was killing him; his back wasn't far behind. Slowly and painfully, he sat up and tried to stretch the kink out of his neck. He'd fallen asleep with the chair against the wall about an hour after Terry's fever had broken. He ached all over. His eyes stung, too. He rubbed his hands over his face.

"What time is it?" he mumbled, extracting himself from the chair to stretch his back.

"I don't know," Terry said softly, sitting up on his elbows.

Fergus passed through the light slanting through the snow-caked windowpane and went to lean against the bed. "You look better," he remarked, putting the back of his hand against Terry's forehead. "How do you feel?"

"Tired, but okay," Terry replied. "You don't look half bad yourself."

"Huh?"

"Your eyes are blue again. Plus, all the bruises and cuts are gone. Someone must have patched you up."

Fergus blinked, reaching up to touch his cheek. "Yeah, actually. A priest."

"Seriously?"

He nodded.

"It's good to see them blue again," Terry said softly, dropping his forearm over his eyes.

A burst of cold wind came down the corridor from the front door. A moment later, Pip and Three slid back the door. Pip looked irritated. He was brushing snow from the back of his coat. Three looked delighted.

"Hi, Terry. How are you?" she asked, coming to hover over him.

"How deep is it?" Fergus asked Pip.

"Only about ankle high, but enough for trouble," Pip grumbled.

"So, good news! I talked to the nurse earlier. She thinks Terry is probably okay to leave, as long as he takes it easy. She said she'd give him some medication, but here's the good part! There's a hot spring nearby."

Fergus turned to Three. "Um, okay?"

"Well, it's got medicinal properties. She thought we could all do with a soak, particularly Terry. How about it? It actually isn't that far away. You look like you could stand it, too, Fergus."

Fergus had to admit, his muscles were cramped and sore. Hot water might not be so bad.

"How do you feel, Terry?" she asked.

Terry sat up, rubbing his eyes. "If it isn't far, I think I'll be okay."

"Let's get you bundled up, then!"

•   •   •

Guillory and Raja joined them at the hot spring with news that there weren't enough materials in the town to properly repair the airship, so they would have to return to Ping City to get it flying again. Fergus wasn't really surprised. It was a pretty small village. The hot water made him feel dizzy, and he wound up having to climb out and sit nearby for most of the time, but he did feel a little better.

They left the sulfuric smelling pools for a lunch of barbecued fish, pickled vegetables, and rice, followed by a short snowball fight, and then returned to the airship to set sail for Ping City. Takafumi was standing by the dock when they arrived, dressed in his full priestly regalia. His hair was pulled partially back, held in place by a tall black hat. Three hurried over to him. Pip hung back, his face full of misgiving.

The two began to chat, nodding and grinning enthusiastically before he pulled a parcel out from behind his back, holding it out to her. Three shook her head, but he pressed it into her hands. She clutched it tightly, and Fergus could see her eyes welling with tears. She sounded like she was protesting, but Takafumi just reached out, putting a hand on her shoulder, and shook his head. He dropped his hand and began to saunter down the dock.

He stopped by Fergus, giving a brief bow. For a moment, he looked unsure of himself, but he cleared his throat and said, "If you call water, it comes." He pointed to Fergus's chest. "Water inside." Then he grinned and – giving Pip a little nod – strolled off.

"Weird guy," Fergus muttered.

Pip snorted and stomped off to the ladder.

"Hey, Three, what'd he give you?" Fergus asked, going over to her.

She looked up, quickly wiping at her eyes. "Oh, this? This . . . " She stared down at the bundle. Her hands shook as she unwrapped it to reveal a gleaming blade with writing at the base. "I think he may have stolen it," she said with a choked laugh. "It's a sacred sword from the temple."

"Really?"

She nodded, gently wrapping it back up. "He said I could return it when I came back. He said . . . "

"What?"

"He said he wanted to grant my wish. We were childhood friends . . ." She trailed off, sniffing back tears. "Just give me a few, would you? I'll be right behind you."

Fergus nodded and went to board the airship.

"She gonna be okay?" Terry asked as he climbed onto the deck.

Fergus turned to look down at Three, who was clutching the sword to her chest, staring in the direction Takafumi had departed.

"Yeah," he said, "I think she's just touched. Come on, you gotta get back in bed."

Chapter Thirteen.

There was no snow on the ground in Ping City, but the wind whistling through the narrow streets was sharper than anything Fergus had experienced in New Peiling. Perhaps it was because the city was open to the sky. Shivering, he returned to his bunk to fetch his winter coat before heading down to the docks. Pulling his muffler a little tighter and his hat down over his ears, he waited for Terry to finish climbing down. Despite the cold, the harbor was bustling. He watched the sailors and merchants behind the veil of his breath.

"Fergus!"

He turned to see Declan strolling down the boardwalk towards them in an expensive-looking wool jacket. He took a deep breath, forcing himself not to grimace.

"And Terry! So good to see you both. I'm glad you returned in one piece," Declan said, stopping before them. His smile lingered on Terry a moment too long. "And Darya is here, too. Just arrived. She was hoping you might turn up soon."

"How did you know we were here?" Fergus asked, failing to hide the suspicion in his voice.

"Well, I do have my sources," Declan said with a chuckle. "Sounds like you caused quite the ruckus back in White Rock. Come, it's freezing. Let's get inside and have a drink. I want to hear all about it."

He put an arm around Fergus's and Terry's shoulders. Fergus's heart gave a violent jerk in his chest. He bit back his anger.

"This time, you simply have to stay with me, all right? I have a grand party planned for the evening. Oh, don't worry, Fergus. No hijinks tonight! Just good food and drink with friends."

"Aren't we underdressed?" Terry asked.

"Oh, not at all. This is not about couture, Terry. Just relaxation."

"I thought Darya rarely traveled this far," he replied.

Declan's smile faltered just a little. "She has taken quite an interest in you. Though I surely wouldn't pressure you, I think you two would make quite the couple."

Fergus pressed his lips together, feeling hot under the skin. He didn't know why he felt angry about it, but his heart was hammering faster than ever, his ears buzzing. He forced himself to take a long breath and count back from ten.

"She is very charming," Terry agreed. "I'll be happy to see her again, though I hope she didn't put herself out for my sake."

Declan laughed, loosening his hold just enough that Fergus could escape from under his arm. He put a few feet between them.

As politely as he could muster, Fergus asked, "Will there be room for us if you've got a big party going on?"

"Of course! You see, it's the Winter Solstice, so we'll be carousing for a few days. As I said, I hoped you'd be back in time, so I was saving a room," said Declan, smiling fondly at Fergus.

Fergus looked away.

"Ah, here we are," he proclaimed as they stopped before the high-rise. "Oh, forgive me. Do you need to run any errands? "

"No, I'm good," Terry replied.

Fergus shrugged and muttered, "Yeah."

"Perfect!" Declan said, clapping his hands. "You may have a hot shower if you like. It will be a little while before the others show."

•   •   •

The party was much more lavish than Declan had described. There were a dozen people putting together decorations when they arrived, and by the time he and Terry came out to join the festivities, the entire place was unrecognizable. The dark blue curtains were pulled shut, obscuring all the windows, and the lights were off, leaving it to a legion of white lanterns to illuminate the way. Above them, someone had draped red cloth over the ceiling.

There were white flowers with curling petals in vases on tables covered by matching red satin cloths. Beside the floral arrangements stood brass incense trays shaped like elephants spewing out Fairy Dust and platters of food. Fergus swallowed, his mouth watering.

Terry was surprisingly quiet. Fergus thought he was on the look out for Darya. He kept adjusting his tie, which only made Fergus wonder if he should have worn one, too. They were better prepared this time, but they still looked like wait staff compared to the other guests, who were outfitted in expensive brocades, rich silks and velvets, and twinkling with rings and necklaces. He rolled his shirtsleeves up to his elbows.

At least, he thought, if he couldn't fit in with this assembly of the wealthy and fashionable, he might as well be comfortable. Terry straightened, releasing his tie, and Fergus looked over his shoulder to see Darya approaching.

Her dress was form-fitting this time, which seemed strange after the lavish, full-skirted dresses she'd worn in Sovnik. It was a light gold, which made her skin look very warm and her hazel eyes very green. Just as before, she was incredibly striking, turning heads all the way across the room as she came over. Fergus, too, was not immune, though he wished that Terry didn't look quite so happy to see her. He snorted softly and edged closer to the table.

"Darya," Terry said. She held out a hand, which he clasped.

"I'm pleased to see you again."

"You came a long way."

Fergus rolled his eyes and turned his back on them entirely, surveying the appetizers before picking up a cracker with something that looked like fish and cream on it. He thought Ursula might like it. He thought Ursula would have liked this party in general. Plus, she would have been much prettier than Darya. It was ridiculous to make such a comparison, and he knew it, but he still felt a little better having thought it.

"Is that Fergus?"

He turned, cracker in his mouth, and swallowed awkwardly. "Hi."

"It's lovely to see you, as well," she said, smiling graciously and brushing a dark curl of hair over her shoulder.

"Yeah, it's good to see you, too," he said, wishing she would stop staring at him with that dissecting gaze.

"You two must be parched," she said, shaking her head as though this was some great travesty. She turned, exposing the long line of her neck, as she looked around for a servant.

"I see you're missing a glass, too," Terry pointed out, gazing at her throat intently.

"Oh, I am, though I just finished one. I don't want to make a fool of myself."

"Nonsense. It's a party," Terry said, putting an arm around her shoulder. She smiled, leaning into him. "Do you want a drink, Fergus?"

"That's okay. I'll get one later."

He watched them saunter away, telling himself that they were not a cute couple at all and feeling great misgivings for how cozy they looked. He turned back to the crackers, picking one up and grumpily stuffing it into his mouth.

"Stupid," he grumbled.

Someone tapped him on the shoulder. "Excuse me . . . "

Fergus turned. Two young women stood before him. One had curly brown hair, cropped short, and green eyes; the other, who might have been from Ping City, had long black hair pulled up in an elaborate coiffure and large brown eyes. They were both very pretty with dark, full lashes and cherry lips. They also were both wearing low cut dresses, which he found distracting.

He cleared his throat, peeling his eyes away, and rubbed the crumbs from the side of his mouth.

"Sorry, can I help you?" he asked.

"We were just wondering where you were from," said the brunette.

"Oh, um, New Peiling," Fergus said. His mouth felt dry, and the words came out thick. He glanced around for anyone carrying drinks.

"Are you thirsty? Here, you can have the rest of mine," said the black-haired girl, pushing a flute into his hand.

"Thanks a lot," he said, taking a drink. "So, where are you from?"

"I'm originally from Sovnik. I work with Declan," said the brunette. "You can call me Nat."

"I'm Lucy. I'm from around here, but my parents are diplomats, so I've done some traveling."

"Nice to meet you. Fergus."

"What's someone from New Peiling doing so far east?" asked Lucy, cocking her head.

Fergus's mouth twitched. He tried to hide it by taking another drink and cast around for Terry, as though seeing him would give him ideas for an excuse, but he was out of sight. He lightly cleared his throat. "Well, we were sent to do an errand for the Count Palatine."

The two women looked at each other, brows rising.

"You know the Count?" asked Nat.

"I've worked for him before," Fergus replied, finishing the flute.

A waiter appeared with a tray full of glasses. Fergus switched out gratefully. Nat and Lucy, too, took fresh drinks. He noticed that both held their glasses very close to their chests.

"So what do you think of Ping City?" asked Lucy, stepping a little closer.

"It's nice. You can see the sky, so that's a lot better than New Peiling."

Normally, it took a few glasses for Fergus to start to feel tipsy, but he noticed, as he sipped his second glass of champagne, that he was already feeling warm and tingly in his fingers and chest, and that his head was distinctly fuzzy. He wondered if Declan had done something with the champagne, or if it was just the Fairy Dust.

"I've only been to New Peiling a couple of times," Nat replied from behind the rim of her glass. Her cheeks were flushed and her eyes bright. They were the wrong shade of green, he thought. Ursula's were much prettier. "At least it's a bigger city than Sovnik and more fashionable than Ping City."

"I'm sorry, you two," Lucy broke in, "but these boots are killing me. Do you mind if we take a seat?"

Fergus blinked. "Yeah, sure thing."

"This way," she said, smiling and putting a hand on his arm.

She directed them away from the sitting room into a little alcove with several brocaded sofas and an antique table. Like the main room, it was dark and adorned in red, lit by paper lanterns. There were a couple of groups congregating in the corners, though no one was seated. Lucy took him straight to the sofa and sat down, pulling him down beside her. Nat took a seat on the other side. They both leaned very close to him. He took a healthy swig of champagne.

"So what do you think of the fashions here? Are they up to date? We can hardly tell. We get so little news from the West," Lucy said, touching his shoulder.

"It all looks pretty good to me," he said, shifting nervously.

Nat scooted closer, though she kept her hands in her lap. She smiled at him reassuringly. "You'll have to excuse Lucy. It's just rare to see a handsome foreigner in the crowd. Well, aside from Declan."

"Nat, you're making him blush!"

Nat laughed, one finger lingering by her lower lip. "Is that so bad? Besides, I don't want you to keep him all to yourself."

Lucy smiled. "We really don't see many new faces at these things."

"Yeah, I guess it is kind of a long trip," Fergus said into his glass.

"It is. I can hardly believe Darya did it, but you know, she really does miss her brother," said Nat, shaking her head, her curls bobbing merrily.

"It seems like it," Fergus agreed, trying to will himself to relax.

"They're so close. I'm really jealous. I have a brother, but he's so loud and crass. I'd give anything to have one like Declan," Lucy sighed.

"Do you have any siblings, Fergus?"

"No, only child."

"What about your parents?"

"They both died years ago."

"Oh, how terrible," Lucy said, leaning even closer.

He felt the curve of her breast against his arm. He wished he'd worn jeans. "It's not so bad," he replied, holding his drink in his lap.

"So you work for the Count?" Nat asked.

"Kind of."

"Kind of? Is there something else you do?"

"Well, sort of. I was in a band," he admitted.

"A band!" Lucy cried from his other side. "Really? What sort?"

"Just rock. It was with my friend Terry. He's also here."

"Oh, was he the one with Darya?"

Fergus nodded, feeling that unpleasant tightness in his chest again.

"Declan is also quite fond of him. He said they got along swimmingly last time you were here."

"That was only like a week ago," Fergus muttered.

"You two must be very close, coming all this way together and having been in that band."

He shrugged.

"Will you sing something for us?" Nat asked, gazing at him from under her lashes.

Fergus looked around. "Um, maybe not. I don't think anyone else would like that much."

"Oh, please do!" Lucy implored.

Fergus laughed uneasily. "I think I need a couple more drinks before I . . . "

"Let me get you a new one," Nat said, plucking the nearly finished flute out of his hand. "I'll just be a minute. Don't make any music without me." As she headed towards the main room, Fergus noticed she had very long legs

"Well, now I have you to myself," Lucy said, smiling up at him.

He had to admit, it really wasn't a bad view, and it had been a pretty long time since he'd had an opportunity to be with a woman. These were Declan's friends, though. Maybe they were just tipsy and excited by a new face, or maybe they had an ulterior motive. He couldn't be sure. But Lucy decided for him.

As she crossed her legs, one happened to slip over his knee. He stared at it for a moment before looking back at her. She looked up at him expectantly, her chin resting on his shoulder. He licked his lips and put his hand on her knee.

"So what do you do?" he asked, his voice sounding pinched even to him.

"Oh, nothing really. Just waiting for my parents to marry me to the right name."

"Really? And you're okay with that?"

"Not at all. That's why I'm here, you see. It's important to our family that I marry well, but that doesn't mean I have to stay locked up until then, or rather, I refuse to stay hidden away."

He nodded, noticing that his head felt heavy.

"What about you, Fergus? Anyone important in your life?"

"Not right now," he replied.

She smiled, her eyes crinkling just a little. Her knee shifted further, pushing his hand up her thigh.

"I'll admit, I'm not sorry to hear that."

He let out a little breath. His heart was beating fast again. "I'm not either," he replied thickly.

"You seem a little tense, though," she said, leaning forward to put her glass on the table. When she leaned back, her hand went to his leg, her thumb running circles inside his thigh. "How can I help you relax?"

His breath hitched. "I'm not sure."

Her teeth grazed the corner of his jaw. "You aren't?"

He turned, and she moved in, pressing her mouth to his roughly. He let out a little sigh, softening his shoulders, and reached up to cup her cheek.

"You two! Didn't I say I'd only be a minute!"

Fergus jumped back, breaking the kiss.

Nat laughed, sitting down, and pushed a drink into his hand. "Don't go getting distracted yet. We can have fun after you sing for us. Right, Lucy?"

Lucy gave a little snort, but didn't extract herself. "I suppose I have the time."

"A toast – to music," Nat said, holding up her glass.

Lucy and Fergus clinked theirs against it and each took a drink. Fergus took a rather long one, nearly finishing the flute. He normally wasn't embarrassed to sing in front of people, but he felt wary about attracting attention here. He lowered the flute, feeling pleasantly disjointed.

"I don't wanna sing alone, so one of you has to sing with me, okay?" he slurred.

"Oh, count me out," Lucy said, shaking her head. "I couldn't carry a tune to save my life."

"Well, I suppose I can help," Nat said, running her hand up his thigh.

Fergus did his best to ignore that. "Tell me a song you know, and we'll sing."

• • •

They sang several songs, and by the time they stopped, his shirt stuck to him uncomfortably, his hands weren't moving with anything like coordination, and both girls were practically on top of him. He rather liked that, though, and he wished that the people lingering in the room would hurry up and leave. Lucy and Nat seemed less concerned about their potential audience, one kissing just below his ear, and the other skirting his jawline. He couldn't move to kiss either back, nor touch them, which was very frustrating and awkward. More than that, it made him feel powerless.

"This is boring," Lucy suddenly said, turning his head towards her to kiss him on the mouth. "Let's go back to my room."

He nodded a little too eagerly, and Nat laughed, sliding off of him and dragging at his arm. Lucy followed suit, wrapping her arms around his waist. They left the room for a darkened hallway. Smears of black and red filled his vision, as laughter and the smell of sweat filled his ears and nose.

They could have led him to the kitchen or to the docks or even to New Peiling for all he could tell. The world around him was very blurry, and his head was spinning. He kept tripping over his own feet. Nat pushed open a door, and the three stumbled into the room. She let go of him to shut it, and Lucy pushed him to the bed. He couldn't control his body enough to sit down properly, and so found himself falling onto it.

Lucy climbed up on top of him, leaning over him. He felt the bed compress, and then Nat was beside her. Their bodies were warm and soft. They smelled rich, like the flowers on the tables, with the lingering scent of Fairy Dust in their hair. Their skin looked very white in the darkness . . .

And that was the last thing he recalled.

•   •   •

He stood at the edge of a vast, black lake surrounded by a field. Overhead, the sky bore down, threatening to swallow the Earth. The grass all around was dead and brittle. It made a thin hissing sound as the wind rustled through it. Something bobbed just above the water in the center of the lake. It was slowly coming closer. Somehow, he felt he needed to go to it. Slipping out of his shoes, he stepped into the shallows.

The dark thing grew nearer, rising out of the water. It was black and spindly and coated with weeds. White eyes flashed. Fergus continued until he stood before the kelpie. It looked down at him, water dripping from its muzzle.

For a long time, they stood, silently regarding each other. Then it drew back its lips, revealing sharp teeth and gums stained with old blood. Its breath left clouds of steam on the air, mingling with his own. Fergus reached out to put a hand on its forehead, but his fingers slipped through, and he fell forward into the water. He pushed himself up with his hands. His hair stuck to his face. He gave it a shake, trying to clear his vision.

The kelpie was nowhere to be seen, and he felt a sudden, terrible sense of loss.

"Where are you?" he called.

His voice echoed over the empty field and lake. The stars seemed very distant and cold, and the world very barren. His chest ached.

"Come back," he said more softly.

His arms and legs sank into the cold, soggy bottom of the lake. The muck covered his hands and then rose up to his wrists, and before he knew it, he had sunken down to his elbows and hips. He panicked, trying to pull himself free, but the mud had the consistency of tar, and though he tried to pull one hand free, he couldn't shake it off. He lost his balance, catching himself on his elbow. Water filled his right ear as he struggled to stay above the surface.

Down, down, down he sank. The cold water lapped at his cheek and stung his eye.

"Help!"

Black ears surfaced, followed by a white eye.

"Help," he cried again.

He was sure he didn't hear the words. He felt them from somewhere in his bones and arteries and knitted layers of flesh.

"We will go together. We are one, you and I."

The mud sucked him under. Water went up his nose, and he screamed.

"Keep him quiet."

People were moving around him. At least he thought they were people. It was hard to tell, because his vision was terribly off. They seemed more like black shapes, twitching and melting in and out of view.

"How were we supposed to know he'd scream?"

"If you rouse Terry, it won't be pretty."

"But Darya is taking care of him, isn't she?"

Fergus felt bile in the back of his throat. He swallowed; it burned as it went down. His heart was beating erratically, and he couldn't seem to breathe properly. More alarming still, he could barely move. He managed to curl his fingers, but the effort was exhausting. He opened his mouth, but only incoherent sound came out. The floor felt like it was melting underneath him. He fought back waves of vertigo and nausea as his fingers skittered along the boards, searching for something solid.

"Is everything ready?"

"This Hunt wasn't nearly as challenging as I'd hoped it would be."

"It's kind of a pity, though, don't you think? He's not bad to look at."

"Are you finished?"

Someone began chanting. It sounded like Declan.

He opened his eyes, trying to sit up. Disconnected hands pushed him down by the shoulders. The ground around him began to glow, illuminating faces. There were at least six people assembled, looming over him. Their eyes looked like black holes in their faces. He screamed again, but someone shoved a hand into his mouth, cutting it off. He bit down. A roar filled his ears, like a gale wind ripping through the room, and someone struck him. His ears rang, and he tasted blood.

Declan leaned over him. His skin seemed to be dripping from his bones. Fergus started to scream again, but was silenced as fabric was shoved into his mouth. He tried to spit it out, but to no avail. Something glistened in Declan's hand. Fergus struggled, trying to drag himself away, but there were hands all over him. He hiccupped, feeling like he might vomit or asphyxiate or both at any moment. White sparks filled his vision, and he stopped struggling long enough to let them pass.

A stinging sensation ran down his throat, then another two over his chest, and then over his hips. Declan straddled him. Words rolled out of his mouth, unfamiliar and garbled. Fergus tried to buck him off, but the hands grew tighter on him.

Don't touch me, he wanted to shout, but all he could make was a muffled moan.

Declan's finger pressed against his Adam's apple and then slid down. The skin burned and bubbled where he touched. Fergus renewed his efforts and managed to wrench one hand free long enough to cuff Declan in the temple. He saw Declan sway and then shake his head.

"Lucy, switch with Lau!"

Figures moved, swayed, shifted, convalesced, and reformed. His right arm was wrenched back, and he let out a grunt of pain. Declan resumed his trail. He was drawing something, and the lines led to Fergus's heart. He had a very bad feeling about what was going to happen if he allowed this to continue. Despite the painful angle of his arm, he tried rolling and twisting.

"Faustine!" Declan barked.

She leaned over him, her blond hair forming a curtain around his face. He saw her fingers shift and change into long, grotesque claws. He jerked his head away.

"Shh, little boy. It will be okay," she murmured, scraping a finger along his cheek and then leaning down to lick it. He felt the strength go out of him instantly. His head lolled to the side, and he groaned, aching for her to touch him again.

"Not too much, or you'll interfere with the ceremony," said Declan from beyond the veil of her shining, golden hair.

Fergus let his eyes fall shut. He felt very warm and comfortable. At the same time, he was aware of a terrible, wrenching pain in his chest. He just couldn't seem to care about that. His body grew heavier and heavier. His eyes seemed sealed shut, and even the thought of opening them was agonizing. Faustine's hand was warm and smooth, gently stroking the side of his face. He still couldn't breathe properly, but that, too, seemed like a distant problem. Something that someone else should worry about. He felt teeth against his collar and cracked open his eyes.

Faustine drew another scratch across his cheek. "Look only at me. You are safe with me." He looked up at her through half-lidded eyes. Her skin seemed to glow. She smiled at him gently.

He was unprepared for the pain that crashed through his comfortable haze. It felt like someone was trying to tear his chest apart. He tried to struggle, but he couldn't even make his fingers twitch. All he could do was scream around the rag stuffed into his mouth until his voice was raw and he was so out of breath that he thought he would pass out. Still, the pain kept increasing, growing to that horrible level he felt the first few times he'd gone from kelpie to human.

It suddenly dawned on him. They were doing the ceremony Terry and Ursula had once warned him about: the ceremony to take another hybrid's powers.

The kelpie's words echoed in his head: *We will go together. We are one, you and I.*

"Stop," he groaned, but the word made no sense, and no one listened. His body shook uncontrollably. Saliva pooled at the back of his throat, choking him. "Terry . . .!"

Something black flew through the air, knocking Faustine away. He heard a fierce growl, and Declan got to his feet, stumbling away. The black beast lunged at him, knocking him down. Fergus heard a shout, and others rushed at the dog. They managed to wrench it away, and Declan retreated to the door, holding his chest while the others grappled with the furious black dog.

Fergus found himself free at last, though his body was unresponsive. He wondered if they had damaged his soul. He wondered if he was going to die now, so close to freedom. He reached into his mind, searching for the dark presence.

Please be there, he willed it.

He felt something uncoil – hungry, powerful, and pleasurable. He latched onto it and his body began to change. The pain seemed very small compared to what he'd just experienced, and this time, he didn't black out. The people around were shouting in alarm, though Terry gave them little time to react. As he felt the shifting and stretching stop, he rolled to his feet.

He felt weak, which was a first. He'd never felt weak in this form, but the world was very unsteady around him, and he was fairly sure that if he even moved an inch, his knees would buckle. He snarled, snapping at the people closest. He managed to catch Lau by the arm and jerked. Lau screamed, and Fergus felt something pop. He tossed him aside and let out an angry bellow.

Declan fled. His panic was infectious, and the others tried to follow. Terry had one man by the shoulder. Another was trying to pull him off, but Terry wouldn't relent. The man glanced at Fergus over his shoulder and paused. Fergus snorted angrily and bared his teeth. The man abandoned his efforts, escaping behind the others. His friend cried after him. Terry released him, jumping up and snapping at him, and the man wasted no time in running. There was a shimmer of air, and Terry reappeared in human form.

"Come on! I left a little something to keep them occupied. Let's get out of here!" he shouted, sprinting for the door.

Fergus didn't think he'd be able to run if he changed back, so he trotted after. He smelled smoke coming from down the hall, but Terry ran right past to the front door and then out into the hallway to a small, hidden alcove.

"We're not gonna be able to make it down. We'll just have to try the roof!" he said, yanking the door open and starting up the stairs.

Outside, the wind was blowing violently, plastering Terry's hair to his forehead. He held up an arm, trying to shield himself from the wind as he slammed the door behind Fergus and searched for something to barricade it with. Fergus wanted to help, but as he took a few faltering steps past the door, his legs finally gave out, and he fell to his side in a heap.

He felt his body turning back, unbidden. He didn't even have the strength to cry out. He just lay there, twitching and helpless as his limbs and torso receded, hooves formed fingers and toes, and eyes returned to the front of his head.

The roof was very cold and rough against his skin, and he realized he'd been stripped down. He didn't want to look at his injuries, and he felt too tired to move, so he just stared at the wall across from him. There were cracks in the concrete. They had grown black with grime. It was funny how many details he noticed in the worn stone. It had been stained dark near the top and bottom, and there were faded areas of blue paint here and there. He could make out at least four different textures in the surface. A black line ran across the center.

He was fairly sure this corroded expanse of concrete was the last thing he would ever see.

He felt Terry's footfalls vibrating as he ran over. They echoed hollowly in his ear. A moment later, Terry pulled him onto his back. His arms felt very warm. Fergus smiled at him, struggling to keep his eyes open.

"Hey, Fergus, come on," Terry said, patting his cheek.

He parted his mouth, wanting to thank Terry, but all he managed was a gurgling cough.

"Don't, okay? Just don't."

Fergus turned his head, leaning his cheek to Terry's chest. He could hear his heart beating quickly but steadily. Once upon a time, he recalled his mother cradling him to her chest like this and singing to him softly. Perhaps he would see her soon. He exhaled, closing his eyes.

"Fergus! *Fergus!*"

Chapter Fourteen.

Terry sat on the edge of the bed – head in his hands, chunks of hair poking through his fingers. Light poured in from the singular cabin window, spilling over his outline and creating an orange-red halo around his head. Loud clangs and shouting emitted from nearby, as the crew worked to finish the last of the repairs in the engine room. Otherwise, the cabin was silent.

Snow fell outside. It was thin and powdery – not even enough to accumulate on the glass. It spiraled slowly, delicately, reaching the window and melting away instantly. A seagull soared past, flapping its wings. It opened its beak, but its cry was muted by the hull.

Fergus shifted. The room seemed very bright and cold and stark. It smelled strongly of alcohol. He wasn't entirely sure where he was, as he blinked against the light. He felt well enough. Nothing in particular hurt, though he felt detached and tired, like he'd overslept on a rainy day. His face was stiff, and he could feel the threat of a headache coming on. He licked his dry, cracked lips and tried to roll onto his side. That was painful, however. He let out a soft, hoarse exhalation.

Terry lifted his head, turning. His face looked shadowed and drawn. He blinked slowly, disbelief in his eyes. Then he sat up and reached out. Fergus saw a dark room with weirdly illuminated hands grabbing at him, trying to silence him, to force him down, to hurt him. He screamed and lashed out.

"Fergus, stop!" Terry said, grabbing him by the shoulders and pinning him to the bed. "It's me. It's Terry. You're safe in the *Returner*. It's okay."

He took sharp, shuddering breaths and stared up at Terry. It took him a moment to register his face – the grey eyes, messy auburn hair, and straight, pale features – but it was most certainly Terry. His eyes looked hollow and bruised and his cheekbones overly pronounced, but it was still Terry. Fergus sighed softly, closing his eyes, and relaxed. Terry released him.

"I didn't mean to surprise you."

Fergus shook his head a little.

"No, I just . . . I should have known," Terry said.

Fergus found he couldn't even open his eyes to look up at Terry. He just gave his head another weak shake.

"Because of what happened, you've been . . . " He trailed off, his voice catching.

Fergus forced an eye open. "Been what?" he whispered.

"I don't know," Terry said, looking away. His shoulders slumped. He clasped his hands in his lap.

"Confusing me," Fergus mumbled.

"Sorry. You've been out of it for several days now. We weren't sure . . . you were gonna make it this time. I wasn't sure." He paused. "It's my fault."

Fergus shut his eye. The light seemed far too bright, and his head was starting to hurt. He thought about asking Terry to shut the curtains, but was struck by a sudden sense of dread, as if darkening the room might wake him from a pleasant dream and send him back into that room with a dozen hands trapping him and white disfigured faces looming over him. He gasped softly and reached up, clutching at the sheets over his chest.

"What is it?" Terry asked, quickly turning to him and putting his hands over Fergus's, trying to pull them away.

For a moment, he couldn't answer. All he could do was focus on breathing and not having a fit at being touched.

"Does something hurt?"

He shook his head, squeezing his eyes shut.

"Let me check."

Fergus relented, and Terry pulled back the cover and began peeling away layers of bandage.

"Looks like they need to be changed anyway," he muttered.

Terry leaned over the side of the bed, rifling around until he came up with a set of scissors and began to cut away the bandages. Fergus lay still, willing away his migraine, and trying not to think about anything at all. He felt the metal brush his skin and jumped despite himself.

"Careful," Terry said softly.

"Thanks," Fergus replied.

"You shouldn't thank me. This is because of me."

Fergus looked up at him through eyes half shut.

"Because I thought they were up to something, but I didn't figure out what it was until too late. I should never have let you come."

"I don't get it."

"Can you sit up? All that talk about the Wild Hunt. At first, I thought it was just a harmless mimicry – a game. When Darya and I went out, we did rough up a human a little, but that was all. She never had any intention of killing anyone. I thought Declan would be the same. I underestimated both of them. I should have realized what was really going on."

"Explain it more simply," Fergus groaned, arms shaking as he held himself up to allow Terry to clean and bandage his wounds.

"The real 'Hunt' was never about playing with humans. I realized something might be wrong after you got sick from eating at Darya's. I figured that she had probably poisoned you. I don't know if she had intended to do so from the start, but she gave us liver. If you and your fairy-soul were too disparate, it wouldn't have bothered you at all, but you were sick nearly immediately.

"I was too selfish. When we met Declan, I just wanted to relax, and you were up in arms. I wanted you to agree with me – to agree that humans should pay for everything they've done. I wanted to punish them, but that's not what it was really about. Not for them." He lapsed into silence, avoiding Fergus's eyes.

Fergus allowed the quiet to stretch for several minutes before asking, "And then?"

"He was so excited about the Wild Hunt thing, but he didn't seem all that interested when we started chasing those guys. I felt like he was waiting for something else, but I didn't think to question what, and what he was really aiming for was you.

"He knew your mother could transform because of the Count, he knew you were close to your fairy-soul from Darya, and he knew that you have a very human sense of right and wrong from meeting you. If you had been more like me, I think he might not have targeted you."

"Go on."

"I'm just guessing, but they probably felt you don't deserve to have as much power as you do. I don't know what they intend to do with that kind of power, but I imagine this isn't the first time they've robbed another hybrid of their powers." He let out a long sigh. "I was a fool. I should have realized they were hunting you."

"How could you have?" Fergus asked, turning his face from the light.

"I don't know."

"Even now, you don't know what they were planning or why, right? The only way to find out would be to ask them directly, so just forget about it. We got out of there, and that's what matters."

Terry nodded mutely. "I shouldn't have left you alone. I suspected they had designs, and I thought if I got close to Darya again, she might give me a hint. We went back to her room, and she tried to drug me. I pretended to drink it. She was getting suspicious, though, when I didn't pass out. I think she wanted me to sleep while the rest . . . But then you started screaming. She put up a fight, but I managed to lock her in the bath."

"What now?"

"We're drifting. The crew is trying to get the airship back in flying order, but no one is sure where to go, since we've been to White Rock and back, and we don't have any leads. Guillory was planning to just return to New Peiling if you had . . . " Terry shook his head.

Fergus snorted.

"So for now, we're repairing the ship and you and avoiding Ping City and its surrounds, and then I guess we'll decide."

Fergus nodded. "Hey, Terry," he started.

"Hmm?"

"Do you think . . . I dunno. Do you think they managed . . .?"

"Managed . . .? Managed what?" Terry asked, leaning over him.

Fergus looked up at him quietly for a moment and then shook his head with a soft sound of dismissal. He wanted to know if his fairy-soul had been injured, or if its powers had been stolen. He wanted to know if he was going to wind up weak and crippled, or mentally unhinged, but he didn't think Terry knew the answer either, and he already looked so pale and haunted.

"Are you okay?" he whispered, shutting his eyes.

"Yeah, of course," Terry said.

"Are you really?"

"Is something wrong?"

"My head just hurts a little," Fergus replied. "What exactly did they do to me?"

Terry sighed, putting his face in his hands again. "It looked like a magic circle, and they were trying to carve or burn something into you. I hadn't seen the ceremony before. I suspect the Count has been involved in one or two, and I've heard of various cases in the slums, but I've never witnessed it firsthand. I think it involves blood. I don't really know the details."

Fergus nodded.

"There were several of them on top of you, so I couldn't tell what they were doing. I just ran in and started attacking. Looks like it's mainly burns and cuts."

"So, not that bad, then?" he asked carefully.

"Since you're awake, it seems not."

"Huh?"

"Well, they haven't damaged your fairy-soul. If they had, you would either be dead, or . . . "

"Or?"

Terry let out another sigh, running his hands through his hair, and straightened. "Probably you would have gone into a coma and never woken up again. I was worried." He turned to Fergus, his cheek highlighted by the beam of light from the window. It made his face look especially white and hollow.

"But you have come to, so I think you'll be okay with some rest. Probably you're still in shock from everything. Luckily, Ursula sent some useful potions with you. I think you'll be up and moving in a few days."

Fergus let out a little sigh of relief. "You know, I thought that might be it, too."

"What?"

Fergus rolled over. His body felt especially stiff where the bandages ran. He could feel an uncomfortable tug on the stitches as his weight shifted. He rolled back onto his back again with a sound of annoyance. "Come closer."

Terry obliged him, climbing into the bed to sit beside him. "Do you want me to close the curtain?"

"No, don't."

"Okay."

"I've had some near misses, you know?" he said softly, putting a hand over his eyes to block out the light.

"Yeah."

"I was thinking I wanted to say thanks. I would've regretted it if I hadn't been able to."

Terry shook his head. "Don't say stuff like that."

"Thank you."

"What are you thanking me for?" Terry asked, voice strained.

"Because if it had been the end, at least you were there. It would have been okay like that."

Terry pressed his eyes to his knees. He was very silent and still, and Fergus wondered if he'd said too much. The door creaked.

"Hey, is he awake?" Three whispered, peeking inside.

Terry uncurled and slid out of the bunk. His back was to Fergus.

"Are you okay?" Three asked, pushing the door open wider and stepping into the room.

"Yeah, fine," Terry said tightly and pushed past her.

Three stared after him, tugging at her hair. Pip slipped into the room from around the corner.

"I probably said too much," Fergus mumbled.

"Fergus!" she cried, hurrying over. "How do you feel?"

"Kinda weird. Really tired."

She crouched down at the edge of the bed, nodding with a comically serious look on her face.

"We were all really worried! At first, you kept struggling and yelling, and then you fell asleep and didn't wake up until now. Well, probably some of it was whatever they drugged you with."

"I didn't hurt anyone, did I?"

"Yes, you hit me," Pip said, looming over Three. He was still short enough that Fergus could see his face from the bed.

"Sorry."

"It's okay," Pip said, shrugging. "I understand. How are the stitches?"

"They seem fine," Fergus said. "Terry just redressed everything."

Pip nodded curtly and went to sit on Raja's bed.

"What happened? How did we get back here?" Fergus asked. He felt exhausted, but his brain was working quickly enough that he knew he wouldn't fall asleep easily.

"Well, that's some story. There have been issues with the airship. Captain Guillory brought on some men to help with repairs, but he thinks they may have sabotaged things instead. I guess they were in league with that Declan guy. You didn't come back that night, which we expected, but Raja said he had a really bad feeling about it. Then a bunch of officers came and said that they were looking for you two. They wanted to arrest you for assault and arson. We let them search the ship, but of course, you weren't there. Pip and I were pretty worried, though."

Pip snorted, but didn't correct her.

"We agreed to go looking for you. We tracked you two to an underground clinic – you know, the kind of place that stitches up criminals and people who don't want to get the law involved. The doctor said we shouldn't move you, but Terry said that if we had managed to find you, Declan couldn't be far behind, so the three of us snuck you onto the ship and departed. That wasn't very easy . . . But we managed!" she quickly amended.

"Anyway, when we started to shove off, the police came back. Luckily, this ship is pretty fast. They only pursued us for about 30 minutes before they gave up and headed back, but we pretty much can't return to Ping City. Captain Guillory and the others are trying to get this thing into flying shape."

"How did we get out of Declan's place?"

"I'm not entirely sure. Terry didn't say, though from what I can guess, you probably escaped over the roofs of the nearby apartments."

Pip nodded from over her shoulder.

"So, how do you feel? Any fever? Headache?"

She reached for him, and Fergus flinched. She stared at him for a moment, hand suspended, and then slowly drew it back. Her brows crinkled, and she looked away.

"Sorry," he mumbled, feeling ashamed.

She shook her head, hair falling over her face. "No, you shouldn't be sorry. They're the ones who did this. *They* should be sorry," she said hotly.

Her tone surprised him. He didn't know what to say.

"Come on, Three. You need to let him rest," Pip said, rising and walking over to put a hand on her shoulder.

She craned her head back to look up at him and nodded. "Okay," she said, very slowly reaching out to put a hand on Fergus's knee. He tried to stay relaxed and even smile. She smiled back, the anger seeping out of her face. "We'll be back later."

•　　•　　•

"For humans, magic is rarely produced without a focus point. This can be any number of things, including a magic circle, charm, wand, crystal, and so on. A human with a hybrid soul has the capacity to use magic using their body as the focus, which is to say without an accessory. Not all hybrids are capable of this. Many find that they do well with one element or particular type of magic and poorly with everything else." Raja looked up from the book. "So that's why it's hard for you to make fire."

He shifted on his stool, turning the page. "There are many theories on how a hybrid might use magic without a focus. This book will explore the more scientific theory behind magic: understanding of the element in nature."

Fergus groaned. "This is giving me such a headache."

"Do you want me to stop?"

"I dunno. Why don't you show me how you make water move again?"

Raja closed the book and put it on his lap. Taking out a sheet of paper, which he'd drawn a circle on, he picked up the glass of water on the floor by the stool and set it on the paper. Closing his eyes for a moment, he pressed his fingers to the edges of the circle, and then he lifted a hand, holding it over the water. Fergus watched as rings formed, and then, slowly, the water began to rise in a thin line, like a small fountain. It brushed Raja's fingers and then fell back into the cup.

"It took me a few years to be at this level," Raja said, taking his hand away from the glass.

Fergus held out his hand. "I'm thirsty."

Raja gave him the water and sat back on the stool. "Truth be told, I'm not that good without a focus."

"Why? Can't you use some kinda element?"

"I'm not really sure."

Fergus swallowed. "What kinda fairy are you?"

"A *ghillie dhu* – a tree spirit. Earth should be my element. Sometimes, I think if I really focus, I can make the dirt under my feet tremble a little, but I'm rarely out in nature, so I don't really know. Maybe with trees or plants, I'd have better luck."

"Were you already . . . uh, well, did you have a fairy-soul when you got to New Peiling?"

Raja shook his head. "I was probably on the cusp of being too old. They usually choose children, after all."

"Why do you think that is?" Fergus asked, continuing to sip.

"Probably because children's psyches are unfinished, so it's easier to insert themselves there than in an adult, who's fully grown mentally and physically."

"Guess that's why the humans are so upset about having hybrids in the city. They don't want their kids to be 'infected.'"

Raja nodded. "I imagine, well, maybe some fairies purposefully visit the children of those who hate hybrids most. It would be a very fairy-like thing to do."

"Yeah, but if they do, they're just dooming that kid to be miserable, too. I'm definitely not gonna do that when I die."

"You probably won't have a choice."

Fergus blew his bangs out of his face. "I still think it's stupid."

"Well, maybe you won't. Maybe you have a nice fairy-soul. It did choose the son of a hybrid, after all."

Fergus wriggled to the edge of the bed, setting the glass down. He felt well enough to walk around a little, but every time he got up to stretch his legs, someone magically appeared to usher him back into bed. He was getting tired of it.

"Can I just walk around for a little while, Raja? I mean, you watch the door and make sure Terry and Three and Guillory stay out."

"Sorry, no can do. I'm not crossing them."

Fergus groaned, pressing his face into his pillow. "It's just cuts and burns," he grumbled.

"That part isn't bad, no," Raja agreed. "It's the magical injuries."

Fergus said nothing.

"Though I think those are probably going to be okay."

"So. Let me get up and stretch."

Raja sighed. "Fine, but I'm not answering to Terry if he comes in."

Fergus sat up, perhaps a little too fast, because spots filled his eyes. However, that didn't stop him as he clumsily spilled out of the bed, stretching his arms over his head. The dots migrated out from the corners, and he swayed. He felt a hand touch his shoulder blade and jerked away, remembering a second too late it was Raja.

"Sorry."

"It's okay," said Raja. "It's only been a few days."

Fergus stared at the floor for a moment before sighing. "I wish I could just forget already."

"Doubt you could ever forget, but it'll get better."

"Think so?"

"Maybe."

"I kinda miss New Peiling."

"Me too. Maybe . . . Maybe we should just head back."

Fergus stared at Raja. "Really?"

He nodded.

"Why?"

Raja looked away. "I know this may sound dumb, but I keep thinking about that seer."

"What did she say to you?"

"She said, 'What was lost soon will be found.' I have a feeling Evelyn is still alive."

"But the Knights . . ."

"I know. I can't explain it, but if it's true . . ."

Fergus nodded.

The ship gave a sudden jerk. Fergus went stumbling straight into Raja, knocking him down. He blinked into Raja's electric blue eyes.

"What the hell?"

"Stay here," Raja commanded, climbing out from under him.

"But . . .!"

Fergus's protest fell on deaf ears. Raja slammed the door behind him. The ship gave another jolt, and Fergus could hear the crew abandoning the engine room to hurry to the deck. He pushed himself to his knees. He just had time to grab the side of his bunk before the ship rolled again. He felt the contents of his lunch at the back of his throat and then a jolt of fear.

They were under attack.

They were too far from White Rock for the organ traders to have caught up – he doubted they would still be chasing the *Returner* anyway – which could only mean one thing. The airship lurched again, sending him sprawling. An explosion echoed from above. He let out a little curse, grappling with the side of his bunk before managing to pull himself into it.

He wondered what he should do. He knew he'd be useless in a fight, but maybe he didn't have a choice. He cast around for something to defend himself with and found a switchblade in Terry's bag. He steadied himself, blade opened, and waited. He could hear footsteps on the stairs. He swallowed, clutching the blade's handle. The door flung open, and Three collapsed to her knees before him.

Fergus dropped the blade, kneeling down in front of her. "What is it?"

She clutched his shoulders, letting out a dry sob. "They took him. They took Pip!"

Chapter Fifteen.

The airship rattled violently. A plume of black smoke stretched out a good mile behind it. Fergus sat with Three on the stairs leading down to the cabins. She said nothing, clutching the bundled sword between her knees and staring into space. There was a nasty bruise on her forehead. Fergus bit his lip and reached out to put an arm around her shoulders. She didn't respond. In his other hand, he clutched a sheet of paper.

I look forward to wrapping up our business, Fergus.

Raja had handed it to him once things settled down. He knew well enough what Declan was playing at, but he didn't trust him to spare Pip if they were delayed. Guillory had just managed to get the engine in working order before setting off in hot pursuit. So far, the other airship was just visible ahead of them, but what with the groans the *Returner* was making, Fergus was worried. He didn't bother reassuring Three. They both were all too aware of what would happen if they were too late.

He heard footsteps at the top of the stairs and turned to see Raja.

"We're gaining on them, but the weather is picking up. Looks like they're flying straight into a snowstorm."

"Can the ship take it?"

"Seems we'll find out. Better brace yourselves."

"Let's go see," Three suggested, rising.

Fergus nodded, following her and Raja up to the deck.

Snow pelted his face, stinging his cheeks. He held his hand before his eyes, squinting. He guessed that Guillory was using a spyglass to follow Declan, because he certainly couldn't see anything other than a wall of grey and bits of white streaking towards him.

"Can we really fly through this?" Fergus shouted.

However, no one heard him over the roar of the engine and the storm. He could hardly hear anyone else for that matter, but there was a lot of shouting all around.

"What's going on?" he yelled.

Raja edged closer, eyes mostly closed, snowflakes catching on his long, dark lashes. "Sounds like we're having trouble! I think we'll have to land!"

"But won't they get ahead of us?"

"I doubt they can fly much further without crashing!"

A crewman rushed past, half-blown by the wind. "What are you doing? Get inside! We're doing an emergency landing!"

"What?"

"Emergency landing! Get inside!"

"I can barely hear anything!" Fergus shouted to Raja.

"He wants us to . . .!"

But before Raja could finish, the airship gave a shudder, sending all three tumbling into the railing. Fergus just managed to grab Three's elbow before she went toppling overboard. Raja rubbed his temple, grimacing.

"This thing is a death trap!" Fergus shouted. "Never taking anything free from the stupid Count again!"

His teeth clacked together as the airship skidded into the ground, and he, Three, and Raja were bounced so violently, they nearly went overboard again. Fergus grunted, clenching his teeth to keep from biting his tongue. The ship, not meant to be on dry land, rolled from side to side. They clung to the rail with all their might until it slowed to a stop, tilting haphazardly to the right.

"Everyone okay?" Guillory called over the loud speaker.

"You guys okay?" Fergus echoed, shakily getting to his feet.

Three nodded, shaking her hair out of her face, and clutched her sword to her chest. Raja groaned, still rubbing the side of his head, and crawled to his feet.

"Now what?" she asked, checking her bundle.

"We'll have to follow on foot," Fergus replied, undoing the rope ladder and unfurling it over the side.

"Is that even possible? Even if they crash, their airship will be so far ahead of us," Three said, voice breaking.

Terry jogged over from the front of the airship. "Everyone all right?"

Fergus gave him a thumbs up.

"Good. We're gonna have to be quick if we wanna catch up. No time for supplies."

Raja gaped at him. "But what if you get stuck out there empty-handed?"

"Wait," Fergus said, "you aren't coming?"

Raja shook his head. "What good would I be in a fight?"

"Then you can follow after us with Orson," Guillory said, emerging from the door. "Just in case we do get stuck out there overnight with no supplies."

"I can do that."

"Are you ready to go?" the Captain asked the others.

"Wait," Terry said, poking Guillory in the chest. "Who says you're coming?"

"How about these?" Guillory said, holding up his coat to reveal the revolvers at his hips.

"He *is* good in a fight," Three said, biting her lower lip.

"He really is," Fergus agreed.

Terry sighed, dropping his hand. "Fine. So how are we going to pursue them?"

"We did a little damage to their ship," Guillory said, pulling a collapsible scope from his pocket. "Their engine is smoking, so if we act fast, we can follow the trail."

"But *how* are we going to act fast?" Terry said, putting a hand on his hip.

Guillory and Three glanced at Fergus and then at each other.

"Well, we were talking . . . " Three started.

"And Fergus can probably run the fastest of any of us."

"Oh yeah?" Terry replied, lifting an eyebrow.

"As a kelpie," Three added. She bit her lip, looking up at Fergus. "If we rode you . . . "

"But . . .! "

"You didn't hurt us at White Rock," Guillory quickly cut in. "This may be the only way. Don't worry. I trust you."

Fergus frowned, glancing at Terry, who shrugged.

"They have a point."

"Okay, let's get a move on," Fergus said, hooking a leg over the railing and climbing down the ladder.

•   •   •

The snow was nearly up to his chest, which made galloping substantially more difficult than planned. He plowed through the drifts at a trot and fell into a canter when he could. Three clung painfully to his mane, and Guillory was holding onto her. He could hear Terry panting several yards behind, running along the trail he'd made. He forged ahead, sending foggy puffs of air through his nose like a steam engine. To either side, all he could see was a few yards of drifts, falling away into a blur of snow and darkness.

He thought he could hear something up ahead. He wasn't sure what it was, though it sounded like roaring and snapping. Wafting in through the wind came the smell of smoke, and he lowered his head against the sleet and snow, putting on an extra burst of speed.

"Fergus, slow down a little! I think Terry's falling behind!" Three shouted, leaning on his neck.

He realized he couldn't hear Terry's panting anymore. He lifted his head, slowing just a little.

"We're very close! I think I see fire up ahead!" Guillory shouted, squeezing his ribs unpleasantly.

Fergus resisted the urge to buck.

"We should proceed with caution," the Captain added.

Fergus slowed from a canter to a trot, lifting his head higher – ears swiveling, nostrils flaring – as he searched for hints of an ambush. The light of the fire grew, cutting through the snowy haze, sending plumes of soot up into the blackness and painting the snow in orange light. The airship had gone to ground, but definitely not on purpose. The hull was cracked, pieces of board scattered across the snow, some still smoking.

He couldn't see into the shadows beyond the snapped boards, but he doubted anyone was inside. A trail led away from the wreckage, disappearing into the blackness. The flames licked higher into the air, as the fire swallowed the fabric of the balloon and skipped down the railing. A dark patch of ground spread out from the wreck. Fergus slowly approached it, Terry falling in at his left shoulder. He snorted, and Terry wagged his tail a little, jogging ahead and sniffing the air.

Fergus halted, watching him go, then tossed his head and stamped his foot. Three and Guillory got the message, sliding from his back into the snow while he concentrated on the memory of orange fish and the ripples of rain on water. They walked ahead as he shifted back to his human form. He tried to follow, but stopped, hands on his thighs and doubled over. He felt acid at the back of his throat and a stitch in his side. He closed his eyes until his head and stomach settled, sucking in the unforgiving winter air.

Looking up, he saw that Three and Guillory had caught up with Terry, who was sniffing the charred debris. He suddenly stopped, tail rising and ears pricked forward. Fergus followed his gaze to a figure silhouetted by the fire. With a last stomach-turning swallow, he walked over to the others. The cloaked figure moved slowly and purposefully from the burning hull of the ship.

Terry growled, hackles rising. The figure stopped a few yards away, regarding the gytrash before turning to the humans. He reached into his cloak with one hand and pulled out an envelope.

"For you, Fergus." It was Lau.

Fergus came forward, stopping just close enough to grab the letter from him. Terry steadily snarled a few feet away. He carefully backed away, not putting his back to the Huntsman, and broke the wax seal with one finger. The light from the fire was enough to illuminate the letter. Three reached out, taking one side, and together they read: *Find the cave. We'll be waiting for you.*

He let Three take it, stepping forward. "What was the point of that?"

Lau laughed unpleasantly from the shadows of his hood. "He likes to stand on ceremony."

"Where is the cave?" asked Guillory.

Fergus turned to him. In the firelight, he looked tall, leonine, and commanding, and Fergus felt reassured.

Lau lifted one hand, pointing at the trail they'd seen before, now partially filled with fresh snow. "Hurry," he cackled.

"C'mon!" Fergus barked, turning on his heel and breaking into a run.

His breath came a lot harder this time, and his side ached. It wasn't difficult for Terry to pass him by and then Three. At least Guillory ran level with him as they hurried along the trail. Up ahead, he could see tree-covered hills rising out of the snowfield. As they drew nearer, it became obvious that they were heading towards a cluster of low mountains. Terry let out a bark, plunging forward with Three as close on his heels as she could manage. Guillory passed him, pulling out a revolver and holding it skyward.

The air burned in Fergus's throat, and his side and diaphragm throbbed. Terry and Three had disappeared into a cluster of pine trees. Fergus slowed to a painful jog, watching Guillory follow.

Just beyond the heavy pines, the footprints led straight to the mouth of a cave. He could see light emitting from its mouth. He couldn't see inside, nor could he hear anything. He was expecting gunfire and growls and shouting, but as he entered the long, narrow tunnel, there was only silence.

Goosebumps rolled down his arms and spine. He bit his lip and edged along the wall, wondering what had happened to his companions. He could see the light growing more intense, and soon there were shadows painted on the wall opposite. Cautiously, he moved away from the wall, slowly shuffling towards a space where the cave seemed to grow wider. There he found Three, Guillory, and Terry. Terry was back in human form, Guillory had his revolver raised, and Three had her sword drawn, but none of them were doing anything. Before them a number of people were assembled, cloaked as Lau had been.

Declan, hood thrown back, stood just beyond them behind a stone altar. He held a massive dagger in both hands, keeping it suspended over Pip's chest. Pip was gagged, but awake. He was making muffled, angry sounds of protest, struggling against his bonds. Darya, the only other Huntsman without a hood, stood by his feet, running her hand up and down his leg with a smirk.

"And here is the man of the hour," Declan gleefully announced.

A few dark chuckles echoed. Guillory glanced back at Fergus. He didn't acknowledge it. Instead, he tried to take count of the people in the room. There were about 10, counting Declan and Darya. They were outnumbered, though he'd had worse odds. Still, he wondered how many of these faceless people were armed and how many could do magic.

"Now, there's no need for violence," Declan said casually, lowering the dagger just a little. "We can establish a fair trade, I think. Fergus, you stay, and the rest of you can take this one and go."

Terry took a step forward, cursing furiously.

"If you'd like, you may imbibe, too, Terry. I still would like for us to be friends."

"Go to Hell!" Terry snarled.

Declan sighed. "I thought we had quite the rapport. We're a lot alike, don't you think?"

Terry said nothing.

Darya moved closer, taking the dagger from Declan and holding it to Pip's throat. He froze.

Declan moved forward, standing before the altar. He held his arms open, shaking his head.

"You know it's true, don't you? This is all we have. Bitter and unfair as it is, this is what we have. So why shouldn't we punish those who have persecuted us? We have the power to do so. We have the power to overrun the humans and take our rightful places as leaders of this world. Wouldn't that be infinitely better than running around after fairy tales?"

"What do you mean?" Fergus asked.

Declan slowly turned to him and smiled. "A little bird told me – you're searching for Tír na nÓg."

Fergus's eyes widened. He glanced at Terry. His brows were furrowed, but he remained silent. Fergus could see him clenching and unclenching one fist as he struggled to keep his face impassive.

"Right on the nail, wasn't I? Yes, I thought that might be good information. There's no such thing. You've already seen what remains of it. That gate won't reopen while any of us are alive. There's no hope. So then, join us, Terry. You don't have to live like an animal anymore. You have the power and talent to take what's rightfully yours."

"No."

"If your conscience is troubling you, then we will soon remove that obstacle," Declan said as he turned to Fergus.

Terry took another step into the room. Darya pressed the dagger to Pip's throat. He let out an alarmed little sound, and Three reached out to grab the back of Terry's coat.

"Why are you doing this?" Fergus asked, not taking his eyes off of Pip, who was looking wildly out of the corner of his eyes towards Three.

"The humans have the upper hand. They rule most of the globe. They have weapons that we would never be allowed to touch," Declan said, nodding at Guillory's revolver. "Whatever our powers may be, we're not immune to iron and steel. We need to cultivate our abilities – to seize power where we can – so that we can rise up against them."

"But what is that gonna solve?" Fergus demanded. "They're just gonna be waiting and building up their strength to do the same thing!"

Declan shook his head. "That sort of weak thinking is why we chose you, Fergus. You fail to see how impossible it would be for them once we are at full strength. We will turn this world into our own Tír na nÓg."

"Then we're no better than the humans!"

Declan laughed. "Oh, but we are. The moment we were chosen, it was decided. The humans corrupted this world with pollution and greed. They caused the Cataclysm. Now they would keep us under their heels, and for what? Doesn't natural selection dictate that the most sophisticated animals will prosper? It's because of weak-minded hybrids like you that we have failed to rise above the inferior humans. Someone like you doesn't deserve that kind of power. We'll make much better use of it. All hybrids will prosper from your death."

"Shut up!" Terry shouted. "I don't give a damn about humans or hybrids. You can all rot as far as I care, but if you think you're gonna lay a hand on Fergus, I'll rip your heart out through your mouth."

"Oh, very scary," Declan cooed.

The hooded figures chuckled.

"Terry," Darya said in a simpering tone, "be reasonable. Think about what we could achieve.

Think about us. You and I – we could do so well together. We could be married, even! You would share in all my fortune and in all our sport. You'd never be unhappy again."

Terry shook his head. "Marry the woman who tried to poison my best friend? Yeah, that makes sense."

She lifted a hand to her mouth, batting her eyes. "I was just having a little fun. I only wanted to have you to myself."

"Shut up."

"But, Terry, surely you must understand," she persisted as Declan returned to her side. "I'm so weary of keeping my head down and hiding my abilities because the humans will panic. I'm so tired of living in darkness. We can find a way to the light. Even if we have to dirty our hands, it's better than letting things go as they are."

"I'm okay with how things are if I've got someone who's not gonna leave my side."

"But I could be that person," Darya persisted, face crumpling. "I really fancy you, Terry. I don't want to fight you. I don't want to see you injured."

Terry scoffed. "Who said *I'd* be injured?" He unbuttoned his coat, letting it fall to the ground behind him, and rolled up his sleeves. "Did 'darling Evan' ever mention who I really am?"

Darya's mouth twitched, but she remained silent.

"I thought so. Seems he wanted to make sure I stayed gone, but someone who has his maid do his dirty work could never become Badb Catha."

Fergus didn't even see what he did, but a violent gale tore through the room, sweeping several of the cloaked figures up and thrusting them into the wall. Terry's hand moved again, and the torches guttered out, the wind whipping to the other side. Fergus could just make out Declan and Darya holding their arms over their heads as another Huntsman was knocked off of his feet and thrown past them.

"Hurry, Three!" Fergus shouted.

She stepped forward, sheathing her sword, and began to make signs in the air. He saw them shimmer to life and fizzle, leaving an afterimage of smoke. Then a rolling stream of fire shot across the room towards the altar. Declan blocked it, sweeping his hand and forming an arc of water in front of himself and Darya. The flames sizzled out, but Three was already running forward, taking out the sword. She swung at the siblings over the altar. Darya blocked it with the dagger, and Fergus saw sparks.

Terry moved forward with the severity of a hangman. With every movement of his hands, fire and wind burst forth, sending opponents flying or throwing themselves onto the ground, rolling around in a desperate bid to smother the flames. For those who managed to get beyond his spells, Terry moved like a dervish, dispatching them easily. He struck one in the chin, and Fergus heard a grotesque crack, which left the man crumpled in a heap.

From Fergus's right, Guillory fired off several rounds, adding to the smoke and noise filling the cave. It was hard to see, but Fergus heard a female voice cry out as the shots echoed. He held his hands to his ears, trying to see somewhere he might help. Many of the Huntsmen's hoods had fallen back. Faustine, Lucy, and Nat shoved past him – screaming, eyes wide with terror – and he noticed Faustine was clutching her shoulder.

For a moment, he wondered what would happen to them, running out into the snow, injured, with no airship to return to, but perhaps they knew of some safe place nearby. They had known about this cave in the first place.

"Fergus, watch yourself!" Guillory shouted.

A shot rang out, lifting the hair from his brow and leaving his ears ringing, and he grunted in pain. He saw the man Terry had bitten in Ping City crumple a few feet away. He shook his head, steadying himself against the side of the cave. Darya and Declan had abandoned the altar, and Three was sawing through Pip's bonds. Declan pulled his sister behind him, pressing her against the cave wall.

There were still three others besides: two long-haired men who could have been twins and a short woman with cropped black hair. The woman was trying to edge away, but the twins were standing in front of Darya and Declan, baring teeth and knives.

Guillory grabbed the girl before she could escape, and Terry descended upon the other two. It seemed like the air around him was crackling. The twins took a step back as he stepped forward. Fergus saw the taller one swallow, saw his throat constrict as his breath caught. His eyes darted to the walls. He let out a little whimper and dropped his knife, trying to make a break for it, but Terry's hand was already in the air, and the man was tossed by a violent wind, striking the ceiling and falling to the ground in a limp pile of black cloth.

His brother made a feral sound and lunged, but Terry deftly sidestepped him. Another horrible crack rang out, and he went down, as well. Terry stepped over him, stopping in front of Declan and Darya. Declan pushed Darya closer to the wall.

"So this is the power of Badb Catha," Declan calmly remarked, but his smile was gone.

Terry didn't reply.

"Fergus," Guillory hissed.

He glanced at the Captain and saw him tie the other woman's hands with the rope cut free from Pip's legs. Three had nearly freed his hands.

"I'm going to leave her here and try to catch the others. Keep an eye on her."

Fergus nodded.

Guillory gave the rope a yank, which caused the girl to let out a soft complaint. He pushed her towards Fergus and turned, reloading, and loped towards the entrance.

"Be careful!" Fergus started to call after him, but he was interrupted as Darya screamed.

He turned to see Declan stagger and fall back against the wall. Blood beaded at his temple, became a drop, and slowly made a path down the side of his face. Terry was standing between him and Darya, whom he had grabbed by the wrist, trying to push her aside. She grappled with him, reaching for her brother. Declan straightened, clutching his side.

"Let her go," he said quietly.

Terry sneered. From Fergus's angle, he could only see the side of his face. The sneer twisted his features, rendering him unfamiliar and frightening. Fergus's heart jolted. Guillory's prisoner made a frightened little mewl, pressing against him. He pushed her away.

"Be still and quiet," he said without looking at her.

He released the girl and cautiously approached the trio just as Darya screamed again, though this time it wasn't in alarm, but pain. Fergus smelled singed flesh. She struggled furiously against Terry's hand, tears streaking down her face.

"Stop! Please stop," she whimpered.

"Stop it!" Declan bellowed and lunged, but Terry knocked him aside with another blast of air. He released Darya, who shied away from him, cradling her wrist to her stomach and making soft, choked noises.

"How touching," Terry said, standing over Declan. "Now imagine if I told you that she was worthless – that her life had no meaning save to harvest her powers." He kicked and struck Declan in the stomach, who grunted and curled up. "Can you imagine it, Declan?"

But Declan did not reply.

Terry crouched down, grabbed him by the front of his robes, and dragged him up to meet his eyes. "You should know, after a man has lost everything, if even one good thing comes along, he'll kill to keep it."

"Terry," Fergus mumbled, taking a step forward.

"Are you going to kill me?" Declan laughed, blood bubbling at the corner of his mouth.

"Yes, I am," Terry replied simply, releasing him. He slowly stood. "I will crush you like the vermin you are." He lifted his foot.

Declan laughed even harder, but didn't move to defend himself.

"No!" Fergus shouted, sprinting forward. He caught Terry around the midriff. "No, don't do it!"

Terry grabbed at him, trying to pry his arms free. "Let go, Fergus. This has to be done!"

"No, don't! We'll find another way!" Fergus cried, only holding tighter, his face pressed to Terry's back. Terry twisted and gave his arm a punch, but Fergus would not relent.

"Damnit, Fergus, let go, or I'll . . . "

Darya shrieked. Fergus turned to see her spring into action. She was a blur of black hair and olive skin and white-rimmed hazel eyes. Her lips were drawn back in a fierce snarl. In her burned and blistered hands was the ceremonial dagger.

"Fergus, move!"

He was thrown backward, skidding across the cave floor. He blinked, vision blurring for a moment, and gasped. Pushing himself up on one elbow, he saw Terry holding Darya's dagger hand in one of his own. A line of blood trickled down the side of his face. His other hand clutched his eye. Fergus's heart sank.

"Declan, run!" Darya shouted, still struggling, though this time with greater success, as Terry stumbled, blood peeking out from under his palm.

Fergus staggered to his feet at the same time Declan did, but Declan did not run. He threw himself at Terry, yanking at the arm that was holding Darya's. Terry was off his guard. The two of them proved to be too much, and Darya shook herself free.

"No!" Fergus shouted.

He shoved Declan away, and Terry fell backwards by luck alone, barely avoiding Darya's uncoordinated flurry of stabs and slashes. Fergus caught him as they hit the ground, and Terry groaned softly, pressing his face to Fergus's neck. Darya loomed over them, her hair sticking out, cheeks red, lips still drawn back, and a maddened gleam in her eyes.

She smiled and raised the dagger, but was interrupted by a sound so loud Fergus couldn't even parse it. It shook the cave, causing pebbles and silt to break free from the ceiling and cascade down. A blinding light filled the cavern and another boom sounded, shaking more debris loose. Not knowing what was going on and unable to move quickly, Fergus threw himself over Terry, clutching him to his chest. Bits of rock pelted his shoulders and neck. Darya dropped the dagger, covering her eyes, and backed towards the wall.

Squinting, Fergus searched for the source of the light and sound. He could just make out Three and Pip standing on the altar. Shimmering in the air over Pip's head was a strange and terrible creature. It looked like a half-formed wolf, growing out of thin air. It was white with blue markings and flashing eyes. Silvery spittle dripped from its semi-transparent jaws, disappearing into the air.

He couldn't see Pip's face, because he was partially hunched over, shoulders heaving, and he was laughing in a very eerie way.

"What is it?" Terry mumbled.

"Pip," he answered quietly, unsure what might happen now.

He couldn't tell if Pip was able to distinguish friend from foe as the ghostly wolf edged closer, looking down at them. Its lips were drawn back in a grotesque grin over impossibly sharp teeth. He could hear Three's soft, insistent pleading. He saw her trying to shake Pip's shoulders as the wolf became more corporeal, alighting on the cave floor. It was at least as tall as Fergus in his kelpie form, if not taller. Behind him, Declan and Darya clutched each other, pressing against the wall.

"Stop it, Pip! Stop, it's over now! They're going to be punished, but not like this," Three said, her voice rising. "Not a second time, okay? Everything is going to be all right now!"

Pip stopped the horrible, cracked laughter, though he remained hunched, and the wolf spirit slowly drew nearer – head low, tail high – snarling and cutting off any chance of escape. Fergus clutched Terry a little tighter. His heart was jumping around in his throat as the wolf closed in on them. Its breath was so cold, it burned his skin. He closed his eyes, ducking his head. He was pretty sure that even doing so, he wouldn't be able to save Terry, but he nonetheless did his best to shield him.

"Declan?" he heard Darya ask tremulously. He didn't catch the reply.

"Pip!" Three screamed. Her voice echoed in the cavernous room, repeating once, twice, three times, and fading softly into a still and pregnant silence.

Fergus held his breath, counting heartbeats, wondering which might be the last. Terry was motionless and quiet against him, though his fingers were tight in Fergus's jacket. The wolf stood over them, leaning down to sniff Fergus's head. His scalp stung with the cold, but he remained perfectly still. It pressed its nose to his neck, and he felt his skin blister. However, it did not bite down on him, but stepped over him and Terry, approaching Declan and Darya.

"Pip," Three said very softly.

"Stop," Pip said.

Fergus risked looking up. Slowly, with Three's help, Pip slid off the altar, coming to stand by the wolf over Terry and Fergus. He put a hand in its fur, unconcerned with the cold it radiated. The wolf turned to look at him.

"We'll let them go for now," Pip mumbled, pressing his face into the wolf's fur. "This time."

The wolf began to loose opacity. Fergus watched it shimmer and fade into thin air.

He let out a sigh. Declan moved away from the wall, but before he could reach the dagger, Three leapt from the altar, trotting over, sword raised.

"No you don't," she said, giving the sword a little slash. Fire flickered in its wake. He could see blue flames curling around the edge. "You're coming with us, if you don't want to die right here."

Declan turned to Darya. "Well?"

She stared up at him for a long moment and then shook her head.

"Put your hands where we can see them," Three said, once again brandishing the sword.

Slowly, the siblings stepped apart, holding up their hands.

"We surrender," said Declan, shrugging.

"Got them all caught up, did you?" Guillory said, panting as he emerged from the tunnel. "Where's the other girl?" he asked, looking around. Fergus realized their third hostage was nowhere to be seen.

"Sorry," he mumbled.

"Well, I couldn't catch the others, either. I have no idea where they've gone, but they didn't return to the airship, and that other man wasn't around either. They're probably long gone. At least you caught these two." Guillory strode over to them. "The ringleaders, aren't you?"

Declan's mouth curved.

Fergus sat up a little. Terry was breathing roughly into his shoulder, hand still plastered to his eye, though now his cheek was coated in blood.

"That looks bad," Guillory noted.

"He'll go into shock," Pip muttered.

"There's a small village on the other side of this mountain," Declan said.

Fergus looked up, eyes narrowing. "Why are you telling us this?"

"I suppose because we've lost. What could it hurt now?" he replied with a shrug.

"You're planning something."

"Well, you won't know unless you give us a chance. He'll die of shock if you don't, though."

Fergus bit his lip, looking down at Terry, who seemed to only be conscious enough to keep grasping his eye.

"Pip, grab those ropes. You two, face the wall," Guillory ordered. "Looks like we'll have to take your word for it, so show us the way to this village."

Chapter Sixteen.

A fire crackled merrily in the hearth, casting shadows over the patches of quilt on Fergus's knees. One had children playing in a swing, another the word "home," and another, on his right knee, had two people hugging. He pressed the thread, feeling it pucker under the pad of his thumb, and watched his nail go white. A log snapped, and the kindling crumpled in the grate.

"Better stir those up," said the old lady, appearing from behind his shoulder.

She went to kneel before the fire, taking out a poker and trying to rearrange the logs once more. Then she brushed her hands together and wiped the soot on her apron. "Do you want another drink?" she asked, coming over to take the empty mug from Fergus's lap. "Or are you hungry yet? We still have warm stew and bread."

He shook his head mutely, hair falling into his face. She put a gnarled hand on his shoulder. There was no strength to her squeeze. She released him, hobbling away.

Terry was in the adjacent room with the local doctor, who'd been roused from his bed to come and have a look. The doctor had only kept Pip with him, sending the rest out. Guillory recruited Three into helping guard Declan and Darya at the local jail: none of them felt it was secure enough to hold the siblings if they really were determined to break free, though no one had yet broached the subject of just what exactly they were going to do with the Abels.

At the moment, Fergus didn't care. All he cared about was the muffled speech coming from the other side of the wall. He felt like an idiot. While he would have liked to say he'd known for a long time, it was only now that he couldn't produce a single doubt about Terry's feelings. Probably, Terry had felt that way all along, but Fergus had been so caught up in whether he was lying, or if he preferred Declan or Raja, that he'd refused to notice.

He ran his hands over his face and through his hair. His eyes burned from exhaustion. He felt woozy, but he was determined to stay up until the doctor had finished. In his way, even with the lies and the doubts and the tension, Terry had always been very earnest. Fergus had to at least apologize for ignoring that. Dropping his hands into his lap, he craned his head back, staring up at the cracked plaster ceiling.

The door opened and the doctor emerged, rubbing one eye behind his spectacles. He blinked owlishly at Fergus before realizing why he was there. He did not smile, and Fergus felt his heart skip a beat.

"What is it?" he asked, pushing out of the chair. The quilt fell in a pile at his feet.

"He's alive, and he'll be fine with rest, but . . . "

"But?" Fergus asked, stepping free of the blanket.

"But we couldn't save his eye. I'm sorry."

Fergus stared at him for a long moment, mouth parted, but he couldn't find the words. He couldn't seem to breathe. He stumbled and then fell into a crouch, one hand gripping his hair, as he stared into space.

"I'm sorry," the doctor sighed. "It's a pity, but at least his life has been spared. Try to get some rest, son."

Fergus wasn't sure if he even nodded. He just kept staring at the same knot in the hardwood floor. It even looked like an eye. He took a shuddering breath and heard footsteps. Pip stepped out, quietly shutting the door. He could feel the boy standing over him, but he didn't move.

"He'll live," Pip said.

"I should have just let him kill them," he mumbled.

"Self-recriminations get you nowhere."

Fergus shook his head, letting his hair shield his eyes. He could see the toes of Pip's scuffed up boots.

"Besides, it is . . . it is terrible to live with that."

Slowly, he raised his head. "To live with what?"

Pip looked away, rubbing at his eyes. "To live with the knowledge that you are a monster."

"But you're not . . . "

"When I killed the man who called himself my master, it was as a monster," Pip said, cutting him off.

Fergus closed his mouth.

"It was the only option, but it is a heavy thing to recall that I killed him in such a way."

"Are you boys still awake?" the old woman called from the doorway. "Come and have some soup and get to bed. You'll die of pneumonia if you get sick out here. Come on. Hurry up," she said, tapping her cane on the wooden floor.

Pip shrugged and shuffled towards the kitchen. Fergus cast a worried look at the door and then rose, following him. It was even tinier than the sitting room. The furniture was made from pine, and the cushions were hand sewn. All sorts of things hung from the walls, from pots and pans to several stuffed deer heads and even a lacquered fish.

"That one's not real," chuckled the old lady. "But it looks so real, I thought it was a work of art. Pull up a stool."

Fergus dropped onto the stool next to Pip, scooting up to the wooden island. It hadn't been cleared off yet, and there were fish scales and leftover pieces of vegetable scattered here and there. The old woman dropped two clay bowls full of stew in front of them and then pulled out a cutting board, picking up a piece of bread and sawing off slices. Fergus could see the bottom was burned, but he politely thanked her as she handed him a few pieces, dipping them into the stew and nibbling at them distractedly.

At the end of the room was an alcove with a window. Flannel curtains blocked out most of the view, but now that the snow had stopped, he could see the stars. There were more than he had ever seen before. They looked cold and sharp and very distant in the black winter sky.

It was at that moment that he noticed that the sky seemed to be discolored just above the curtain.

"What's that?" he asked around the piece of bread.

"What's what?" the old lady asked, looking up from her battle with the burned loaf.

"That weird color in the sky. Just above the curtains."

"Oh, that," she chuckled, putting down the knife.

Pip glared at him as she shambled away, forcing him to reach over Fergus to procure bread. Fergus didn't notice, though. His eyes were on the window as the woman hobbled over to it, her cane clacking against the floor with every step. She pulled back the curtains. The casing was coated in snow, and the glare of the lanterns made it a little hard to see anything on the lower half of the glass, but looking up, Fergus could most definitely see a green haze highlighting the mountains beyond from behind.

"We have no idea what that is," the old woman chuckled. "It just showed up a few years ago. My son and husband have been out to search for it at least a dozen times and haven't found a thing. Some say it's just the Northern Lights, but if so, they must've been on vacation for nearly 70 years. I've never seen the likes of them before now, and I grew up in this town, mind you."

She let the curtain fall shut, hobbling back over to them. Fergus stared at the hint of green still visible from the top of the fabric. His heart was beating so hard, he could hardly even hear.

"Is something wrong?"

"No, I just," he started and turned to see Pip staring at him with grumpy exhaustion and the old lady cocking her head. "You said they couldn't find it?"

"They walked all around those mountains in daylight, but they couldn't find it. It must only show up at night, and it's far too dangerous to travel those mountains then. Besides, I think it's a lot further away than it looks, or else I'm sure they would have found something."

Fergus nodded, swallowing too fast and choking. He beat his chest, eyes watering. It was the same green light as in White Rock. Hadn't the fortuneteller said that he would find the gate when he stopped looking? And what with Terry being injured and Declan trying to steal his fairy-soul and Pip being kidnapped, he hadn't thought of Tír na nÓg at all.

He knew it in his bones: that green light was the new gateway.

•   •   •

The next morning, he and Pip traded places with Guillory and Three. Rather than go rest like Three, the Captain set out with Raja and the crew to "clean up," as he put it. Pip was quieter than usual, staring at the jail floor with his jaw set. Declan was awake, though said nothing, for Darya was still asleep, leaning on his shoulder. Even dirty, disheveled, and exhausted, they were still quite the pair.

Fergus sighed, craning his head back against the wall. This jail was more comfortable than the one in Ping City, though he was on the other side of the bars this time.

"So, Fergus, what's the hold up?"

Pip stiffened.

Fergus turned to Declan. "Not sure what you mean."

"I think you do. Are we waiting for Terry to heal up enough to finish the job, or will you hand us over to the human's 'justice'?"

Fergus blew his bangs from his face, staring at the ceiling. "You'd deserve it if I did let Terry have you."

Declan chuckled. "That's rather scary for you."

"Not like you're sorry at all."

"I'm not." Declan smiled thinly. "I believe in what we've been working towards."

"Sacrificing other hybrids, hurting humans who aren't even involved . . . Even if you have a reason, it isn't good enough to excuse what you've done. You can't change things that way."

"And how can we change them, Fergus?" For the first time, a little heat crept into his voice. "It's easy to sit back and condemn, but where are your answers?"

Fergus said nothing.

Pip lifted his head. "We can get along with humans if we respect them."

"And that will make them respect us in return? I may die of laughter."

Darya opened her eyes, regarding them sleepily without raising her head. "Humans won't respect us. All they can do is fear us. They struck first, condemning us to poverty and squalor," she said softly. "There is no reason we should have to live in fear of them."

"Maybe they fear us because of what we do to each other," Pip said darkly, looking away.

"We needn't be enemies," Declan replied.

"You wanted to steal both our powers. How is that different from an exorcism? How are you better than the bad humans?" Pip asked.

Fergus jumped in. "Even if I agreed with what you're saying, Pip's right. If nothing else, doing things your way has led you here. Not a good situation, is it? I'd say even if I don't have an answer, you've already proven your plan sucks."

Declan chuckled, running his hand over his face. "Perhaps you have me there."

"Stop laughing," Pip snarled.

"Easy," Fergus muttered. "We'll figure something out working together and thinking about what's gonna really last."

"Saint Fergus, you are naive," Declan said with a shrug.

Fergus didn't reply, and the room lapsed back into silence.

•   •   •

He returned to the inn around lunchtime where the old lady handed him a tray of fishy smelling soup and freshly burned bread and sent him off to check on Terry. The room was very narrow with a low ceiling, and unlike the kitchen and sitting area, hardwood from top to bottom. It made Fergus feel claustrophobic. Terry looked very small under the mountain of quilts and throws. He was awake. One eye was heavily bandaged, the cloth wrapped several times around his head.

"Help," he mumbled.

"What is it?" Fergus nearly dropped the platter as he rushed over.

"I'm being crushed by some blankets."

"Don't scare me," he grumbled, putting the tray on the bedside table. He began to peel back layers of quilt.

"Why are you so jumpy? That's much better."

"I'm not jumpy. Just worried."

"About my eye? I think it's done for."

Fergus didn't reply.

"Not going to laugh? Guess I don't really feel up to it either." Terry sighed, lifting his arms over the covers and clasping them over his chest. He turned his good eye to the little window in the corner. "Open the curtains, will you?"

"Are you hungry?"

"No. Smells like ocean water anyway."

"I think it's some kinda fish." Fergus came over, drawing up a chair. "Bread's not too badly burned this time."

"I'll live."

"Sorry."

Terry let out a long sigh.

"I know it doesn't change anything, but . . . " Fergus began.

"Please don't. This is hard enough without thinking of you agonizing over it. Just let it be."

"But if I let you just do it, you wouldn't have lost your eye."

"Who knows what might have happened? Maybe I'd be fine, and they'd be dead. Maybe Darya would have stabbed me in the back. Maybe she'd of gotten you. All we have to work with is what happened, and between my eye and you, I think I did the right thing."

Fergus stared at his hands.

"That seer said I'd lose something important. I'm glad it was this instead of my best friend. That's all there is to it."

He looked up at Terry. His pale face was set in earnest lines, though after a moment, he winced and put his hand to the bandage over his right eye. Fergus watched the muscles of his throat glide up and down as he swallowed back the pain. He wasn't even sure that Flynn would have made this kind of sacrifice for him. He didn't know what to say. "Thank you" felt far too paltry. Apologizing again would be belittling what Terry was trying to tell him. Making a joke seemed insincere.

He snorted, mouth crooking, and shook his head.

Terry smiled thinly. "Told you, you're the only one I'd call friend, and, you know, I am kind of a dog."

"Loyal?"

"To those who deserve it."

Knowing that there was someone who cared for him this much, who was happy to give up something this big and terrible for him, and who would do it again with a smile felt so big he couldn't digest it. Fergus leaned forward. Terry blinked at him, a little curious and uncertain, but said nothing.

For a moment, Fergus studied the purple veins crisscrossing his eyelid. His eyelashes were surprisingly long, but they were so light, it was hard to see. A thin path of freckles crossed his nose from cheek to cheek, though they looked faded. He couldn't tell if it was from the pain, or because it was now mid-winter.

Fergus cupped his cheek. Terry's mouth twitched, but he remained silent – his body tense under the covers – and Fergus thought he might be holding his breath. He leaned down and kissed him.

It seemed they were both surprised by it. It only lasted an instant before Fergus quickly drew back. Terry blinked owlishly and drew his lower lip between his teeth. Fergus wondered if he ought to apologize. They stared at each other in silence. The cuckoo clock ticked away in the other room. It struck the hour, and the annoying, high-pitched chime sounded.

"Are you going to start doing that every time you feel guilty about something?" Terry asked with a crooked smile.

"That wasn't . . . "

"I'm joking. Besides, I didn't say it was bad."

Fergus's mouth jerked, but failed to form a smile. He looked down at his hands again.

"So? What was that, then?"

"I'm not really sure," Fergus admitted.

"That's a little awkward."

"I know." He reached up, scratching his cheek, and turned to the stew. "So, you don't want any of that?"

"Tear off the burned parts, and I'll eat the bread," Terry said, and Fergus thought he detected a sigh.

"Hey, Terry," he said, picking up the bread and peeling away the burned parts of the crust.

"Yes?"

"I think we've found it."

"Found it?"

"Yeah, the gateway. I think it's nearby. Well, maybe not that nearby, but you can see it from here."

Terry started to sit up, but Fergus hurriedly put a hand on his shoulder to stop him. "Not right now, but at night, there's a green light over the mountains just like in White Rock. Maybe if we take the airship in that direction . . . "

Terry relaxed, sinking back into the pillow. He stared up at the ceiling. For a moment, he started to lift his hands, and then let them drop again, shaking his head. "Wow."

"Yeah."

"Seers are pretty scary, huh?"

Fergus snorted, scratching his cheek with his knuckles. "Seems so. I haven't said anything to the others yet, though I think Pip might have worked it out."

"As soon as I'm out of this bed, we're going."

"Okay, but you better be healed first. Who knows what we're gonna find there?"

There was a rap at the door, and the old lady stuck her head in. "Everything all right in here?"

Fergus quickly passed Terry the unburned bread. "Just fine, thanks."

"Let me know if you want more stew."

"Thanks," Terry said. He waited until the door was shut. "You should tell Guillory, so he doesn't start planning to pack us all up and return to New Peiling."

Fergus nodded. "Yeah, but later. If I leave you alone in here, that old lady's gonna come in and spoon feed you herself."

•　　•　　•

It was hard to fully grasp that they were teetering at the edge of discovery. That night, he pointed out the green light to Guillory, who agreed that it did look a lot like the light at White Rock. He didn't look particularly happy about redirecting to find its source, but he didn't argue either. Instead, he sent Fergus out on a final shopping trip to pick up supplies lost in the last few go-rounds with the pirates and the Huntsmen.

Fergus took Raja with him to buy new coats, dried meat, oil, and candles. Guillory also suggested arming themselves in case they had to set out on foot.

He picked up a hat made of rabbit fur, pulling the flaps down over his ears. "You know, this *is* a lot warmer," he said, looking into the mirror. "Makes my head look weirdly small, though," he added, pulling it off again.

"Well, it's fur," Raja said, considering a fluffy grey hat with a frown. "I don't like the smell."

"There are a ton of woolen ones, too," Fergus said, drifting over to a display of knitted caps. "Gonna need something, I think."

"Do you think it really is the gateway this time?"

"Huh?"

"I overheard Pip and Three talking. Plus, I saw the light, too."

"Oh yeah. I don't know, but the old lady at the inn says it only appeared recently. Plus, the color is right. Same as White Rock."

"And have you decided what you'll do yet?"

Fergus sighed, putting down a black knit cap and then picking it up again. "I dunno. Maybe I'll only figure that out when I'm right there in front of it. You're gonna go?"

"I'm not sure. I'm a little afraid to. I've never transformed before, and . . . "

"And?"

But Raja just shook his head, putting the cap on and wrinkling his nose. "Maybe knit is better. Animal skins reek of death to me."

"Well, they are dead," Fergus pointed out. "So what is 'and'?"

Raja made a show of taking off the cap and examining it before he replied. "Just what the seer said, you know?"

"What was it again?" Fergus asked, putting on the black cap.

"That I'd find what I lost."

"Oh, right," Fergus said a little uncomfortably. He stared at his reflection in the mirror beside the display. His eyes were still blue. He smiled faintly before glancing at Raja. His smile faded. Clearing his throat, he muttered, "Evelyn."

"Maybe it isn't her. For all I know, it could be a button. But if it is her, I have to find her. If they have her, I have to get her back somehow."

Fergus tucked his hair into the cap, not replying. He thought he understood a little of how Terry must have felt all those times he'd been so bullheaded and idealistic that he just wouldn't listen. He didn't want to say that he didn't think that if Evelyn was alive, she'd be in a state Raja could rescue her from. She'd be luckier if she had quickly died before the exorcism or whatever else the Knights had done, but he knew how cruel it would be to say. Yet perhaps his silence said it best.

Raja sighed, putting the fur cap back where he found it. "Even if she was just a vegetable, I still don't want them to have her. I don't care what it takes. I just want her to be safe from them."

"Guess you really love her, huh?"

Raja smiled weakly. "Yes."

Fergus pulled off the cap, putting it in the basket on the floor between them. He ran his hands through his hair, trying to get it to fluff up a little more. "How are you gonna find out?"

"I have no idea, but if I return to New Peiling, I'm sure I can find something."

"And what if you find out she is long gone? What if something happens to the gate, and you can't just easily get back to it if you want to?"

"I'll find something to do with myself."

Fergus felt goosebumps suddenly prick up along his arms. He cleared his throat uneasily. "Yeah." He paused, took a deep breath, and then added, "But what if the fortune means Tír na nÓg? Something your fairy-soul lost could be something you lost. All our souls essentially 'lost' Tír na nÓg during the Cataclysm."

"I've thought of that. It's not impossible."

"I just don't think revenge is worth much in the end."

"Surprisingly skittish coming from you."

Fergus picked out a second black cap, thinking Terry might like one, too, and put it in the basket. "Maybe," he said with a shrug. "But it's not like killing all the Knights would bring Flynn back, nor Audrey. If Evelyn is gone, then it won't bring her back, either. I don't think you'll feel any better having done it, even if you could."

"I know," Raja said. Fergus turned to see him staring at the ground, hair over his face. His hands were clutched at his sides. "I know. I couldn't even handle those Huntsmen people. Still, if I could even do a little . . . "

"Then Evelyn would be happy?"

"Probably not."

"Then you would feel satisfied?"

"Probably not."

"What then?"

"Maybe it could save someone else."

Fergus nodded. "That makes more sense. If it's for that, it might be worthwhile."

"Thanks," Raja grumbled and began to irritably rifle through the woolen hats.

"That's what Niamh's creed is, isn't it? Finding a better way, peacefully?"

"Most of Niamh is dead now, and who says the fairies will be kinder than the humans?"

"You used to hope they'd be," Fergus replied.

"I don't want to talk about it anymore, Fergus," Raja snapped.

Fergus jumped a little. He looked away, muttering, "Sorry."

Raja didn't reply.

"I'm just gonna take some of this stuff up to the register. Bring anything you want when you're ready, okay?"

Raja nodded halfheartedly, and Fergus didn't know what to say to console him, so he picked up the basket and headed to the front of the shop.

Chapter Seventeen.

The green light grew more intense as the little airship doggedly chugged through the mountains. Fergus stood in the control room with Terry – still heavily bandaged – and Guillory. Fergus's eyes were glued to the light burning away the profiles of the mountains. Terry leaned heavily on the wall, staying out of the way as much as Fergus was in it. Crewmen coming down from the deck kept trying to maneuver him aside, but something about the intensity of the light left him transfixed.

"We couldn't find a trace of them," Guillory was telling Terry. "We searched all over that cave, but it was like no one had ever been there. I have no idea if they were still alive and escaped, or if the women who escaped went back for the bodies. I doubt we'll need to worry about them again one way or another."

"They'd be very stupid to come after us," Terry muttered.

"Fergus, you're leaning on the controls."

"Oh sorry," he mumbled, taking a step back, but a moment later, he began to edge forward again.

Guillory put an arm out to stop him. "This is a tricky bit of navigation. One wrong move, and we'll crash into these mountains. This airship is on her last leg, in case you couldn't tell. For the love of . . . Bridges, take him, *please*."

Fergus scowled, but let Terry take him by the arm and drag him back to the wall.

"I swear, it's the most annoying light I've ever seen. I can hardly tell where we're going," Guillory grumbled.

"It's so warm," Fergus said, held in place by a tug on his arm. "And fresh. It looks clean."

Terry snorted. "Well, it does feel warm. Magic's thick in the air. I *wouldn't* be surprised if the area around here is too rough to cross at night."

"Then let's hope we don't crash," Guillory said waspishly.

"I thought you were the best of the best," Terry replied.

"Best of the best is still only a man."

Fergus found himself drifting towards the window again, but Terry pulled him away. "Come on, let's check on Pip and Three. I don't think they should be left alone with those two for too long."

Fergus reluctantly left the control room and followed Terry down to the cabins. They stopped on the landing, listening carefully for the sounds of anything amiss. He could just barely detect the soft hum of Three's voice.

"Sounds like it's okay," he said, stepping forward and bumping into Terry. "Whoa, sorry, I forgot . . . "

Terry's mouth crooked to the side as he turned his head enough to fully look at Fergus. "Yeah."

Fergus looked away, biting his lip.

"I don't want another guilty kiss," Terry said softly, failing to look amused.

"It wasn't because of guilt," Fergus insisted, turning back to him.

Terry said nothing, watching him silently, and Fergus felt antsy. He didn't want to move away, though he knew he should. He continued worrying his lip, trying to guess from Terry's expression what was expected of him, but he'd never known how to do that in the first place. It wasn't a look he was used to; it drew him like the light. However, it wasn't particularly inviting either.

He started to raise his hand, and Terry subtly shifted away.

"We may be only a few days – maybe only a few hours or minutes – away from making a decision that will change our lives completely," he said softly, not meeting Fergus's eyes. "I think it's better if we don't add to the confusion."

"You just had hair in your face," Fergus muttered. He turned to the cabin door, opening it with more force than necessary.

Three jumped. "Don't do that!"

"Sorry."

"They're asleep, so you don't have to worry," Pip said from her other side.

Sure enough, Declan and his sister were both passed out, slumped against the far wall.

"Guess we should be quiet."

"No, I drugged them," Pip replied, lifting his chin a fraction as he stared at Fergus.

"Not a bad idea," Terry said, hovering outside the doorway.

"I wouldn't leave them alone, but they should be out for a few hours at least," Pip said, lowering his chin, but adopting a smug look.

"Do you have anything that might help the Captain see? Says the light's blinding him."

Pip and Three looked at each other and shook their heads.

"Is there trouble?" she asked

"Not yet."

Three blew her hair from her face. "That's *so* not reassuring."

Terry shrugged, giving her a contrite smile.

"You two look strange," Pip said with the kind of bluntness that made Fergus want to strangle him.

Three cocked her head. "Hmm? Yeah, you do a little! What's up?"

"Nothing, I'm just going to go see if we're any closer," Fergus said.

"Nothing, I just wanted to see if either of you need a break," Terry said simultaneously.

Three laughed. "That *is* weird, you know. You aren't fighting again, are you?"

"No," Fergus said.

"Wait," she said, catching his sleeve. "I want to see, too. Do you mind, Terry?"

"I did offer."

She followed Fergus up the stairs, close at his heels. "Are you okay?"

"Of course."

He heard her stop and sighed, turning around.

She tugged on her hair, eyes cast to the ceiling. "Seems like this really could be it, doesn't it? Pip says the air feels different. Thick or something. It seems like there's a lot of magic here, like at the shrine. It's like that feeling before lightning strikes."

"I don't like lightning."

She laughed and began ascending the steps. "Well, I bet it'll be nicer than that."

He grunted a little and hurried up the rest of the steps. He wasn't sure if it was because he just didn't want to be too close to Terry at the moment, or if it was the draw of the light, but he felt he had to hurry. The green bathing the control room was no different from when they left it. Guillory glanced at them over his shoulder.

"No leaning on the controls."

"I wasn't gonna," Fergus grumbled, crossing his arms and leaning against the wall.

"Wow, you know, this is a little eerie," Three said, looking around at the green-tinted controls. She stepped closer to the steering wheel. "We must be close."

"Actually, I'd give us about a day," Guillory replied. "From what we can see on the scope, there is a visible center to the light, and it isn't close."

"What's it look like?"

"Don't you lean on the controls either. They said it looked like a bubble."

"A bubble?" Fergus asked.

Guillory nodded. "Are you sure you really want to get close to this thing?"

"Yeah, we didn't come all this way not to."

The Captain sighed. "You should try to rest. I have no idea what to expect once we're there."

Fergus turned away from the green burning itself into his retinas. He blinked, seeing flashes of light behind his eyelids. His heart was jumping around in his chest, and he felt too tense to sleep.

"Are you sure it's not closer?"

"Very."

"Okay," he sighed, turning to Three.

Her face looked alien, painted in the green light. It made her eyes look very black. She pursed her lips. "What?"

"Nothing. I was just wondering if Pip had any more of that sleeping draught."

"Oh yeah, there's still some left."

"Can I have it?"

"Of course. Come on, I'll get it for you."

•   •   •

The glass was rattling so hard that a crack had formed and was steadily sneaking up the windowpane. Fergus's teeth clacked together. Somehow, after all the trouble they'd had with this airship, he couldn't feel particularly alarmed at how much the ship was shaking and groaning. It seemed almost natural that the hull would crack now and expel them into the valley below. The wind snuck through the crack in the glass, creating an annoying, high-pitched whistle.

He groaned and rolled over, hoping that if he at least pressed his face to the mattress, his teeth would stop smacking together. "What time is it?"

"About 5 p.m. Seems we're right on it," said Raja. "We made better headway during the day when the Captain could see. Now, though, seems like he's just trying to keep it together."

"Why aren't you up top?"

"He said everyone except the crew should stay below."

"Terry?"

He heard a muffled groan from overhead.

"I think his face is hurting from all the rattling," Raja said softly.

Fergus slid out of bed and zigzagged across the room to the window, grabbing the casing to try and steel himself as he peeked out. All he could see was the green light, broken up now and then by a ghostly patch of grey.

"Are we inside?"

"Not yet."

"I'm gonna go talk to Guillory."

"You probably shouldn't disturb him."

"Hey, I can look into the light without being entirely blinded," Fergus replied. "I might be able to help."

Raja opened his mouth to argue, but Fergus was already stumbling out the door. Getting up the stairs was not particularly easy. He was tossed from wall to wall and only avoided falling backwards by clinging to the railing. He managed to climb the steps and forge his way into the control room.

Guillory was bathed in a light so intense, he seemed only a fragment of his usual size. At the center was a great, rotating cloud like a waterspout, climbing high into the heavens and melting into the night sky. Beneath it, the green light rose in a haze under the storm cell. Rings of light illuminated the mass at intervals, poking through where the clouds grew thin.

"That doesn't look like a bubble."

"It did from afar."

"Can we actually fly into that?"

"We're about to find out."

The giant, circling monstrosity grew steadily larger in the window. Fergus gulped. Guillory strained at the wheel, trying to force the ship to stay on course.

"Let me help," Fergus said.

He got a little winded grunt in reply, which he assumed meant, "yes." There wasn't much space for his hands, so he stuck them over Guillory's.

"To the right," Guillory said through gritted teeth, and Fergus began to slowly push away. "That's a little better. At least the wind's only going in one direction."

A tree, ripped up by the roots, suddenly blocked out the light, speeding past the window. He heard shouts on the intercom over the roaring of the wind.

"We lose anyone?" Guillory called.

"No, Captain!"

"Steady, men!"

"Maybe we should pull out," Fergus said, watching debris bouncing off of the glass.

"That chance's already passed. We're going in or down. Only way now."

"Captain, the casing's coming loose!"

"Fergus, go down and get the others, but tell them not to get in the way."

He quickly nodded and jogged down the steps, tripping and sliding down the last few in his haste. He rubbed his back, wincing, but got up and limped over to Three and Pip's door.

"Bring them up. Everyone to the control room!" he shouted, hurrying to the next room. "Guillory wants us above!"

Three and Pip hurried past him, pushing a very groggy Declan and Darya before them. A moment later, Terry and Raja stumbled out, searching for anything to steady themselves with. Raja reached the banister first and managed to catch Terry just before he ran straight into the wall. Fergus lunged after them.

"What's he want us up top for now?"

"Maybe he thinks it's better if we all die together," Fergus said, clutching the railing with both hands as his feet were ripped out from under him. He went down on one knee, cursing in pain, before righting himself.

They made it up to the control room, everyone grabbing whatever they could to keep from being thrown.

"How is the crew doing?"

"Tied themselves on, so they won't be blown away. We're going full speed ahead. Better that way, I think. Brace yourselves."

The foggy light crept over the deck, sliding towards the window, and obscuring everything in front of it. Fergus held his breath, listening to the crackling and popping of the intercom. He wondered if even that would give under the force of the storm. He could hardly even hear the crew, though once in a while, a shouted order would slip through. And then the air grew still and silent. The walls stopped shaking, and though the boards still complained disconcertingly, the wind ceased.

"What's going on out there?" Guillory called, but the intercom had gone entirely silent. "Bloody Hell. Fergus! Three! Go look!"

Fergus nodded and rushed up the stairs to the deck, Three close behind. He swung open the door to find a strange, silent world. It was like being in the middle of a snowfield. The fog was so thick, it seemed to suck up all sound. He felt around behind him and located Three's arm.

"Hold onto me!" he shouted, but his voice came out like a whisper.

He felt her fingers catch around his arm and squeeze, and he began to creep forward. He stumbled over a web of branches that had been blown onto the deck and had to stop to extricate his feet.

"Is anyone out there?" Three murmured.

"Hello?" he called.

One of the crew ran straight into him. Fergus didn't see him until he was right there, clipping his side and going down.

"Are you okay?" Fergus asked, wheeling around. He could just barely make out the form of the man as he got to his knees and then stood.

"What is this place?"

But before Fergus could answer, he was up and disappearing into the mist towards the door. They found several more crewmates, but all of them seemed to be befuddled, on the verge of panic, and vanished into the fog before Fergus could sort them out.

"Guillory's certainly flying blind now," he said more to himself than Three, because he was sure she couldn't hear him.

"Fergus?" Three tugged on his sleeve. "Fergus?"

"I'm right here. Stay calm."

However, she began to climb his arm until she was right on top of him. She threw her arms around his middle. She was shaking, eyes rolling as she looked around.

"What is this?" she whimpered.

"It's okay. Just stay calm. I think it's clearing up."

And sure enough, the fog seemed to be thinning. It had a glittering quality, like particles of glass or sand. The air was warm – so warm that sweat began to form around his temples and at the back of his neck. He freed up a hand from Three's arms to unbutton his coat. It smelled pleasant, like fresh water and crushed grass. Despite the fact that he was quickly going from warm to hot, the air still felt fresh.

He took a deep breath, closing his eyes, and felt just the faintest brush of a breeze on his skin. Opening his eyes again, he saw lights filling the air. At first, they hung there, highlighting the fog in golden spheres. Then they began to move, slowly cutting through the mist, leaving shimmering trails. One flew past him, and Fergus saw that it was shaped like a butterfly. He reached out, trying to catch it, but it burst into dust and slipped through his fingers.

"Amazing," he mumbled, looking at the dust on his fingers.

Three relaxed, and he managed to peel her off. She held out her hands, letting one of the light butterflies land. Fergus watched it explode into glitter, shooting out like fireworks, and coat her hands, as well.

"What are they?" she asked.

He shook his head. "No clue."

The airship had slowed to a crawl. It shuffled forward like a blind man exploring an unfamiliar room. Fergus heard something scrape the side. He could see dark shapes through the thinner patches of fog on either side.

"Looks like we're right on a mountain. Better warn Guillory!" he said, catching Three by the wrist and pulling her along as he hurried back to the control room.

Pip glowered at him as he and Three returned, stopping to catch their breaths. He let go of her arm. The rest were still glued to the window.

"The mountains . . . " Fergus started.

"Already saw them," said Guillory.

"Oh."

"We should be okay if we take it slowly. Could you see anything out there?"

Fergus shook his head. "Not really. No more than you apparently."

Guillory took a hand off the wheel, reaching around in his jacket, and pulled out a collapsible telescope, holding it out for Fergus. "Take this and have another look."

"Wait, I'll come with you," said Raja.

"Me, too," added Terry.

Pip and Three nodded, as well.

Fergus shrugged and led them back up to the deck. The fog was steadily dissipating, and now the mountain to their right was, if somewhat mottled, mostly visible behind the screen of green air. He carefully made his way to the front of the airship, unscrewing the scope and holding it up. Beyond the remaining mist, he saw the mountains spreading out from their right to the fore. A bright light broke their watery outlines.

"Looks like there's a cave or something ahead," he mumbled, lowering the scope.

Terry took it from him, holding it to his good eye. He was silent for a long moment before nodding. "I think that's the center of it. I'll let Guillory know." He handed the scope back to Fergus.

It seemed like the airship was barely moving. Fergus fidgeted with the scope, twisting and untwisting it. His bangs stuck to his forehead. He shrugged out of his coat, leaving it in a pile at his feet as he wiped his face on his shoulder. The mist was nearly gone by now, revealing the stark mountainsides all around. Fergus could see the mouth to the cave, the light spilling from it like spotlights on a stage. If he went in there, he would never step onto a stage again, he thought. If he passed through to Tír na nÓg, he would never do anything human again. He probably would never see the human world again.

He stared down at the green light glinting off the brass scope. Despite the heat and humidity emitting from the cave up ahead, it felt very cold and heavy in his hands. If he went to Tír na nÓg, he wouldn't be able to see Three or Pip anymore, nor Raja or Guillory. He turned to Raja, his face highlighted in Kelly green. His long, shaggy black hair was in his eyes, which looked bluer than usual and a little sad, like he was watching a close friend leave.

Niamh had been searching for this for years. Probably the thought of giving it up in exchange for the tiniest shred of hope was hard, and Fergus wished he had anything to say, but he didn't, so he turned to Three, who was wide-eyed and excited, tugging on Pip's arm every few seconds, as though they were making any ground.

The highlights in her hair had nearly grown out, leaving the ends bleached and faintly tinged with red. She bit her lip, grinning around her teeth, as she turned to him. Pip looked ahead with an inscrutable expression. His dark eyes looked a little less suspicious than usual, but by the twitching of his eyebrows, Fergus thought he must be turning things over very carefully in his mind.

Fergus looked back down at the instrument in his hands, catching sight of his reflection. His hair was looking wild and too long, there was scruff along his jaw, and his eyes looked tired. He smiled halfheartedly at himself and felt a little depressed at the expression mirrored back at him. He tucked the scope into his pocket and turned to see Terry hauling Declan and Darya onto the deck.

Darya was mumbling furiously against her gag. Terry pushed her, and she tripped on her skirts, falling to the deck beside her brother. She stared at Terry murderously before fixing her glare on Fergus. He looked away.

"Are we taking them with us?"

"Yes," Terry replied.

Fergus nodded silently.

The first mate, Orson, jogged up to them. "We're docking here. Looks like there's a path you can take. We're going to secure the airship. Assemble by the ladder."

Guillory was waiting for them there. "I'm coming, too. I want to see what we've risked life and limb for."

"Okay," said Fergus. "Who else is coming, and who's staying?"

"The crew will stay with the ship. Most are too superstitious to continue anyway," Guillory replied.

Fergus turned to the others. "Raja? Three? Pip?"

Three opened her mouth, but Pip cut her off.

"We will stay."

"But, Pip!"

"The only place I want to be is with Three, so I don't care about Tír na nÓg. I don't want to even see it."

"But what if you saw it and really wanted to go?"

"You couldn't come with me," he said, shaking his head, "so even if I wanted to, it's no place for me. It's easier this way. This is how I feel, and I don't want to second-guess myself for any reason."

Three opened her mouth and then shut it. She quickly looked away, scratching her quickly reddening cheek. "Okay."

Fergus tried not to look amused. He cleared his throat. "Raja?"

"I want to see it. Besides, if you go, the Captain will be on his own coming back. It might not be safe for someone without fairy eyes."

Guillory smirked, but shrugged.

"So, Terry, Raja, Guillory, those two, and me," Fergus said, his voice catching a little. He ran a hand through his hair, feeling his throat tighten. He didn't want to say good-bye to Three and Pip yet. Realizing everyone was looking at him, he let out a choked laugh. "Uh, guess that's our party."

Three suddenly flung her arms around his neck. "Fergus! Fergus, if you don't come back . . . "

He stiffened and then bit his lip, putting his arms around her. Her tears were warm against the side of his neck. "Yeah."

"I'm so glad we met," she said between sniffles.

He swallowed, unable to reply, and patted her back. It was a long moment before she finally released him and stood back, wiping her eyes on her sleeve. He took a deep breath, forced a smile, and turned to Pip. Pip gave him a little smile, rolling his eyes.

"Take care of Three," Fergus managed.

"As though I wouldn't," he replied, making a face. He paused and then glanced at Fergus. "You aren't all bad."

"Same to you."

"All right, let's get going before this place disappears," said Guillory.

• • •

They crept along the narrow trail. Below swirled the remains of the mist, obscuring the valley. Fergus tried not to look down as he edged, back against the rock, up the path. The dancing lights were all around, breaking up the green light with their warm glow. His legs were starting to ache. He licked his lips and glanced back to see Declan, Darya, and Terry. Darya's skirts were torn to her knees to keep her from stumbling and falling over the ledge. Terry had transformed and was snapping at their heels to keep them moving. Probably, it was also just easier to navigate the path as a gytrash.

The path led to a narrow land bridge that cleared the gap between path and cave. Guillory trotted over it like a mountain goat, though Raja was much warier, half-squatting and very slowly shuffling forward, both arms straight out at his sides. Fergus stepped up onto it and began to carefully put one foot in front of the other. He found that he had to look down to make sure he didn't step too close to the edge. He couldn't see anything except gaping darkness below.

He swallowed, trying to keep his breathing even and focus on each step. Bits of rock broke free and fell down, down, down until they were swallowed by the blackness. Fergus's vision swam, and he stumbled. He could tell before he put his foot down that his balance was off. For a split second, there was nothing but the promise of empty air and hard earth far below, and then Guillory and Raja grabbed him by the shoulders and hauled him onto the ledge. He fell to his knees.

"Thanks," he mumbled.

Rubbing his forehead with the back of his wrist, he got to his feet. Guillory clapped him on the shoulder. They waited a moment for Terry to shepherd the Abels across the pass. Once safely on the ledge, Terry turned back into his human form, quickly fixing the bandages. For a second, Fergus could see bruised, swollen skin, but before he could spot the missing eye, Terry had the bandages back in place.

He reached over and ungagged Declan and Darya. Declan spat at him, and Guillory stopped Terry from backhanding him.

"Not out here. We're still too close to the edge," he said, releasing Terry's wrist.

Terry shrugged. "You heard him: get moving."

Fergus turned to the mouth of the cave. He couldn't see anything beyond the light. Holding his hand in front of his eyes, he led them inside. The light became very intense at the entrance, and he hoped there was solid ground at the other side as he stepped through.

The glow was dimmer on the other side. The inside of the cave mirrored the ledge somewhat. It had a dome-like shape, the walls stretching up to form a ceiling high over their heads. The floor gave way about midway into the cave. Beyond the interior ledge was a screen of light, green around the outsides, turning whiter towards the center. It shimmered at odd intervals, like grass stroked by the wind. The five of them stood just inside the entrance for a moment, staring at it.

"You finally made it," said a familiar voice.

Fergus turned.

Standing to the right side of the gateway was Jane.

Chapter Eighteen.

She wore an emerald-colored hood, which she presently pulled back. Her red hair was pulled up in a messy twist, clipped in place by silver butterflies that let out a little jingle when she moved her head. Her eyes were painted as green as her cloak. She cocked her head, smiling her typical, coy little smile at him with round, pink lips, and tucked a stray curl from her face. She looked nearly as stunning as Darya, much as she had the night of the Count's ball. Slowly, she walked towards them, and Fergus saw that her feet were bare.

"Jane? How can you . . .? Is it really you?"

She stopped and chuckled. "Oh no, but I thought this form might make you comfortable."

Fergus's eyes narrowed. He edged forward. "Who are you?"

She shook her head, still smiling. "I wear many faces."

"Not helpful. Are you Jane or what? *Is* there even a Jane?"

"Of course, there is. I met her many years ago, after her parents had died. She was a sad, lonely little girl, and she was very happy to have a friend. I wore her face and said we could be sisters." She sighed, closing her eyes. "She is one of my favorite humans."

"Human? She's not a human. She's a hybrid just like us."

"Oh, hybrids are the same as humans to me," she replied. "So close and yet always so far from us."

"Us? You mean, the fairies?"

The woman nodded.

"Wait, you're a real fairy?"

"Yes. We've met before, Fergus."

"How do you know my name?"

She didn't answer his question, but instead continued, "Shall I show you? It's not as pretty as this face." She lifted her hands, covering her face, and the air distorted, turning bright a moment. She withdrew her hands to reveal the weathered features of the old woman from the forest outside Peygham.

"What the hell is this?" Fergus asked, recoiling.

"Who is she?" Terry asked.

"Back in that forest, after the airship crashed and we were separated, when I transformed the first time, she was there. She took me to her hut and fed me, and I turned back into a human. Then she . . . " Stabbed him and made a wild fairy-dog attack him, prompting him to turn back into a kelpie. He eyed her with a little frown, feeling that it was probably unwise to express ingratitude to a true fairy.

He cleared his throat. " . . . showed me how to turn into a kelpie again."

She cackled in that unpleasant, toady way. "That's right, my pretty pony. I taught you in exchange for a song. I see this face disturbs you." Lifting her hands again, she changed back into Jane.

"So, what? You've been following Jane and me around?"

"In a way. I've wondered if anyone would find this place. You see, I am Niamh's true Fand. Are you surprised? Haven't you ever wondered why Jane was so dedicated to Fand, or why she seemed to be the only one who'd ever met with her? You have wondered, haven't you, Raja?" She said, smiling at him over Fergus's shoulder. "Or maybe you've wondered why so many people thought she *was* Fand?" She turned her attention back to Fergus.

"Yeah, I guess," he replied, scratching his head. "But what about all the political stuff? People said they saw you going in and out of the Mayor's office and all."

"That was Jane. I don't really care for human politics, but she took it upon herself to try. I thought it was a hindrance. That's why I was so very pleased when I found you. I just couldn't get close to you," she replied, frowning at Terry.

"So basically you've been manipulating Jane all along?" asked Raja.

"Manipulating? I don't believe so. She sought my advice, and I gave it."

"But to what end? You already knew where this place was. Why didn't you just tell her?" Raja demanded. "If you'd just told her, then Evelyn, Flynn, and Audrey . . .!"

"I didn't particularly care if she found it," Fand said with a shrug. "It's not that I wished to harm her or any of our followers. I do like humans, which is why I've stayed in the mortal world. However, remaining here becomes tedious. The decades pass so slowly when you have nothing to do, so I thought I would provide some entertainment for you and for myself. I dropped some hints, waiting to see who might put the pieces together, and Jane's clever young lover was the only one who did."

"Flynn . . . " Fergus muttered.

"He kept it to himself, though. Perhaps he stopped trusting her, because she was so close to the other humans."

"Wait, is there some relationship between Jane and the humans?" Fergus asked.

Once again, the question was ignored. "However, even though Jane took all of Flynn's notes, you managed to find just the one to lead you here. I think that means you've won."

"What is Jane's relationship with the humans?"

"I did say she was a very trusting girl, didn't I?" Fand said, waving her hand dismissively. "But that is of no consequence."

"It is to me!" Fergus said, stepping forward. "What did Jane do? Did she cause the Knights to find out about Niamh?"

Fand stared at him impassively. "Here you are at the threshold of our world. Two of you can even take your fairy forms. Once this gate closes, there will not be another for 50 years. If you remain in the human world, you will very likely be dead by then." She cocked her head. Her barrettes tinkled softly, glittering in the light. "What will you do?"

"These two will be going." Terry pushed Declan and Darya forward, yanking their bindings free.

Declan rubbed his wrist, looking between Fand, Terry, and Fergus. Darya clung to him wordlessly, staring reproachfully at Terry. "A death sentence, is it? You make it sound so easy to toss away the yoke of humanity, but if we could, we wouldn't have needed him," he said, jerking his chin at Fergus.

"That's right," said Terry. "But at least you'll have a chance to survive. You weren't offering Fergus the same. Besides, now you won't have to worry about humans anymore. Be thankful."

"Forgive me for not being terribly appreciative at the prospect of being toyed with over a hundred years and then torn apart and eaten." Declan turned to Fand, but her face remained unreadable. "Seems like that's as good as a, 'You're right.'"

"Declan," Darya whimpered, pressing her face into his back.

He reached around, patting her, and sighed. "And so the hunter turns prey, and the hero executioner. But I warn you, Terry, if we do manage to escape – be it five years or 50 – or if you follow us into Tír na nÓg, we'll find you, and we *will* have our revenge."

"You can go on your own, or I can force you. Which is it?"

Declan lifted his chin, narrowing his eyes. "We'll go on our own, thank you."

He turned to Darya, who let out a strangled sob, shaking her head, and Fergus felt a twinge of sympathy.

"Don't," muttered Terry.

"I wasn't gonna do anything."

Declan put his arm around his sister's shoulders, turning back to Terry. "I wonder: Are you really a fairy, or are you just an angry man?"

Terry's eye narrowed. Fergus grabbed him by the back of his coat.

"Oh, that is quite scary. Fine then. Come along, Darya. It will be all right."

Slowly, the two turned away from the group towards the light. It cast a green halo around their dark hair. Darya was half-collapsed against Declan. He looked to be dragging her a little. She made quiet, desperate little sounds, but he went forward without hesitation, and they disappeared into the light.

Fergus let out a shuddering sigh.

"Funny," Guillory suddenly said, "how you say you like humans, but you just let that happen."

Fergus turned to him, following his gaze to Fand. She cocked her head, confused by the accusation.

"Didn't you feel sorry for them at all?" Guillory asked.

"Well, why didn't you do anything, then?" Fand replied evenly.

Guillory looked away, shoulders slumping.

"Because it's a far kinder punishment than they deserved," Terry supplied, glaring between them. "If you took them back to New Peiling on charges of attempted murder, they'd be hanged without trial. That's what they would have deserved. Instead, they can fend for themselves and see just how much they like a world without humans. Maybe it'll teach them a lesson."

Guillory remained silent, staring at the floor.

Fand chuckled, touching the side of her neck. "You have caused me trouble, but I've enjoyed watching you, Terry. Now, who is next?"

"Not me," said Raja, stepping back. "I just wanted to see what we lost so much for. I wish it had been more than this."

"Tír na nÓg is a paradise," Fand replied. "You don't think it was worth it?"

"I think you made a game of our lives, and we're the ones who lost."

Fand just shrugged. "Fergus? Terry?"

Fergus stared at the wall of light. It hurt his eyes, but it was comforting at the same time. The undulating colors beckoned him forward. Once again, he wondered what it would be like to resign himself to living as a kelpie, never straying from his lake for the rest of his life. All he would think about was eating and – if the occasion presented itself – mating, and there wouldn't be anyone trying to steal his powers, no one to reject his feelings, no more living hand to mouth, no more cold, lonely, jealous, tired, sick, betrayed . . .

He could leave behind the intricacies of human emotion. He could break away from the painful truth that to be human was to be lonely and always wanting for something.

It wasn't up to him to save the world. It wasn't like there was some grand calling dictating that he had to protect humans from people like the Abels, nor that he should protect hybrids from people like the Knights. How could one person change anything anyway? No matter how much power he amassed, there were millions of humans to contend with. It was an uphill battle, and he wasn't going to change it one way or another.

But then, he was one of the few people who believed the world *could* still be saved. There weren't many like him left from what he'd seen. Wasn't this basically running away from responsibility? He wondered if he would regret it when he was resting at the bottom of his dark, tranquil lake. Would he still wonder how Raja and Ursula and Pip and Three and Guillory were doing?

To leave now would be to abandon them. They weren't weak people, and he wasn't responsible for them, yet he felt he was just a little. They were, after all, his friends. They were the people who had been beside him, protecting and supporting him, all along. All of them had accepted that he might choose to leave without condemning him. They all wanted the best for him. He owed it to them to want the best for them, too.

He lifted his head and realized he'd drawn close to the light. He could see his reflection in its surface, except it wasn't his face, but a large black horse with flashing white eyes and fangs. It threw its head, pawing the ground. Its coat gleamed, and its mane lifted as though touched by an unseen breeze. It was beautiful and powerful and carefree. He caught himself reaching for it and then pulled away, taking a few steps back and shaking his head.

"No."

"You won't go?" asked Fand.

Fergus shook his head again. "I'm staying," he said quietly, feeling a wave of regret even as he said the words.

"But, Fergus!" Terry stepped in front him, grabbing his shoulders. "We don't have to live like this anymore. We could go there and be happy. We could live like true fairies. We don't have to worry, because we have the power to do it. There's nothing here for us anymore!"

Fergus looked away. "I won't stop you if you have to go, Terry, but I can't. If you went . . . " He swallowed thickly. "If you went . . . I just . . . I'd be alone. The most important thing I've found would be gone, but I have to stay here."

"But *why?*" Terry asked, desperation thick in his voice.

"To give someone else the opportunity to have what I've had." He glanced back at Guillory and Raja. "Because I think all this time, I was just running away. I didn't know what to do about the humans who hated us, so I thought it was just better to escape them. I wanted to get away from Ursula and my mom's ghost. I wanted to stop feeling bad about everything. Probably, if I went in, I could do all of that, but deep down, I'd know it was running away."

"You're not responsible for anyone else, Fergus. Look at me," he said, shaking Fergus's shoulders. "You don't have to worry about them. If they wanted to be here, they would, and they're not, so there's no reason you should worry about anyone else."

"Maybe that's true," Fergus agreed. "But I don't want to forget how I felt about Ursula or about Flynn or about you. All along I've been saying there's got to be a better way. Well, I wanna stop running and start looking. I wanna find it."

"Nobody cares about what you've said. No one is expecting you to put your money where your mouth is. You might die without ever finding it."

"I know, but *I* expect it. My mom killed herself. She was so scared of losing her mind that she ran away. My dad found out something he didn't like and ran away, too. When they left, they screwed everything up. My mom was never the same after he left, and when she left, look at what happened.

"They both wrecked the lives of the people around them by choosing to avoid what was hardest. Living with humans, trying to find a way to get everyone to get along, is hard. Being treated like this is really hard. I know everyone has given me their blessing to do this, but I want to make my *own* paradise."

Terry's grip loosened. His lips were drawn back, brows knotted. "Fergus," he groaned, shaking his head.

Fergus gently took him by the wrists. "I'm a human, and I'm a fairy. That's what a hybrid is. I can be both of those things and still be me. That's the only me that's really me. If I chose to just be a kelpie, I wouldn't be me anymore. All that would be left of who I am now is just that little bit of regret at the back of my head."

He released Terry's hands, and Terry let them fall to his sides. Slowly, he turned to the light, his back to Fergus. Fergus wanted to reach for him, to beg him not to go, but Terry wasn't arguing anymore, and he knew he couldn't ask him to stay when Terry wasn't asking him to go.

"I hate you a little bit right now," Terry said softly. "For so long, I've just wanted to stop all this. I never wanted to be the one who punished people. I never wanted to degrade myself. I wanted to change things, but all I could do was the dirty work, and nothing ever changed, so I just wanted to let that all go. I wanted so badly to say good-bye to Terry Bridges, to Badb Catha, to the pathetic me in a human body that couldn't fix anything. I wanted to have a better life.

"I had a better life once, and losing it was irreconcilable. If I step through that light right now, I won't have to clean up anyone else's mess ever again. I'll never have to worry about where I'm gonna sleep, or if I'll be able to find something to eat. I won't have to feel dirty or angry or alone, because a gytrash is happiest alone, and fairies don't think about filth." Fergus heard his voice hitch, saw his hands form fists at his sides.

"And if you would just go, too, then everything would be pretty much perfect. The only person I really care about is you. The rest can go to Hell. Maybe I could forget you, if I just step through. Maybe it wouldn't matter, but I think the part of Terry that was left would still be thinking of Fergus, and I'd know. You're my best friend. I wanted more than anything for you to want to go there with me, but . . . because of that, I guess I always knew you wouldn't."

He turned back to Fergus, looking stricken. "So I can't go either."

"Bravo! How touching! So monsters have feelings, too."

Terry's eye widened. Fergus felt as though he'd been dashed by ice water. Hardly daring to breathe, he turned towards that unpleasantly familiar voice.

Ashton Harriet stood at the entrance, dressed in full Air Guard regalia. It was the bright red jacket that Guillory had once worn. The sneer on his face made his scar stick out more than usual, giving him a demonic look.

"Ashton!" exclaimed Guillory, looking confused, but pleased. "How the devil did you find us?"

Harriet shook his head, lifting a hand to his forehead. An even uglier smile stretched across his face. "Oh, that was hardly difficult." He snapped his fingers. "Bring her in."

Fergus glanced at Terry, but Terry looked equally confused. A short, raven-haired woman stumbled through the entrance.

Raja let out a garbled cry. "*Evelyn!*"

He started to lunge for her, but Guillory caught him, shaking his head. His expression was no longer welcoming – eyes narrowed and brow furrowed.

"Why have you come here, Ashton?" Guillory carefully asked.

Harriet chuckled. "We have a few items to contend with. First and foremost, we were to find this place and destroy it."

"What?" Fergus said.

"That's right," Harriet replied. "Make sure none of the nasty fairies come out anymore. That's our first order of business."

"And the second?"

"Arrest the traitor ex-Captain."

Guillory jerked back, mouth parting, but was too shocked to speak.

Harriet sighed, and for a moment, he didn't look so triumphant. "Mother is very persistent, you know. I honestly hoped we wouldn't run into you here. It would have been better if you were still off searching." He looked away from Guillory. "Seize him."

Men in uniform filtered through the entrance, swarming the Captain. Guillory turned his head rapidly from side to side, but as they closed in on him, he didn't resist.

"Well, I half expected it, if we're being honest. I'm glad, at least, that you were man enough to do it yourself, Ashton. Stand back, Raja."

"What the hell are you doing?" Fergus shouted. "Isn't he your hero? How can you arrest him?"

Harriet turned to Fergus, curling his lip in disgust. "Orders are orders. I don't expect an animal to understand."

"Say that again," snarled Terry.

"What are you going to do with the rest of us?" asked Raja, who was suddenly a lot closer to Evelyn. She didn't seem to recognize him. She didn't seem aware of her surroundings at all. Her eyes were half-lidded, and she was smiling in a dull way. The men didn't even bother restraining her.

"We will exorcise you, just as we will exorcise all hybrids, so that the world can be at peace."

"You!" Fergus growled. "You're behind the Knights!"

He laughed. "Yes, I am. Allow me to introduce myself. They call me 'Bedevere.'"

"You're Bedevere?" asked Terry, a look of horror crinkling his features.

Harriet smirked. "That's right, and you are Badb Catha. By all rights, I think this makes us mortal enemies."

"How do you know about that?" Fergus demanded.

"Oh, this little tramp isn't the only one we've rounded up, and we have our ways of extracting information. Take them away," Harriet said, gesturing to Guillory and Evelyn.

One of the men grabbed Evelyn by the arm, dragging her through the entrance. The rest pushed Guillory along behind.

"Wait!" shouted Raja, chasing after them.

"Raja!" Terry and Fergus shouted, but it was too late. He disappeared through the entrance after the Knights.

"So now it's just the three of us," Harriet said, sauntering closer.

"No, there's also . . . " Fergus looked around and realized Fand was gone without a trace. He felt a wave of despair wash over him.

"Also?" Harriet asked, lifting an eyebrow. "Were you hoping for some kind of *Deus ex Machina*? I'm afraid it really is just the three of us, though, Irvine. Now, we are supposed to be exorcising all the dirty little hybrids, but I was thinking it might be funnier if I just shot you both here and left you to haunt this lonely mountain for all eternity." He pulled out his revolver, cocking the hammer with a flourish. He pointed it at Terry and then at Fergus.

"Which one should I deal with first? Bridges, I think you'll give me the most trouble, but, Irvine, I just plain hate you."

Terry tensed beside him, muscles bunching as though he was thinking to run at Ashton. Fergus stepped in front of him, holding out his arms to keep him back.

"Fergus, what are you doing?" Terry asked, trying to pull him aside.

"We're not just gonna stand still and let you shoot us, you know," Fergus said, struggling to keep Terry at bay. "And when you run out of bullets, I'm not gonna hold him back."

Harriet's mouth quirked. "You're on."

The gun went off with a small *boom*. Fergus grabbed Terry's arm, wrenching him to the side as they both went tumbling to the cave floor. A second shot struck the rock next to his knee, ricocheting and striking him in the thigh. He grunted in pain. Terry grabbed him by his shoulder, trying to pull him to his feet.

"And now you die," Harriet said coldly.

However, before a third bullet could be fired, a burst of flame shot across the cave, separating them from Harriet. Three stood just inside the entrance, panting, flames licking down her blade. Pip was right behind her.

"Come on, while there's still time!" he shouted.

Three released another wall of fire, as Terry hauled Fergus to his feet. Together they limped to the entrance. Harriet shouted in pain, but Fergus dared not look back to see what had happened as Pip pushed him and Terry through. The airship was hovering just over the ledge, the ladder dangling down. Pip herded them to it. Fergus could feel the mountain trembling under his feet. He looked up and saw the morning sun rising beyond the peaks, painting the sky a rosy pink.

"Hurry, Three!" Pip shouted as Terry put the rope in Fergus's hands and urged him to climb.

It was painful. He could feel blood running down his leg, and he thought the bullet might have taken a chunk out of his skin, but he bit his lip until he tasted blood and forced himself to climb as quickly as possible. He dropped onto the deck, head spinning with pain. Terry was not far behind. Pip scrambled up after him.

"Three!" Pip shouted, leaning over the railing. Fergus could feel the airship start to lift into the air.

"What are they doing? We can't leave her!" he gritted out.

"We have to go. Whole mountain's been shaking since the sun first showed, and I don't want to stick around and see what happens next!" shouted Orson, rushing up to them.

"Three!" Pip called again.

Fergus dragged himself to the railing. He saw the end of the ladder blowing back and forth, slowly drawing further away from the ledge. Three appeared from the fading light at the entrance. She stopped, casting another fire spell with her sword, and then turned. She looked up at the ladder in alarm and then jumped.

"Three!" Pip and Fergus shouted together.

Her fingers slipped on the rope, and she began to fall, but caught the next rung down. She managed to get a second hold on the ladder with her sword hand, but her feet dangled free. She bit her lip, looking down.

"Haul her up!" shouted Orson, and he, Terry, and Pip began to drag the ladder up until Three was close enough to be pulled onto the airship.

"So close," she gasped, clutching her chest. The sword fell from her hand with a clatter.

"Are you hurt?!" Pip asked, leaning over her, clutching her shoulders.

She shook her head. "Sorry, I couldn't capture him. I thought we could make them give us the others back . . . "

Fergus saw Ashton escape the cave and sprint over the land bridge, his form growing smaller and smaller. He turned to see the enormous Air Guard airship hovering nearby.

"We better move it before they shoot us down."

"Already on it!" said Orson, disappearing inside.

The airship jerked to life, ascending quickly into the air just as an explosion rocked the side of the mountain. Chunks of rock fell to the ledge. Another blast rocked the air, striking the mountain over the cave entrance and knocking several boulders loose. Fergus thought he saw a bird fly free of the debris, but it was gone in a flash as another cannonball struck the mountainside.

"They really are destroying it," Fergus said.

"It's bought us some time, so let's be thankful!" Terry said, springing to action and rushing off with Three to help the crew.

"Let me see your injury," Pip said, crouching beside him.

Fergus pulled his hand away. He couldn't see anything but blood welling under the tear in his jeans.

"Guillory didn't even resist. What was he thinking?" he muttered, looking away from the wound.

"He probably has a plan."

Fergus frowned. He couldn't see the other airship, but he could hear the continued cannon fire pelting the side of the mountain. He had a bad feeling that if Guillory had an idea, that idea involved talking sense into Harriet, but if Harriet was willing to go so far as to arrest him as a traitor, Fergus didn't think his odds were very good.

"I think I'm going to have to stitch it. Can you stand?"

Fergus nodded, letting Pip help him up.

"Get inside."

They limped down the stairs, but Fergus stopped outside the control room where Orson had taken Guillory's usual spot. In the window, he could see the sun rising, and then the airship jolted and took off, shooting forward. He barely managed to catch the doorway to brace himself. He heard Pip grunt as he was thrown into the wall.

"We have to follow them!" Fergus said.

"We're no match," Orson replied, shaking his head.

"But they have Guillory and Raja and Evelyn!"

"They'd shoot us down in a second. Besides, I bet the Captain has a plan. Your friends will be okay as long as he is. Best thing we can do now is beat 'em back to New Peiling."

Fergus bit his lip. "Set a course straight for New Peiling."

"Roger that!"

"Come on," Pip said, tugging at him. "It's going to get infected!"

Fergus allowed him to lead the way down to the cabin and strip him out of his jeans.

"Let me get you something to drink. This is going to hurt," Pip said, standing.

Fergus turned from him to the window. A dark blur momentarily blotted out the sunrise. He blinked. He was sure that a little bird had just flown past. Getting up, hand clutched to the wound, he limped over to the window and saw a single black feather caught against the sill. He pressed his face against the glass, but the bird was long gone.

"What are you doing?" Pip asked, sounding exasperated as he came over to drag Fergus back to the bed.

"I think she got away," Fergus said, taking the glass of whisky and carefully sitting. He threw it back and lay down.

"Who?"

"Fand."

"What's that mean?" Pip asked, blotting at the wound.

"I'm not sure yet, but I have a feeling things are gonna get a lot worse. You sure— *Ow*! *God*! You sure you wanna stick around?" Fergus said between clenched teeth.

"It's up to Three, but we heard an old 'friend' was heading in that direction."

"That guy?" Fergus asked breathlessly.

Pip nodded.

Fergus let out a little whistle and then grunted as Pip drew the thread tight. "Guess that makes it double trouble."

"Shut up and lie still."

Fergus pressed his palms to his eyes, doing his best to acquiesce. "Screw the whisky. Gimmie more of that sleeping potion and wake me when we get to New Peiling."

GLOSSARY

Banshee: A female fairy that foretells death with her cry. Example: Lady Gemini.

Boobrie: A fairy that appears as a large bird with a large hooked beak and webbed and taloned feet. Often steals farm animals to feed on. Example: Rosslyn.

Cait Sìth: A cat fairy with a white marking on its chest. Example: Ursula.

Gancanagh: A male fairy that seduces human women, causing them to die of love for him. Example: The Count.

Ghillie Dhu: A tree guardian, which appears as a dark haired man dressed in leaves and moss. Example: Raja.

Gytrash: A large black dog fairy with glowing eyes. Sometimes considered a harbinger of death; at other times a guide. Example: Terry.

Kelpie: A fairy that appears as a black horse, luring travelers onto its back and dragging them into the water to eat them. Example: Fergus and Ainslee.

Púca: A shape-shifting fairy that often appears as a black horse. It sports a fondness for taking drunkards on wild rides across the countryside. Example: Evelyn.

Selkie: A fairy that appears as a seal, which can shed its skin to become a beautiful woman. If a man steals its skin, he can force the selkie to marry him. Example: Jane.

Tarbh Uisge: A gentle water fairy that appears as a black bull with no ears. Example: Flynn.

ABOUT THE AUTHOR

Addison Lane was born and raised between a small town in the Deep South and the Big City. Though wanderlust ever calls, she presently resides on the East Coast, where she's a mild-mannered web designer by day and literary crime fighter by night. *Stealing Terry* is the sequel to her first novel, *Hanging Flynn*. She is presently working on the third and final volume of the *Fairypocalypse* series.